SWEET TALKING MONEY

Harry Bingham was born in England in 1967. After graduating from Oxford University, he worked for ten years as a London-based investment banker. He spent time in major American, Japanese and European banks where he gained first-hand knowledge of the world of billion-dollar deals, hostile takeovers, and company bankruptcy. In 1997, he left banking to care for his disabled wife and to write his first book, *The Money Makers*. He lives in Oxford with his wife and an increasing number of dogs. He now writes full time.

D1242491

SWEET TALKING
MONEY

Harry Bingham

severn
House

This first hardcover edition published in Great Britain 2002 by
SEVERN HOUSE PUBLISHERS LTD of
9–15 High Street, Sutton, Surrey SM1 1DF,
by arrangement with HarperCollins*Publishers*.
This title first published in the USA 2002 by
SEVERN HOUSE PUBLISHERS INC of
595 Madison Avenue, New York, N.Y. 10022.

Copyright © 2001 by Harry Bingham.

British Library Cataloguing in Publication Data

Bingham,   Harry
    Sweet talking money
    1.   Stocks - Fiction
    2.   Speculation - Fiction
    I.   Title
    823.9'14 [F]

        ISBN 0-7278-5804-1

Dedication quotation from *Selected Poems, 1923-1968*
by e.e. cummings, published by Faber and Faber.

Except where actual historical events and characters are being
described for the storyline of this novel, all situations in this
publication are fictitious and any resemblance to living persons
is purely coincidental.

Printed and bound in Great Britain by
MPG Books Ltd., Bodmin, Cornwall.

For my beloved N.

lady through whose profound and fragile lips
the sweet small clumsy feet of April came

into the ragged meadow of my soul.

Books are books. But if books were films, then I was the writer and director, while the producer, editor and assistant director was my wife, Nuala. This is an acknowledgement in the most straightforward sense: a formal recognition of her part in the forming of this book. This book was written by one, but created by two.

ONE

1

Sometimes you have to go crazy before you can come to your senses. Sometimes you have to lose everything to find the one thing that really matters. Sometimes – Hell, forget about sometimes. Here's what happened.

2

It was eight thirty-five on a chilly Boston evening, and the scientists were beginning to ramble. Enough.

'Let's call a halt,' said Bryn. 'Who's writing up?'

He knew the answer. A scraggy scientist, looking like something put together from rags and pipe-cleaners, raised his hand. 'Dr Lewinson. Excellent.' Bryn turned on his smile, maximum beam. His show of goodwill was brief and insincere. Of the eighteen people in the room, fourteen would be fired as soon as the deal concluded. Bryn knew that because he was the architect of the whole transaction. The others didn't, because they weren't.

The meeting broke up.

As Bryn began to pack away, a further racking cough rumbled painfully from his chest. It was his second trip across the Atlantic that week, so his jet lag, coming at him from both sides, was having an echo effect on his battered system.

'Dammit, look, I wonder if you can help,' he said, grabbing one of the departing scientists. 'I really ought to see a doctor.'

'A medical doctor? Hey Steve, you're not a doctor, are you?'

'No. Why don't you try what's-her-face, Dr Dynamite downstairs?'

'You think that's safe?' The scientist laughed. 'Only kidding, really. She's great, just . . . No, really, she's great.'

As he spoke, the scientist fussed around with pass keys and swipe cards, taking Bryn downstairs, past empty laboratories, silent storage rooms, the hum of computers. They emerged on to a corridor on the ground floor, dark except for the glow of streetlamps spilling in from outside. They raced along until they arrived at a lighted doorway, where a brass plate advertised its owner, Cameron Wilde, MD, PhD. 'Here you go,' said the scientist, shaking hands. 'Good luck.'

Bryn raised his eyebrows in enquiry. 'Dr Dynamite, huh?'

'She's kind of explosive. That's part of the reason, I guess.'

'And the other part?'

'Nobel prizes. Built on the profits old Freddie Nobel made out of dynamite.' He nodded at Wilde's door. 'She's a future winner, if ever I've seen one. And I have, actually. Several.'

Through a frosted pane in the door, lights burned. There was a dark shape, which might or might not have belonged to a future Nobel Prize winner. Bryn put his hand to the door and knocked.

3

The room was a good size, thirty foot by twenty, lit by three or four anglepoise lamps. On the wall where Bryn entered was a small pool of tidiness, somebody's workstation, a secretary's, probably. Everywhere else was chaos. Stacks of paper on every surface. Sheaves of computer print-out. Journals, textbooks, e-mails, binders. Yellow Post-it notes tacked anywhere and everywhere. There was a workbench jammed with two PCs, a portable, a couple of printers, a scanner, and wiring arrangements designed by a five-year-old. There were two further work areas crowded with microscopes, two high-capacity clinical fridges, boxfuls of needles, blood collection tubes rolling around loose in cardboard trays, plus other equipment Bryn didn't recognise. The room's built-in shelving had long ago buckled beneath the deluge, and sheets of chipboard standing on concrete blocks acted as emergency reinforcements. There were four chairs in the room and on one of them sat Cameron Wilde, MD, PhD.

'Dr Wilde?'

'Uh-huh.'

The doctor sat in a pool of light cast by one of the lamps, her face partly hidden by the hair which fell across it. She was pale-skinned, skinny, not much to look at.

'I apologise for disturbing you. I've been working with the team upstairs and I needed a doctor urgently. One of them suggested you might be able to help.'

Wilde was working on a stack of documents. She didn't seem over-anxious to greet her new arrival. Holding her pen in her mouth as she sorted papers, she said, 'What's the problem?'

'Flu. Had it for weeks. I got a prescription in England, but didn't have time to fill it before I left.' He held out the piece of paper, which was no good to him in an American pharmacy. 'I apologise for bothering you.'

She looked at the prescription, and let the pen drop from her mouth. 'It's no bother.'

'Thanks.'

'Your doctor gave you this? For flu?'

'Right.'

'Uh.'

'Anything wrong?'

'Wrong? Depends on what you want. If you want to get rid of your flu, this won't help at all. If you just want to cover up the symptoms so you can go right on doing whatever it was that gave you flu in the first place, then this is just the stuff.'

'Right. OK. I'll take my chances. Thanks.'

'And the more you go right on doing whatever it is you do, the longer the flu will stay.'

'Like I said, I'll take my chances.'

She shrugged. 'OK.'

The pen went back into her mouth and her hands went back to sorting her papers. Bryn couldn't see a prescription pad anywhere, but then again there might be five hundred of them hidden round the room.

'You can give me the prescription?'

'Can. Sure. But won't.' Each word came out with a little puff, as she began shifting big piles of paper to get at documents stuffed away at the bottom.

'Won't?'

Bryn was incredulous. At thirty-four, he was a Managing Director of Berger Scholes, one of the world's biggest and most successful investment banks. Last year, his bonus had been £625,000 and his group, which handled company acquisitions in the pharmaceutical industry, had advised clients on transactions worth over sixty billion dollars. That wasn't all. If he looked brutish on a bad day, he was hand-some on a good one. He weighed two hundred and ten pounds, not much of which was flab. He was broad, heavy, strong; a corporate bruiser with brains. A Welsh farmer's son, Bryn had taken himself to Oxford University, then for the last fourteen years crashed successfully through the investment banking jungle. The way he saw it, he'd go crashing on for years to come. If he wanted a prescription to relieve him of flu, he wasn't going to let some self-righteous doctor with a face that last saw daylight in the Reagan administration stop him.

He pressed his chest with thick fingers, coughing as he did so. He wouldn't plead, but he would make his point.

'Dr Wilde, I understand that you would like to cure my flu outright, and I respect you for it. Unfortunately, to the best of my understanding, there is no cure for flu. But right now, this very minute, I am tired, I am in pain and I have a full day of work ahead of me tomorrow. I must therefore insist that you, please, give me the medication specifically designed to relieve people in my situation.'

Wilde quit doing whatever it was she was doing, and swung around to face Bryn. The anglepoise lamp was directly behind her head, so her face was more or less invisible to view.

'I didn't say there wasn't a cure.'

Barely holding on to his temper, Bryn said, 'OK. If you'd prefer to try me on something else, I'd be happy to trust your judgement.'

Wilde consulted her watch, angling it to catch the light. 'I don't have much time. Maybe half an hour.'

'Half an hour . . . ?' Bryn wondered what prescription could possibly take half an hour to write. 'Sure. OK. Whatever.'

5

'And no guarantees. I don't do too much human work these days.'

Things had gone beyond strange, Bryn decided, and he let this remark pass without comment. Just as well. Wilde had her head buried in one of the clinical fridges, searching for something. In the light streaming from the open door, Bryn could see rows of glass beakers, stoppered vials, glass trays, and neatly labelled cartons. Wilde emerged with a glass tray divided into twelve compartments. In each compartment, a little fluid sloshed around.

'Any health problems? Serious ones, I mean.'

'No.'

'Any history of illness in the family?'

Bryn had injured his knee playing school rugby. His brother had been invalided out of the Pontypridd scrum with a femur fractured in three places, and his dad had damaged his ankle so badly in a game of pub rugby that when the bones healed, they had all fused together and the foot ended up as stiff as a board. Even Bryn's grandfather had twice ended up in hospital having his stomach pumped after post-match celebrations that had started too early and ended too late. But still . . . 'Nope. All healthy,' he said.

'OK. Good. Thumb, please.'

'My thumb?'

Bryn held out his hand. Wilde picked up a cylinder just about big enough to hold a toothpick, held it to his thumb and clicked a button. Bryn felt nothing, but when the cylinder came away, blood welled from a small puncture wound.

'Good. One drop in each compartment, please.'

She peeled away a cellophane cover from the tray, and Bryn held his hand out, dripping blood into each compartment. As he did so, his chest was racked by a deep and painful cough, and blood splattered untidily around the tray.

6

'One drop per compartment. Please.'

Bryn held his thumb steadier as his cough subsided. 'Can I ask what you're doing? Is this for diagnosis?'

'Diagnosis? I thought you said you had flu?'

'Yes, but . . .'

'What's to diagnose? You get stressed, you get flu.'

'I am not stressed.'

Bryn hated that. He hated it when those without the balls for the job assume that every successful banker must be stressed just because they're successful. Bryn was successful, but he wasn't stressed. Those who worked for him might be, but that was their lookout.

'Sure you are. Stand.'

Bryn's thumb had completed its duties, but nobody had mentioned the fact to his circulatory system, which continued to push blood out through the miniature wound. Since no cotton wool was on offer, Bryn stood up, thumb in his mouth to stop the bleeding. Meantime, Wilde stood up too, surprisingly tall in her flat shoes, lanky as anything, her labcoat looking as if it hung on a hanger.

'May I feel?' She approached Bryn, putting out her hand.

He opened his jacket, making it easy. With a sudden movement, her hand balled into a fist and shot forwards into the dead centre of his chest. The pain astonished him, rocking him backwards and momentarily winding him. He gripped the edge of the table behind him, careful not to dislodge any of its tottering piles.

'Jesus!' he said, as soon as his voice had emerged from a fit of agonising coughs. 'Jesus Christ!'

'Stress. That's stress. Biological stress. Unhappy cells.'

Bryn held his hands over his heart. The pain in the rest of his body had mostly washed away, although a general ache still sang its reminder. He was about to make some comment, demand some explanation, but Wilde had already moved away from him and was bending over the glass tray with a pipette. Following the drop of blood into each compartment was another drop of something else.

'OK. Let's look.'

She thrust Bryn in front of the microscope and he forced his bleary eyes to focus through the eyepiece, as a glass slide slid into view. Round balloons swam in some kind of fluid, along with bigger, more ragged-looking shapes, gently shifting position in the warm currents generated by the microscope bulb. What the hell was he doing here, he wondered.

'See the macrophages? Keep an eye on them.'

'Macro- . . . ?'

'Macrophages. Not the round ones, they're your red blood cells. The big, irregular white blood cells. They're what protect you against flu.'

'Right. Only not.'

'Watch.'

Wilde took the slide, added something from her pipette, and slid it back beneath the light. Little strands of blue had joined the throng beneath the lens, and Bryn watched as slowly, slowly, the macrophages sought out the little blue strands and began to engulf them.

'They're eating the little blue things. Is that good?'

Wilde pushed him away and peered through the scope. 'Hardly. Your white cells are barely moving. I've just sprayed them with a ton of foreign protein and they ought to be going crazy. They don't know if I've given them AIDS, or just a bit of chicken.'

'And?'

'And what?'

'AIDS or chicken?'

She glanced at him briefly, as though not taking the

8

question seriously. 'Chicken-derived polypeptides,' she said. 'It's the reason why you got flu, now it's the reason why you can't shake it.'

Bryn was blurry with illness, tired from too much work, and disconcerted by this strange doctor. His mind felt foggy and dull. 'Chicken?'

'Your white cells. They're exhausted. We need to juice them up.'

Rudely shoving Bryn aside, she began working with the glass tray. She'd scraped her dull, sandy-coloured hair away from her face and secured it at the back with a rubber band plucked from some packaging discarded in the wastebin. Unconscious of her appearance, unconscious of anything except her work, she took a few drops from each compartment, dropped them on to a slide, and studied the slide under the microscope. She took about five or six minutes, working in silence, with little tuts of dissatisfaction emerging as she failed to find what she was looking for. Bryn looked around for somewhere to sit. The chairs were mostly either inaccessible or piled high with research documents, so he eventually settled for a stack of paper tottering somewhere in the darkness. He watched Cameron working intently in her pool of lamplight, and as he watched, he felt the ache from the punch settle down and begin to mingle with his other aches, disappearing into them, making itself at home. Eventually, with the eleventh compartment tested, she looked up.

'We've got something. Not a perfect match, but the best I've found.' She looked him up and down, like a butcher at a cow. 'And you're not in such awful shape. It shouldn't take too much.'

She shoved him across to the microscope, as she went over to the larger of her two fridges. In the round image picked out by the lens, Bryn saw the same thing as before, only massively different. The lethargic white blood cells had gone hyperactive. As soon as they located a blue protein strand, they enveloped it and gobbled it, then went charging off to look for the next one. Even as Bryn watched, the microscope slide cleared of all invaders.

'Wow,' he said. 'And what if that had been AIDS, not chicken?'

But Wilde wasn't listening. Her hands pattered down rows of glass bottles in the fridge, then stopped and pulled out a beaker. Next she found a syringe which looked like a church steeple joined to a zeppelin, and began to fill it.

'What's that?' asked Bryn.

'Same solution as I used to beef up your white cells under the scope. It's a mix of nutritional factors. Fuel for blood cells.'

She swabbed his arm with alcohol, and Bryn felt the familiar cooling sensation.

'Is this what you do? Your research area, I mean?'

'Huh? This? God, no,' she said, waving her needle. 'This is crude, painfully, painfully crude.' The alcohol had evaporated away, and Cameron wiped the vein a second time. The syringe looked bigger close up, huge in fact. 'With real diseases, serious disease, you actually need to reprogram the white blood cells, literally write strings of program code to remind them how to do the job.' She poked at his vein to make it stand out. 'Not silicon chips, obviously, the body needs chemical code. Amino acids. Peptides.' She levelled the syringe. 'Little prick.'

'I have not,' muttered Bryn, trying not to watch.

'I beg your pardon?'

'Nothing. Forget it.'

Dr Wilde had found the vein without difficulty, and with calm expertise, slowly and smoothly injected the solution into his arm. It was almost totally painless.

'Done,' she said. She pulled the rubber band from her hair and shook it into its previous uncombed mess.

'Thanks. Like I say, I have a full day of meetings tomorrow, so anything which helps . . .'

'Tomorrow?' She snorted out through her nose, possibly her version of a laugh. 'You'll need to cancel.'

'I can't cancel. That's the point. That's why I came.'

She shrugged. It wasn't her problem. 'Try to eat properly while you're recovering. That means no caffeine, no alcohol, no sugar, no dairy, nothing processed, not much fat, no additives, no allergens.'

'Grass. I'll eat grass.'

'Organic, where possible. Thirty bucks for the injection, please. You can give me another twenty for the consultation, if you feel like supporting my research.'

Bryn rolled down his sleeve and groped for his jacket.

'It's nice to work on humans every now and then,' she continued. 'Mostly I just stick needles into rats.' Her words came out in grunts as she cleared her microscope bench of the litter. The compartmented tray, now rejoicing in twelve drops of finest Welsh blood, she waved in the air. 'Human blood. A prized commodity. Can I keep it?'

'Be my guest. Punching people is part of your research? Or was that just for fun?'

Wilde was nonplussed. She didn't understand jokes, it seemed.

''It wasn't research. I just wanted to explain . . . Sorry.'

Bryn pulled a hundred bucks from his wallet. 'Can you give me a receipt?' He needed it to claim his expenses. She looked vacantly round the mountainous paper landscape in its inky darkness and pools of light. She didn't do receipts. 'OK. Don't worry. Just keep it. Good luck with your research.'

'Thanks. Sorry I hurt you.'

'That's OK. Not to worry. It's fine. Thank you.'

'Here, have this,' she said abruptly. She found a business card and scribbled on the back of it, a hundred dollars, received with thanks. He took it and caught a taxi back to his hotel downtown, musing on what he'd witnessed.

He'd seen blood cells recharged and reinvigorated. He'd seen blood cells destroying invaders like Schwarzenegger on speed. He'd seen a failing immune system rebuilt under the microscope.

This time, of course, the invaders had been chicken, the magic show no more than a party trick. But if, as she'd implied, Dr Wilde could repeat her trick with serious illness, then it wasn't just a trick she'd discovered. It was the Holy Grail.

4

Bryn had as much intention of spending the next day in his hotel room as he had of giving all his money away to charity, but there are times when things move beyond your control. By eleven p.m. his temperature had shot up to 105°F and hung there all night. Shivering underneath a mountain of duvets, he cancelled everything he'd had arranged and waited for the crisis to pass. By evening, his temperature had come down, his chest had cleared, and his appetite returned with a vengeance. Other than a little temporary weakness, he was as fit as a fiddle and ready for action.

Making a rapid check of flight times, he made a dash for the airport through rainswept streets, catching the last overnight flight into London. He slept well through the journey, woke sufficiently refreshed to manage a king-sized breakfast, and was first off the plane on arrival.

Strictly speaking he should have gone straight into work, but it was a grey and chilly morning at a grey and ugly Heathrow, and he found himself asking the cabbie to take him home instead. He'd shower, shave and have a second full-size breakfast, before going into the office.

And there was another motivation. For several years his marriage had been poor, possibly even collapsing. He and his wife, Cecily, had their fair share of relationship problems, of course, but on top of that, theirs was a banker's marriage. It wasn't that Bryn cared about his career and Cecily didn't. On the contrary, she had been brought up to consider money to be more important than oxygen. But there was a cost: work came first, the marriage came second. Out of their last fifty-two weekends, only five had been completely free of work.

And so a stop for breakfast and a shower wouldn't just be pleasant, it would be Bryn's way of showing Cecily that she still mattered to him, a small step towards reconstructing their relationship. He'd been taking a lot of such steps recently, hopeful that they were clawing their way towards something better.

Outside his tall, white-fronted Chelsea home, he paid off the cabbie, climbed the steps, let himself in, called upstairs and downstairs, got no answer – and then saw it, a note, folded on the hall table. He opened the note and read it.

5

And read it again, in a mounting blur. 'Dearest Bryn,' – that was nice, wasn't it? A good affectionate start. No problems there. 'This is just to say that I've decided to leave you.' Bryn gripped the banister and collapsed heavily down on the lower stair. What do you mean, *'just* to say'? What's *just* about that? 'Dearest, this is just to say I've burned the house down, murdered the kids, slaughtered the neighbours, eaten the cat.' Bryn breathed deeply. Maybe he was missing a trick here. Maybe she'd meant to say something else altogether. 'Dearest Bryn, I've decided to leave you . . . some breakfast in the oven, some gloves in your pocket, a photo, a love letter, a *billet doux.'*

No, it didn't say that. Definitely not.

He rubbed his eyes roughly, and blinked to focus. Try though he might, he missed the next few sentences and only caught up with Cecily's beautiful handwriting several lines later. 'I'm sorry, darling, I could see you really trying to mend things, but I believe it wasn't meant to be. I've realised that it's important to me to begin again, and that's what I intend to do. Please don't be silly and try to pursue me – it won't work. You know me well enough by now, to know that my decisions are for ever.'

He did, and they were.

6

For a long time, at the foot of the long staircase, Bryn sat stunned and stupid, yet in a way not even surprised. These last few months, he'd felt like a man trying to rebuild a house during the earthquake-volcano-hurricane season: heroic, maybe; a loser, for sure. He crumpled the letter and threw it away. The scrumpled ball hit Cecily's bow-legged rosewood table and made one of her Meissen vases ping with amusement.

Work. There was always work. At least at Berger Scholes he could harness all his energy into bullying the world into submission. It didn't compensate for a failed marriage, but, by God, it was a good distraction. He heaved himself up and stumbled off to work.

A mistake.

On his desk waiting for him was a corporate memo, sent from Head Office, addressed only to him.

TWO

1

'What the hell is this?'

Bryn shook the memo furiously at his boss, a Dutchman, Pieter van Ween, head of the bank in Europe. Van Ween – blue eyes, fine silver hair swept back over a clear complexion – spoke calmly.

'I'm sorry you found out this way. I tried to phone. I couldn't reach you, so I thought it better to drop you a line –'

'I don't care how I found out! I do care about Rudy Saddler coming to piss on my patch.' Bryn's voice came across as unnecessarily gruff – the voice of a man two hours after getting off an overnight flight, forty minutes after finding his wife had left, three minutes after finding out his job was dissolving. He rubbed his chin, which was rough and unshaven.

'No one's going to be pissing anywhere.' Van Ween was puritan enough to dislike foul language, banker enough to tolerate it. 'The pharmaceutical industry is a big area. Plenty of transactions. What was it? Sixty billion dollars' worth we did –'

'*I* did –'

'The bank did last year. Saddler's going to co-operate,

not steal your show. He's already told me how much he welcomes your local knowledge. I know he respects your work.'

'Respect, bullshit. I've built the best pharma team in Europe and he gets to put his name on the door. Are you trying to send me a message?'

Van Ween understood this game. He played it often. He played it well.

'There's no message. I didn't ask for Saddler. He wanted to come. I have guys I wanted to send to New York. It was all part of the deal.'

'You traded me.'

'This is a bank, Bryn. I did what was best for the bank.'

'I don't know about that. I do know that I work my arse off and my reward is to be demoted –'

'There's no demotion –'

'– demoted to second in command of the team I built. You may say there's no message, but I've got to tell you, Pieter, I'm hearing one.'

'Are you saying you will not accept the position which is being offered?'

The question shifted things into van Ween's favour. Bryn could act the martyr, but unless he had something lined up elsewhere, he couldn't afford to reject anything. Van Ween wanted to make him say it. Bryn sighed. He was devastated by his wife's disappearance, shocked by the news about his job. 'I'm not here to give you any ultimatums,' he said wearily. 'I just wanted to let you know I was unhappy.'

'I understand. It had occurred to me you might not be altogether happy. There is something else I had in mind. It's a critical area. Something we're keen to expand. Begin to make some real money. And from your point of view, I think it's a good career move. It's the kind of position that gets noticed in New York.'

Bryn opened his hands to invite more information. He didn't want to sound excited. In truth, he wasn't excited. Pieter van Ween would have pitched the position the same way whether it was running the trading floor or counting paperclips. The Dutchman paused to register the fact that Bryn was making a request, then continued.

'It's emerging markets: Russia, former Soviet Union, all of Eastern Europe, Asia as far as India, Africa. You'd have the biggest territory of anyone in the bank and everything except trading would report to you. You'd report directly to me. I'd give you time to get to know the area, then we'll sit down and talk. If you think the business flow will justify increased resources, you can have them.'

'Do we have lending authority?'

'We can lend money in Poland, the Czech Republic, Turkey. Maybe South Africa, I'd have to check.'

'Not Russia? Not India?' Van Ween stayed silent. He wouldn't participate in Bryn's effort to belittle the job. 'How much did we make last year?'

'In emerging markets? About fifteen, twenty million bucks. But focus on the future.'

'That's less than I made on the Claussen deal alone.'

'The job's about possibilities, Bryn. You're giving reasons why we need to beef up our effort, why we need you.'

Bryn thought about it. Half the world under his command, but the wrong bloody half. If the bank wouldn't risk its money – for fear of coups, collapse, or craziness – then there wasn't much Bryn could do to earn it. There was always consultancy work, but in these Godforsaken markets the businesses were too small, too cheapskate to stump up real cash. He was being offered an empire, but it was an empire of sand, a dirt track into the desert.

Van Ween noticed the hesitation. It was a lousy deal, he understood that. But he needed to accommodate Saddler's

18

arrival and he needed somebody to do the emerging markets job. Hughes was a good guy, headstrong and cocky for sure, but most decent bankers were. Van Ween decided to offer some more inducement.

'If it's the travel that's worrying you, then I understand that. It's demanding. We've got some big energy projects in Kazakhstan right now. A privatisation in South Africa. We'll need you to be there on the ground, of course, but I don't want you to compromise your family life. Take time off when you need to. I know I can trust you to strike an appropriate balance.'

'Jesus, the travel. I hadn't even thought . . .'

Bryn trailed off. Nothing on earth could afford less pleasure than business travel to the places van Ween had outlined. He'd heard nightmare stories – true stories – about bankers stranded on an airfield someplace in Russia, minus fifteen outside and falling, the plane's pilot pointing to an empty fuel gauge, telling the Westerners to buy fuel or stay grounded. Mobile phone two thousand kilometres from the nearest signal. Company Amex card a stupid joke. Dollops of cash, pushed across a table in a green-painted hut; men shouting in an alien language, arguing over maps and cash and vodka; and all the time the temperature outside falling.

'I hadn't even thought about the travel.'

'As I say, I know you'll want to talk it through with your wife . . .'

Those words – 'your wife' – almost sent an unaccustomed spurt of tears through Bryn's rusted-up tear ducts. *His wife.* He'd had his problems with Cecily, no question, but she was his wife – or, rather, had been. He felt desolate and betrayed. 'There's nothing else?'

'We'd like you to work with Rudy Saddler as his number two, if you could see your way to sorting things out with him. But either way . . . it's your call. Let me know when you've talked to your wife. Cecily, isn't it?'

'Yes. Cecily.' Bryn was stuck in his seat for a moment, cloddish and uncertain. He was a skilled negotiator, but van Ween was no pushover and van Ween held all the aces. Bryn could give up half his empire and more than half his glory to a newcomer he didn't get on with, or travel the world's least glamorous corners slogging his guts out for a penny here, a nickel there. 'Thanks, Pieter. I'll think about it. Get back to you.'

There was a third option which neither of them mentioned but both were aware of. Bryn could call a headhunter. Clear out. See what he could get somewhere else. It didn't feel great, but it was an option.

'OK.' It was a dismissal, but friendly. 'And believe me, Bryn. You have a good career here. Think long-term. Don't make the mistake of moving on because of – because of a hiccup.'

'Yeah. OK.' He stood up to go.

Van Ween watched him carefully, appraising his man, knowing that Bryn's 'yeah, OK' was as good as meaningless.

'And Bryn, I understand your frustration, but we've put a real offer on the table. We won't be sympathetic if . . . if you choose to head elsewhere.'

Bryn understood van Ween's meaning. As with any senior banker, much of Bryn's wealth was tied up in deferred bonuses, a hostage kept to encourage loyalty. The money was Bryn's as long as he stayed with the bank, but it became the bank's money if he chose to quit. Sometimes, if the bank nudged people out, it was generous, it decided not to add to the misery by hanging on to the precious cash. But van Ween was telling Bryn not to hope. If Bryn called a headhunter and quit, he'd wave goodbye to three quarters of a million pounds.

2

'There's one more here. The last of our hepatitis controls.'

'Oh no, really?' exclaimed Cameron. 'That's too bad.'

She went over to the cage – hardly a cage, even, more like a rat playground, full of fluffy white sawdust, plastic toys, feeding trays and hidey holes. The last of its inhabitants lay stretched out, nose just poking out of the darkened night area. Cameron snapped off her latex gloves, opened the cage door and reached in, picking out the little white corpse and stroking it, smoothing its whiskers. 'Dammit,' she said. 'It's Freddie. We didn't need that. I was hoping that at least Freddie would survive.'

Cameron's lab assistant, a delightful graduate student called Kati Larousse, rubbed Cameron's shoulder and said gently, 'At least it improves the stats, Cameron. And the experiment's over now. This is the one hundred and eightieth day.'

'We didn't need the stats to look any better. They're good enough already. Hell. I wish I'd stopped all this at a hundred and twenty days. Even ninety. We were way into statistical significance already by then.'

Larousse gave her boss a hug. 'You're the only researcher in the world who'd react like this. You carry out the most successful animal experiment ever undertaken in this field, and all you do is worry about your controls dying on you.'

'How are the others?'

Cameron reached for the door to the neighbouring cage. A sign above it read 'Herpes', along with warnings about animal handling.

'Gloves, Cameron. Careful.'

'Damn my gloves.'

Cameron reached into the cage. This group of rats had

been deliberately infected with the herpes virus one hundred and eighty days ago, and all but four were now dead. The ones that were still alive were lethargic and glassy-eyed, about to follow the twenty-six rats that had preceded them to the pearly gates. Cameron stroked the rats regretfully, apologetically even.

'How about the others?' she asked after a while.

'HIV, you know. All dead. Hantavirus and Ebola virus, we've got eight and six left respectively.'

'And the treated rats? No problems there?'

Larousse moved to the cages on the opposite wall. The cages were identical, except for one thing. The rats weren't dead, they weren't even dying. One hundred and eighty days before, they had all been injected with the exact same deadly viruses that the control groups had received, but nothing had happened. The rats bounced around their cages, coats glossy, eyes sparkling, squabbling over toys and fighting their way through tunnels and up ladders, like so many healthy puppies. They didn't know it, but they owed their lives to Cameron's Immune Reprogramming. Larousse used her hands to check inside the sleeping area, but they came away empty.

'Nothing. No problems at all. Oh, except that this one has lost part of its tail.'

Cameron inspected the rat. It was thinner than the others, a constant target of playground bullying. 'Benito. Shame. He had such a nice tail.'

Larousse let her boss linger round the cages a little longer before interrupting. The end of an experiment is the busiest part, collecting all the data which records the precise success or failure of the work. 'I guess I should start taking blood samples from all the survivors?'

'Right. Get it centrifuged and refrigerated. We can begin the lab analysis tomorrow.'

'OK, sure. And ... the controls, Cameron. These little guys are dying. You want me to ... ?'

'Oh, sure, yes, of course. I mean, right away.'

'How do you want me to do it?' Larousse was gentle. Most experimenters didn't care what happened to their animals at the end of an experiment, but Cameron Wilde wasn't like that. There were different injections you could give to put a rat to sleep, and Cameron was bound to have views on the kindest method.

'You know,' said Cameron, 'exactly like we did the others.'

'I don't understand. We didn't do the others. They just died.'

Cameron stared at her assistant, slowly understanding what she had meant. 'Oh, no. We're not putting them down, Kati. I'd never ... No way. We're going to try and get the little guys well. Build them up again. We're going to do the full Immune Reprogramming on all of them.'

'Do the whole thing?' Larousse was astonished. After a long and complex development period, Cameron's Immune Reprogramming technique had been put to the test in this one amazing experiment. Nothing in scientific history had ever worked better – not on rats, anyway – but it was still time-consuming, laborious and expensive. 'Do we have the funds, even?'

Cameron's eyes flashed with anger. 'I don't care if we've got the funding. I'm not going to let these little guys die just because we can't be bothered to cure them. Christ, if we don't owe it to them by now ... We're going to get them better, and then they're all going to go off to PEACH. If I can't afford that, I'll keep the little guys myself.' PEACH was the Post-Experiment Animal Care Hostel – a pricey but deluxe outfit run by a couple of dedicated Boston animal-lovers.

'Yeah, sure, Cameron. That's fine. Actually, I'm delighted. That's great news. God, I love working with you.'

Cameron stared around the room. Since the discovery of penicillin, medical history has all been about the search for the magic bullet: pills which wipe out a bug, leaving everything else intact. With bacteria, the search was successful. One by one, killer diseases like tuberculosis, scarlet fever, whooping cough and diphtheria began to fade out of existence – slain by the magic bullets of antibiotics. There was a time when scientists were optimistic that all diseases would follow suit, that infectious disease would literally be eliminated.

But then the failures began. Viruses began to shrug off vaccinations. Bacteria grew resistant to antibiotics. New diseases sprang up out of nowhere. Scientists don't say so out loud, but they're worried. The drugs companies won't admit it, but their bullets are failing.

Cameron wasn't surprised. The way she figured it, drugs can *never* defeat infectious disease. Bacteria reproduce every twenty minutes, five hundred generations in a week. In the time it takes a new drug to be developed, approved and marketed, the bacteria it was designed to kill have evolved far, far away from the original specimens.

Cameron's alternative was simple. What's the only known way of killing *all* viruses and *all* bacteria, no matter how weird and wonderful, no matter how foreign or strange? Answer: the human body. Most of the time, our bodies deal with everything: viruses and bacteria, prions and moulds, insect bites and toxins. You can put fifty people in a room packed full of influenza virus, but only five of them will come down with flu – the five who are stressed, or unhappy, or malnourished, or sleep-deprived, or recovering from some other illness. The other forty-five just deal with it.

24

And that was Cameron's answer. To reprogram the human immune system to deal with its failures. To teach the immune system to do what it does best. This had been her mission in life ever since entering Harvard Medical School as an exceptionally gifted sixteen-year-old. Now aged just twenty-nine, she had carried out the most ambitious experiment in the history of viral disease, and come away with the most brilliant results ever achieved. But that was rats. The next step was to repeat the trick with humans.

Cameron looked at the rat cages once again: the empty ones where the controls had been, the others where the treated rats hurtled round in skidding clouds of sawdust.

'Let's make this the last animal experiment we ever do, OK, Kati?'

Larousse grinned approval as she busied herself with needles and collection bottles. 'Have you thought more about publication?' she asked.

'Uh-huh,' said Cameron. '*The Journal of the American Academy of Medicine* are quite keen, I think.'

'Keen? They'll bite your hand off.'

'I hope so. The next phase of this is going to be pricey. We'll need a decent write-up to secure our funding.'

Larousse put down her rats, needles and bottles.

'Listen,' she said. 'There are a hundred and fifty rats in this room who ought to be dead or dying, and just look at them. Not a trace of disease. None of them. Not in half a year. Your problem isn't going to be getting money. It'll be how to fight it off.'

Larousse was wrong, of course. Dead wrong. As wrong as wrong could be. But don't blame her. Larousse was a scientist, and what do they know about money?

THREE

1

The loneliest place in the world is easy to find: a luxury hotel in a foreign city and a phone with no one to call.

It was six weeks now since Bryn's life had broken to pieces on the rocks. Cecily had promised him that her decisions were for ever – or, to put it bluntly, that she was as stubborn as a donkey. Bryn knew this. He'd have been less surprised to meet Mount Rushmore on walkabout than to find Cecily changing her mind. All the same, he'd done what he could. On the assumption that she'd gone home to her parents, he'd tried to call her there. It was Cecily's mum who answered.

'Oh God, Bryn, it's you,' she'd said, not unkindly.

'Yes, I was hoping that I could maybe speak to –'

'Yes, yes. Of course you were.'

Her voice was sympathetic and unhappy and Bryn then knew straightaway that Cecily hadn't just left him, she'd left him for somebody else. 'He's a rich sod,' her mum went on to say. 'Taken her off to some horrible mansion in the Caribbean. I met him once, Bryn, *hated* him. I'm so sorry.'

But sympathy from his about-to-be-ex-wife's mother was little comfort, as he began to search the ruins of his life for a path leading out.

Once, that path would have been work. He was still at Berger Scholes, of course – back in Boston finalising his biotech deal – but his career there was coming to an end. He wasn't going to knuckle down as Rudy Saddler's number two, and he wasn't going to trudge the world of emerging markets, hunting for nickels. He'd called a head-hunter, who was even now lining up new places, new jobs. Bryn Hughes would start out all over again: new job, new start, and in time, perhaps, a new woman, perhaps even a family.

Meantime he was lonely. No one to visit. No one to call. It wouldn't be different tomorrow or the next day. Welcome to life without a family. Welcome to life without direction.

He wasn't hungry, but ordered a giant salad from room service anyway, giving himself something to pick at. Putting his hand in his pocket, searching for a couple of dollars to tip the waiter, his fingers met the sharp rectangular edge of a business card. He pulled it out with the money. A receipt for a hundred bucks, received with thanks, scribbled in pencil on the back of a card. Cameron Wilde, MD, PhD. Bryn tipped the waiter and stared at the card.

A Boston number, someone to call.

2

Over on the university campus, a phone rings in the surrounding silence. Cameron Wilde, working late, answers it.

'Cameron Wilde.'

'Dr Wilde, it's Bryn Hughes.'

'Brandon . . .'

'Bryn. Bryn Hughes. A patient of yours.' Still no recognition. Bryn gave her the help she needed. 'I came to you with flu and you punched me in the chest.'

27

'Oh. Sure. You were the guy who said he wasn't stressed.'

'Right. It was around then you started hitting me . . . I was calling to say that you totally sorted me out. One day in bed, then as right as rain.'

'As right as what?'

'Rain. A British expression. Something to do with our love of bad weather, I suppose.'

'You're welcome.'

'I wanted to thank you. Perhaps I could take you out to dinner somewhere. That is,' he added, joking, 'if you know anywhere which doesn't serve coffee, alcohol, sugar, fats, additives or dairy.'

'No, sorry.' Her no was flat, no hint of apology.

'No?'

'No. I don't know anywhere. Uh . . . you could eat at my place if you wanted. Did you mean tonight?'

'Yes. Tonight. Unless you're doing anything.'

'No. Sure. Fine.'

And shortly Bryn was in a cab crossing Boston, watching the darkened winter streets pass by, feeling as he hadn't done for years.

For the first time since his life had smashed upon the rocks, here was an edge of excitement, a tiny nibble of adventure, a step into the unknown. He sat forward in his seat, unaccountably excited by what lay ahead.

3

The air that night had come down from Canada, and shivered with the possibility of snow. Bryn stamped his feet in the lamplight spilling from the apartment block's lobby, careful with his once-injured right knee on the frozen pavement. When, following his second ring, the buzzer buzzed the door open, he made his way across the over-heated lobby towards the stairs and Cameron Wilde's apartment.

'Here. I brought this.' Bryn held out a bottle of champagne he'd bought at the hotel before leaving. Cameron looked at it, but made no move to take it. Her face was white, drawn, shocked. 'Are you OK? Is this a bad time?'

She shook her head, turned, and walked into her living room, leaving the door open for Bryn to follow.

The room was pleasant enough. Pale floorboards, strewn with rugs. A couple of lavender-blue sofas. Walls stone-washed and decorated with a handful of anonymous prints. No TV. You could look at the room for an hour and know nothing of the person who owned it. Until, that is, your eye arrived at the corner devoted to Cameron's work: paper stacked high on shelves and the surrounding floor; PC and printer; graphs, notes, equations tacked up on the wall above. If the room was coloured according to the intensity of life in its various parts, then the whole large living space would be a pale, almost icy blue; the study area, a vivid, glowing scarlet. Cameron crashed down on one of the sofas, looking like death.

Bryn read the situation quickly and crouched in front of Cameron, squatting awkwardly with his weight skewed on to his stronger knee.

'Dr Wilde, I don't know what's happened in between my phone call and now, but I can see you're in shock. If you want me to go, please say.'

She said nothing.

'Right. I'm going to stay. Now I can help you best if I know what's going on. What is it? Some kind of attack? An intruder?'

There was no sign of forced entry, and Cameron was on the third floor, but it was best to be sure. The scientist gave no response.

'An intruder? No intruder?'

Bryn bashed at her with his voice, studying her face carefully for information. It seemed to him she was telling him 'no'.

'OK. What else? Perhaps . . .' Bryn was about to try other avenues when he noticed a fixity in Cameron's expression. She was staring at a letter lying open on her table. 'This letter? You came home from work, found this letter, and it gave you a shock? May I read it?'

There was no sign in her face, so Bryn went ahead. It was a short note, from the editor of the *Journal of the American Academy of Medicine*: 'Thank you for your recent submission to this office. Unfortunately, we do not consider this paper to be of sufficient interest to our readership at this present time.' There was another sentence or two of blah-blah. A pretty standard rejection, as far as Bryn could tell.

'You submitted an article to the *Journal* and it was rejected.' Bryn hesitated. The American Academy of Medicine published the world's most prestigious medical journal. If medical science was athletics, then publication in the *Journal* was like running in the Olympic finals. 'Cameron,' he said, using her Christian name for the first time, 'it's not surprising to get a rejection like this. Even great scientists get rejected sometimes. There are tons of other places where you can get your article published.'

'Right. The *Redneck County Medical Gazette*. The *Baldhead Mountain Parish News*.' Cameron's eyes were large and smoky-blue, but the skin around them was puffy and grey, and the eyes themselves red-rimmed and desolate.

'No. Real journals. Respected ones.'

Cameron slowly shook her head. 'No,' she said. 'No. You don't understand.' Then, after a long pause, finding what she had to say almost impossible to speak, she continued. 'They told me . . . they said they . . .' Just as it seemed she had petered out, she burst into life. 'Oh, goddamn it! They told me my results weren't acceptable. They thought I'd fixed my data.'

'Fixed? They thought you cheated?'

But she had snapped shut again, her screen of hair falling forwards over her face. All the same, you didn't need to be much of a psychologist to see that Cameron had no more fixed her data than she had swum the Atlantic. He gripped her by the shoulders and forced her face up towards him, brushing her hair back from her eyes.

'They thought you cheated, but you obviously haven't. So there's a mistake. And mistakes are fixable.'

'Fixable?'

Bryn wished he'd used another word. 'Correctable. Mendable. They think you fixed your data. You didn't. So sort it out. Ask for independent checks, whatever.'

Cameron shook her head. 'There's an ethics committee,' she said. 'Apparently, I've got to collect my work. Hand it over for investigation.'

'First step,' said Bryn, ignoring her. 'Find out how the mistake happened. What did they say? What did they think went on?'

Cameron stared at him, trying to make up her mind whether to trust this battering ram of a stranger. In that instant, Bryn realised that her silence up till now had been less because of her shock, and mostly because of her uncertainty over him. Still uncertain, she continued. 'They didn't say. They wouldn't say, but personally I . . .' She shook her head, reluctant to continue.

Bryn took her by the shoulders again. 'Speak, Cameron. I do better with words. What are you saying? You have a suspicion about something? You don't know, but you have a suspicion?'

She nodded, slowly.

'Who? You have colleagues, co-workers, lab assistants? Anyone you argued with? Had a fight? Fired?'

'No. Kati, my lab assistant, she's my best friend. She wouldn't. Not her. But . . .'

'Yes? But? But, who?'

'Look, I don't know, but . . .' She shook herself, as though physically shrugging away her shock, as though literally stepping into a more aggressive, defiant state of mind. 'Listen. Our Head of Laboratory Services used to be a creepy guy named Duaine Kovacs. One night I found him down with my rats. Late at night. I don't know what he was doing there. I screamed at him.'

Bryn didn't quite follow. 'You think he knifed you, because you screamed at him once?'

Cameron shook her head. 'When I found him, he was clearing up a spillage. Blood. He'd cut himself. After he left, I looked at a few drops under the microscope. Good stuff, blood, it tells you everything.' She sighed. 'Anyway, Kovacs was in a state. Unhappy blood. Like, way worse than yours. I ran some tests. Alcohol. Dope. Cocaine. Prozac. Tons of stress factors. I reported him, of course. I mean, I wouldn't care. If someone wants to take coke, that's their problem, but in a laboratory – in my laboratory, messing around with my rats . . . I wasn't having it. He was fired.'

'OK. So we have our mole. Question is, why on earth would the *Journal* believe him rather than you? He was fired after all.'

Once again, Cameron's face clouded and Bryn probed hard to read what was written there. 'Something else, Cameron. There's something else you're not telling me.'

She sighed, a sigh which began down in the soles of her feet. 'Damn right, there's something else.' She paused again, gauging her little-known visitor. 'The night Kovacs was fired, he was drunk, high, I don't know what. He burst in on me, yelling abuse, how my experimental results would never see the light of day, how they were going to see to it.'

'They who?'

Cameron shrugged. 'I don't know. That's the point. They ... whoever.'

Bryn felt a flicker of excitement flashing from nerve to nerve across his body, like a lightning flash that briefly illuminates an entire landscape. He didn't know why or what, but he knew he was on to something important. He leaned forward. 'Let me understand. When you send a paper to the *Journal* or any other scientific publication, they get it reviewed, right? Half a dozen independent reviewers comment on whether the article is good enough to be accepted. Did your paper go out to reviewers, or was this rejection just based on the editor?'

'Oh, no. The editor, he was keen – I mean, *was* keen.'

'Do you know who he chose to review your paper?'

'Sure. I'm not supposed to, but I found out.' Cameron gestured at the mountains of paper surrounding her desk. 'In the yellow binder, there.'

Bryn found the binder and pulled it out. Pasted to the inside flap was a list of six reviewers, names and numbers.

'Good.' He brought the list back to the sofa. 'Now, I need you to think. Look at these six names. Tell me if you can think of any reason why they might be hostile to you or your paper.'

Cameron looked at the list for about two tenths of a second, then shook her head. 'No. Why be hostile? It's only science, for God's sake.'

Once again, Bryn did his bully-boy act, squeezing Cameron's shoulders so that she was forced to look up into his eyes. 'Listen,' he said. 'Nothing in the world happens without a reason. Nothing. If a handful of intelligent scientists chooses to believe some coked-up laboratory manager without even checking with you, then there's a reason. Once we work it out, we probably know who's behind all this. OK?'

Cameron looked back at the list, more intently now. But the names still revealed nothing to her. She dropped the list. 'I can't think of a reason.'

'OK. Who does your paper hurt? It's about – what? How to juice up rat blood?'

'It doesn't hurt anyone,' she said, a little sharply. 'My medicine is about helping people.'

'Helping people, right. But what about your rats? What was in your article?'

Cameron shrugged, as though unimpressed by her own achievements. 'I took a hundred and fifty rats, gave them five kinds of killer disease, then treated their immune systems. Reprogrammed them. Programmed them to be incredibly good at killing whatever virus it was I'd given them. I wrote up my results and sent 'em to the *Journal*.'

'And what about the rats?'

'They lived, of course. Otherwise my paper wouldn't have been very interesting, would it?' Bryn gripped Cameron's arm, tightly, more than was polite. He delivered his next question with barely controlled intensity. 'To cure your rats. Did you use drugs? Were their recoveries in any way drug-dependent?'

'Oh, who cares?'

Cameron sought to free her arm, but Bryn tightened his grip, as his nerves danced with urgency. 'Please, Cameron. It's critical that you tell me.'

She quit struggling. 'Some of the rats benefited from very small doses of immune stimulant pharmaceuticals. In real life, not an experiment, I might have wanted some further drug support. But in general, no. The rats didn't get better because of any drugs.'

Bryn's flicker of excitement burst into flame, seizing hold of his entire body. He leaped back as though on fire. 'Jesus Christ! Jesus, Cameron, I thought you said your paper didn't hurt anyone. There are billions – no forget that – there are tens, *hundreds* of billions of dollars invested in drug technologies which you could be putting at threat. It's not if, frankly, it's who . . . Let me think. Jesus.' He took the list of names again, thrusting them in front of the scientist, inches from her face. 'Do you recognise any of these names? Is there a common link? Any company, or organisation?'

Cameron looked at the names. 'They're all OK. This guy, Professor Durer, he's quite good. Had a real interest in my work. Rucci . . . The name rings a bell, but . . . Now, Freward. He's a grade-A creep, but an OK scientist . . . The others, hell, the others, who cares?' Her insightful analysis stumbled to a close.

Bryn drummed briefly on the table. Then, pulling out his phone, he began to dial.

4

First London, where it was two o'clock in the morning. He called three of his junior analysts, two of whom were asleep in bed, one of whom was at work, finishing up a spreadsheet for one of Bryn's other projects. Bryn began to bark instructions, getting the two sleepy analysts into work as soon as possible, pulling the third off his existing project for the time being. He thought briefly, then, for the sake of completeness, he called a couple of associates in New York and set them the exact same task, with the same urgent deadline as he'd given the others. What one group missed, the other might find, and vice versa. Before he was done, he interrupted himself briefly. 'Fax?' he asked Cameron. 'E-mail?' Wordlessly, she pointed to her filofax which lay on the desk. Bryn flipped to the contact information, and gave it to the associates on the other end of the line. He switched off his phone and tossed it down.

'There we go. We'll have some answers pretty soon.'

'Answers to what? Except whether you're a nice guy to work for.'

Bryn allowed himself a tiny smile. 'We pay 'em enough.'

'Can I ask you something?'

Bryn looked up in surprise. 'Of course.'

'Who *are* you? How come you know about the pharma industry? More to the point, what the hell made you come see me tonight?'

With a jolt, Bryn realised that Cameron knew nothing about him. She'd shown no personal curiosity in him the night they first met, and this evening the normal social exchanges had been obliterated by the steamroller of Cameron's distress. 'I'm an investment banker,' he said, briefly explaining who he was and how come he was in Boston.

'That doesn't explain how come you're in my apartment.'

He shrugged. Why was he here? Because his wife had left him and he thought that some weird Dr Dynamite scientist type was going to make him feel all warm and cuddly again? He shook the question away, and crossed to Cameron. 'We should have some data coming in by now.'

He booted up Cameron's PC and went into her e-mail. Before long, e-mails began to fly in from London and New York. 'Data dumps,' he said. 'Everything you ever wanted to know about your six reviewers, plus the *Journal*'s editor. Everything which has ever appeared in print, anywhere in the world. Pharma company appointments, educational bulletins, research reports, internet stuff, you name it.'

36

'You have systems which do that?'

'Not systems, people. The information is out there, it's finding it which is hard. Now, let's see . . .'

For two and a half hours he worked, expertly skimming the mass of information flooding in, printing, marking and putting to one side anything he thought possibly relevant. Before long, seven piles mounted up: Durer, Regan, Rucci, Czarnowski, Booth, and Freward – the six reviewers – plus Goldbach, the editor.

At length, he took a break.

'OK,' he said. 'I think I'm close. Of the six reviewers, I can connect four to one company, Corinth Laboratories. Durer is the one who connects tightest. His research lab has a major multi-year contract with Corinth. I doubt if Durer would stay in business if Corinth moved away. Regan and Czarnowski have both done paid experimental work for the group, plus Regan – no, Czarnowski – has done paid lectures, expert witness work with the FDA, that kind of thing. Then Booth is working to get a hospital extension funded. His co-chairman on the committee is an ex-CEO of Corinth. It's not a strong connection, but if they're hoping for funds, you never know. That leaves Freward and Rucci. I can't find anything. Not yet. But there's more stuff coming.'

He carried on speaking, but Cameron had turned to stone.

'Rucci,' she said. 'I've just remembered where I heard the name.' She walked to a shelf and pulled down an old edition of an industry magazine, *Pharmaceutical People*. She flicked through the pages and found the item she was looking for: a sickly-sweet mother-daughter feature, adorned with a cheesy photo. 'The mom, Paula Rucci, was my reviewer. Her daughter, Gabriella, is Vice President in Corinth's Veterinarian Division.'

'Ha!' barked Bryn, flying back to his sheaves of paper.

He flicked quickly through his stacks and came away with a sheet. 'Gabriella Rucci has recently been promoted to Executive VP. How nice. Her mum may be clean, but her daughter certainly isn't. And if dear little Gabby comes home one day and tells her mum all kinds of crap about you, who's she going to trust? That just leaves Freward.'

Cameron shook her head. 'Uh-uh. Freward's the worst.' From a pile on her desk, she pulled a photocopied research piece, *Quantificational errors in omega pathway modelling of digestive enzymes*. Among the list of authors, Freward's name had been circled with a handwritten comment next to it, 'Pillock!' Bryn looked blankly at the page.

'Freward's a good scientist,' said Cameron, 'but he devotes his life to these kind of knocking pieces, always trying to shoot good work down. He's a director of – what's the name again? – the Katz-Jacoby Research Foundation and –'

'And Katz-Jacoby is exclusively funded by Corinth.' Bryn finished her sentence, triumphantly. 'We've got it, then. The smoking gun. The only weird thing is the coincidence. The editor seems clean, so how come he ends up with six Corinth stooges out of six? That doesn't add up.'

'Uh-uh. It figures. The editor will most likely pick one lead reviewer first, and talk to him about a possible slate of names. The most likely guy on this list is Freward. Like I say, he's a jerk, but a good scientist with a decent reputation. Maybe the editor comes up with some suggested names, maybe Freward comes up with them all. Any case, by the time they're done talking, Freward has packed the jury.'

'Plus they've got Mr Smack-head Kovacs running around spreading rumours about you, just in case.' He looked at Cameron admiringly. 'They really took care to sabotage you,' he said. 'They must really respect your work.'

'Thanks.'

'No, really. You can't beat the compliment ... And Corinth. It makes sense. I might have guessed.'

'You mind telling me why?'

Bryn paused to inspect his questioner. She was dressed in old jeans and a thin T-shirt which ran into puckered ridges at the shoulders. She was pale and thin, hair a mess, tear-stained eyes a visual disaster area. All the same, she wasn't exactly bad-looking. All that high cheekbone stuff that women are meant to have, she had.

'Corinth Laboratories,' said Bryn. 'An outstanding company. A decade ago it was a bit-part player. Some good drugs. Some bad drugs. Nothing much in the pipeline. But then they struck gold. They hired this guy Huizinga from outside the industry. Chemicals, I think, was his background. He shook up the company, top to bottom. He began licensing drugs, buying up small biotech outfits, research labs. And focus, he gave it focus. Before Huizinga, Corinth did a bit of everything. A chemo drug. A bit of respiratory stuff. Some anxiety medications. He ditched all that. The one good product they had was an anti-viral, Zapatone. It was big in AIDS –'

'Zapatone? God, it's toxic. Toxic as hell. There was a British study which showed –'

'There was a British study which showed it shortened the lives of three quarters of the patients who took it. But that was Huizinga's brilliance. He *boasted* about the study, made his salesmen lead with it. He went out and told the world that no drug in the history of the world had ever had such impressive anti-viral properties –'

'Anti-patient properties –'

'Whatever. They made a few tiny modifications to the drug administration protocol. Meaningless changes, but enough that they could say the British study was irrelevant to the way the drug was now administered. And that was that. Zapatone took off, and that was Huizinga's cue. Ninety per cent of Corinth's sales are now in anti-viral drugs, with just a couple of other sidelines they haven't yet bothered to sell. Mostly now, the drug industry is looking for less toxic solutions. It's a kinder, gentler industry, that's the idea. But not Huizinga, not Corinth. They recognise that there are plenty of doctors out there who like the macho stuff. Toys for the boys, and guns for their chums. They put out these publicity handouts for Zapatone, overlaying a picture of the drug with photos of B-52 bombers.'

'It's criminal.'

'Genius. Corinth was worth a couple of billion dollars when Huizinga came in. It's worth fifty times that today – a hundred billion dollars, no less. If there were Nobel prizes for business, Huizinga would be a cert.'

'I do not believe you!'

'I'm not saying I approve, I'm just telling you how the world works. And say what you like, they're smart. They've got the world's biggest stable of anti-viral drugs. Your medicine is a threat. You said it yourself: under certain circumstances, your technology might be complemented by conventional drug therapy, but by Corinth's slash-n-burn stuff? No way. As Huizinga sees it, it's him or you.'

It was a tactless phrase on which to finish. Cameron's eyes skated back to the letter still lying open on the table.

'Right,' she said grimly. 'And at the moment, it's him.'

And it was then, at that precise moment, that Bryn took leave of his senses.

40

FOUR

1

To begin with, the only sign of the craziness which had come over him was a very rapid beating of his hand on the table, accompanied elsewhere by the focused stillness of concentrated thought. For three whole minutes, he stood there, oblivious of Cameron, unconscious of the world.

Then: 'I'm a bloody fool!'

'Excuse me?'

'Fool,' said Bryn, thumping his chest. 'Moron. Cretin. Idiot. You mentioned an ethics committee. Tell me about it.'

'I don't know. Where bad scientists go to be interrogated, I guess.'

Bryn shook his head and stared wildly at her. 'Kati. Your co-worker, Kati. Can we go and see her?'

'It's gone midnight.'

'Is it? Damn. Well, come on then. There's no time to lose.'

Cameron had no car, so they took a taxi over to her offices. The night was freezing, and frost sparkled on the grass. Above them, the sky was bright with stars, but a dark band in the north spoke of a weather front moving in.

'Do you mind letting me know what's going on?' Cameron hurried along in Bryn's turbulent wake, frightened by his bulldozer energy but also reassured.

'Due diligence,' said Bryn, storming up the steps leading to Larousse's apartment. 'That's banker-speak for look before you buy.'

'Honestly, she'll be asleep,' said Cameron. 'Can't we wait?'

'Uh-uh,' Bryn disagreed, pressing the doorbell solid for fifteen seconds. 'She's awake.'

A bleary Larousse came to the door in tartan flannel pyjamas, and stumbled through to her small living room, blinking to get the sleep from her eyes. She was one of those enviable souls, pretty even when caught in the worst possible moment. Clear-skinned and petite beneath a mass of dark-rosewood curls, she twisted her hair into a tie at the back so that it hung in a Pre-Raphaelite halo around her face. Cameron's looks worsened in contrast. It wasn't that there was so much wrong with her – apart from maybe her limp, mousy hair drooping down in front of her eyes – but she seemed to want invisibility, to avoid being looked at or admired. Bryn obeyed the silent instruction and concentrated his gaze on Larousse.

Cameron talked her through the events of the past few hours, ending with the broken-hearted admission: 'They don't believe us. They think we cheated. We're under investigation, Kati . . . Oh, Kati!'

Bryn studied her carefully as Cameron recounted the story, but it was absolutely plain that Larousse was totally shocked, stunned by the very suggestion that they might have twisted their facts. Larousse and Cameron huddled up on the sofa together, cuddling and tearful. Bryn was almost totally sure of what he was about to do, but there was one last check he wanted to make.

'Cameron, would you mind getting me some coffee, please?'

Larousse looked hard at her visitor. Cameron had barely introduced him and here he was, like some bear out of the Maine forest, bursting into her apartment at one in the morning, ordering her boss to make him coffee. 'I'll go,' she said, starting to get up.

'No. Please. I want a word alone. I have three – no four – questions to ask you privately. Cameron, would you mind . . .'

Cameron left to go into the kitchen, and Bryn turned to stare directly at Larousse.

'OK. First question. Did you and Cameron cheat on that experiment? In any way at all? At any time?'

Colour rose in the young scientist's face. 'No. Absolutely not. Never. No way.'

'OK. Good. I believe you, but I needed to ask. Second question. Your Immune Reprogramming worked on rats. Are you sure you can get it to work on humans? I mean, assuming you've got time and money.'

Larousse wetted her lips. It was unnerving, this giant man, his unwavering stare, his barely controlled intensity. 'Not certain, no. Nothing in science is certain until you've done it. And one critical difference is that the peptide chains we rely on are species- and disease-specific.'

Bryn looked blank.

'What I mean is, our Reprogramming works by using little bits of chemical code, which literally floats around the body instructing it how to fight disease. Trouble is, every species has got its own way of coding these things. That means all the work we've done on rats has to be done over with humans.'

'So the answer is?' prompted Bryn.

Larousse shrugged. 'It'll be a lot of work. The experimental protocols will be way more complex, for one thing.

You can't just give hepatitis to humans and see how they do. But I don't want to be too cautious. I'd say we had every chance of success. Every chance in the world.'

Bryn nodded. It seemed like he hadn't blinked since sending Cameron from the room. 'Good. Third question. The way Cameron talks, you and she are on the cutting edge of research in this area. How do you know? Maybe there are scientists in, I don't know, California, Germany, Japan who are ahead of you.'

'Possible. That's always possible. All I can say is, we've never heard anything of the sort. There are others in the field, of course, but no one even approaching our level of success. And then, of course . . .'

'Of course?'

'There's Cameron. She's not just good, you know. She's extraordinary. Passed out in the top two per cent of every exam she's ever taken. She got bored during her Harvard medical training – would you believe that? She got *bored* – and did a PhD in biochemistry at the same time. The *same* time. Without even telling them. It's unbelievable. She's not just good, she's the best.'

Bryn breathed out and sat back. The glare left his eyes, and Larousse began to relax. Cameron, peering round the corner from the kitchen, re-entered the room.

'A fourth question,' said Larousse. 'You said you had four questions.'

'Right, you're quite right. Kati, do you know anywhere round here we can get some pizza?'

2

Despite the hour, the pizza restaurant was busy. It was as though, all across the city, the snow pattering down outside had stimulated people to go out into the whitening streets in search of food. They took seats in the window, and watched cars glide by them in silence across the dim, phosphorescent snow. Kati had just pulled warm clothes over her nightwear, and the flannel collar of her pyjama top poked upwards out of her jumper.

The two women claimed not to be hungry, and agreed to share a no-cheese, no-flavour, thin crust Marinara, while Bryn ordered a fourteen-inch Massachusetts Gobbler Special and a pitcher of beer. The two scientists sat together, wondering why they were here, wondering about Bryn.

He wolfed the first slice of pizza and downed a long draught of beer. 'That's better,' he said with a belch. 'Cameron, you ought to be famished. No? OK. You want to know what on earth is happening. More to the point, you want to know what the bloody hell I'm doing here.'

Kati nodded, and Cameron looked alert.

'First the bad news. Brent Huizinga and Corinth Laboratories have sabotaged your research. They've done it once. They'll do it again. They'll go on doing it until they've driven you from the scene.' Bryn gestured broadly with a wedge of the Massachusetts Gobbler. Dollops of ground beef and chilli dropped off on to the melamine table. He took another bite, and with his mouth full asked, 'That night you found Kovacs in your laboratory, you know what he was doing?'

Cameron shook her head.

'He was planning to screw up your experiment. Kill off your rats, or whatever. Don't know, doesn't matter. Wherever you go, whatever you do, Huizinga is after you. He's got a hundred billion dollars to protect, so even if it costs him a few million bucks to do it, he's going to silence you.' He prodded at her with his lump of pizza. 'This time. Next time. The time after that and the time after that.'

The colour – what little colour there was – emptied from Cameron's face in less than a second.

'How dare you –' began Kati, but Cameron interrupted her with a gesture.

'It's not true what you say,' she said icily. 'From here, our next step is human research. Nobody's going to believe that we fake results there. Every single patient we work with will be able to corroborate us.'

'Yes.' Bryn took another vast bite. 'And how much will it cost, the next phase?'

'Five million bucks, maybe ten,' said Cameron.

'And who's paying?'

'Anyone,' said Cameron, 'anyone at all.' She tore a crust off her pizza and rolled it into a ball, rolling it round and round her palms like a six-year-old with Plasticine.

'As far as the world believes, you did some experiments with rats which failed. You faked the results, wrote them up, and had your paper rejected. That's not worth five million bucks. That's not worth anything at all.'

'For God's sakes,' said Kati to Cameron, 'we don't need to sit and listen to this.' But once again, Cameron motioned her silent. This was a duel she had to fight.

'So who?' said Bryn. 'Who's going to fund you?'

'OK,' she whispered. 'It'll be tough. Either the people funding me at the moment will go on doing it, or else I'll need to repeat my animal work using independent labs and outside experimenters. That way, no one can possibly accuse me of cheating.'

'To repeat your animal work elsewhere you need money, which you don't have. And Huizinga can infiltrate outside labs even more easily than he can get into your own. Wherever you go, whatever you do, he'll make sure he finds a Duaine Kovacs to foul up your experiments. No one will need to accuse you of cheating, because your tests will fail.'

Cameron's voice had shrunk away to nothing. It was the ghost of a whisper, the echo of a croak. 'Then the people who are funding me now, the biotech crowd, will go on. They'll believe me, not Kovacs.'

'Cameron, I know for a certain fact that your funding is about to be cut off.'

Her voice had vanished, but her eyes asked how.

'Go easy,' warned Kati. 'Take care.' But Bryn ignored and overrode her.

'I know, because I'm working for the buyers, remember? I've worked on their acquisition plans. I've sat in on their strategy meetings. They're going to cut you off.'

'That's not what they ... Every decision ... its own merits.' Her voice faded in and out of audibility.

Bryn bashed away one last time. The family motto: if at first you don't succeed, thump it. 'Of course they say that. They want to close the deal. They'll say anything. I tell you, I know their plans. They're doing the whole deal for one drug, Biloxifan. They're going to sell a couple of the other drugs in development. They're going to relocate some research staff. Then –' He snapped his fingers. 'They'll fire everyone else, sell the buildings. I know, Cameron, I know. I'm their banker.'

'It was your idea, wasn't it?' said Kati, eyeing him sharply. 'You told them what to do and they're doing it.'

Bryn denied nothing. 'I advised them in their commercial best interest. It's my job. When I advised them, I hadn't met Cameron and I hadn't met you.'

'I'm finished,' said Cameron. 'You're quite right. Thanks to you, I'm totally finished.'

Her voice began to turn into a yell, and from round the restaurant people began to stare.

'You should be ashamed of yourself!' said Kati furiously. 'Don't you think she's suffered enough tonight without you rubbing her face in it?'

'Rubbing her face in what?' asked Bryn, tearing off

another gigantic slice of pizza. 'Don't you even want the good news?'

3

And so, at a quarter past two on a snowy night in Boston, Bryn outlined his plan.

Crazy as it sounded, Bryn had made up his mind. He wouldn't stay at Berger Scholes. He wouldn't take the jobs his headhunter was bringing him. He'd quit. Wave goodbye to his deferred bonuses. Wave goodbye to banking, where every year is a bumper year, every bonus bigger than the last.

'I don't get it,' said Cameron. 'I see why I benefit. I get funding. I get to carry on with my science. But I don't understand what's in it for you?'

Bryn bent across the melamine table, pushing his pizza crusts to one side. Two o'clock Boston time was seven in the morning London time. Bryn's time-zone-delirious body was long past caring. The brain called the shots, and the body was happy just to swallow the pizza and guzzle the beer.

'I set up a company. The company employs the pair of you to carry out your research. I'll fund you. I'll give you all the support you need. In return, I get to exploit your findings. We'll push your discoveries so hard that they're doing your Immune Reprogramming in every hospital from Tokyo to Toronto.'

'Exploit my findings? You mean, like, commercially exploit?'

'Yup.'

'Patents, and royalties, and the stockmarket, and all that stuff?'

'Exactly.'

'Right. OK. I get you. No.'

'No?'

'No. I didn't go into medicine to make money. If you have a discovery which benefits patients, you just have to put it out there. Let people use it for themselves. Not try to make a dollar every time somebody gets sick. I'm sorry. I don't know what I'm going to do next, but not that. No way.'

She glanced across at her neighbour, asking for support. Kati gave it. 'I agree. What we're doing is for the good of humanity. It's not for sale.'

'You're crazy, absolutely crazy,' he said. This was the one sort of opposition he hadn't expected, and for a moment he was utterly unsure of how to handle it. It was like a modern astronomer trying to argue with someone who thought the world was flat, that the sun orbited the earth, that the heavens were full of angels singing. 'You're making a mistake,' he said lamely.

'I appreciate all that you've done – '

'Why should you?' asked Kati. 'He hasn't done anything, except cut off your funding.'

'But I think I should go. Really.'

The two women stood up, Cameron tall, skinny and evasive; Kati, with her halo of hair and her deep-brown spaniel eyes. They were getting up to go.

'No. Stop. You've got to hear me out.' His voice had a desperate edge, and he ordered himself to master it, adding more calmly, 'Sit down, just listen to the arguments.'

The two women looked at each other, and, taking the lead, Cameron sat, followed by Kati. But it was edge-of-the-seat sitting, nothing more than a hair's breadth away from leaving again. Anything Bryn said would have to be good.

With a hoarse voice, he spoke. 'In the medical world,

when it comes to choosing how to care for patients, what does it come down to really, truth or money?'

Cameron took a moment to absorb the question. Then, calmly, 'It's truth, of course. One bunch of scientists does its best to come up with solutions. Another bunch of scientists tests them out. They publish their results. And that's it. Doctors adapt their treatments. Patient care improves. It's that simple. It's got nothing to do with money, whatever you might like to think.'

'Really?' asked Bryn. 'Really? Then tell me, how much money do we spend on preventing disease, as opposed to treating? Two per cent of the total? Three per cent?'

Cameron laughed, a kind of snort as though dismissing the question. 'Well, OK, we don't spend anything like enough on prevention, it's true. But –'

'But what? What's that statistic again?' He appealed to Kati for help. 'If you take Vitamin E, it reduces your risk of heart disease by . . . by how much?'

Kati pondered the question in silence. It was as though she had the answer at her fingertips but was wondering whether to release it. After a long pause, she made her decision and spoke. 'There was a big study done recently,' she said with a sigh. 'Ninety thousand patients followed over two years. All taking Vitamin E. Heart attack risk was reduced by nearly half –'

'*Half!*' said Bryn.

'But other studies have been done using bigger doses of the vitamin. Those studies suggest the real figure is more like three quarters.'

'Exactly,' said Bryn. 'So there you go. If we wanted to, tomorrow, we could cut heart attack deaths by three quarters. *Three quarters*. With one simple little vitamin. So how come we don't? How come people still die needlessly? Hundreds of thousands, every year. What's stopping us?'

His question was greeted by silence. Pizza crust cooled on the melamine table, but at least up above, in the glassy heavens, the angels had stopped their singing. Cameron licked her lips which had gone dry. She was listening.

'I'll tell you how come,' he continued. 'There's no damn money in it. Vitamins aren't patented. Anyone can make 'em. The profit margins are no better than you get from selling potatoes. But – surprise, surprise – drugs aren't like that. Profit margins can be ninety per cent or better. You know that. Annual revenues in the US cancer trade are a hundred billion dollars. Each year, every year. The heart disease business comes a good second. Who cares that we can prevent most of that disease? Who cares if people die? Why should some bloody little vitamin salesman be allowed to poop that party?'

The silence continued. Bryn wondered if he'd done enough, or gone too far. It was Kati who spoke next, and when she spoke, Bryn realised she'd become an ally.

'It's true. And it's not just drugs. It's surgery. It's been estimated that eighty per cent of heart bypass operations are unnecessary, arguably nearly all of them.'

'Right,' agreed Bryn. 'Absolutely right.'

'And then there are the drugs which actually do you harm,' continued Kati. 'Cholesterol-lowering drugs which give you cancer. AIDS drugs that have been shown to shorten your life. Chemotherapy drugs which shrink tumours but have no impact whatsoever on life extension, though the doctors never tell you that.'

Cameron was very pale, and Kati too stopped, wondering if she'd pushed things too far. But again, when Cameron managed to find words, they were words of support. 'Arthritis,' she whispered. 'My grandmom suffered really badly from arthritis. I was real mad when I found out in med school that standard drug treatment actually makes the illness worse.'

'Exactly. My granddad, too. Good example,' Bryn encouraged her.

'Best-practice treatment of arthritis,' said Cameron, 'would be diet, plus allergy interventions, plus maybe some natural cartilage-builders.'

'Right.'

'But no drugs.'

'Nope.'

'So no profits from drugs.'

Silence.

'Anti-depressants,' said Kati sadly, after a while. 'The best ones are all non-pharmaceutical, but no one uses them.'

Bryn nodded in agreement. 'No one.'

'No money in them, right?'

'None at all.'

Silence.

Cameron looked out at the snow. As they had been speaking, a soft blanket had fallen, muffling the city. People and cars, when they appeared at all, moved slowly, treading cautiously, slowing right down at the bends. Then she brought her gaze back into the room, first down at her hands, then up, sadly, very sadly, to Bryn's face. The white tabletop reflected chilly light on to the underside of her face, as though she too was wandering outside, lost in the moonlight and the snow.

'Well, I guess this has been my night of lost illusions.'

'It must be hard.'

'You always do this when you invite a girl out to dinner?'

He smiled. 'I'm sorry.'

'So tell me again. What you want us to do.'

Bryn repeated his ideas, going slowly, making sure he brought Cameron along with him this time. 'I'll set up a company which will help you to develop your research, and then market it when it's ready. You say you hate the way

Corinth does business. OK. So put them out of business. Not by publishing research papers. Who's ever heard of a corporation going under because of some damn research paper? Hit 'em where it hurts: their bottom line. We'll pitch our salesmen against their salesmen, our results against theirs.' He put his hand on Cameron's arm and said very gently, 'It sounds mad, I know, but the stockmarket is your friend. You fight them in the laboratory, and I'll fight them in the marketplace. If we get it right, the whole world will be reprogramming its immune system and nobody, but nobody, is going to be popping Corinth's little poison pills.'

The scientist paused. 'Why are you doing this? You want to save the world? Or do you just want to make your million?'

'Make a million?' Bryn smiled sympathetically. 'No. I'd like to get rich, seriously rich, a hundred million rich. If I do a little good along the way, then that's great. But I don't pretend that I'm doing this for the good of my soul.'

'Uh. Well, that's clear enough, anyway.'

The world fell silent as Cameron thought. This was the biggest decision of her life, the hardest, the most painful. But also, as she thought about it, the easiest. Her reputation was gone, her funding, her hopes of scientific acclaim. Her only hope was sitting in front of her, a battered-looking steamroller of a man, someone she scarcely knew.

'OK,' she said. 'You win. I give up. Let's do it.'

4

The U-Haul depot opened at dawn and Bryn was first in line. He was about to sign out a mini-van, but Cameron shook her head. 'Too small,' she said. So Bryn hired a truck and bought a hundred and twenty orange crates at five bucks each.

'You an experienced driver?' asked the boiler-suited rental guy. 'Them streets outside are an inch of snow laying atop of an inch of ice.'

'Finalist in the Welsh all-terrain truck-drivers' championship,' said Bryn. 'Would've won 'cept some bastard shunted me.'

'You don't say?' The rental guy took a different set of keys from the board behind him. 'Here, take the Toyota. Transmission on the Volvo is shot to shreds. Same price. Don't mention it. Finalist, huh?'

It was a good job the rental guy chose to stay reading his *Off-Road Biker* inside his oppressively warm glass booth, else he'd have seen Bryn slide twice coming out on to the road and only miss a negligence suit by the fewest of inches as an outraged motorist swerved angrily away from the outcoming truck.

'You even know how to drive?' said Cameron.

'I'm a quick learner.'

Once in Cameron's office, they worked fast, with Cameron's spirits rising rapidly as her sense of adventure took hold.

'Kati?' she said.

'Uh-huh?' Kati shifted a stack of paper into a crate and stood up, flexing her back.

'Our new colleague, Bryn. Part crazy, wouldn't you say?'

'You've found a part that's sane?'

'Paranoiac, for sure, and what do you think? A little hypomanic, could be?'

'Uh, I guess. Mental health. Not my field.'

Bryn said nothing, just worked to clear the office as fast as he could. He'd filled sixteen crates and already his back was beginning to sing out warnings.

'Bryn?' said Cameron.

'Yes?'

'There are some pretty good drugs these days. I could put you on something.'

'Lithium,' said Kati. 'Have you thought about lithium?'

'Yeah, good, start you on lithium, maybe? Or you want me to refer you to a specialist?'

Bryn dropped the crate that he was holding.

'Your ethics committee,' he said. 'The one that was going to investigate you. Have you ever heard of it in your life before?'

'I've never been framed in my life before.'

'They wanted you to collect up all your research data, protocols, everything.'

'Just like a committee, wouldn't you say?'

'Then hand it to them.'

'Not much point collecting it otherwise.'

'Corinth. Not an ethics committee. Corinth. Fantastic idea. They just ask you to collect everything significant from your last five years of research and hand it over to them. Perfect. That's why we need to clear out tonight. Make bloody sure that they get nothing, nothing at all.'

Cameron paused. Then, 'Not just paranoia, Kati. Schizophrenoform psychosis. Florid stage. Lithium, for sure. But I'd have to think about chlorpromazine. Maybe clozapine, risperidone.'

'You think I'm nuts,' said Bryn. 'You find me any reference to that ethics committee, anywhere, ever.'

'Kovacs had the run of this office and my lab,' said Cameron. 'If they wanted stuff, they could have just taken it.'

'For God's sake, woman,' said Bryn, more impatiently than he'd intended. 'Have you ever actually opened your eyes in here? Look at this place.'

Even after twenty-four crates of paper had been cleared and stacked, the room was still overflowing with paper. Cardboard trays of collection bottles sat on top of computer keyboards which rested on paper foothills that led up to the mountains all around. The four anglepoise lamps sat like herons pecking nourishment from the sea of clutter. Cameron looked around.

'It's kind of . . . crowded, I guess.'

They worked on for a while in silence. It was back-breaking labour, and one by one the two women, short of sleep and short of food, dropped out, leaving Bryn to finish. His own back complained angrily now, and his dodgy knee had twisted badly on the icy pavement outside. At length, with the office empty but for the computer hardware, the anglepoise lamps, the bare workbenches, and the sheets of chipboard idle on their concrete blocks, Bryn stopped. Cameron had collapsed with exhaustion and delayed-onset shock and was snoring away on one of the chipboard sheets, covered up with Bryn's greatcoat.

'OK, then. One at a time,' said Bryn, beginning to load the PCs into crates.

Kati hesitated, instead of helping him. 'Technically –' she began.

'I know. Technically, these PCs belong to the biotech crowd, not you. But then technically, as an employee of Berger Scholes, I shouldn't be doing what I'm doing. And technically, Brent Huizinga didn't do anything criminal by destroying your reputation and sabotaging your work.'

He yanked out the power cords and Kati, silently and solemnly, helped him to steal them.

5

The final stage was the laboratory. Kati took a quick inventory of the place where she'd spent so many hours.

'This PC,' she said. 'And this.'

She placed her hand on a domed chamber about four

feet in diameter. It was built of white metal, had a control panel at the side, and a number of leads connecting it to the computer.

'And this would be ... ?'

'The correct term for this would be the White Blood Cell Immune Modulation and Reprogramming Facility.' Kati stroked the domed surface with affectionate familiarity. 'But since it's where blood cells come to learn how to be better blood cells, we usually just call it the Schoolroom.'

Watched anxiously by Kati every step of the way, Bryn hefted the Schoolroom to the truck.

'No, not on the crates. It needs cushioning. Don't just drop it. Gently. There.'

Kati settled some old blankets under the Schoolroom and all around it, till it was swaddled like a baby on New Year's Eve, peering up at them like a giant white eye.

'D'you want to feed it?' he asked. 'Get it some treats for the journey?'

Kati looked at him, her face still clear and pretty after an exhausting night. 'Don't joke,' she said. 'The Schoolroom is your future now. You'd better take care of it.'

The comment shot home like a crossbow bolt. *The School-room is your future now* ... Was he really going to throw in one of the most lucrative careers open to a human being, in favour of ... what? Some twenty-something scientist who did good things for rats, whom he'd met properly little more than twelve hours before, who'd had her paper rejected by a top American medical journal, who'd been accused of cheating and was unable to clear her name?

'I must be mad,' he said, settling the blankets more closely round the big white dome. 'Mad as they come.'

6

There remained one last ritual of departure.

Bryn woke the sleeping Cameron, and let her blink and stretch her way into wakefulness.

'Oh my God,' she said. 'If I'm not still dreaming, I'm in trouble.'

'Good morning,' said Kati, stroking her hair clear of her eyes.

'What's good about it?' said Cameron, shaking it back again. 'I am still dreaming, right?'

Kati ruefully shook her head.

'Delirious? Suffering from a rare idiopathic brain disorder?'

Kati shook her head.

'Maybe to all of those,' said Bryn, 'but we still need to get out of here.'

Cameron stared at him: the ultimate proof of the weird turn her life was taking. She stretched some more, allowing the kinks and pressure points down her spine to give a full report on their night's entertainment. 'God, could you guys really find nothing more comfortable than chipboard?'

Bryn gave her a sheet of paper and a pen. 'You need to write a message,' he said. 'Everyone's going to wonder why you've just upped and gone. You need to give them a reason.'

'Reason? Well, hell, that's easy. *Dear Everyone, I cheated and now I've gone to hide.* Or how about, *Dear Everyone, this English guy I hardly know thinks that everyone's out to get me and it turns out that paranoia is infectious.*'

'Welsh,' said Bryn. 'I'm Welsh. Say anything except the truth.'

Cameron ignored him and wrote fast, holding the paper so only she could see it. Once done, she folded it, addressed it, and left it in plain view for anyone to find. Despite her self-control, her hand trembled slightly and her ears burned at the shame of finding herself in this situation. Bryn didn't ask to read the note, Kati gave her boss a supportive squeeze, and the three of them marched to the loaded truck.

Bryn put the key into the ignition, but before switching on, he made a speech.

'From now on,' he said, 'secrecy. Our first and only rule. Other companies have assets. They have mines, or power plants, or aeroplanes, or shops, or miles of phone cable, or factories, or warehouses. We have none of that, just knowledge, the information that's in this truck, and the genius that's in your heads. We need to take care of it.'

'Better get another driver, then,' said Cameron.

'Buckle up,' said Bryn, doing as he advised and checking the empty road in his wing mirror. 'Corinth went to considerable trouble to ruin you – trouble and expense. They'll be watching carefully now, to see which way you jump.'

'And?' said Cameron. 'Which way are we jumping?'

Bryn grinned at her, turning the key in the ignition until the big truck vibrated with the desire to leave. 'You're not just jumping,' he said. 'You're going to disappear.'

FIVE

1

The Arctic Circle was having a good month for the export trade. Not content with dumping a shedload of snow on Boston, it had delivered a country-sized blanket overnight express to the British Isles, with further deliveries already in transit. At London Heathrow, nervous air traffic controllers watched their disappearing runways and reached for the panic buttons.

Somewhere off the west coast of Ireland, Bryn's jet nudged its course northwards by a few degrees and a not-very-apologetic pilot informed the passengers that their new destination would be Birmingham, not Heathrow. A ripple of conversation flowed through the economy seats at the back of the plane, but up in business, where Bryn sat, there was barely a flutter of interest as the travel-hardened veterans of the air revised their plans and helped themselves to sausage and egg.

At Birmingham International, Bryn hired a car and pointed it not south-east down the M40, but southwards down the M5. Six weeks since Cecily's departure, he still hadn't admitted the fact to his parents, and the time had now come.

As he drove into Wales, climbing out of the Wye valley

into the Brecon Beacons, the snow on either side of the road thickened to a mantle six inches, sometimes a foot deep. For all his initial swerve in the truck in Boston, Bryn was well used to driving through snow, and he negotiated the ascending lanes skilfully, coming to rest at a farm on the top of the road, the last farmland before the open hills. He honked his horn, a clear note in the crystal air.

Hearing the sound, his mother came anxiously to the door of the slate-roofed farmhouse. She looked at the unknown car with suspicion, before lightening into a flurry of smiles and greetings as Bryn swung his bag out of the boot. Welcoming him, scolding him, offering food by the bucket-load, she bundled him indoors.

'If only you'd told me, I'd have got something ready. As it is, there's nothing except a couple of pasties and last night's shepherd's pie and a bit of beef left over from the weekend and I could warm up –'

'Mum, please. It's eleven o'clock in the morning, and I had breakfast on the plane.'

'On a plane again? There was a crash last week. In Delhi, was it? I wish –'

'Not last week, the week before. And it wasn't a crash, it was a near-miss. And as you say, it was in Delhi.'

'So not Delhi, then?'

'No, Mum – coffee, please, yes, but no beef, honestly – I was in America. Boston.' Gwyneth Hughes' expression puckered in a look of renewed concern, as America was, to her, a land awash with gangsters, guns and drive-by shootings; the only place on earth more dangerous than London. 'And yes, I was careful. And yes, I did get Dad some Jelly Beans.'

Her next two questions having been taken care of, her frown smoothed away, although a hint of caution remained in the eyebrows as though reserving the right to be worried at any time. 'And Cecily?' she asked. 'How is she? No news, I suppose?'

The question meant, 'Have you got her pregnant yet?' As the daughter of one sheep farmer and wife of another, Gwyneth had always known that fertility is the first and most important property of the female.

'No, nothing like that, anyway.' Bryn breathed out in a long sigh. His mother's anxiety to be hospitable had released itself in his coffee. Six spoonfuls of coffee granules, a splash of water, and milk so thick it was virtually cream. He sipped it, knowing that he had to finish, even though he had a passion for real coffee, carefully blended, properly made. 'Cecily and I have decided to separate. She's gone her own way. We'll get a divorce through in time.'

'Oh, I see.' Gwyneth stood at the sink, apron on, tap full on, staring out on to the farmyard, her last dark hairs turning grey. 'You're sure, are you? Maybe she just needed a holiday. Goodness knows there are times I've wanted one.'

'No, Mum. It had stopped working. It's final.'

'Final, is it? Bryn . . .' Gwyneth tailed off, but her son knew what she wanted to ask.

'No, it wasn't anything I did. There wasn't another woman involved. Cecily did find . . . She's with another man now. Lives in the Caribbean.'

'The Caribbean? Oh, Bryn.' She rinsed her hands and composed her face before turning round. 'My poor love.'

Bryn nodded, a bit too choked to respond. As the weeks had passed, he'd come to see that Cecily had been right. Over the years since their wedding, they'd floated too far apart for any amount of emergency repair work to mend the damage. If you leave a hill farm neglected for too long, the hill will claim it back, no matter what you do at the last. All the same, however sensible it might be to cut his losses, the fact remained that he had to start out all over again. He turned his head away and set his jaw against the possibility of tears.

'It's all OK at work, though?' said Gwyneth, tactfully reading the need for a different subject. 'It can be a blessing, work, staying busy.'

'Work's fine,' said Bryn, regaining control of his vocal cords. 'But I don't know, I'm thinking of leaving, to be honest.'

A surge of relief swept into his mother's voice. 'Oh, I do hope so. Your dad could use the help, Bryn. He's not been so well lately and I know Dai has his hands full.'

Bryn's elder brother Dai, the family success story, had retired from professional rugby a few years ago through injury and started up a construction company, specialising in agricultural buildings for local farmers. Nothing would please his mother more than Bryn joining forces with Dai and helping his dad out on the farm in his spare time.

'Lord, no. Not that. I've got a lot of options, but I'll probably end up setting up on my own.'

'Oh . . . I didn't know you could do that.'

'Do what?'

'You know, set up your own bank, just one person. I thought you needed . . .'

Bryn laughed. In the fourteen years of his banking career, his mother had understood nothing about how he earned his living beyond the fact that he worked for a bank. 'No, I won't set up my own bank. I'm thinking of going into health technology. Medicine.'

Gwyneth searched her repertoire for an appropriate response, but came away empty-handed. She raised her eyebrows, put her hands to her perfectly set hair, and gave her son a big multi-purpose smile. 'Medicine,' she said. 'That's nice.'

Meanwhile, outside, the first flakes of a new snowfall

began to cover up the tyre tracks and footprints that had speckled the yard outside with black.

2

'You're kidding.' Cameron wasn't fazed.

'I know. I ought to be joking. I bought it over the phone. I was snowed up in Wales, and all I had was my dad's blurry fax machine. It looked OK in the photo.' He gestured around, trying to explain how he'd got drunk with his brother Dai one lunchtime, stumbled across to the farm office, peered at a string of small and fuzzy fax images of buildings, selected one on the basis of price alone, and then faxed through a signature on the contract before he'd had time to take a second look.

'You're *not* kidding? Seriously?'

They were standing inside, but their coats were on and their breath built castles in the freezing air. From a hole in the roof water dripped, joining the pools of water covering the floor.

'It's not all bad,' said Bryn. 'It's cheap. We can fix it up. And it's big. We wouldn't have got this much space, if –'

'If you'd actually bought, like, a building. You know, those things with walls, a roof, lighting, heating –'

'No water on the floor,' said Kati. 'No concrete slipway heading into a river.'

'No boats. No smell of muck that's been allowed –'

'Oh my God,' said Kati, as a fat black rat ambled out of a stack of rotting timber and lolloped across the floor to a hole in the wall before disappearing. 'No rats, for heaven's sake. I mean, don't get me wrong. I like rats, but there are limits.'

They had a point. Cameron and Kati had obediently done what Bryn had begged them to do. They'd gone home to their parents, in Chicago and Vancouver respectively, and spun some yarn about looking to start the next phase of their work with a new research institution, possibly in Europe. They'd sent out letters to a handful of American colleges and research companies, deliberately weak applications that would be quite likely rejected even if Corinth wasn't quick enough to stamp on them.

And then they'd disappeared. They took holiday flights down to Mexico City, went by bus north to Tijuana, then via a couple of further flights moved on into Latin America before catching a mainline British Airways flight direct from Rio to London. As Bryn had said, 'Not even Corinth is going to keep up with your movements. They'll probably catch at least some of your application letters, and I wouldn't be surprised if they snoop around your parents' neighbourhoods, trying to pick up your trail. All they'll see is a story of failure. Most likely, they'll assume you got some research post in Europe. As far as your folks are concerned, you should let them think the same thing. Corinth will keep an ear to the ground, but they'll never find you. Not here.'

Cameron poked an oil-spattered tarpaulin with her foot. Water sloshed around in the folds, but at least any wildlife under the surface stayed put. 'You can hardly blame them,' she said. 'This isn't exactly where you'd expect to find us.'

Bryn sighed. The Fulham Boathouses had certainly been cheap, and yet, in Bryn's half-inebriated state, the estate agent's photo had been deeply misleading. In the foreground of the picture there had been an old Victorian wharf reconfigured as modern offices, and it was this Bryn thought he'd been buying. Dominating the rear, the boathouses had stood untouched since the Fulham Boating Association had gone bankrupt in 1973. The wooden walls were wet to the touch, and large areas of timber were so rotted away that Bryn could easily enough have put his fist through the side of the building. Inside, apart from the rats, there was little enough: rowing-boat hulls covered with tarpaulins or left to rot along with everything else. The only object of any grace was a lofty barge-style houseboat, of the sort that the Oxford colleges used to keep.

And yet, there were compensations. The boathouses were located amidst a cluster of wharves, where the Thames sweeps south from Hammersmith. They were only a brisk walk from Fulham Broadway and the King's Road, and not more than a stone's throw from the heart of London. At the end of the main boathouse, wide double doors twenty feet high opened out on to the river. Thrown open, and assuming a warm summer's day instead of the miserable February weather that actually surrounded them, the view would be spectacular, the far side of the Thames a mass of elderflower and rosebay willowherb, tumbling down the cobbled bank into the water.

'You know, it's not so bad. My brother's a builder and he'll help sort this out. He won't charge much, and besides, buildings are easy. We've got a much more immediate problem.'

'We have?' said Cameron. 'Do I want to know?'

'You certainly do,' said Bryn, and told her.

3

'Pick a disease, pick any disease.'

It was certainly an excellent selection that the young man had to choose from. A small cupboard tinkled with glass-stoppered ampoules, each one labelled with an acronym denoting the killer disease inside.

'We've got a good range of retro-viruses in at the moment,' continued Cameron. 'Our spuma viruses are a little short, but we've got all the herpetic viruses, filoviruses, a very nice O'nyong-nyong fever . . . How about the arbo-virus? You get some really interesting brain diseases, you know, generally fatal. I can offer you a wonderful Vene-zuelan equine encephalitis, some Russian spring–summer encephalitis, a pretty fair Japanese –'

The young man began to look pale as Cameron rambled on. He was a venture capitalist called Malcolm Milne and Bryn was hoping that Milne, or one of his competitors, would be able to solve the young company's most immedi-ate need – funding. But while there was every reason to impress Milne, there was no need to terrify him.

'Why don't you choose, Cameron? This one, for example.' Bryn grabbed an ampoule at random.

'Kuru virus!' she exclaimed in delight. 'New Guinea laughing sickness. Ex-cellent choice. Slow-acting. Fatal. Vir-tually wiped out the poor old Foré tribe. Not something we see so much now. Transmitted exclusively via cannibalism, you know. All those raw brains lying around. Mm-*mmm*. Very tempting.'

Jiggling the ampoule in pleasure, she bounded off to the temporary microscopy bench set up in Bryn's living room. Cameron's scientific clutter looked incongruous amidst Cecily's carefully chosen furniture and costly paintings. On the whole, Bryn knew which he preferred, and he watched contentedly as Cameron drew blood from Milne, and added it to the virus solution. When she was done, Kati took the tube and slid it into the white dome of the Schoolroom, checking the connections into her PC. They were short of tables, so the Schoolroom just sat on the Persian carpet, like a mosque in miniature. 'OK to start,' she said.

'OK,' said Cameron, 'get this. Inside the Schoolroom now, in that tube of blood, there are good cells and bad cells. The good cells are going to munch up the kuru virus, the bad cells are going to sit on their butts.' She moved to the PC monitor, where a crowded data panel was being continually updated. 'Look here. The Schoolroom is calculating your percentage of successful cells. This number here shows your score.'

Milne looked. 'Two per cent?' he said, obviously gutted. 'Isn't that awful?'

'Against a real nasty kuru virus? No, no, I'd say that wasn't bad at all. But, OK, you need to do better. Now, tell me, what would you do about it?'

'What would I do?'

'Sure. Think of your immune cells as soldiers, as a miniature army. What would you do?'

Milne thought about it. 'I guess an army needs guns and ammunition. It needs equipment. Food, obviously . . .' He shrugged. What do armies need? 'Boots?'

Cameron was nodding vigorously, as though Milne was expounding some brilliantly technical scientific theory. 'Pre-*cise*-ly,' she enthused. 'That's it. Guns, ammo, food, boots. And that's what your immune system needs. Vitamins, minerals, amino acids, antioxidants, catalysts, enzymes, co-factors. You name it. The right amounts, in the right mixtures.'

'That's your technique?' said Milne, disappointed. 'You dole out vitamins?'

Cameron shook her head. 'No. Think about the army again. You've got it equipped, rested, fed. What next?'

'Next? You attack the enemy, I suppose. "Once more unto the breach, dear friends, once more." '

Shakespeare hadn't been on the Harvard med school syllabus and Cameron looked momentarily puzzled. 'Right,' she said. 'Exactly. You attack. But how? You've got tanks, planes, infantry – I don't know, what do they have in armies? – artillery, missiles, all kinds of stuff, but do you just blaze off with everything, or is there some sequence you're meant to follow? Do you just charge in, or do you co-ordinate things?'

Now it was Milne's turn to look puzzled. 'Well, you have a commander-in-chief, I suppose. He gets information, develops a strategy, sends out orders . . .' He shrugged again.

Once again, Cameron looked radiant, as though one-to-one with Einstein. 'Pre-*cise*-ly. Exactly right. Communication. Armies use radio, computers use program code. The human body uses – well, a whole bunch of stuff, but among other things, it uses peptides.'

Milne began to nod. 'Peptides, right . . . program code. This is the Immune Reprogramming part, correct?'

Cameron nodded and tapped the Schoolroom on its baby-smooth dome. 'Now watch.'

Cameron nodded to Kati, who hit some keys on the PC and threw a switch on the Schoolroom. The Schoolroom's hum increased, and its faint vibration could be felt working its way through the thick carpet on the floor, creeping out towards Cecily's expensively tasteful wallpaper.

'Like I say, we can't promise much,' said Cameron. 'The peptide sequences are very specific. We don't know the code for humans, and we certainly don't know the code for kuru viruses in humans.'

'So what are you doing?'

'We can get your army properly equipped. Vitamins, minerals, all the rest of it. And we know some parts of the code, peptides which seem to be associated with a generalised performance in immune activity. It's kind of basic, like getting your plan of attack from a training manual. But still, at this stage it's as good as we can do.'

Milne nodded.

The Schoolroom hummed in the surrounding silence. On screen, the percentage of good cells ticked slowly upwards:

3%, 4%, 5%, 6%, 6.5%. The rate of increase slowed to a halt. It stopped. Cameron glanced across at Kati, who caught her intention and instructed the Schoolroom to stop. The hum died away. A grey cardboard tray of needles stopped its tiny glassware chatter.

'That's it?' said Milne.

Cameron peered intently at the screen, reading the hundred-and-twenty or so data parameters caught and measured by the Schoolroom. 'This virus pretty much wiped out the Forés of New Guinea. I told you it was nasty.'

'And don't underestimate what we've just done,' added Kati. 'Your immune system was at two per cent competence. It's now at six and a half per cent. You're already three times better at fighting this disease, and that's our most basic possible treatment programme.'

'We could try to juice things up a little,' said Cameron. 'Now, if you were a rat, of course . . .' She spoke briefly with Kati, discussing the on-screen data, and they agreed on some changes. Kati removed one tray of fluids from the Schoolroom and slotted another one home.

Their guess seemed to be an accurate one. The percentage of reprogrammed cells began to creep upwards once again: 7%, 8%, 10%. Then, all of a sudden, the numbers shot upwards: 25%, 67%, 98%. Error messages flashed on-screen and Cameron and Kati sighed in simultaneous disappointment.

'Isn't that good?' asked Milne. 'Ninety-eight per cent? That virus is dead meat.'

'True,' said Cameron, 'but so are you. We overcharged your immune system and it's gone crazy. Your army isn't just attacking the enemy, it's attacking you. You've now got a highly serious auto-immune disease. If you were a patient, you'd be dead.'

70

Kati typed an instruction on the PC, and the School-room's hum died away. A little click of glassware indicated the arrival of a bottle in a dispensing chamber. Cameron withdrew it and shook it up against the light from the broad sash windows, then dropped it regretfully into a clinical waste bin.

'OK. We failed. Shame you're not a rat.'

'And if I were?'

'Then instead of throwing away that bottle, I'd have injected it back into your arm.'

'Reprogrammed cells only, right?'

'Right. We chuck the bad ones. And we wouldn't take a little ten-millilitre sample from you, we'd take half a pint. Every day. Until you'd licked the disease.'

'And it's OK just to throw away the cells that don't make it?'

'It's not OK, it's actually good. It stimulates the body to grow more cells. And since we're saving the good ones and chucking the bad ones, you head towards a situation where most of the cells in your immune system are highly trained at destroying kuru viruses.' She raised her hands, as though to show that she could do no more. 'There's no way you can stay ill under those circumstances. None at all.'

Silence fell.

Bryn looked at Milne. Milne looked at Bryn.

'OK,' said Milne, at last. 'I'm interested.'

4

'Ha, ha, ha, Bryn, you're a right berk, you are.' Dai, Bryn's brother, the former glory of the Pontypridd rugby pack, swung his leg back and kicked a hole right through the collapsing timber. 'I must be a bloody ghost, like,' he said, crashing against the side of the shed with all his weight and emerging in a shower of rotten wood on the other side. 'I can walk through walls. Here, look here.' He was about to give another demonstration of his supernatural powers, when Bryn intervened.

'OK, OK, Dai, I can see the wall's rotten, thank you. I was wondering whether you might be able to fix it up as well as knocking it down.'

Dai clambered back through the hole he'd made, meditatively ripping off another chunk of planking on his way.

'That all depends on the load-bearing timber.'

He used a pocket knife to scrape at one of the main timbers supporting the roof. There was a layer of green slime on top, but underneath the wood was hard and good. He walked along the wall, testing the thick oak pillars. 'Seems OK. Have you looked in the roof?'

'Yes. The beams and roof trusses are basically fine. The rest of it's a disaster.'

'Ha, ha, ha, by God, Bryn, it's a good job you didn't get really drunk, otherwise God knows what you'd have bought. Dad's cow barn looks a bloody palace compared.'

He laughed, but all the time his eye was assessing what needed to be done. It wasn't long before he delivered his verdict. 'I'd say we can clean up the main structural timbers, rip away the rest of it – that'll be a short bloody job, and all – and just put up a new shell, tongue and groove, shiplap, whatever. Then the roof basically the same. What do you want? Cheapest would be sheets of ply with weatherproofing. 'Course, you'd have to –'

'Insulation.' Kati had appeared from one of the rooms to the side of the main boathouse. She was wearing gumboots and was wadded like a doughnut in fleece-and-down jackets. Her perfect curls were stuffed away into a woolly hat and her cheeks shone pink and clear with the cold. 'Insulation,' she said. 'Lots of it.'

'Insulation, Bryn? I'll use eighteen-mill tongue and groove. Can't see you wanting insulation as well.'

Kati opened her mouth to protest, but Bryn waved her quiet. 'My brother's idea of a joke. We'll stick in a ton of fibreglass.'

'Mineral wool's better,' said Kati. 'Non-carcinogenic.'

She explored the building's timbering with her hands, trying to visualise how the insulation would work, and Bryn stepped close to her, not touching, but working alongside her, their breath forming one cloud which rose above them into the vastness of the roof. 'Mineral wool it is,' he said, without stepping away from her side.

'Eh, eh, Ewan,' said Dai. 'We need to sort out some rooms in here. No point putting in insulation if you've got a thirty-foot ceiling. And what d'you want to do about the observation tower? Rip it down or fix it up?'

Bryn reluctantly left Kati's side and continued round the derelict buildings with his brother, identifying problems, suggesting solutions. He was a good builder, Dai, and his business would have done well even if it hadn't been the automatic choice of every Pontypridd fan within forty miles.

'We going to use local labour, or d'you want me to bring my men?'

'Use yours,' said Bryn. 'I don't want to pay London wages if I can help it.'

'I'll tell that to my lads, see if they want to come.'

'They'll come.'

'And they'll have to stay somewhere.'

'They can stay with me.'

'I'll try, I promise, but no guarantees.'

'How many men d'you need!'

Dai looked around. 'Half a dozen, plus trades. Sparky, plumber, decorator.'

Bryn pulled three wads of tickets from his pocket. 'Six

Nations rugby,' he said. 'England–Wales at Twickenham, Ireland–Wales at Lansdowne Road, Wales–France at the Millennium Stadium. I'm still trying to get Wales–Scotland, and the Italy game. Transport and beer thrown in as well.'

'By damn,' said Dai, fanning out the tickets in admiration. 'You're right, they'll come. Bloody hell, Bryn, we'd even get Dad up to London for this, except he's under the weather all the time now.'

After Dai had left, notebook crammed with notes, rugby tickets cosseted like the Crown Jewels in his breast pocket, Kati spoke to Bryn.

'Nice guy, your brother.'

'Salt of the earth, and just as thirsty.'

'He called you Ewan. Why?'

'We had a sheepdog called Ewan when we were lads. It's just a nickname.'

Ewan was the name of a sheepdog, alright, but not just any old dog. Of all the many collies bred and trained by Bryn's dad, Ewan was without question, beyond a doubt, and past dispute the randiest of them all. Dai had noticed Bryn's not-so-casual closeness to Kati, and the nickname was invoked by either brother when they saw the other in pursuit of a skirt.

Kati nodded solemnly as though Bryn's bland explanation made sense, knowing that it didn't. Later that day, when Bryn took advantage of Cameron's absence to take a meal alone with Kati, she laughed at his jokes, was merry and outgoing, was happy to talk about herself and her family, and showed a warm interest in Bryn and his family. But when the meal ended, she refused a 'cup of coffee at my place', kissed Bryn high on the cheek, and took a separate cab home to her Notting Hill flatshare.

'Eh, eh, Ewan,' said Bryn to himself as he watched her go, 'never give up, boy, never give up.'

74

5

Starting in business is like jumping a ravine. Getting it right is terrific. Getting it nearly right is so bad, you'd better not have jumped at all.

Bryn knew that. He'd seen businesses take the run up, make the jump, lose their footing ever so slightly on take off – and then sail through the air, destined never to make the other side, destined to fall in appalled slow motion a thousand feet to the boulders and thorn bushes strewing the canyon floor.

He didn't want to be like that. He took precautions, and one night he drew up a contract and brought it to Cameron, who was sitting in Bryn's living-room-turned-laboratory.

'Hey there, Money Man,' she greeted him.

'Hey there, Medicine Woman.'

'Found me my money yet?'

'Nope. Still looking. Found a cure for AIDS yet?'

'Nope. Still looking.'

They laughed. Because he was laughing, Bryn spilled his coffee (Jamaican roast, double espresso, a hint of sugar). The coffee splurged out on to the sofa, staining the pale yellow silk. 'Don't worry about it,' he said as Cameron leaped up, ready to mop it up. 'Leave it.'

'You don't like the sofa? It's kind of nice to spoil.'

'It's OK.' Bryn shrugged. 'But Cecily wants it back. As well as that,' he said, pointing to a little Venetian chess table. 'And that, that, that and that,' he said, pointing to most of the other objects in the room.

'She's cleaning you out, huh?'

'She's helping herself to the contents of one pocket. The business is taking the contents of the other.'

'So what does that leave you?'

Bryn laughed. 'I don't know. My trousers? Here. I've got a contract.' He handed it over.

Before she took it, she held his gaze a little longer. 'Don't drive yourself too hard,' she said. 'You need to look after yourself.'

'Don't worry, I will. I am.'

She dropped her eyes and peered at the agreement. 'I thought I already signed a contract.'

'An employment contract, yes. This is an assignment of intellectual property rights. It transfers your research to the company. It's required for insurance purposes. Doesn't mean anything.'

'If it doesn't mean anything, why do it?'

'Because it's required for insurance purposes.'

'I hand over everything I've worked on for the last five years, because some damn insurance company wants me to?'

'Cameron, there's no problem in signing this. I won't stop you doing what you want with your research, absolutely anything that's reasonable.'

'I can still publish what I like?'

'If you want to tell Corinth what's going on, you can.'

'But in principle. If I wanted, I could publish?'

Bryn shrugged. 'If Corinth weren't a factor, then as far as I'm concerned you could publish whatever the hell you wanted.'

Cameron peered again at the contract, hoping it would say something in plain English so she could understand it. It didn't. Bryn had taken care to draft it that way. She shrugged and signed.

That was a mistake.

Bryn had lied.

The insurance company cared a lot about a lot of things. It cared about fire extinguisher maintenance records and whether there was going to be non-slip matting in the bathroom. The insurance company didn't give a twopenny damn about Cameron's research, but Bryn did. Since he had staked everything on Cameron's genius, he'd decided he'd better make sure of her. An employment contract wouldn't keep her from walking. Holding on to her research would.

It seemed like a minor deception. Bryn felt bad about it, but not too bad. How was he to know that everything, but *everything*, would one day be set at risk?

SIX

1

Five weeks later.

The boathouse now more than a third of the way towards total renovation, Dai and his men working dawn to dusk, foul timber all stripped and burned, new walls flying up, a smell of wood primer and sawdust, gathering excitement, and huge views out over the river filling their new world with light. So far, so good.

The medical side had been attended to as well. Cameron and Kati drew up a wish-list of lab equipment, expecting Bryn to argue every single item, as their old employers always had. But not a bit of it. 'Sure this is all?' he'd said, waving a chequebook, and now, every day, vans arrived at the boatyard, asking repeatedly if this was really the right place, and unloading crate after crate of beautiful new equipment: blood spectrometers from Germany, medical glassware from Sweden, computers from California, centrifuges from Canada, clean air filtration systems from France and Britain, and clinking bottles of chemicals from Italy, Japan, Switzerland and America. The boathouse had an old observation tower – formerly the spot from which the jolly old Fulham rowers watched the jolly old boat race – and Cameron had seized upon it as her office, and was already nine tenths of the way towards filling it with junk. So far, so good.

By now, several venture capitalists had been introduced to the emerging technology under conditions of the strictest secrecy, enforced by the fiercest confidentiality agreement Bryn had ever drawn up. Two of the finance houses were still thinking, the third – Malcolm Milne's – had come back with a strong positive response and an offer of funding on excellent terms. So far, so excellent.

Buoyed up by the signs of success, Bryn had incorporated the company, drawn up articles of association, registered for VAT, opened accounts and done all of the hundred other things that a young company needs. They were now officially Fulham Research Ltd, described in official documents as a company 'involved in research and development in the area of human biology'. The vaguer the better, as far as Bryn was concerned, anxious to hide from Corinth as long as he was able. But of Corinth, there was no sign at all. So far, so good.

Romantically, Bryn had been making the most of his brother's hint and had done what he could to woo Kati. Kati liked him well enough, that much was clear, but she'd just been dumped virtually at the altar by a cheating fiancé, and she was in no hurry to get started with anyone else, least of all her boss. Bryn was disappointed, but didn't lose hope. He took care over his appearance (as far as was possible when he had half a dozen Welsh builders sharing his bathroom) and went out of his way to be charming. He liked Kati, and wasn't in a rush. So far, so satisfactory.

Adding to his workforce already, he brought across Meg Tillery, his former secretary, from Berger Scholes. To Bryn's delight, Meg had taken only about half a minute to listen to his proposal before saying yes, and only about half an hour from saying yes to leaving Berger Scholes with her personal belongings tucked into the traditional black bin-liner. So far, so good.

Of Corinth's henchmen, there was no sign. Cameron and Kati had cautiously sounded out their parents and it had transpired that, just as Bryn had predicted, there had been a stranger snooping round their home neighbourhoods, asking for information. Since Kati and Cameron had been vague and unspecific, Corinth would have learned nothing of value. Bryn felt sure Huizinga would keep an ear to the ground, but without knowing where Cameron was, there was little more he could do. So far, so good.

But all was not well. In fact things had grown so bad, Bryn was beginning to wonder if he'd committed the worst mistake of his entire life.

2

'Let me get this straight,' said Bryn, clamping down hard on his voice so he didn't actually yell. 'I've found twenty million pounds' worth of funding, and you're telling me you don't want it?'

'Right.'

Muscles fought in Bryn's jaw as he composed a reply. 'Cameron, you do understand that we need this money? That the company relies on obtaining this money?'

'Wrong. We need money. Not twenty million pounds, maybe only a quarter of that. But whatever the amount, we don't need this money. Not from Milner.'

'Milne.'

'Whatever.'

It was late at night in the boathouse, the only time it was usable, when Dai and his lads had downed tools and were doing their worst in London's nightspots. A couple of the smaller downstairs rooms were all but finished and

Cameron had been setting them up the way she wanted: bloodwork facility, microscope workshop, computer pods, library. She was dressed in her working outfit: jeans and a T-shirt, with a labcoat flung on top, hanging from her skinny shoulders as from a broomstick scarecrow. A thick rubber band of the sort dropped on the pavement by postmen twisted her hair away out of sight. Once, as Bryn had watched, an end of hair escaped its grip once too often, and she reached for a pair of surgical scissors and snipped it off at the root. 'Damn hair,' she muttered.

Now, ignoring Bryn, she pulled over an unpacked shipment of dyes and solvents and began to rip away the brown packaging tape. Bryn reached for the box and tugged it from her grasp.

'Please stop that,' he said. 'We need to talk.'

She looked irritated, glance wandering around the room, visibly thinking through how best to arrange her stores. 'Now?'

'Yes, now.'

She gazed round the room again, before grunting, 'Uh, OK,' figuring that the quickest way to get rid of Bryn was to hear him out. 'Upstairs, then. I've left my tea.'

They walked up the spiral staircase to Cameron's office. Windows looked out in each direction: north and east over central London, south and west over the river. 'You'll be a bloody princess in here,' Dai had said as he'd finished the room, 'all you need now is the knight in shining armour.' The tower room did have something of the fairy-tale about it, but what Bryn thought of was ivory towers, academic scientists cut off from the real world, out of sight and out of touch. Cameron rummaged amongst her rapidly growing mounds of papers and found a long-cooled cup of camomile tea. 'Ugh,' she sipped it and put it down. 'Forget that. OK. Shoot.'

'Good.' Bryn found a wooden storage cupboard that hadn't yet been swamped by clutter and sat down. 'First point, we need money, lots of it, I estimate twenty million pounds.'

'So you keep saying. I don't see us needing more than five.'

'Look. Five million pounds only covers your human research phase. It gets you to where you've already got to with rats.'

'Right. Which, as I recall, was a one hundred per cent cure of all viral diseases tested.'

'Good. That's the hard part, but not the most important part.'

'Oh, for God's sake. What's this? A lecture on the profit motive? You're confusing me with someone who gives a damn. Please get this. *I – don't – care.*'

She stood up and reached for her tea, wanting to move it to a safer spot, but Bryn interrupted. He was in a fury of impatience. He was the boss, head of the company, chief executive. At Berger Scholes he'd been a Managing Director, able to snap orders at nearly anyone in the firm and have them obeyed. Yet here he was, for all his notional power, unable even to hold a conversation with his most critical employee. He leaped to his feet and, as Cameron reached for the tea, he grabbed it first and slammed it down on a window sill.

'No,' he snapped. 'This is not about profits. It's something you need to hear. Please.'

Cameron breathed out in a sigh. 'OK. Go ahead.'

'Good. Now, you just told me that you can cure all major viral diseases in rats.'

'If we get 'em early. If the disease has progressed far, then –'

'OK. If you get 'em early, a hundred per cent. Now, tell

me, could I do that? Take the Schoolroom, cure your rats?'

'What? *You?*'

'Yes, me. Could I personally cure a rat with an early-stage viral disease?'

'No way. Never.'

'How about a doctor, let's say an infectious diseases guy in a busy hospital? A nurse? A lab assistant?'

Cameron blew out through her nose and glanced unceremoniously at her watch. 'Listen, Kati and I can cure those rats because for the last five years we've worked on nothing else at all. We know our rats. We know our blood. We know our viruses. We know the Schoolroom. We know –'

'Exactly,' said Bryn, holding up his hand. 'Thank you. Now tell me, once you've finished your human work, and you and Kati are getting a close to one hundred per cent cure rate, it's going to be the same, isn't it?'

Cameron looked blank, unsure what he was getting at. He continued. 'You've got a technique for curing people, but no one knows how to use it. By your own statement, it takes five years of training to use the Schoolroom competently, which is four years, eleven months and two weeks too long.' Holding his hands in front of him like a conductor damping the orchestra's sound, he said, 'The point is your technology's useless unless people use it. Me, a nurse, a busy doctor, a lab guy. With training, of course. A week or two. Even a month or two. But not five years, plus a medical doctorate, plus a research doctorate, plus a brain the size of a planet which everyone tells me is going to get a Nobel Prize one of these days.'

He stopped abruptly. It was an odd way to deliver a compliment. She wrinkled her mouth in embarrassed acknowledgement of the praise.

'Uh. I see your point.'

'Right. So five million pounds for your clinical trials. I've allowed eight million, because these things run over. Then another dozen or so for development. Turning the School-room into a box of tricks which anyone can use, me, a nurse, a lab guy, whoever.'

'Hence twenty million.'

'And hence Malcolm Milne.'

Now that Bryn no longer had to force his words at his recalcitrant partner, the space between them had grown too narrow. Cameron swivelled to look out of the window, where the black Thames marched silently towards Chelsea, Westminster, and St Paul's. London was a new city for her, a new adventure. She still didn't know whether her escape from Boston was the smartest move she'd ever made, or the stupidest. Bryn moved back, scuffing some piles of books on the floor. Cameron glanced at her watch, then returned her gaze to Bryn. 'OK. I get the money part. I take the point.'

'I knew you'd –'

'But Malcolm Milne, no way. Sorry, but no.'

3

'I *heard* him,' said Cameron patiently. 'He was talking about exit. He was talking about selling the company.'

'Yes, it's how venture capital works. Milne has to sell out to repay his investors.'

'How long before he sells?'

'Five years, maybe seven, maybe one. It's his call.'

'Who'll control the company? You, or Milne and his cronies?'

'The Board controls the company. The shareholders appoint the Board.'

'That's a bullshit answer.'

'OK. It depends how much of the business I sell. Since

all we've got at this stage is an idea, I'll probably have to sell seventy or eighty per cent to raise enough money. But even if I could persuade Milne to take just forty-nine per cent, he'd still require a say in all major decisions.'

'So Milne either controls the company or he has a veto?'

'It's not in his interest to screw things up.'

'His interest, huh?' There was another, longer pause. Cameron found a rubber band on the bench beside her and pinged it out into the dark, out on to the sleeping river. 'And when his time's up, who does Milne sell us to?'

Bryn spread his hands at an impossible question. 'Maybe he floats us on the stockmarket. Maybe he sells us to a company in a related business, maybe ... Well, anyone, whoever offers most.'

'Such as a drugs company scared by our technology?'

'Cameron, he can sell us to anyone he wants. He needs to make a profit. It's the rules of the game.'

'The rules of the game say he can sell us to Corinth?'

Bryn shook his head. 'Yes, that's possible, but really –'

'Really what? Back in Boston, you said that – what's-his-face – Hosanna –'

'Huizinga.'

'– saw this as a him or us situation, a game worth one hundred billion dollars to him. Why wouldn't he buy us? Buy us, then drop the technology? That's a crazy risk to take.'

'It's a risk you won't be able to take, without funding.'

Cameron stared out into the black night. Across the water, streetlights shone orange through a screen of winter trees while upriver, moored in a line below Hammersmith Bridge, a group of houseboats stirred slowly in the breeze, red lamps warning where their sterns jutted out into the current. Her breath misted the window.

Bryn let her think. There was no option except to take

Milne's money, none at all. She was a smart woman and she would see that, she'd have to. When she turned on her heel to answer him, he was ready for anything except what she actually said.

'Then we have a problem, because I am not going to put my ideas into hands that I don't trust.'

'Milne's OK. Don't worry about Milne.'

'I don't care if he's Mother Teresa, he'll still sell to the highest bidder. He *has* to. You just told me he does.'

'Cameron.' Bryn's voice was hard-edged again, hard and desperate. 'You need to be realistic.'

'True.'

'You're killing this company. This is the only way.'

She brought her face to within a few inches of his. Close up, you no longer noticed its pallor, the brusque way in which its owner treated it, all you saw were its commanding grey eyes, ablaze with intensity and passion.

'Listen, I have a chance to develop a technology which will save lives. Potentially hundreds of thousands of lives, millions, even. The Schoolroom doesn't have to be expensive. Peptides don't have to be expensive. This is a medicine which can wipe out some of the nastiest diseases in not just the rich countries, but the poor ones, too.

'You're asking me to take a chance on Milne. Fine. If it was just me, just my career, just this company, I'd be happy to bet everything on him. But the patients? The AIDS sufferers, the hepatitis victims, all those grannies who die just because their poor old immune systems can't cope with a simple flu bug?' She shook her head. 'I can't do it, Bryn. I won't.'

Bryn pursed his lips. He felt small for thinking the thought, but it bothered him when he heard Cameron talking about selling their technology cheaply. Not that he wanted to rip people off – not that he wanted the Third

World to suffer – just . . . Well, after all, he was a business-man and this was his business.

He sighed. 'I know, Cameron. I understand, believe me. But we have to face facts. We need the money.'

Cameron dropped her eyes and picked up the offer letter from Milne which had prompted the whole conversation. Tearing it into shreds and leaning far out of the window, she threw it into the river, where the white fragments began to float away, caught by the silent midnight ripples.

'I agree,' she said, 'we need the money. But not from Milne. Not now. Not ever.'

SEVEN

1

The immense and mouldering college barge which had been sitting in the main boathouse had been hauled down the slipway to sink or swim, and after a brief hesitation, it had swum quite happily, moored up against the side of the boat-house, slapping against the wood at every change in the wind. It made a nice place to sit and watch life, and Bryn sat on the roof of the barge, protected from the green mould by a dustsheet left by Dai.

Meg, Bryn's former secretary and a bouncy brunette who was just a few years younger than him, came round the corner of the boathouse, down the jetty, and scrambled breathlessly on to the roof. 'Coffee,' she said, dumping a bag down beside her. 'And yes, it is from the Italian shop up the road, and yes, it is a double espresso, and yes it is continental roast, and yes, you are the most finicky coffee drinker in the whole world ever.'

Bryn took the coffee with gratitude, and began telling her about Cameron's refusal to take money from the venture capitalists.

'Twenty million quid,' said Meg. 'She tore it up?'

Scraps of the ripped-up offer letter still floated down by the side of the barge, trapped in a debris of floating twigs, plastic bottles and a kind of nameless oily scum. Bryn gestured at it with his coffee cup.

'There it is. All gone. Shame.'

Meg had tried lying back on the roof to catch some early spring sun, but the sun was so feeble it was scarcely worth catching, and her head had poked over the edge of the dustsheet, quickly gathering an assortment of moulds, lichens and algae. Picking the green bits from her hair, she mused aloud. 'Cammie had a point, though. It would have been gutting if you'd succeeded with everything, just for old Malcolm Milne to sell the whole kit an' caboodle to Corinth.'

Bryn smiled wryly. 'Right. Not that gutting, since I'd stand to make a bloody fortune from the sale. Besides, there'd be no reason for Milne to sell to the bad guys. It's not as though he cares one way or the other.'

'Cammie's point exactly, sweetie.' She looked at the green stuff collected in her hand and hurled it at a gull, missing by miles. She continued to gaze after it, then sprang to attention. 'What the hell is that?' she demanded, jabbing a finger downstream past the red-brick wharves towards the empty trees of Bishop's Park.

'It's a tree, Meg, a willow tree.'

'It's what's in the tree, matey. Look.'

Bryn rolled on to his elbow. In the bare branches of the willow tree, there was a blue-green smudge. 'Bloody hell, you're right. It's a parrot.' The blue-green smudge nodded its head and began to preen, as though to confirm the sighting.

'Must have escaped,' she said. Then, 'Good on you, parrot!' she screamed.

Bryn shook his head. 'Actually, I doubt it. They're meant to be quite common, apparently. Escaped parrots started breeding and London's warm enough these days for the birds to survive through the winter. I'll bet you we're looking at a genuine wild parrot.'

'Wild? Who's wild? I don't call you a wild Welshman, do I? It's free, a free parrot.'

Bryn laughed and swigged at his rapidly cooling coffee. Meg continued gazing, mesmerised, at her find.

'It's a pity you had to go elsewhere for money,' she said reflectively. 'I know you. You wouldn't sell out to the bad guys, however much you think you would.'

'It's a pity I'm not a multi-millionaire, Meg.'

She looked sharply at him, about to cross the unmentionable gap between banking secretary and banking boss. 'You must be pretty close, though,' she said. 'Big swinger at Berger Scholes and all that.'

Bryn sighed. 'I've had to split things with Cecily. She gets all the savings and most of the furnishings of any quality. I get the house, my deferred bonuses – ha, bloody ha – and sod all else. I'm not far off being a pauper.'

'What's ha bloody ha?'

'All gone, Megsy, m'dear. You forfeit your deferred bonuses if you leave. I left. I forfeited them. Three quarters of a million quid.'

'Bloody hell, you're a madman.' Meg pondered the notion of having three quarters of a million pounds and then losing it. 'I wouldn't have left if you'd dragged me by my hair. I'd have glued myself to my desk. I'd have nailed my –'

'Yeah, well, your sympathy is duly noted.' A pause. 'That just leaves my house. It'll fetch getting on for a million, though I had sort of planned to live in it . . . Anyway, even a million's no good. This company needs way more than that.'

Meg rolled on to her belly, poking her head over the side of the barge, staring at her reflection in the turbid waters. 'Why not borrow the money? Then we wouldn't have to have horrible investors, just horrible banks.'

'You can't simply go out and borrow. You have to have assets to borrow against. If you don't have assets, you have to have cash flows, revenues, profits. Old fashioned things like that.'

'Well, there you go, then.' Meg rolled round the other way and sat up. 'First get some cash flows, then borrow some money. Honestly, some banker you are.'

Bryn swirled the last of his coffee round his cup. It was stone cold, but he drank it anyway. For the past forty minutes, the sun had shone like a pale disc through cloud, and the day was too cold for long periods on top of dank and festering barges. If he was a parrot, he'd stay indoors. He stood up to go.

'Thanks for the brainwave, Meg. The Schoolroom works on rats. How about we charge them . . .' As his voice tapered off, he suddenly froze. 'By God, though, you never know . . .' His posture changed; became charged with energy. At the end of the barge, there was a dried-out tin of paint left by one of Dai's workmen. Bryn repositioned the tin with care, and took a few paces backwards. 'That pleasure boat, there. One minute to go, two points needed for victory. Bryn Hughes to take the kick.'

Meg looked at the launch making its way upriver, twenty yards distant, its roof dotted with passengers. 'What are you – ?'

But Bryn ignored her. He checked his pacing and settled his eye on the distant boat. Taking a quick run up, he gave the tin an enormous kick and watched it sail in a huge arc into the air, narrowly clearing the upper deck of the startled boat. The splash into the water on the other side was hidden from view. A couple of passengers who'd been watching cheered and waved. In an imaginary stadium somewhere, fifty thousand Welshmen stood and applauded.

'Is he Bryn Hughes, or is he Neil bloody Jenkins?'

'Neil who?'

But he was off, leaping off the boat, on to the bits of planking which acted as a jetty, and on into the boathouse yard.

'Cameron!' he roared. 'Cameron, Kati!'

Meg stood up. The wind was chilly. Her boss was mad. She tipped her coffee away and began to thread her way through the surrounding wharves towards the willow tree, watched by its exotic resident. 'Hello, parrot,' she said.

2

When Meg caught up, Cameron and Kati were already jammed into a pair of seats, watching Bryn as he strode around. Meg caught sight of the handsomest of Dai's workmen, winked at him and sat down.

'So that's the whole idea,' said Bryn. 'We're going to use your know-how to make some money, right here, right now. We pop the research and development outfit under the wing of a parent company, and use the parent company to generate cash. We'll use the cash to fund our research, and once we're making some serious money, we'll go out looking for some loans as well. All we need is a way of putting your existing knowledge to commercial use.'

Ten minutes earlier, Cameron and Kati had been involved in a deep conversation about new methods of peptide fractionation. Since Bryn had whirled in like a storm demon, shoving them into chairs and haranguing them, they had understood virtually nothing. They exchanged glances.

'You want us to sell something?' asked Kati.

'Yes. No. Well, OK, yes and no.' Bryn took a deep breath and another step backwards into the realm of the intelligible. 'Look, between the two of you, you know an awful lot about viruses and an awful lot about viral illness. Stuff which no one else knows.'

'Loads of people know parts of it, but maybe no one knows all of it. No one except us. Right,' said Kati.

Cameron sat imprisoned in her chair, writing chemical equations in biro on her white labcoat, and waited for something that Bryn said to make sense.

'Good,' said Bryn. 'Exactly. Now I know for a certain fact that you can put that knowledge to use. I went to Cameron with flu and she cured me, no messing.' Cameron groaned in pleasure, as she found what she was looking for in her chemical equations, then looked up to find everyone looking at her. 'Flu, did you say? Sure, but that was easy. You were an easy case. We couldn't begin to guarantee those kinds of results.'

'No, I know that, but patients don't need guarantees, they just need the best treatment available. That's you. You and Kati. You two, plus other doctors who we'll hire and train in your techniques. Obviously, we wouldn't be doing the full Immune Reprogramming at this stage, we'd use conventional drug treatment, supplemented by everything else you guys thought was useful. As time goes by, and your research matures, your treatment methods will improve too. We won't just have research papers to prove our results, we'll have patients. Hundreds of them.'

Cameron wasn't looking at her equations now, she was staring at Bryn. 'You think I ought to spend time with patients?'

'Yes. You spend time on them. They spend money on you. That's business.'

'But my research? Isn't that more –'

'More important? Yes. But we need to pay for it. This is a way to pay for it.'

'And when you think about it,' said Kati, 'we've always

wanted to have better access to patients. That way we can watch the clinical progress of disease, not just its blood chemistry.'

'Uh, 's'true,' said Cameron, still amazed. 'But you know, Bryn, can you see me with patients? I mean, when you came to see me, I hit you.'

'Did you?' said Meg. 'Good for you.'

Bryn ignored her. 'OK, no hitting. No assaults of any kind. No doodling on your labcoat while your patient is telling you their life story. And we'll make sure Kati or someone is there with yóu, so if you do accidentally lay into someone, there's someone to say sorry.'

'Uh, OK,' said Cameron, still bemused. 'Patients? Sure. Why not?'

3

And finally that week, a minor incident, hardly worth the mention.

Cameron's father, a mathematician at Illinois State University, was extremely fond of Lewis Carroll. Following a suggestion of Bryn's, Cameron bought him an expensive but special birthday gift: some early editions of *Alice in Wonderland and Alice Through the Looking Glass*. Sending them special delivery, she dispatched them in good time for his birthday, but when the day arrived, the books had not. Another week or two passed, the gift was still mislaid, and Cameron ended up claiming compensation for the full amount from the Post Office. She didn't mention the loss to Bryn or anyone else, not liking to appear naïve or incompetent in her dealings with the outside world.

And that was all. A minor incident, hardly worth the mention.

EIGHT

1

For businesses as for people, childhood is meant to be a time of happiness and freedom from care. The funding is meant to be in plentiful supply, the business concept is still untarnished by excessive contact with reality, moods are good and tempers are sunny.

Meant to. The emphasis is on *meant to.* That's not always how it works.

2

The boathouse was finished off. It looked glorious – better than glorious. The white-painted interior turned the palest spring light into a glory of watery fire, with ripples from the Thames reflected upwards through huge waterside windows on to the beams and trusses of the vaulted ceiling. A horse-shoe of consulting rooms hung like a mediaeval minstrels' gallery around the former boathouse, connected by a sweeping spiral staircase of natural oak. Round the back, Cameron had her laboratory, her library, her office up in the tower, her storeroom, and all the other requisites of a serious research programme. The building was a joy to look at and a joy to use.

Ordinarily, Dai and his crew would have been exhilarated at the end of a job. But as it turned out, the grandstand tickets supplied by Bryn had magnified a dismal Welsh performance in the Six Nations rugby to a disaster of such epic proportions that one of Dai's men had looped a rope from the ceiling rafters and tied a noose in the end. A joke, of course, but only just.

Meanwhile, Bryn had put his house on the market. The estate agent had confidently valued it at a round million, delighting Bryn, who had expected less. Unfortunately, as things turned out, it was Bryn that proved to be right. When the buyers came to view, the house was still full of at least six large Welsh workmen, each of whom was like a kind of Shake-n-Vac dispenser for builders' dust, and the kitchen, living room, bathroom, and bedrooms were full of enough beer cans to threaten a glut on the aluminium market. Offers when they came were scanty and low, and Bryn ended up settling for eight hundred and fifty, pleased to get even that.

'Where are you going to live now?' asked Meg.

Brandishing a wire brush, a boiler suit, and twenty-five litres of white paint, Bryn pointed from the reception room windows. Seagulls wheeled in the empty sky above while, beneath them, the barge they shat on, like a tarnished crone, swayed uneasily on the oily water.

'You're kidding,' said Meg.

3

Like a cross-Channel swimmer hesitating at the waterside, the first two weeks had been spent with Cameron and Kati locked in anxious theoretical discussions about the best way to handle patients.

'It's a challenge for us,' admitted Cameron during a rare interlude. 'Rats can't launch malpractice suits, and if you get it wrong, you don't have to spend too much time worrying if someone else could have done it better. Patients are different. I mean, after all, they're people.'

Kati's big spaniel eyes blinked slowly in agreement. 'On the other hand,' she said, 'it's true, we do know a lot about nutrient therapy. Like, a lot. Combining that with conventional medical care could be of incredible benefit. But still . . .' She shook her head, unhappy with the responsibility that came with looking after people instead of rats.

'Maybe we should focus on a particular disease group,' said Cameron. 'Hepatitis A, perhaps. Even flu.'

'Or how about just one patient a month?' queried Bryn sarcastically. 'Have you actually made any progress at all? Apart from working out that patients are people, that is.'

'Got anywhere?' repeated Cameron. 'Sure. We've identified some real issues, a laundry list of points to get thinking about.'

'OK,' interrupted Bryn. 'You know what? I think you should start seeing some patients, and soon. We'll open for business on Monday.'

4

On the following Monday, they threw their doors open to a wondering public, ready for all comers. On Monday evening, they closed them again, not having admitted a single patient; no one except a lady who'd wandered in asking for directions, and a bloke from the Eternity Wharf industrial estate who'd cut his finger and wondered if they had any plasters.

On Tuesday it was the same, except that no one asked for directions, and the bloke next door now had a packet of Elastoplast and no further need of medical attention.

On Wednesday, Bryn got serious about advertising.

5

London is an expensive place in which to advertise.

You can buy space alright – space on hoardings, space in papers, space on the tube trains, space on radio, space on TV, space in the freebie magazines shoved in your face at Underground stations, space on those green or pink photocopied fliers that crowd London's air like pigeons. There's no shortage of outlets for your advertising pound, but that in itself becomes the problem. Londoners close off from advertising. They develop a kind of sight-blindness which cuts out the excess of noise. To catch their eye and hold it, to keep their reading gaze for enough seconds to transmit the required information, you need to buy a mountain of space, an unmissable island in the info-cluttered sea.

'Damn it,' said Bryn, slamming down the phone. 'How the bloody hell do people get started round here?'

He picked up the sheets with his advertising budget and began to redo the numbers, trying to trim a number here, cut a figure there, knowing in his heart he should be doubling the numbers, not halving them. He was sitting with Meg in the new reception area. A cleaned-up boat hull topped with waxed oak boards formed a reception desk and Meg sat behind it reading a gossip magazine. 'Maybe I should retrain as an aromatherapist,' said Meg. 'Most of the calls we get are from people who hope we do aromatherapy and that thing they do with feet. Foot poking.'

'We'll get patients. Just a question of time.'

'Reflexology,' said Meg. 'That's it. What you need, matey, is a bit of free publicity.'

'Thanks, Meg. I'd stick to foot poking if I were you.' Bryn's voice skirted an edge of irritation. He wasn't angry at Meg but he was frustrated with the way things were going and was worried that he'd miscalculated badly.

'No, really. I mean it,' she said, returning to her magazine. For a few minutes there was silence, then Cameron wandered in, distractedly, looking for Kati. Meg interrupted her.

'Hey, Cammie. How good are you at fixing mysterious viral illnesses which have baffled literally dozens of America's best doctors?'

Cameron shrugged. 'Depends on the virus, depends on the blood.'

Meg passed over her magazine and Cameron read briefly before commenting, 'Probably virally induced mitochondrial collapse. Enteroviruses, one of the retro-viruses, could be anything. Result is what we'd call CFIDS, what you guys would call ME. It's a serious illness, in bad cases very nasty indeed.'

'Can you fix it?'

Another shrug. 'Look, with time and resources, I reckon Kati and I could fix pretty much anything. But we've only got three patients in the whole of next week and somehow I don't think she's one of them.'

Meg passed her magazine over to Bryn.

'Free publicity,' she said. 'Always listen to your Auntie Meg.'

NINE

1

Money.

It's famous for making the world go around. It's equally famous for being unable to buy you love.

But right now, Bryn wasn't concerned with love, how to buy it or how to obtain it. He wanted, roughly speaking, to make the world go around, the way he wanted and at the speed he wanted. For that, he needed money, and failing money he needed publicity, but until his house sale was completed, still a month or two away, he was as poor as a church mouse and as anonymous.

He looked again at Meg's gossip magazine. Access, access, access. The whole trick would lie in obtaining access. But how?

He drummed his fingers and came to a decision.

2

He drove home.

Upstairs.

Over his bed hung two pictures, one of them an etching by Picasso, the other an etching by Matisse. They were both of them signed, both wedding presents from Cecily's parents, and both now in Cecily's half of the divorce settlement. Too bad. He took them off the wall and carried them downstairs.

Down to the car, five seconds ahead of a traffic warden. On to New Bond Street, home to jewellers and art dealers. Bryn found the gallery he was looking for: Gellman Modern Masters. He went in, etchings tucked under his arm. The gallery was white-painted and almost empty, its street wall formed by a single sheet of plate glass. On the remaining walls there hung a couple of dozen pen and ink drawings by David Hockney, each one distantly spaced and separately lit. Neat white cards gave details of titles and dates, but there was no mention of price. Behind a glass-and-steel desk, a girl, too beautiful to be handled, sat adjusting her hair.

'I've got some pictures. I'd like to sell them.'

The girl flapped briefly, as though being spoken to was outside her job description. Then her eyes happened to fall on the telephone in front of her. She pressed a button. 'Mr Fraser . . . please,' she murmured. She replaced the handset. In the meantime, something terrible had happened to her hair, and she began to attempt an emergency resuscitation. Mr Fraser appeared.

'May I help?'

'I've two etchings I want to sell. Picasso and Matisse. I've got the certificates of authenticity and everything.'

'Indeed. I'll be happy to look, though certificates aren't always conclusive, of course.'

'They'd better be, since they've got this gallery's name on them.'

'Ah, yes, I see. Perhaps I may view the pieces?'

Bryn laid the pictures on the glass desk. The girl rolled back on her chair, worried about close contact with human beings. Her hair seemed OK for now and she sat still, worried that movement might damage something. Mr Fraser examined the etchings.

'Matisse. Yes, an earlyish piece. Perhaps 1916 or thereabouts. 1918, is it? Yes, an interesting piece, well presented, even if the print run is a little on the lengthy side. The Picasso's a bit more ordinary perhaps, but let's see. Only the fourth print to be taken from this particular plate, and good condition. You wanted to sell both?'

'Yes.'

'I could offer, perhaps, eleven thousand for the pair. Roughly six for the Matisse, just a little less for the Picasso.'

'Done.'

'Perhaps you would like to arrange with Persephone here a time to bring them in and we'll have a cheque ready for you.'

Persephone rolled closer to the desk in an act of bravery and picked up a sharp pencil, as though to prove she knew how to use it. An appointments book lay open before her, empty as the room, blank as her mind.

'I have brought them in,' said Bryn, 'and I'd like the cheque now.'

'Now?' said Fraser. 'Yes, very well. A moment, please. Persephone, perhaps you could look after this gentleman, while I . . .'

Fraser drifted off behind a white door at the back of the gallery. Persephone executed her looking-after duties by offering Bryn a smile which barely wrinkled her skin, but was no doubt intended to chop him off at the knees. Bryn left her and strolled round the gallery, looking at the Hockneys. Swimming pools, dogs, a clothed woman, a couple of naked men. Bryn thought of his dad and how little he would appreciate these works.

Fraser reappeared soundlessly, holding a sealed envelope addressed in an italic hand to Bryn Hughes, Esq. Fraser followed Bryn's gaze to one of Hockney's naked men.

'Beautiful draughtsmanship, is it not? If you should require our assistance in the future, please don't hesitate. We have many more pieces available at the back, should you wish . . .' Fraser drifted off, as though finishing a sentence would insult the art.

'Modern art,' said Bryn. He flicked the picture in a place where the naked man would be most likely to feel it. 'If you ask me, it's mostly cock,' then, turning his head so his gaze took in the rest of the gallery, 'and bull.'

Out on the street, cheque in his pocket, he dialled a number salvaged from one of Cecily's gardening books. It was the Royal Hallam Nursery and Arboretum, a regular supplier of out-of-season or unusual plants to the Chelsea Flower Show, offering horticultural perfection at eye-popping prices.

'Can I help you?' asked the girl who answered the phone.

'Yes,' said Bryn. 'I'm very sure you can.'

3

The day Fulham Research Ltd (or rather, the Fulham Clinic, as it had now become) got its fifth full-time employee was a day everyone remembered. Cameron and Kati had declared their need for serious computer assistance, and they'd begun to interview a wearisome succession of IT types, rich in jargon but apparently devoid of real programming ability. Until Mungo.

He shambled in, half an hour later than his appointed time, wearing a grubby T-shirt, a pair of enormous khaki-coloured trousers studded with unnecessary pockets, and a pair of luminous trainers which you could probably cross the Channel in, if you could have tolerated the smell.

'Wicked place,' he commented, looking around Bryn's

high-ceilinged, big-windowed office and offering no apology for his lateness.

Bryn and Cameron looked at each other, wondering whether to sling him out and wait for an adult with a working knowledge of the rudiments of hygiene.

'OK, briefly – er – Mungo, our major priority is some programming work which will be conducted under Dr Wilde's supervision, as well as –'

Bryn broke off. Mungo was shaking his head in ever larger side-to-side movements. 'No way, man. Priority number two, could be.' He ran his words into each other. *Could be* sounded more like *coo-be*, or even just *c'be*. 'You need to get some kick-ass security going first. What you've got is ropy, man. Row-peeee.'

Bryn smiled thinly, very thinly. Eavesdropping assiduously from the reception desk, Meg overheard his tone and moved closer, anxious not to miss the forthcoming explosion. 'Our IT security has been professionally installed, and as I say our main –'

'OK. Go into MS-DOS, and I'll show you.'

'MS-?'

Mungo swung Bryn's keyboard away from him and with practised fingers closed down Windows and moved into the Disk Operating System – territory deeply unfamiliar to Bryn.

'Type "tiger".'

Mungo swung the keyboard back to Bryn.

'Tiger?'

'Yeah. As in, you know, *tiger*.'

Bryn typed the word and instantly the screen filled. 'WARNING. This computer system has been tiger-teamed. The following security defects have been detected . . .' There followed a long list of problems, none of which made any sense to Bryn. 'Recommended actions: Hire Mungo.'

'You did this?' asked Bryn stupidly. 'From outside?'

'Yeah. Always do with new jobs. Check it out. Trouble is most places do what you do. Hire some drongo in a suit who farts around for a few days, then tells you what a wicked job they've done. You say, "Wicked job? Oh, I say, top hole. Here's a big pile of wonga, please spend it on your lady wife." You've been ripped, man, but course you're not going to know.' (This last bit pronounced roughly: nu-gu-nu-no). ''S not their fault mostly. Only kids.' At a guess, Mungo himself was nineteen, maybe twenty.

'Tiger-team?' said Bryn, looking back at the screen. 'As in SAS, huh?'

''S right. It's a bit of an overstatement, seeing as how this particular tiger-team consisted of me and a big bag of smoky bacon flavour pretzels. Mind you, I did use to do a lot of samurai work for the telcos, before they got too square.'

'Samurai?' asked Bryn weakly.

'Bust in to the telecoms networks. Left an e-mail telling 'em how I did it. Asked them to make a contribution to the Mungo-for-Mayor appeal. Trouble was when the droids got involved – suits, man, droid equals suit without the humour – first they started sending me cheques. I mean, *cheques*. To a fourteen-year-old? I ask you. Plus then they got all "Oooh, criminal activity" about it. Dweebs, man, total dweebs.'

Bryn stared at Cameron. Cameron stared at Bryn. They'd never seen anything like Mungo before, never would again.

'Mungo, we'd love you to join. When can you start?'

Mungo stared at Bryn as though he was a halfwit. He rapped on Bryn's monitor where the warning sign was still displayed. 'No, man, don't you get it? I have started.'

4

It's tough being rich these days. Any fool can own a sports car. Designer labels slum it in the supermarket. Any tomfool accountant who sticks at his job can get the big house and the tennis court, maybe even the place in the sun.

Flowers are an example. Roses in January? It ought to be impossible, the laws of nature forbid it. Yet a hundred quid will buy enough January roses to fill your home. How is money meant to talk, when the jingle of small change sounds so loud?

Bryn had solved this particular problem. As he crossed the lobby, eyes turned at the tree he drew behind him on a trolley. The tree was miniature, eight foot tall and already mature. But that wasn't what caught the attention. On to the dwarfing root stock, not one but two trees had been grafted. The lower section belonged to an early-fruiting cherry, the upper section was taken from a late-flowering crab apple.

On the streets outside, a thin sleet hesitated on the verge of snow and pedestrians passed quickly in a huddle of coats and scarves. But Bryn's tree knew nothing of this. Bred by geneticists, born of surgery, reared under computer-controlled lamps, the tree had waited all its life for this day and this moment. Its upper branches were crammed with blossom, its lower boughs hung with cherries, well formed and glossy, although inedible. It was a miracle, eight thousand pounds' worth of miracle.

'I have a gift for Miss Cheryl Kessler.'

The receptionist eyed Bryn and the magical tree behind. The hotel was used to celebrities, and the annoyances that came with them. House policy was to refuse all requests for autographs and similar nuisances, but to accept gifts, which were taken upstairs at the end of every day. The policy was a strict one, but the tree was beyond policy. You couldn't ask a cherry tree which flowered and fruited all at once to wait in line, like any old bunch of flowers.

'I'll have it taken up right away.'

The receptionist was nervous, expecting Bryn to challenge her right to take the tree off him, but he was all smiles.

'Excellent. If Miss Kessler wishes to see us, we will be seated over there.' Bryn pointed to the sofa in the lobby where Cameron waited. 'Please mention to Miss Kessler that there is a note with the gift.' He indicated an envelope nestled in the snow-white down of the blossom.

The receptionist nodded and summoned a bell-boy, then, thinking that such a gift needed an escort, found somebody else to serve behind the counter while she and the bell-boy bore the miraculous gift upstairs.

'Now we wait,' said Bryn.

'I don't see the point,' said Cameron.

'Cheryl Kessler is ill. Conventional medicine hasn't been able to find a cure and there are millions of fans praying for her recovery. Don't you want to make her better?'

'She's only one data point and I don't see why we've started to pay our patients in trees.'

'Publicity. We need to put ourselves on the map. And I wish you'd stop calling our clients data points. They're not data points, they're patients.'

'You call them revenue units.'

'Well, we won't have any bloody data or any bloody revenue if things don't look up.'

Bryn scowled at himself: no use in letting Cameron know he was tense. He apologised for snapping. Cameron muttered something sarcastic, then turned back to a pile of research papers she had brought with her. Time passed.

'Cameron. Sorry. Would you mind sitting up a bit straighter?'

'What?'

'It's just that we need to make a good impression.'

Cameron's slouch didn't change. Bryn had forced her to put on something smart – a dark skirt and jacket, which she hated – but she'd refused absolutely to mess around with her hair or face, and the best that Meg and Bryn had been able to do was to persuade her that a purple scrunchy with a bit of shine in the fabric was preferable to a rubber band.

Bryn's smile froze, then loosened. A gorilla of a man, three hundred pounds of him, was buying postcards at the hotel gift shop and using the opportunity to scrutinise the lobby.

'Look at me and smile as if I've just made a joke,' said Bryn.

Cameron pulled a face.

'We're being inspected,' said Bryn, still smiling. 'We need to show them we're not wackos.'

'You've given somebody you don't know a tree worth twelve thousand dollars and you want to show them you're not a wacko?'

The gorilla was pink with pricklish yellow hair. He made a call from his mobile, his gaze now openly fixed on Bryn and Cameron. Bryn crossed his legs and picked up his paper again. He'd selected *The Times* as the safest bet: conservative, recognisable to American gorillas, but not as stuffy as the *Financial Times* or the *Wall Street Journal*. Cameron, of course, had piles of research papers in front of her, which she devoured as intensively as ever. Out of the corner of his eye, Bryn noticed the first gorilla being joined by his big brother, a black guy, unnervingly dressed in a three-piece suit. The bodyguards decided something and came over.

'You want to see Miss Kessler?'

'Yes, indeed. Allow me to introduce Dr Wilde here, formerly of Harvard University, and myself, Bryn Hughes, proprietor of the Fulham Clinic.'

'You know how many people want to see Miss Kessler?'

Bryn wanted to stand up, shake hands, be polite, but the gorillas stood too close to let him stand. He maintained his unnatural, oily politeness.

'All of London, I'm sure. Did she receive our gift in good condition?'

'London?' said the blond gorilla. 'London, England?'

'Everybody wants to see Miss Kessler,' said the black guy. 'Everybody in the world.'

'Yes, of course.'

'You a psycho?'

'No. Cameron here is a doctor and –'

'Oh, she's the doctor,' said the blond gorilla. 'She's the doctor and you're what? Her dancing mistress?'

The black gorilla turned his attention to Cameron for the first time.

'You send Miss Kessler the tree?'

'I guess,' said Cameron. She didn't seem unnerved by sitting beneath a wall of American beef. She was more interested in her research material.

'You think you can fix Miss Kessler?'

'I should think so.'

'You hear that?' The black gorilla spoke to his pink partner. 'This little lady thinks she can cure Miss Kessler. Two hundred doctors don't know what's wrong with Miss Kessler and this lady says she can make her better.'

'You send trees to all your patients?' The black gorilla bent down, tucked his fingers beneath Cameron's arms and lifted her upright. In a single movement, his hands swept down, checking her for weapons.

'Miss Kessler would like to see you about your tree,'

said the pink gorilla. 'She wants to know why the cherries ain't ripe.' He shook briefly, which is probably gorilla for laughter.

The two giants walked off, with Cameron sandwiched in between. Bryn they ignored. He walked behind, unable to find a way through the human wall in front, then crammed himself into the lift, leaping between the closing doors. The top floor was given over to penthouses and suites, and Cheryl Kessler had taken the lot. Technicians, PR types, production staff, money men swarmed around; drones humming round the one queen bee.

At the entrance to the Royal Suite, the two gorillas shifted position. Before he knew it, Bryn found himself flung against the wall, arms and legs spread, while fingers big as bananas explored his body. The exploration wasn't gentle and wasn't meant to be. With a final cautionary jab, they discarded him and opened the door.

The room was dark, curtains drawn, lamps off. Against the far wall, something white gleamed in the blackness and there was a scent of spring in the air. Cherry blossom. As his eyes grew better able to handle the gloom, Bryn made out a heap of pillows and quilts. A pale oval marked the face of the world's biggest rock star. The face spoke.

'I puked after the show last night.'

Somebody needed to reply, so Bryn did.

'I'm sorry.'

'It was your fault I puked?'

'No, I'm sorry you felt ill.'

'That why you sent me a tree?'

'No, I –'

'You ever consider I might have allergies?'

'Allergies?'

'The tree's got pollen, right? Or is it too screwed up to have stuff like that?'

110

This was no good. Time to take control. 'Miss Kessler, I sent you the tree because I believe that Dr Wilde here can cure you. The tree was to get your attention.'

'A chat-up line?'

'In order to get you well, we're going to need to take some blood, some urine, run some tests, then we'll be back to you with a treatment plan.'

'I've done a million tests. I'm running out of blood.'

'We'll keep the blood draw requirements to a minimum, I promise.'

'How come you're talking? I thought you said the other one was the doctor.'

Cameron stepped forward.

'I'm Dr Wilde. You want to tell me what's the matter?'

'Didn't you read the piece in *Vanity Fair*?'

'No.'

'*Rolling Stone*?'

'No.'

'You see my Letterman interview?'

'Oh, for God's sake, I've got better –'

'You even know who I am?'

'Know? Yes. Care? No. You're a singer.'

'Right, I'm a singer. You hear that, boys? I'm a singer.' The gorillas grunted and shifted their weight. 'Only now I'm a very sick singer.' And Cheryl Kessler, the tough-as-nails megastar, began to recite a list of symptoms with an invalid's absorption.

Cameron, who had no sense at all of being in the presence of one of the best-known celebrities on the planet, interrupted freely with her questions. Skin disorders? Food sensitivities? Faintness on standing? Temperature regulation? Kessler acted tough, but she answered everything. Ever since the mystery virus had hit her, she'd cancelled most of her obligations and where she'd refused to cancel, she'd given her concerts lying in a vast four-poster bed draped in sheets of scarlet satin. The newspapers speculated openly about whether she was genuinely ill or whether the whole thing was a gimmick. But the truth was that Kessler was seriously unwell and desperately anxious to find out what was happening.

'Photophobia?' asked Cameron.

'Fear of photos? Me?'

'Not photos. Light sensitivity.'

'Joke, OK? It was a joke. They have those in med school? Yes. Light sensitivity, pretty bad.'

'Menstrual problems?'

'If you're from the press, I'll kill you. I'll get the boys here to jump up and down on your heads. I'll get –'

'Don't worry about that,' said Bryn. 'I can assure you –'

'I don't need your assurances. Ben and Bobo are my assurances.' The gorillas flexed their hands and made little white crescents with their teeth. 'Sure I got problems.' She went on to list her menstrual problems in enough detail that Bryn realised why she was concerned about the press. Here was a six-figure story if ever he'd heard one.

Eventually Cameron was done asking questions and got out her needles. She took four tubes of blood, with her usual surprising expertise, and even persuaded her patient to go to the bathroom to fill a large screw-topped beaker with urine.

'D'you dance?' asked Kessler, returning, pale and sick, from the bathroom.

'Dance?'

'Yeah, for God's sake, you must know what dancing is.'

'No, I don't dance.'

'Huh, shame. You've got the body for it, and I'm short a female dancer at the moment.'

'Well, I suggest you go hire yourself a dancer.'

112

'Yeah, OK. Jesus.' She was tired and Cameron was packing up. 'Ben, Bobo . . .'

The gorillas emerged from the gloom and cracked their fingers a few millimetres away from Bryn and Cameron. Bryn was keen to make his exit without assistance and hustled her to finish.

'You coming to the show tonight?' Kessler's voice from the dark.

'Uh-uh. Sold out,' said Bryn.

'Well, maybe next time. Thanks for the tree.'

5

With no gorillas to fill it, the elevator was spacious.

'You think you'll be able to cure her?'

'Don't know. Depends on what Kati and I turn up in the lab.'

'Can you give a probability?'

'No way. I could if she was a rat.'

'You think you'll be able to find out what's wrong?'

Bryn was nervous and his nerves made him batter away at Cameron, as though he was still a banker and she was his junior analyst. Her lips compressed with annoyance.

'Oh, I already know what's wrong,' she said.

'Well?'

'She's got a virus.'

Bryn snorted. 'What kind of virus? One you can do anything with?'

'How would I know what kind?'

'Will your lab tests tell you?'

'No way. They're not those kind of tests.'

'Well, how are you going to kill it, if you don't know what it is?'

'I won't be able to kill it. But still,' Cameron shrugged,

'it'll give us a whole new data point and we can keep the blood stored for future analysis.'

'Jesus, Cameron!' Bryn was appalled. 'What the hell do you mean, you can't kill it? What the hell is the point of coming here if you can't even kill the damn thing? We can't spend eight thousand quid every time you feel like taking blood from someone.'

Cameron's face had whitened to something even more bloodless than its normal sun-free pallor. She said nothing and just stared ahead. Bryn relented. 'I'm sorry. You said that with enough time and resources you could cure pretty much anyone. That's what matters.'

'I said that? Sorry. I can't cure her.'

They were in the lobby now, about to leave. There were a few people at the check-out desk, a dozen or so more at the bar. They all got to listen to what came next.

'You can't cure her?' Bryn thundered, voice bouncing around the marble walls. 'What the bloody hell do you mean you can't?'

'What I said. I can't kill the virus. I can't cure her. Clever things, viruses.'

Bryn was beyond shock now. It was stupid, really, the whole bloody idea. Take some wacko doctor. Stick a brass plate on the wall. Cross your fingers and hope for a miracle. Jesus Christ! How could he have been so stupid? He whacked his head with his fist. 'Jesus!' He took a breath and tried to calm down, see if there was anything to salvage.

'Maybe there's something you can do. Check her nutrition, for instance. Maybe poor nutrition is making things worse.'

'Maybe.'

'We could still come out with credit if we can alleviate things, even if we can't cure her.'

'I guess.'

'Give her some of your magic juice, like you did with me.'

'Uh-huh.'

'Improve her immune system, get it cranking as hard as it can.'

'Sure. Like I say, doctors can't do much against viruses. Nothing to beat the body's own immune system.'

Bryn stared at Cameron. Cameron stared at him. Around the lobby a couple of dozen people stared discreetly at the pair of them.

'You're going to do it, aren't you? You won't kill the virus, you'll just get Kessler's immune system to do it for you.'

'More or less.'

'And you'll be successful, won't you?'

For the first time, a smile twitched at Cameron's mouth. 'That's the plan.'

Bryn exhaled, with a mixture of anger, relief and a sudden sense of spreading safety. 'Jesus, Cameron. Don't ever let anyone tell you you're easy to work with.'

The smile that had twitched before now burst out into the open with a clear, pealing laugh. She pulled off the purple scrunchy at the back of her hair, tossing it into a waste basket and running her hands through her hair to restore it to its normal uncombed, unkempt appearance. She pushed him playfully with her hand on his chest.

'God, you sure wind up easy,' she said.

Bryn opened his mouth to reply, but she was already walking away from him, laughing as she went. Bryn watched her from behind: this enigmatic, infuriating, dedicated genius of a woman. He paused for a moment, then started forward, hurrying to keep up.

TEN

1

Back at the laboratory, it was an excited fivesome that rigged the microscope to the slide projector and slotted a slide containing Kessler's precious blood beneath the lens. Bryn drew down the blinds to cover the river-facing windows. Meg and Mungo took seats quietly at the back, like kids allowed in to an adult entertainment on condition of good behaviour. Mungo munched noisily from a bag of pretzels, spilling handfuls through a tear in the packet. As the blinds came down, the image sharpened. Drawn in red and black on the wall, the secrets of the world's biggest rock star came into view.

'Wow. That's Cheryl Kessler,' whispered Meg.

Cameron had centrifuged a blood sample to extract white blood cells only, and it was this that they looked at, the big ragged shapes swimming gently in their fluid, unaware that they were no longer running in some of the most famous veins in the entire world. Kati and Cameron watched for a while, the slow movement, the gentle change of shape. Bryn, Meg and Mungo waited in silence, waiting for a commentary to illuminate them.

'Seems OK,' said Cameron at last. 'Let's hit 'em with something, see how they cope.'

A pipette of chicken protein dropped on to the glass slide, which slid back beneath the lens. The familiar blue invaders filled the picture and now the white blood cells – the macrophages and natural killer cells, the B cells and the neutrophils, and all the rest of the trillion-celled army – were called upon to act. As usual attention focused first on the macrophages, the all-gobbling vacuum cleaners of the blood. Slowly, like giant marine animals in some unfamiliar zoo, they began to attack their opponents. To Bryn's uneducated eye, they looked like they were doing a good job.

'How are they doing?'

Kati and Cameron glanced at him, as though wondering if he was serious. Mungo muttered something about how, 'It's not really fair servin' chicken without BBQ sauce, or maybe one of them hot-hot-hot Jamaican things with all pepper and stuff. It's no wonder, they're all *woooh* about it.' Mungo fluttered his hands to imitate a macrophage insulted by the lack of an adequate condiment selection. Meantime Cameron turned her gaze back to the wall, back to the slow motion battle-to-the-death. It was Kati, as usual, who volunteered to act as interpreter.

'OK. There are a number of problems you can have. One is you may not have enough white blood cells. That's not a problem here. If anything, and we'll get some data on this shortly, I'd say Kessler was oversupplied. That means her body recognises a threat and is churning out white cells in response.'

'So that's good?'

'Right, that's good. But it's one thing to have a lot of soldiers, it's quite another whether they can fight.'

'And?'

As they had been speaking, one of the larger macrophages in the middle of the screen had turned full circle, struggling to engulf a blue-stranded piece of chicken

117

protein. Kati turned her eyes back to the screen, her clear face sombre in the reflected light.

'These macrophages are immature. They're privates dressed as generals, kids in uniform. In the whole time we've been watching, we've seen a lot of huffing and puffing, but not a single kill. Not one.'

Cameron had seen enough. She pulled the power cord from the projector and the image vanished as the room fell dark. The four others awaited her verdict. She flicked the lights on, and pulled her labcoat over the jeans and T-shirt which she had exchanged for her earlier temporary smartness.

'You've picked us a tough one to start with.'

Bryn smiled a keep-your-spirits-up kind of smile. 'Shame she's not a rat, then.'

Cameron shook her head. 'She's got a serious illness, which is now a full-blown, late-stage, fully progressed disease. Even if she was a rat, we couldn't be certain of getting a result.'

'And?'

'And what?'

'And do you have a prognosis, doctor?'

'Sure,' said Cameron. 'I'd say we're not going to go home tonight. Right, Kati?'

2

They didn't go home that night or the night after or any night for the next two weeks. Meg and Bryn, Cameron and Kati brought bedding into the boathouse, slept when they were exhausted, and woke themselves six hours too early. Although Mungo offered his services, there was no real computing work to be done and he was a clumsy crisp-scattering liability in the laboratory, so after the first

118

temper-fraught day, Bryn told him to leave the lab and get on with his work elsewhere.

Meanwhile, for fourteen days the others worked non-stop. They had, as ever with Cameron's work, two targets. Step one was to find the combination of nutrients which did most to boost Kessler's immune cells. Step two was to find the peptide molecule which would act as the ELIMIN-ATE VIRUS command in the body's programming sequence.

They began, logically enough, with step one, attempting to locate the precise combination of more than forty nutrients which would do most to support Kessler's blood cells – a task which sounded simple enough, until Kati told them that 'the number of possible combinations is far greater than the number of stars in the universe. You can't get there using guesswork, you have to know what you're doing.'

In order to work most effectively, they divided themselves into teams. Cameron and Kati prepared the solutions, Bryn and Meg tried them out. Fairly soon, the two non-scientists were able to spot the obvious failures, and when they were in doubt, they called from their microscopes to one of the others, who came over to review the image. In every case what had looked to the laypeople like an encouraging sign, quickly disappeared on a more professional observation. As Bryn and Meg learned their trade, the number of times they called excitedly for help tailed off. When they did request a second opinion it was in a voice without hope.

And so they slaved.

3

Four days into their marathon, at eight o'clock on Saturday night, Meg turned off the lamp of her microscope, rubbed her red-rimmed eye, and shoved the tray of glass microscope slides away from her with distaste. She got up.

'Saturday night is party night,' she announced.

'You're going out?' said Bryn, incredulously.

'I need you to help me reformulate my BCAA complex,' said Cameron, in a tone halfway between surprise and warning.

Meg ignored them. She disappeared upstairs to the consulting room which had been pressed into service as her bedroom, with its roll of foam and sleeping bag for her bed, a suitcase for her wardrobe, and a two-kilo bag of bird-seed, with which she had vowed to befriend her precious parrot. She emerged fifty minutes later in a short black dress, clicking downstairs on heels two inches higher than could be comfortable, hair done, nails French-polished and gleaming, make-up perfect, leaving wafts of perfume on the air behind her.

She walked back to the wet bench, where chemicals were made into exact solutions under Cameron's eagle eye. She sat down in front of her calibrated beakers, her pipettes and her electronic balance, and began work once again.

'Like I said,' she explained, 'Saturday night is party night.'

4

'How long have we got?' asked Cameron.

Bryn shrugged. 'She was meant to be on tour in the Far East, but she cancelled all of that. In theory she has a few dates in Europe, then another Wembley gig, then back to the States, but the fact is no one knows. She's sick enough she could go home at any time.'

'That's not the only problem. I only took four tubes of blood. We're on the third tube already, and somehow I don't see her giving us more, not unless we have anything to show for it.'

She was right, of course, but it was hardly comforting.

The next day, with step one still no closer to completion, they began on step two.

5

'Urine,' said Cameron, holding out a collapsible plastic container which would expand to about a gallon when full.

'Urine?' said Bryn.

'Yes, please. As much as you can manage.'

Bryn expanded the container like a concertina. 'I hate to tell you, but I don't think –'

'I know, I know,' said Cameron impatiently. 'I've already given Kati and Meg jars to fill. I wasn't too sure about Mungo. You think he does drugs?'

'Think?' said Bryn.

'OK. Not Mungo, then. I'm about to go and do mine. You do yours. Between us we should get enough.'

There was a pause.

'Enough for what?' said Bryn.

6

It turned out that Cameron's sudden obsession with urine collection was a smart shortcut for getting to step two.

'It's pretty simple,' Kati explained. 'There are basically two reasons why Kessler's sick. One is her blood cells have gotten very weak. Two, she's missing some of the command data her body needs to get it up and running.'

'Command data? Peptides, in other words?'

'Right. Now you can find peptides in blood, but it's kind of easier to look for them in urine. Our plan is to compare some average healthy urine – that's you, me, Cameron and Meg – against Kessler's sample. If the healthy urine is packed with one particular peptide, and Kessler's urine has none of it, then you can be pretty damn sure that the missing peptide is the one that you want.'

'You mean the missing peptide is saying something like KILL THAT VIRUS.'

'Exactly. I mean it's a whole lot more complex, obviously. Like a *whole* lot more.' She paused. There was this thing that scientists get, where they're almost unable to let a simple explanation suffice when a more complex one is available. Kati wrestled with her conscience for a moment, before the angels won out. 'But sure,' she said. 'You've got the idea.'

7

And as it turned out, step two – normally the tricky bit – was as easy as pie, just as step one – normally the simple part – continued to defeat their best efforts.

They began their morning by exposing the two urine samples to a stream of heated air, evaporating the liquid and leaving them with a soft white residue, which Meg poked with a sterile glass rod, saying, 'So *that's* a piece of piss.' Cameron and Kati then put the delicate powder through a string of processes to separate and identify its ingredients, mapping the results out in a complex black-and-white banding pattern on computer. Each band on the screen related to one particular peptide cluster, and the bigger the band, the more common the cluster.

For the most part, Kessler's urine looked pretty much the same as everybody else's. Where the normal sample had a big band, Kessler's sample also had a big band. Where the normal sample just showed a pale grey strip, hinting at the presence of a chemical in tiny quantities, then usually Kessler also had a pale grey strip, about the same in size and coloration.

But there were differences, too.

Most of them, Cameron dismissed. 'She's sick, remember, and sickness produces all kinds of changes in the body. Most of the peptide differences have nothing particular to do with this illness, they're just telling us that she's ill.'

But as she and Kati bent over the computer, using the tab keys to inch along the complex structure, they suddenly, simultaneously, gave out a yelp of delight.

'K3-34a!' they shrieked.

Meg and Bryn, who had been sent back to the tiresome and unrewarding labours of step one, looked at each other and smirked.

'Not K3-34a,' said Meg.

'The old bugger,' said Bryn. 'Fancy good old K3-34a popping up here.'

As the two scientists descended from cloud nine, Kati divulged an explanation. 'We were half expecting it,' she said. 'Once, a long time back when we were only just starting, we had a patient a little like Kessler. Back then we didn't have the Schoolroom or anything like that, we were just improving our peptide banding techniques. That patient had a hole at a spot called K3-34a, where everyone else had a perfectly normal dark band. We may be having problems with the first phase here, but we've as good as got the key to phase two in our hands.'

But for all the short interval of joy, the gloom was quick to descend again. The peptide code was useless, unless Kessler's blood could be made strong enough to use it. The weary routine began again. Millilitre by millilitre, the precious tubes of blood drained away.

8

The following Saturday, it wasn't just Meg who dolled herself up for an imaginary dance floor. Kati, too, getting into the spirit, disappeared off with Meg and came downstairs an hour later in the closest approximation of a party outfit that her bag, so hastily packed eleven days before, had been able to offer. Both women had shimmer eye-shadow, party hair, and 'you can't see 'em, matey, but our toes are stunning'.

Bryn smiled at the new arrivals. 'You look gorgeous,' he said to them both, but with eyes only for Kati. 'You look fantastic.'

'You're in luck, then,' said Meg, ''cos looking is all you're going to get. And how about you, Cammie? I've got a dress you can borrow, and I'm dying to get my hands on your hair.'

But Meg's entreaties were entirely disregarded. 'Uh-uh. No way,' said Cameron, checking the rubber band at the back of her head for tightness and rubbing her cheek on her labcoated shoulder, as though to remove any possibility of make-up from it. All the same, it was easy to see she wasn't quite cool with the question. Her cheeks flushed pink in the lamplight, and it was with an angry fluster that she switched the conversation abruptly on to gel electrophoresis and cellular protein synthesis. Her sharpness of temper lasted all through the night, and was only truly gone when dawn broke the following day.

9

The following Wednesday. One millilitre of Kessler's blood left in their fridge, all the rest of it gone in their fortnight's fruitless quest.

124

'We'll try one more day, then give up,' said Bryn.

He was close to despair. No cure, no publicity. No publicity, no clients. No clients, no money. And without money, they could never turn Cameron's potential into a usable product, and he'd have gambled everything he had, only to see every last bit of it lost.

Cameron held the precious millilitre in her hands, tossing it in its glass container from side to side. Outside, it was evening. The sun was setting somewhere to the west, over the Thames, that big, strong, bridge-stapled river. The barge still bumped against the jetty outside, still covered in filth. Fifty yards downstream, the setting sun tangled in the branches of the willow tree, where a blue-green parrot enjoyed the last of the day, waiting for Meg to bring its now regular evening feed.

'No, we've done enough for now,' said Cameron. 'Let's go home, get some sleep, have a bath. When we reassemble tomorrow, we'll see if any of us has had a brainwave. It's not as if another couple of experiments is all we need.'

She was right, and they agreed without discussion. Bryn called a cab – they all lived close enough in West London for it to be worth sharing – and they each went to their rooms to shovel dirty clothes into a bag for an overdue clean. Bryn hadn't shaved for the last three days and he looked like a barbarian, a barbarian with a head-cold.

When the taxi came, they drove away in silence.

10

The cab nodded out into the traffic. Twilight sank like a depression into the city.

'God, it's gloomy,' said Kati. 'Work all day in a darkened lab, then come home in the dark.'

No one answered.

'At least we tried. If anything in biochemistry could have cured her, we'd have found it.'

'I blame Cheryl Kessler,' said Meg. 'Bloody woman for having an incurable disease. And for her horrible music.'

'Cobblers,' said Bryn. 'You were humming it all last week.'

'I hate it now.'

For the last several days, Cameron had been silent and withdrawn. Although they tried not to let it be felt, everyone knew that this was Cameron's hour, her moment of glory or failure, and as the shadow of failure lengthened across the days, the strain of it had told. She stared out of the taxi window, looking at the meaningless traffic, the din of lights, the empty residential streets and the still-busy commercial ones. Conversation fell silent.

Then something in her sprang to attention. She quivered like a wolf-pack catching a scent.

'My God, Kati, you're totally right.'

'What do you mean?'

They were moving fast in the outside lane of the Cromwell Road, in a London where traffic became more careless and more aggressive with every year. Cameron grabbed for the door handle and wrenched at it desperately. But the taxi doors locked automatically and the door stayed shut. Like a wolf caught in a cage, she bent round, with her back against her route of escape.

'Chemistry. We tried everything. That's exactly our mistake.' She scrabbled at the handle once again. Red lights were forcing the taxi to slow but it hadn't yet stopped. 'For God's sake, what's with this goddamn cab?'

The hunting-frenzy had seized her. Invisible scents were calling her, and nothing would stop her escape.

'Cameron, wait. When the cab stops –'

'If you want, we can –'

126

She ignored them. She probably didn't even hear them. Her nails scratched repeatedly at the fake leather of the door panel as she scrabbled at the handle. 'Working in the dark, Kati. It's not gloomy, it's lunacy.'

The cab squealed to a halt, the locks released, the door flew open, and Cameron was out on the road. Bryn tried to give chase, but, unlike his quarry, he wanted to avoid being flattened by a truck, and Cameron had raced through three lanes' worth of fifty-mile-an-hour metal moving in a blaze of car headlamps and blaring horns. She almost collided with a cab, whirled round its bonnet to find its light on, leaped inside, and was soon carried off on the steel-and-rubber tide.

Bryn got back into the waiting taxi. 'Should we chase her?'

'No,' said Kati. 'This is how all her best work is done. Late at night. On her own. In a frenzy.'

'You know what she's on about?'

'Only what she told us.'

And what she'd told them had amounted to just one word, screamed through an open window above the roar of traffic and the cursing of car horns.

'Physics,' she'd shouted, 'don't you see? Physics.'

ELEVEN

1

This time the curtains were open and the eight-thousand-pound tree looked much the worse for wear. Its blossoms had fallen or gone brown and the leaves below were beginning to curl. The cherries remained as hard and glossy as ever.

'Not much of a gift,' said Kessler.

'Have you kept it watered?'

Kessler snorted. 'Just because I've got to stick to water, doesn't mean everything else has to. Ben and Bobo have been keeping it tanked up.'

Bryn sniffed at the half-empty bottle which stood beside the tree. Gin. He emptied the remaining liquid over the roots.

'Better get it soused. Nothing worse than a half-drunk cherry tree.'

Kessler looked him up and down slowly, the way most men would look at most women most of the time if there weren't such a thing as harassment laws. He was a bit brutish, Bryn. It's hard to be over a certain weight and yet stay perfectly in proportion, and the bigger you're built, the harder you have to work to keep in shape. Bryn was neither well proportioned nor in regular training, but then again

Kessler was reputed to enjoy a little bit of rough with her smooth, a little bit of slap with her tickle.

'I've trashed your tree,' she said. 'The doc here has fixed me up. Anything more we need do?'

Kessler was in a dress so short, it was politer to call it a T-shirt, except that whatever you called it, it had shrunk so badly you might as well admit that it was fit for a tramp and leave it at that. Long black boots guided the eye up the leg, as if anyone's eyes needed guiding. She had dark hair, pale skin and a crimson slash for a mouth.

'We need to keep you well,' said Bryn. 'Cameron?'

'Sure. The virus is still in your system. It will be for the rest of your life. Your immune system has it under control and, if you keep your immune system happy, there's nothing you need to worry about. I've got a list here of dietary recommendations, plus a list of supplements, plus I want you to have a six-monthly check-up for a couple of years at least.'

Kessler's foot tapped on the carpeted floor, practising a dance routine. Every time she practised, though, her foot ended up an inch further away from the other one. Bryn watched with the intensity of a professional choreographer, though a choreographer would probably have been looking at the feet and not let his eyes be guided anywhere by a pair of black leather boots.

'No alcohol,' said Cameron, ticking the points off on her list.

'Cocaine?' asked Kessler.

'Cocaine?' Cameron was brusque, but truthful as always. 'It could be preferable in some respects, but it's hard to say. There hasn't been the same amount of work done on cocaine.'

'Everyone I know goes to work on cocaine.'

'I'd recommend you drink a pint of fruit juice and a pint of vegetable juice daily.'

'When you say vegetable, do you mean actual coma victims or can I make do with paralytics?'

Cameron dropped her pen. 'You want to stay well? Or you want to screw around? Your call, I honestly don't give a damn.'

'OK, sorry. Fruit juice. Veg juice. Not too much cocaine.'

'I'd advise you to take better care with your diet than you have done in the past.'

'I'm a man-eater,' whispered Kessler, not looking at Cameron and with her feet now too far apart to be of any use on the dance floor.

'Any recurrence of symptoms, call me immediately.'

'Itches, for example.' Kessler scratched herself in a place where she might have been feeling itchy. It was a gesture which would have attracted anyone's eyes, especially given the dress she was wearing, but as Bryn's eyes were already firmly on the spot, his weren't in need of further attracting.

Cameron scowled, and anger burned in the tips of her ears, but first and foremost she was a doctor, and her duty was to help the sick. 'I don't give a damn if you get scabies, leprosy, psoriasis and eczema all rolled into one. But any fever, giddiness, photophobia, exhaustion, give me a call right away.'

'OK, doc.'

'That's it. Normally, we'd charge for our services, but I guess that since we've already given you an eight-thousand-pound tree, giving you a check at this point would be a little meaningless.' There was bitterness in her voice.

'Thanks, Cameron. I'll settle up with Miss Kessler.'

'Yeah, right.'

Cameron showed no sign of moving.

'Thanks, Cameron. I'll see you later.'

Cameron waited another moment, but Bryn was firm and she had no option but to leave. She left, pale and furious.

She said not another word to Bryn, but as she packed her briefcase, her hands were visibly shaking.

'Miss Kessler, my fanny,' said the rock star, tugging Bryn into the bedroom. He was a big man, but he tugged easy.

Ben and Bobo, the gorillas, had been banished into the bedroom during the medical stuff, but now they were banished back again. Bryn smiled at them as they left.

'Thanks for getting me well,' said Kessler.

'Pleasure,' said Bryn.

'Are you and your doctor friend an item?'

'Christ, no. Just partners. Business partners.' Kessler had read something else into Cameron's anger, but whatever it meant, it wasn't her problem. 'How much publicity do you want?' She hooked a thumb into the top of her dress and pulled. The Lycra fabric sprang off and rolled itself into a ball. 'Big, huge, or gigantic?'

Bryn sat on the bed and removed his trousers.

'Gigantic,' he said.

2

Physics had proved to be their unlikely, not-conceived-of salvation.

After the event, Cameron had been able to explain it calmly; explain in sequence what had not come to her in sequence, what had come to her in a single blinding flash, like a hilltop rider seeing lightning illuminate the entire floodplain beneath.

'As Kati said, we'd taken the chemistry as far as it could be taken. I don't mean we'd explored every possible combination, but what was weird was that nothing we tried even made a shadow of difference. It's like our patient had pneumonia, and all we had was sugar pills. There had to be some totally different approach, something which would allow all our brilliant biochemical techniques to take effect. What could it be? It was obvious really. Here was our patient lying in darkness, hadn't seen daylight for God knows how many weeks, her blood was crying out for something which isn't even a part of chemistry . . . Light is a nutrient, after all. You can get light-deficiency diseases, just like you get vitamin-deficiency diseases. In Germany, they shrink tumours by exposing blood to polarised light.'

'So all Kessler really needed to do was open her curtains?'

'No, of course not. She had a serious viral illness, which needed the Schoolroom plus all our chemical techniques. It's just that for all our good stuff to take effect, we needed to supply one extra critical ingredient. That's all.'

And so it had been. They'd bathed their last millilitre of blood in an ocean of full spectrum polarised light, using a protocol which Cameron had obtained from a senior German researcher. Then, going right back to the very first series of chemical baths they'd used, they tried out Kessler's blood for signs of life. They got what they were looking for straightaway. They exposed the rejuvenated blood to the K3-34a peptide, and on its very first run, the Schoolroom achieved an excellent first-time score of 24%. With further experiments they hoped to push the figure up beyond 60%, but that had been for the future. All that had happened in the present was that Cameron powered down the Schoolroom, patting it on its white-domed head, congratulating it.

'We've cracked it,' she said. 'We're there.'

3

From that moment on, Bryn and Cameron, who had been working so closely together, began to move in different worlds. There was still a lot of work to be done on the

132

science side, and adapting the treatment to Kessler's veins was going to mean a whole ocean of challenge which Bryn didn't understand. But meantime, Bryn was busy with his own projects.

There was the barge for one thing. His house sale was due to complete at any moment, and when it did Bryn would be homeless. On fine days, and not-so-fine days, and on evenings which stretched far into the night, Bryn scrubbed at the barge with his wire brush until he'd exposed the strong clean wood beneath the mould. He painted the woodwork white, picking the barge boards and stovepipe chimney out in black. He cleared out the dank interior and burned the ancient and mildewing furniture in a pile on the riverbank. He prised open the windows and oiled their hinges. He sold most of the rest of Cecily's furniture and paintings (despite increasingly spiky little notes from her about returning it all) and bought himself some new furniture: a couple of vast old chesterfields rescued from a Portobello junk shop, an iron-bound oak chest bought at auction in Brecon, and a huge double bed which dominated the great stern cabin with its views south, east and west over the river. There was still masses to be done before the barge was finished, but at least it was habitable. Meg brought in armfuls of daffodils and set them down in vases, jugs and milk bottles all over the barge. It was airy and spacious, fresh and inviting; a one-person apartment to house Bryn's new one-person life.

But more important, there was the Fulham Clinic, still little more than a brass plate on a wall and a crazy idea for a global medical research company. But Bryn was long past rejecting things just because they were crazy. He called phone engineers to expand the switchboard to take twenty outside lines. He began to draw up plans for extending the clinic by building a series of consulting rooms in a kind of lean-to arrangement at the side. Meantime, Bryn retained a specialist medical recruitment agency to begin the search for a half-dozen senior doctors, a similar number of nurses, and two or three receptionists.

'The Fulham Clinic?' said the girl from the agency. 'I'm not sure I've heard of it.'

'Oh, don't worry,' said Bryn. 'You will.'

4

The final night of her European tour, Kessler was booked for a last sell-out performance at the Wembley Arena. On stage, shoved away at the back, was her band. In front, dominating the stage, was a massive bed, front legs lower than the back, tilting it like a display case. It was covered in sheets of red satin, piled with furs, heaped with pillows of scarlet and purple.

A thrill surged through the fans, a thrill they couldn't quite explain. Rumours passed from person to person: tonight was a biggie, tonight was special, tonight would make history. Nobody was aware of starting the rumours – nobody except the people paid by Kessler to start them – but they gained in size and velocity as they shot from mouth to mouth. Tonight was huge; tonight was extraordinary; tonight the world would catch its breath.

The lights fell. The stage sank into blackness, the huge bed briefly invisible. A quick movement in the darkness, sensed not seen. The lights rose, the band struck up, an instrumental number, but popular. The first howls rose from the audience. Then, tempo rising, the music gathered itself into a thunderclap, the topmost sheet was pulled from the bed, and there was Kessler, dressed only in a black satin chemise. The howls rose into shrieks as the gig got into its stride.

Kessler performed the first three numbers from bed, lying

quiet, showing none of the energy she had once poured into performance. Upright or prone, Kessler was good enough to command the absolute attention of her fans, but still, somehow, even in the midst of the concert, the rumours swirled. Tonight was stupendous. Tonight was astounding. Tonight would shake the world. Nothing appeared to support the rumours – nothing except the fact that since Kessler's illness, her performances had always seen her draped in more than a flimsy silk nightie: sometimes furs, sometimes velvets, once a kind of goose-down ball dress trimmed with ermine; anything at all, but always warm, always enveloping. It wasn't much to go on, but still the rumours hurtled.

Then the fourth number. Drumbeats and a bass line, unfamiliar chords. A melody sketched over the top on synth and saxophone. The audience listened to the first couple of bars, then doubt settled into certainty. This was a new song, one never heard before. The rumourmongers sensed imminent vindication. Howls and cheers, clapping and stamping, rose from the audience and fell back. History was being made. It was too important to miss. For the first time since becoming ill, Kessler sat up to sing.

'*Dead man doctors, bullshit spivs . . .*'

Wild cheering. Cheering not for the song or the merit of the song. Cheering because of all her gigs to date, this would be her most famous: bigger than her sell-out gig in Central Park, bigger than her first discovery in an Atlantic City nightclub, bigger even than the Vatican City concert where she'd burned an effigy of Torquemada, the Spanish inquisitor.

'*Condemned me to prison, life behind bars.*'

Artistically, musically, it wasn't a song which would live long in the annals of rock. But that didn't matter. Something extraordinary was happening. Kessler was rising from her bed, throwing off her sheets. The bass line, which had been quiet, became louder, impossible to ignore. '*Eeeee-ooooo-oough.*' Kessler screamed, leaping to her feet, standing at the foot of her bed. '*They were wrong.*' She leaped to the floor, then hurled herself to the ground: a forward flip, a cartwheel, another forward flip. '*They were wrong, wrong, wrong.*' The huge bed began to roll backwards into the darkness of backstage. Kessler leaped around it, hurling pillows into the audience. '*They were wrong, wrong, wrong.*' She kicked, flipped, and kicked again; but her breath held steady as she roared out her words.

The screams of the fans reached the point of actual hysteria: emotions so big they no longer knew what to do with themselves. Medical teams hauled the first faint-victims from the crowd, treating them quickly, clearing the decks for the next crop. From the wings, Bryn and Cameron waited and watched. Cameron was bored. She didn't see the need to be there in person, she didn't like the music and Bryn had stopped her from bringing anything useful to read. She was absent and unco-operative.

Bryn was aware of his partner's discontent, but he didn't care. After the concert, Kessler was holding a press conference. Her awesome PR machine had pulled together twelve TV stations from around the world, all of the UK press, most of the European and US papers big enough to have a London correspondent. The international press agencies would be there, photographers on assignment, as well as freelancers looking to syndicate their pictures. Editors in London had been warned there was a big story pending and produced mock-ups of their early editions with big blanks on the front page. Phone and satellite links had been tested, expanded and tested again. When the story came out, it would reach the world in seconds.

Kessler had promised gigantic. She would deliver humungous.

5

But later that night, as Bryn made his way home to his barge tired but happy, another emotion began to intrude: fear.

The publicity was good news for the clinic, good news for Cameron, good news for the entire venture. But there was a catch. Up till now, they had been walled off from the outside world, hidden, invisible, beyond reach. Tonight that had changed, and changed for ever. When Brent Huizinga picked up his morning paper, he'd know that Cameron Wilde was alive, well, and more dangerous than ever.

Bryn licked his lips. The fight was on.

TWELVE

1

In the clinic's high-vaulted reception area, morning light streamed horizontally from the east, reflecting from the Thames. The boat-hulled reception desk looked submerged as the room filled with watery light right up to the white-beamed rafters. The waiting room table was littered with the morning's papers and there was a jugful of coffee (mocha Mysore, regular blend) brought in by Bryn, steaming hot from the barge. But it was the headlines which caught the eye, big as banners in the tabloids, front page even in the broadsheets.

'Revolutionary approach cures the incurable', said one of the more sober papers. 'Rock star first to benefit from immune technique'.

That wasn't what the tabloids talked about, at least not on the front page, and not in the two-page photo-spreads. 'Kessler cured – and it's straight back to bed', commented one. Or even more simply: 'Welsh boyo beds Kessler'.

'Get this,' said Meg. 'The *Sun*'s got a league table listing Kessler's celebrity shags. You're number four on the list ahead of Warren Beatty.'

'Bloody hell, that I could live without.' But he reached for the paper.

Meg held it away from him, reading titbits out loud.

'Kessler rated thirty-five-year-old hunk, businessman Bryn Hughes, as her best shag of the year. We give him eight out of ten for sex appeal.'

'It's like you've been cloned,' commented Mungo, examining the multiple images of Bryn which lay on the table, prodded and fingered by shafts of sunlight. 'Bryn Hughes, Replicator Man.'

'Sounds like you can replicate without cloning, Bryn, m'boy,' said Meg. 'Here, it goes on to say, "Hughes has so far refused to comment on Kessler's own performance, except to say that she responded well to treatment". Well, how was she?'

Then something extraordinary happened. Cameron, who'd been sitting silently, exploded from her seat.

'Oh, for God's sake!' she snapped. 'This is a research establishment, not a goddamn whorehouse.'

Kicking her chair away from her, she marched into the laboratory, slamming the door hard in her wake. The sound crashed around the room before fading out amongst the rafters. The others looked at each other guiltily. As they shifted in their seats, Bryn's leg happened to fall against Kati's. He didn't move his. She didn't move hers. Bryn could feel the warmth of her calf bleeding through the fabric of his trousers.

He caught her eye. 'I'm sorry,' he said to no one in particular. 'The Kessler thing meant nothing. It didn't mean anything at all.'

Kati smiled. She was smart. She knew that. Her leg continued to rest against Bryn's, his against hers. From the laboratory, sounds of Cameron's anger continued to trickle out: drawers being closed with unnecessary force, glassware being slammed down on to worktops, an angry mutter. Kati moved her leg away. Bryn continued to smile, his face bathed in light.

2

One week later, and the clinic was running full blast.

The clinic had already recruited four full-time doctors as well as Cameron, with more on the way. They'd chosen an outstanding clinical virologist, Dr Rauschenberg, to act as the clinic's medical director under Cameron's overall supervision. Rauschenberg, a tall, bearded, German-accented doctor of twenty-five years' experience, was already a complete convert to Cameron's style of medicine.

'When I was a young medical student, training in Heidelberg, many of us believed that if we studied to be virologists, we would need to train again before we retired. We were going to defeat the virus, *ja*. No virus, no virologist. But now? We are as far as ever, maybe further than ever, from winning. But this Reprogramme technique is incredible. Again now, I think maybe I need to retrain myself.'

Until Cameron had finished her research, of course, patients couldn't obtain the full Immune Reprogramming from the clinic, but, as Rauschenberg was quick to see, there were countless ways in which Cameron's expertise could be used to enhance the standard drug-oriented medicine on offer. 'With Cameron's technique, we understand so much more about blood. We can test our patients to see which drugs are working best for them, and in which doses. We find out what support materials they need. We are still using mostly drugs, *ja*, but the right drugs hopefully, in the right amounts.'

And if the doctors were enthused, the patients rang the phone off the hook. Meg kept an appointments book running eight weeks ahead of the current date. Every Monday morning, she opened up a new week for appointments, and by eleven thirty every Monday morning the entire week was booked solid.

The mood was good.

3

April. Each day was busier than the one before. Nurses came and went. Upstairs, in the consulting rooms, doors banged, and doctors barked instructions, advice and orders.

Downstairs, the clinic's waiting area – a horseshoe of green sofas by the huge windows overlooking the river – was already overflowing. One morning, as Meg was marshalling the stream of patients, there came a tap at the window, fifteen feet up on the river side. Meg stared. A blue-green shape looked down at her and gave another brusque tap of impatience. Meg's face broke into a broad smile as she ran to open one of the lower windows. The parrot flew down, perched for a few moments on the lip of the window, then with another sharp downward nod of its head, flew straight in, alighting on the back of Meg's chair. 'You little darling,' said Meg. 'I thought you'd never ask.'

4

She wasn't the only one to have similar thoughts that day. Since arriving in England, Kati had been staying with a friend in Notting Hill, but had recently found herself a flat of her own in a quiet residential area off Shepherds Bush. Ever attentive, Bryn had offered to help her with the move and arrived at dusk, a few minutes on the late side.

As he began to park, he glanced up and glimpsed light spilling from an open door, Kati in a state of shock, and two kids racing off up the road. Bryn leaped from the car and thundered off after them, yelling. They looked round, saw the size of their pursuer and dropped the handbag they'd stolen, whilst continuing to run like the wind.

Panting heavily, Bryn retrieved the handbag and jogged back down the road.

'Your bag,' he puffed.

'Thanks. Are you OK?'

'No. Bloody unfit is what I am. Are *you* OK?'

'Fine. I came outside to see if I could find you. The two boys walked right past me, then just turned around and demanded my bag. There was nothing inside, really. I was just worried they might produce a weapon.'

'You did right.'

'But thanks. It wasn't like I wanted them to have it.'

'You're welcome.' They were just inside the doorway now. Kati's flat shared a communal hallway, and it smelled like communal hallways always do: carpet which ought to be replaced, mould, the smell of old wallpaper and other people's kitchens. The passage was narrow, and Bryn and Kati were forced close together. 'Are you sure you're OK?' he said.

She put her hand to his cheek, then the back of his neck. She nodded. Her hand felt nice, as did the smell of her hair, and the look of her upturned spaniel eyes. He felt a surge of fondness and a sweet, sharp stab of lust. Aside from his brief, albeit well-publicised, fling with Cheryl Kessler, he hadn't so much as touched a woman since Cecily had left, and Kati wasn't just a woman, she was a particularly nice one.

'I'm really glad you came tonight,' she said.

'Me too,' he nodded.

He put his hands to her cheek, then his lips to hers, cautiously at first, not knowing if she would accept.

She did. It had been a lonely haul for her too, and Bryn had been lovely to her right from the start. She kissed him back, first with fondness, then with passion. They backed through the door into her flat, and got no unpacking done that night.

5

And meantime, on a field sloping steeply up to the downward thrust of the Brecon Beacons, a man is sitting on a sandstone boulder, as fluffy spring clouds skitter across a glorious blue sky. All is not well. A dog alternately licks the man's hand and barks. The man strokes the dog automatically, an impulse no longer guided by the brain. The man isn't old – at least, not unless you count a weather-beaten sixty-ish as old – but there's a dazed look on his face, a blinking attempt to make sense of a confusing world.

He doesn't know how long he's been sitting there, but the dog, Rhys, knows something is out of the ordinary, and in the ways that animals can be worried, Rhys is worried.

A long distance below the man and his dog, there's a grey-haired lady stepping out into the stone-flagged farmyard, calling out a name. 'Mervyn?' shouts Gwyneth. 'Mervyn? Mervyn?'

Rhys barks. Something's wrong.

THIRTEEN

1

The internet is badly named. It's not a net, it's an ocean. You, you're the net. If you want to find treasure in the deep, dark sea of nonsense, you've got to be skilful, patient and usually lucky as well.

Right now, Bryn wasn't leaving a whole lot to chance. Like Gari Kasparov playing three games of chess simultaneously, or a circus stuntwoman riding three horses bareback round the ring, he had three computers and three printers on the go, trawling for information with drag nets and dynamite. Meg hovered round, sorting and stacking the paper, feeding the printers extra paper or toner as needed.

Mungo shuffled in, trying to fit a can of Diet Coke and a lump of cold hamburger into his mouth at the same time. He'd set up the computers on the green sofas of the waiting area, because, once the clinic was closed for the night, the reception bay offered the most space for work. He inspected his babies, unhappy with what he saw.

'I can get you into Dataworld for free,' he mumbled.

'That's OK, Mungo.'

'MediaScan too, probably. Those outfits don't spend much on security. Their clients aren't street enough to try anything smart.'

'Right. Where "not street enough" equals honest.'

'Those databases are two hundred quid an hour, some of them.'

'No, Mungo. Just no. OK?'

'OK, OK. Chill.'

There was a pause. A dark shape bobbed up on the reception counter, emitting little squawks and demanding attention.

'Good girl, Tallulah,' said Meg. 'Good girl.' She found some seed for the parrot and scattered it on the counter. The parrot began to peck away on the waxed oak boards.

'Tallulah?' said Bryn. 'You're serious?'

'Yes, matey. Short for Tallulah Belle.'

'Good name,' said Mungo. 'Parrot – Tallulah – very sound.'

Bryn shook his head, baffled at their logic. 'Mungo,' he said, changing the subject. 'Any chance of your getting inside Corinth?'

Mungo sniffed vigorously. 'Well, I wasn't going to tell you, man, least not unless I cracked it, but I've sort of been poking around.'

'Trying to hack in?'

'*Crack*, man. Crack. Hacking is holy, cracking is dark side only.'

'Trying to crack them?'

Mungo nodded. 'Jus' the basics. Ping sweep. ICMP queries. Port scanning. TCP fingerprinting. That sort of thing.'

'You think you'll get in?'

'Gimme enough time and I could probably get inside the Darth Vader's knicker drawer, but it depends on how pushy you want to be. There's always the risk of tripping a crack-alert, see. I mean, if they were awake, they probably already saw my ping sweep.'

'They mustn't know we're trying.'

'Like mustn't? Or like mustn't-mustn't?'

'Big mustn't.'

Mungo wiggled his eyebrows. 'You can't make an omelette without breaking eggs,' he advised. 'Least, not without spending one pound twenty-nine pee on a cheese an' onion microwave omelette, with a crinkly bit of lettuce leaf as the most extremely imag'native serving suggestion.'

'You cracked us easily enough.'

'Yeah.' About six syllables were crammed into the one tiny word. 'To be honest, man, any teeny-bop lamer could have cracked you. The Brothers Lame of Lamesville, Arizona could have cracked you. I tell you, man, even –'

'It wasn't as bad as –'

'Angus Lame McLoser and his mum –'

'OK, Mungo. OK.'

The youngster trailed off. 'Wee Jane McLimpie ... Course, there might be another way, but it's *see*-ree-ously difficult.'

'And that is?'

'Crack the phone system, then crack Corinth.'

'You can do that?'

Mungo shrugged. 'Used to do that kind of thing when I was a kid, but they've made it tougher now.'

'You'll give it a go?'

'Yeah, man. I'll try. Wish you hadn't got me started on omelettes. Me belly's doing a Dance of the Seven Gurgles now. Time for a chocolate waffle.'

He sniffed again, rubbed his belly, looked sadly at the money wasting away on-screen, shot a longer and fonder glance at Meg, then shuffled off again, a skinny little character in enormous trainers with his big saucer-shaped eyes. Bryn felt briefly paternal towards the youngster before turning back to the printers and the rising mounds of data on Corinth.

146

'What's this all for?' asked Meg. 'Aren't we maybe going a bit O-T-T?'

He grimaced. 'First rule of warfare, Meg. Know your enemy.'

2

Rescued, restored and now resplendent, the barge had returned from the dead.

The outside gleamed white-and-black with the brightness of new paint. Inside, Bryn had sanded back the grimy oak floor and brought it back to life with endless coats of linseed oil. The brass window fittings gleamed a spotless pale gold. The wood-panelled walls were hung with Bryn's things – signed rugby photos, some decent oil paintings of the Welsh hills, photos of his mum, dad and brother, and a couple of framed newspaper stories commemorating his biggest deals. The room was comfy, male, welcoming. It smelled of linseed oil, candle smoke and old leather – and, best of all, the only lingering signs of Cecily were some faded but gorgeous Persian rugs that had somehow evaded the auctioneer's hammer.

'Nice,' said Cameron, who hadn't seen the finished article until now. 'Very you.'

'Yeah, thanks,' said Bryn. 'It's a welcome change, to be honest. Cecily's taste was – well, she was talented, very *House & Garden*, but it was all a bit dainty for me. I don't like a room you can't belch in.'

Cameron went momentarily boss-eyed, then produced a small but definite belch. 'You're right,' she said. 'It works.'

He grinned at her and belched back, like a donkey braying. The burp happened to coincide with the bow-wave from a passing boat, and so the barge rocked up and down as though in awe of Bryn's prowess. 'Show-off,' said Meg.

A couple of wrought-iron candlesticks made by his father's blacksmith threw a flickering yellow light on to stacks of documents beneath. They helped themselves to drinks – beer for Bryn, red wine for Kati and Cameron, white for Meg – took dried fruit and nuts from bowls on the table, then turned to business.

'OK,' said Bryn. 'Now, we know that Corinth became aware of Cameron's work about a year or two back. They understood that she threatened to knock out a medicine based on carpet-bombing everything that moves, and the way they saw it, she put at risk every single cent of their hundred billion dollar market value. Now, imagine you're Brent Huizinga, the Corinth chief exec. What would you have done?'

Kati shrugged, thinking about Bryn's face, how it looked by candlelight, how the shadows moved across him as he moved or the candles sputtered.

'We know what they did,' she said. 'They tried to ruin Cameron's career. As far as they know – or knew, rather – they succeeded.'

'OK. But if it had been you, wouldn't you have done something else as well? You'd have tried to take out Cameron, definitely, but meantime wouldn't you also begin to reorient your company, steering it away from what you know is a dangerous area?'

'I guess, maybe. But I don't . . .'

Kati tailed off, her mind still half on her new boyfriend's appearance. You couldn't really call him handsome, but he was seriously attractive in a second-hand-bulldozer sort of way. She put her finger to her mouth in an unconsciously flirtatious gesture.

'Well now, that's the point exactly,' he said. 'You *don't* see it. Think about it . . . We've got data here on the last dozen acquisitions they've made. Every single one has been in the realm of slash-n-burn medicine. Solano Virology Inc, Velmar Pharamaceutech ... You name it, their acquisitions pushed them ever further into the danger zone.'

Bryn paused, assuming he'd made himself clear, but Cameron, Kati and Meg were waiting for him to finish.

'The point is, they're not changing strategy, they're *hardening* strategy. If they've got products in the softer end of the market, they're actually looking to ditch them.'

Kati nodded, but Bryn continued lest any doubt remain.

'So once again, if you're Huizinga, and you're determined to hold fast to your original strategy, what do you do when Cameron disappears from your radar screens, then re-emerges in a blaze of publicity?'

Kati shook her head. She didn't know.

In a soft voice, Bryn spoke again. 'Well, that's just it. We don't know.' He gestured out of the open windows, where night air floated in from the Thames and a dark city spread out beneath a fluorescent sky. 'But they're out there somewhere. Working to destroy us, cost no object.'

Throughout all this Cameron had been sitting, a picture of concentration, red wine disregarded in her hand. Then, as the silence began to fold round Bryn's last speech, she began to shake her head, first just a little, then stronger and stronger as her thoughts took hold.

'Cameron ... ?'

She looked up to find the others staring at her. Her grey eyes were huge and solemn, her voice low and grave.

'Oh, we know,' she said. 'We know alright. This is Corinth, remember, Corinth. They're doing the one thing that we can't handle. The one thing that'll kill us.'

3

'Anita Morris,' she said. 'That's what gave it away. She was a professor out at Yale. Pretty good, but real ambitious, totally focused on her own personal bottom line. A perfect candidate. Just who I'd have picked if I were Huizinga.'

She helped herself to some of the dried apricots which Bryn had set out. They were unsulphured organic ones, and their dark-as-black-tea complexion gave no clue to the sunburst of sweetness within. 'Uh, good,' she commented, before pulling a magazine from the stack in front of her and waving it at Bryn.

'*Pharmaceutical News*,' she said, 'a trade magazine. Date –' she checked the cover – 'two months back.' Clearing her voice, she began to quote, '"Anita Morris, well-known Yale immunologist has been hired by Corinth Laboratories to head up a new research team at Corinth's Norwalk, Connecticut facility. The exact nature of the research has not been revealed, but both parties commented on the exciting and ground-breaking nature of the work. Professor Morris will have a substantial working budget, and will report directly to corporate office."'

Bryn froze for a moment, not understanding what he was being told. Then it clicked.

'Oh, shit,' he commented, with feeling.

'That's not all,' said Cameron, ignoring them all. She tugged another sheet of paper from her pile, this one a print-out from one of Bryn's innumerable databases. '"FDA listings of human trials cleared for implementation." Blah, blah, blah. "Institution: Corinth Laboratories. Project Director: Anita Morris. Type of Project: Human Trial, non-product, confidential."'

'Non-product? You mean it's not a drug?'

150

'Exactly. Isn't that nice? Corinth interested in something it can't sell.'

'Oh shit. Isn't that exactly like Huizinga? Hell, damn, bugger and blast!'

'Will someone please tell me what's going on,' said Meg, as a sudden sharp breeze whirling in through the windows caused the candles to gutter and shrink.

'As Cameron says, this is the worst news of all. They've hired Anita Morris to do what we're doing. Research into human Immune Reprogramming. They want to race us.'

'So what? They can't own knowledge.'

Bryn snorted. 'Oh yes, they bloody well can. They'll patent their findings. Then they'll work on alternatives and patent those. Everything. They'll patent everything.'

The London night all of a sudden seemed darker and more menacing than before. The gentle lapping of water against the boat's hull no longer seemed like the rhythm to a lullaby, it sounded like the tap-tap-tap of destiny, a soundtrack from a horror film.

Then Kati spoke again. 'I'm really sorry to say this, and I know there's a possible financial issue for us, but strictly from a medical perspective . . . in a way, isn't it good news that a big company has gotten interested in this? If Corinth is serious about Reprogramming, it'd be amazing.'

Dear Kati. Dear, sweet, pretty Kati, who could never be as nasty or duplicitous as the world she lived in. Bryn looked at her with fond incredulity. 'Well, for one thing,' he said, 'that possible financial issue is the difference between my financial destruction and . . . But put that aside. Think about it. Corinth is worth a hundred billion dollars. Immune Reprogramming will never be worth that. *Never*. They don't want the patents so they can use them. They want them in order to bury them.'

'You mean, *not* use them? They're allowed to do that?'

151

'Of course they're allowed to do that.'

Kati swallowed. Bryn's world was a rougher, nastier one than she had ever bargained on encountering. It was the one discordant factor in their otherwise happy young relationship. He was so familiar with the cynical brutality of the pharmaceutical industry that it often seemed as though he shared its logic, agreed with its assumptions. Cameron's mouth had tautened too, her gaze unblinking and hard.

'But surely,' said Kati, 'Immune Reprogramming is better medicine, so it must be worth more money. Why . . . ?'

Bryn softened his jaw a little, trying to make sure that his anger towards Corinth didn't come across as aggression towards Kati.

'Take AIDS,' he said gently. 'How long does Reprogramming take to eliminate the virus?'

Kati shrugged. 'We don't have any human data. But in rats, it takes around two weeks. Sometimes three if we have trouble.'

Bryn nodded, still keeping his voice low and soft. 'Right. Now, medically speaking, that's a great result, wonderful, fantastic, just what the doctor ordered. But commercially speaking, if you don't mind me saying, it's a disaster. Corinth doesn't *want* drugs that cure you. They want you to live long, be sick, and take drugs. Think about it. AIDS drugs, anti-depressants, certain types of heart drugs, Viagra, for heaven's sake – the most profitable medications are all ones which don't cure you, but just make you go on taking them. Reprogramming is a wonderful thing, Kati, and it'll make us plenty of money. But Huizinga will never sell it instead of his drugs. Never.'

The silence grew louder.

Upriver to the west of London, a band of low pressure gathered and intensified, and the breeze increased in strength and force. The draught plucked at the papers on the desk, it twitched at Cameron's unbound hair, it snatched at the candle flames, causing them to tremble and smoke.

'What do we do?' asked Kati.

It was Cameron who answered. 'Only one thing we can do. We race 'em. We get there first.'

'More specifically,' said Bryn, 'we have to beat them to the Patent Office. And that means you two have got to forget about your blood juicing, and forget about the School-room. It's the peptides that matter now.'

Although Cameron was nodding with big arcs of the head, Kati was still puzzled. 'That's not logical,' she said. 'Scientifically –'

'Forget science. Think economics,' said Bryn.

'Think . . . ?'

'Think about it, Kati,' said Cameron. 'Corinth can't patent the Schoolroom, because we already own it.'

'Oh, I see.'

'And they can't patent blood juicing, because there's nothing there to patent. All we do is inject a whole bunch of natural substances, and you can't patent vitamins and you can't patent injections.'

'Ah.'

'But peptides – well, they may be natural and we haven't invented them, but for some reason some damn fool bureau-crat decided that people could patent them –'

'Precisely,' nodded Bryn.

'Presumably because the same damn fool bureaucrat cared more about the profits of pharma companies than he did about people's health –'

'Perhaps.'

'Just like the same bunch of morons decided you could patent human genes, even though that's kind of like taking out a patent on gravity –'

153

'If you like.'

'But either way, if we want Reprogramming to work, we need to patent our peptide sequences before Corinth gets anywhere close.' Cameron shook her head at the size of the task ahead of them. 'And that's not going to be easy. Each disease has its own peptide encoding. It's a massive undertaking.'

The breeze ratcheted up another notch, and shadows began to swing around the room, like the banners of a mobilising army. On the walls, Bryn's framed pictures began to rattle and shake. Once again, it was Kati who broke the silence, speaking to Cameron.

'Anita Morris,' she said. 'How good is she? Is she good enough to beat us?'

Pale and serious, Cameron nodded. 'She's OK and she's got money. She'll have a huge lab, as many research staff as she wants . . . If it was a fair race, we'd win it every time. But it isn't and God help the sick, Kati, God help all of us, if they win.'

And as she spoke, a moth fluttered in through the open window, helpless to control its movement through the unpredictable air. It staggered briefly around, as though looking for something to land on, a place of security. It was a short struggle. The breeze lifted it and drove it straight into one of the candles. The flame flared briefly as the wings caught light, then fell away.

A smell of burning filled the room.

4

'Goddamn the goddamned – *goddamn* it!'

The test-tube shattered in her hand as her legs skidded from under her, and a stray elbow caught a beaker full of fluid as she tumbled to the floor. She landed with a painful

154

bump on her bottom, and the beaker tumbled with her, splashing her with betaine hydrochloride and smashing on the floor. 'God – *damn* – IT!'

Meg burst in, took a look at the scene. Cameron had tears in her eyes, which she scrubbed angrily away with the sleeve of her labcoat. Having corrected her eyes, her hand wrenched at the back of her head to make sure no hair had escaped the inevitable rubber band. In a voice loaded with rage and frustration she said, 'It's OK, Meg. I just slipped.' She clambered upright, using her hand on the worktop to support her, then yelped in pain as a glass splinter stabbed her. 'Ow, *shit!*'

Meg bundled the scientist into a chair, and like a mother with a child, drew the splinter from her hand, forced Cameron to sit quiet as she washed the wound, then put a plaster on top. She swept the floor, disposing of the broken glassware in the sharps bin, and mopped up the betaine hydrochloride whose fumes were filling the room. She opened the door and window to allow a draught in.

From outside, music coming from the barge drifted in on air laden with scents of an urban riverbank May evening: waterlogged wood and traffic fumes, river ooze and elder-flower. A tinkling laugh – Kati's laugh – rose above the Mozart, while the knocking of the barge against the jetty growled an answering rhythm.

Cameron kept trying to help with the clean-up job, but Meg wouldn't let her. 'Not yet, babe, you'll only break something else.'

'I am not a six-year-old,' muttered Cameron.

Meg put her mop away and looked searchingly into the other woman's intense grey eyes. 'Time of the month, is it?'

'No. I just broke something. That's all. Jesus. What's this, the Cockney Inquisition?'

Pursing her lips in annoyance, Cameron rose and

slammed the open window shut. The Mozart and the tinkling laugh were cut off with a bang. The room filled with
silence, bringing a flash of startled understanding to Meg.

'Oh my God,' she said. 'You've got the hots for Bryn,
haven't you?'

'I have not.' Cameron's denial was instantaneous, but a
rush of scarlet up her cheeks betrayed the truth.

'Oh my God, you've really got a bad case of it.' Cameron
shook her head, but tears began to tumble from her eyes,
confirming the truth beyond any doubt at all.

Meg put her arm round the scientist and let her cry, big
heavy tears penned in for too many weeks of silent suffering.
Eventually, as the weeping began to die down, Meg asked
gently, 'How long has it been, sweetie? How long have you
fancied him?'

Gulping for words, Cameron answered. 'I don't know,
really . . . When he crashed on to the scene, I thought . . .
I thought . . . God, Meg, I don't know what I thought. I
guess I thought he wasn't doing all this – you know, rescuing
me, my work, everything – just for money. I didn't think
people did things like that. I thought it must be, just a
little bit, even just a tiny bit, because of me. Shows what a
dumb-ass I am.'

Her voice trickled away as she battled with her tears,
while Meg continued the story. 'You thought he must have
had some sort of attraction to you, because you didn't
believe him to be the self-centred, money-grabbing, male
bastard that he turned out to be. Meanwhile, you've been
working here right on top of him, seeing him every day,
working yourself into a right big tizz over him, getting yourself more and more upset every time he and Kati spend a
night together.'

'Which seems to be every night at the moment.'

'They're not serious about each other, you know. They've

156

both just come out of heavy relationships, and what they need is –' Cameron's gulping and eye-wiping became more anguished the longer Meg went on. In a hole of her own making, Meg stopped digging. 'Sorry, I suppose that makes it worse.'

Cameron allowed herself to cry once more, while Meg rubbed her back in long, slow circles of comfort.

Then, on an impulse, Meg put her hand to the scientist's head and pulled away the rubber band. Her shoulder-length sandy hair fell around her face, still kinked where the band had gripped it. Meg ran her fingers through the hair like a hairdresser before a restyle, then put her hand to Cameron's chin and lifted it, gazing into the brave but grief-battered face.

'You don't really give yourself a chance, do you?'

'What d'you mean?' asked Cameron, old defensive patterns at the ready.

'Look, tell me if I'm going too far, but you're not exactly experienced, are you? Have you ever had, like, a proper boyfriend?'

'Have I ever had a proper boyfriend? I'm not a virgin if that's what you mean. There were a couple of guys at grad school, and we had intercourse and everything. But, Jesus! They were juveniles, Meg, more interested in Budweiser and bowling than anything else. I wanted to work. I knew I had it in me to do great work in medicine, and I couldn't see the point in fooling around, really. If I ever met a man who was actually grown to adulthood, it might be different, but till then, I don't really give a damn. At least, I didn't until . . . until . . .'

'Until Bryn conned you into thinking he might be a grown-up.'

'And it's not as though sex is all it's cracked up to be. Not for me it wasn't.'

'It can be quite nice with the right bloke, and you know, Bryn's not such a baby. He's into commitment. I know he was cut up about his marriage. I think his fling with Kati is just a holiday until he's ready to start looking for the one true one again.'

Cameron's expression moved comically between anger and tears, uncertain which way to turn. Meg continued to play with her hair, wiping her eyes and forcing her to look straight ahead.

'You're right about one thing, Cammie.'

'Uh?'

'Even the nicest men are nine-tenths brain-dead when it comes to looks.'

'Ah!' Cameron snorted angrily and reached for the rubber band which would take her hair out of Meg's inquisitive hands and away from sight and reach. Meg stopped her.

'Cammie, for God's sake. You're a bloody pretty woman and you act like you've got something to hide.'

'Look, if men want me, they better want me. I'm not going to dick around playing stupid little cutesie games for their benefit. If they want me, they can come get me.'

Once again she reached for the rubber band in order to lock her hair back under house arrest. 'Damn it!' said Meg, who fought for the band and cut it into pieces with some surgical scissors which sat nearby.

Cameron was white-faced and angry. 'Screw you, Meg! This hairstyle works for me, and I'm not going to monkey around with it for you.'

'Too bloody right it works. Why don't you just tattoo *sorry not interested* on your forehead and have done with it?'

'Where do you get off telling me how to live?'

'Listen, gorgeous, when it comes to physical attraction, men have brains the size of pickled walnuts, not even located in their skulls, and it's no bloody wonder that they don't look twice. You choose, Cammie. You can go through life guarding against the possibility of romance, and feeling bitter because romance never comes. Or you can go out looking for it, and bloody well find it. On everything else in the world, you're the original braveheart, scared of nothing. But on this subject, you're the ace, king and queen of wimps.'

Meg flung down her challenge with a flourish, then stopped, wondering if she'd gone too far as Cameron sat, face down, plucking thoughtfully at the corners of her mouth. At last, she looked up.

'You think I'm pretty?'

'No, babe, you're gorgeous.'

'Honestly?'

'Honestly.'

Cameron accepted the information with a tiny nod, then went back to her thoughts and her mouth-plucking.

'OK, then. I'll do something with my hair. If that makes men run after me like dogs after a bitch on heat, then more fool them. But I'll do it. Only nothing I have to fuss over the whole damn time.'

'Listen, sweetheart, spending a few minutes on your hair would be good, but that's only the start of it. There's clothes, there's make-up, there's flirtation, there's getting out of the laboratory and actually meeting people. The hair's only a start.'

'Meg, I am not going to spend my life –'

'How are you going to spend it? Single or with someone? That's the choice. And if you want to spend it with someone, you've got to join the human race.'

Cameron paused, tugging at her hair as though using a leash to pull her back. Eventually she decided. 'No, Meg. Sorry. I'm not a coward. Not about my hair, not about

159

anything else. But in the end I don't give enough of a damn. If a guy wants me for me, then that's fine. If he wants me because of a bit of make-up, then forget it. I'll wait for a grown-up to come along.'

'You'll wait for ever.'

Cameron held the other woman's eyes for a moment, smiled sadly, and went back to work.

5

Night-time in the boathouse. Outside, the barge nudges against the little jetty, creaking. Inside, everything is dark and still, except upstairs in Mungo's tiny attic room, Pod Mungo, as it's known.

The room is crowded. It has three computers, two printers, a fax machine, four phone points (one voice, three data), mounds of junk food, a microwave, handfuls of computer CDs and manuals, and all the other nameless piles of rubbish which form Mungo's chosen habitat. The carpet is rich in a kind of alluvial layer of discarded food, and the air is strong with the scent of printer toner, hot wires, and piles of dust and paper warmed by the stacked-up electronics.

Mungo isn't there, yet he's hard at work. His three PCs are switched on and busy, running a simple computer program. The job they have is this: to dial phone numbers in the Connecticut area. For each three-digit exchange code, they begin dialling at xxx-9800, and then go on up: xxx-9801, xxx-9802. It's dull work but the PCs don't mind. Knowing them, they probably enjoy it. Each time they ring, they're looking for the characteristic response signal of a modem. Each time they find one, they transcribe the number to a data file, hang up, and dial again. xxx-9803, xxx-9804, xxx-9805. And once they get up to xxx-9999, they move on, to the next three-digit exchange, and the next, and the next, right through the night, every night.

6

Bryn's dad is sick. No one recognises the illness, and Mervyn Hughes is too old, too stubborn, too damn bloody-minded to see a doctor. If he calls it anything, he calls it flu and goes about the farm as best he can.

It's not a very good best. The jobs which have to be done are done, but all those things like mending fences, digging ditches, dunging fields and rehanging gates just aren't happening. The farm is beginning to slide, and a sliding hill farm is hard to stop.

Mervyn, in his lethargy and brain-fog, is the only one who won't admit the problem. The others – Gwyneth, Bryn, Dai – admit it, talk about it, worry about it. But until the stubborn old man consents to change, there's nothing much they can do. Dai does what he can for the farm in his spare time, and Bryn, too, goes up at weekends. But it's not enough. Once again, and with more urgency than before, Gwyneth has asked Bryn to come home and settle.

FOURTEEN

1

Mungo drifted in, walking gingerly, like an insect with half its legs broken. A bruise hung over his forehead like a cloud of purple smoke, and the smell of tobacco, mixed with other popular combustible inhalants, clung to his refugee-style streetwear.

'Heavy weekend, Mungo?'

Mungo pointed to his knees and elbows. 'Skating. Wounds of honour. Came off doing my first switch tailslide. Had another go and did it. Sweet.'

'Congratulations.'

'Bit sore today, though.'

Bryn smiled. 'Yeah, well, take it easy.'

Mungo hadn't had much of a childhood. His father had been a brief visitor at the best of times, and his mother suffered from bouts of mental illness which had left her unable to care for her family. Mungo and his two sisters had been in and out of care, in and out of foster homes, all their lives. JoJo and Dar, the two younger girls, had always depended on him for mothering and fathering, as well as simply big-brothering. In some ways, Mungo was as old as the hills, in others he was hardly grown up at all. Given a different start in life, he'd have been an internet zillionaire, or a top video game author. Or perhaps he'd simply have been ordinary and happy. As it was, Bryn liked him, relied on him, and was happy to play the kindly father that Mungo had never had.

'I'm going to see if I can get some of that ethanol off Cam'ron. Paint myself with it.' He mimed dabbing the ethanol on his wounds, then hopping as it began to sting, then smiling seraphically as it anaesthetised the cuts.

'It wears off after a few minutes. And it'll sting.'

'Yeah, but it's wicked. I'm going to try, anyway.'

Bryn nodded permission with a smile, then turned to business. He pulled out a sheaf of phone bills.

'See these, Mungo?'

Mungo looked and nodded.

'Spot anything wrong?'

Mungo shook his head.

'They're about one quarter of what they ought to be. I thought maybe you'd taken it into your head that we were paying too much for our online research services.'

'You were being ripped, man.'

'I don't care, Mungo. We can't just nick things when you don't like the price.'

'No, man, I know. You already told me.'

'Well, look, can we just go back to the old-fashioned way of paying for what we use? Think of it as a generation gap thing.'

'No, man.' Mungo sought a way to explain the obvious. 'I've been grafting. Took a data compression system off the net, and hooked up with New Zealand for our data feed. It's cheaper. Big bandit problem here, man. Suit-bandits, worst sort. It's all pukka, man, straight-up. I thought you'd be pleased.'

'I am, Mungo. Thanks. You've done a splendid job.'

Mungo's frown of worry passed into a radiant daybreak of delight. 'Alright. So we're sorted?'

'Yes, indeed. We're sorted.'

Mungo did something involving his nose, his sleeve and the back of his hand which caused all three to be briefly connected by strings of green mucous, before a vigorous rubbing on the seat of his trousers disposed of the evidence.

'Oh, yeah. Meg asked me to give you these.'

Mungo passed over some letters. 'Dear Mr Hughes. Thank you for your recent loan application. While we were impressed by . . . blah, blah . . . we regret that . . . blah, blah,' he read. There were two others, both of them all but identical to the first. 'Wunch of bankers,' said Mungo, illustrating the thought with a hand gesture.

But Bryn wasn't listening. He was frowning in thought, knuckling his jaw as though trying to muscle a way through. Eight loan applications sent. Six rejections received. That didn't add up. Right now, the Fulham Clinic was riding a wave of public popularity. Bryn had a stellar record in business and finance. Yet the rejections didn't even invite negotiations. They just said no, plain and simple. It was strange, unexpected.

He began to thump his first into his palm. If at first you don't succeed – thump, thump and thump again. The rhythm of his fist softened into a slow, meditative pounding. Rays of light wove gentle lightning around his head.

At length he looked up, almost surprised to find Mungo still there. 'Can you get Meg in here, please? I think it's about time I asked my old friends at Berger Scholes for a loan, don't you?'

2

Mungo left, clearly surprised that Bryn hadn't previously thought of anything so obvious. But when Meg came in a moment later, followed in a series of short flaps by an increasingly confident Tallulah, her surprise was for a different reason.

'Berger Scholes won't give you a loan for a few million, will they? I thought they didn't touch anything under fifty million bucks.'

Bryn shrugged. 'Not usually, no. But for one of their favourite ex-employees, you never know.'

'If you say so,' she said, deeply sceptical.

'Get a set of loan application documents together, can you?'

Meg nodded and turned to go, but hesitated. As she paused, trying to make up her mind about something, a speedboat passed outside. At its wheel was a young man driving too fast, and a young woman standing up, getting her face wet in the spray. The girl was pretty and wore a short skirt, which lifted as the boat accelerated. Bryn raised his eyebrows and smiled. Meg's hesitation came to an end.

'Honestly, what is it with you? I know you used to have your problems with Cecily and everything, but at least you tried. Where's all that commitment stuff gone? All you need is the sight of a girl's legs to make you all creepy and adolescent again.' Meg's tone of voice came out more ferocious than she'd intended, and Bryn waved her into a seat.

'Listen Meg, I can't remember when I appointed you guardian of my romantic life, but for what it's worth, I'm very fond of Kati and she's very fond of me. But that's as far as it goes. We enjoy each other's company, and every now and then – not as often as you might think – we have sex. When we do spend a night together, it's about fun, it's not about all eternity. She was really cut up about her fiancé leaving her, and I was upset about Cecily. When I got married, I intended to stay with Cecily for the rest of my days, and I'm just not yet ready to start down that path again. Maybe in a month or two. Maybe in a year or two. When

165

the time comes to separate with Kati, we'll deal with it like responsible adults. I am not going to let you guilt-trip me over my one and only casual relationship in ten years.'

'Yeah, OK, I didn't mean to get heavy. Sorry.'

'That's OK.' In the corner of the room, Tallulah had begun to peck at the training shoes Bryn had been out running in that morning. 'And get off my shoes, you revolting bird.'

'You go on, Tallulah,' Meg said protectively. 'Eat the horrible man's trainers if you want to . . . And if he wants a meaningless relationship with the second-best-looking woman in the clinic, then I suppose it's none of my business.'

'It's not meaningless, Meg, it's just not church bells and wedding dresses. And I hate to let you down, Meg, but she's not the second-best-looking, she's top.'

Meg shook her head. 'Second.'

'Sorry. There's always you, of course, unless you meant one of the nurses. I suppose Karen is quite –'

'Not me, you idiot. Cammie's top by a bleeding mile. Knocks the rest of us into a cocked hat.'

'Don't be ridiculous!' Bryn laughed.

'Ten pounds says she is.'

'How are you going to prove it?'

'Are you on?'

'OK, but I say you owe me a tenner.'

'Well, she may not look it, but she's a stunner.' Bryn was about to object to her logic, but Meg was unstoppable. 'She's tall, thin, good face, full lips, big eyes, good skin, hair you could do anything with. She doesn't use any of it, but she's got the lot.'

'Well, I'll just have to make do with number two, then, won't I?'

'You don't, actually. Cammie fancies you like mad. Truly, madly, deeply.'

'Cameron? Meg, you're joking. No.'

'She does.'

Bryn closed his eyes and breathed in deeply, so that his barrelled ribcage rose steeply with the in-breath. He exhaled. 'Please tell me that you're kidding. Please.'

'She started falling for you back in Boston. She's been falling ever since. Right now, she's head over heels in love with you. Even when I tried to talk her out of it, listing all your bad points – it's quite a long list, actually, when you start to spell them out – she didn't listen. It's still all you.'

'Oh, *shit*, Meg.'

'*O-shi!*' squawked Tallulah, making a sudden break-through in her understanding of human communication.

'Good girl!' said Meg encouragingly. 'Good parrot.'

'Honestly, Meg. I've never done anything to lead her on – never, I swear.'

'Yeah, I know. Her girl-meets-boy skills are a little rusty – well, OK, they're completely rusted up – but, yes, Cameron loves you. I had a long chat with her last night. She told me all about it.'

Bryn was still disoriented. Cameron was so closed down in some ways, it had been fairly easy not to think of her as a sexual creature at all: just a brilliant intellect, whose chosen body-form happened to be female. Bryn hated the idea of hurting her, but he'd be just as likely to go out with a mainframe computer as with her. Speaking gently, he said, 'I hope you told her that I . . .' He shook his head.

'She's nice. She's amazingly intelligent. She's passionate, warm-hearted, committed. She's a totally brilliant all-round human being, even if she can be a bit odd. Plus she adores you, I don't know why, but she does. And she's not the teeniest bit stuck up, not like your oh-so-delightful ex.'

Bryn's oh-so-delightful ex had begun to deluge him with

short sharp letters, asking him how come her paintings and furniture and other valuable items hadn't yet been shipped as agreed. A fair question, and one not so easy to answer, given that the whole lot had now been sold and the money plunged irreversibly into the clinic. But still, that was a problem for another day.

'Meg, no,' he said. 'Definitely not.' Still Meg paused. 'Definitely,' he added. 'Definitely, definitely, definitely.'

'And good-looking, I promise you.'

'She could look like Claudia Schiffer, Meg, she'd still drive me nuts.'

'Not Claudia Schiffer. More like Julia Roberts without the hair – no, I know, she's like a skinnier version of –'

'Meg, no. Just no. Definitely not. You're on to a loser here. Have you ever even heard me and Cameron in a room together without us getting into an argument within about ten minutes? The very first time I met her, she punched me.'

'You're both Aries. You should expect a fiery relationship.'

'Meg, please. I'm really sorry that Cameron should be in this position. But just make sure she knows she needs to look elsewhere. Don't tell her I said so, but head her off. It's the last thing on earth I need right now. The last thing she needs. Last thing the company needs, for God's sake.'

'It's your funeral. I'm not going to let her stay single for long.'

'Bryn Hughes, RIP,' said Bryn, crossing himself. 'And you can take that damned bird with you when you go.'

Summoning Tallulah with a snap of the fingers, Meg went back to the door, wondering whether to tackle Bryn one last time, but her boss was deep in thought again. Having his medical director deeply in love with him was one problem, but it didn't threaten the company's existence.

His hand reached for his Rolodex, twizzled the cards, dialled a number.

'Rudy Saddler? Hello, it's Bryn Hughes . . .'

3

Meg didn't know it, because Cameron never told her. And Bryn never knew it, because Cameron never let him see. But the fact was that Cameron heard what she was never meant to hear. Standing with her hand on the handle of Bryn's door, she heard the whole conversation between Meg and Bryn, including his final savage summary of his feelings: 'It' – 'Cameron, in other words – 'is the last thing on earth I need . . .'

The last thing on earth that Bryn needed slunk away, out of the boathouse, past the wharves, through the residential streets leading up towards the Fulham Palace Road. On a granite kerbstone, a river of snarling traffic before her, a dirty pavement behind, Cameron Wilde MD, PhD sat down and cried like a baby.

It was the second time in so many days that she'd cried. As far as she was concerned, that was twice too often. She wasn't the crying sort. On returning to the boathouse later that day, she tugged Meg straight into her tower office, her mind made up. There, with London spreading like a map at her feet, she took the decision that would change her emotional life for ever.

'I've been thinking,' she said.

'That's what you're paid for.'

'Screw Bryn.'

'Yeah, right. Screw him.'

'I want to go for it.'

'Go for it?'

'Make-over. Hair, clothes, whatever. The whole shebang.'

169

'Cammie, really?'

'What's that phrase you're always quoting?'

'Sex appeal – please give generously?'

'Not that,' said Cameron crossly. 'About flirtation.'

'No flirtation without preparation. No reproduction without seduction.'

'Right. So let's prepare and seduce.'

Meg grinned, more and more broadly as she saw the valley of opportunity widen in front of her.

'Make-over, then manhunt,' she said.

'Huh?'

'When a pretty girl feels lonely – make-over, then manhunt. Top tip from Auntie Meg.'

'How do you go manhunting?'

Meg shrugged. 'How does a lady-ape go man-ape hunting?'

'That's different,' said Cameron. 'Their bums swell up to five times their normal size and go purple. Then man-apes beat each other up till there's only one left.'

Meg grinned. 'Same difference. We'll go clubbing Saturday night. But before we go, I'm taking you to a beauty salon, get your arse painted purple. Deal?'

'Jeez, Meg. I appreciate it, you know, but I'm not sure, I think –'

Meg kissed her partner on the cheek. 'I don't care too much what you think, gorgeous. You and me. Saturday night. I could use a good shag, and frankly, Cammie, I think you could too.'

4

Mungo's PCs have done their job. Mungo now has a list of literally hundreds of phone numbers in Connecticut which are answered by computer. He hasn't dialled every number in the state, but, thank goodness, he doesn't need to. The American phone companies, God bless 'em, always locate the keys to their vast networks, the big computer switches, up in the 9800s or 9900s. If they didn't, Mungo would have the devil's own job locating them, but for some reason, they always do.

The next step is harder. Only one of Mungo's phone numbers will lead him to the switch he wants, but which? And when he finds it, how will he fool the computer into believing that he's an authorised user? There are no pre-set answers for such questions, only painstaking work, moments of brilliance and a strong dash of luck.

He begins the next stage, knowing this is a task he can't delegate. He dials the first number. Somewhere out in Connecticut a modem chats briefly with his and connects. His screen displays a single character: '?'. He's being asked for an instruction.

Mungo knows his way around the British telecoms system, and he figures that a lot of what works in Britain should work just the same in the United States. After all, the basic hardware components of each system are pretty much the same. He tries his UK tricks. Nothing. Just a persistent question mark. He figures this number, whatever it is, probably isn't the one he's after.

He moves on to the next number. It's a lot of work, but unlike most of Mungo's previous adventures in cyberspace, this time it matters. High up in the boathouse roof, Pod Mungo is all but dark. Two of the three PCs are powered down, and the only light in the room comes from Mungo's one solitary screen. This is how cracking is meant to be. Late at night. Dark. Full of the excitement of the unknown.

On screen, a single character flashes. It's white on black, the old-fashioned colours of MS-DOS. The character is a question mark. It's Mungo's move.

FIFTEEN

1

Friday evening. A wine bar in the City.

Huge champagne bottles line the walls: bottles as big as barrels, big enough for a child to hide in, relics of the high-living 1980s, when bankers competed to see who could piss away their income in the most offensively show-off fashion. Well, guys: you were all winners, the whole stripey-shirted lot of you. Rudy Saddler sat among the trophies, sipping at a glass of water.

Bryn Hughes had brought him here, for a reason presumably. Hard to see what. He hadn't said anything worth saying. Nothing about his loan application, nothing else, either.

'If you'll excuse me,' he murmured, rising to go to the loo.

Bryn watched him go. Jerk. He still disliked Saddler for stealing his job, though he also knew that Saddler hadn't done anything that he, Bryn, wouldn't have done in the same situation. Who cares? What law is it says you have to be consistent? Bryn waited till the door to the loos slammed shut, then reached for the other man's jacket, found his wallet, and withdrew his Berger Scholes security pass. Bryn put the pass into his pocket and Saddler's wallet back where it was. Bryn finished his beer. Saddler finished his pee. They exchanged banalities, made their escapes.

2

Saturday afternoon.

Cameron had been accused of cowardice once, and it wasn't going to happen again. Grim as the angel of death, with a face of iron, she sat in front of the hairdresser's mirror, swathed in a black polyester cape. The hairdresser ran her fingers through Cameron's hair, fluffing it up and letting it fall back.

'How do you want it?'

'Just the way it is,' growled Cameron, 'but I'm not allowed, apparently.'

Meg stepped forward with a conciliatory smile. 'What she means is . . .'

Then the shampoo went on, the scissors came out, and Cameron was in the process of losing a hairstyle she'd had, unaltered, since the age of eight. As they left the salon an hour or so later, Meg pinched her partner's bottom.

'What are we, babe?' she whispered.

Cameron grinned, secretly thrilled with her sleek new hairstyle. 'Purple,' she said. 'Purple and proud.'

3

Midnight on Saturday and the time had come. Wearing a suit, Bryn walked straight into the main reception.

'Evening,' said Bryn.

'Morning more like,' said the Berger Scholes security guard, shoving a night visitors' book at Bryn.

Bryn signed himself in: 'Rudy Saddler'. He headed towards the turnstiles.

'It's after hours, mate. I need to see your pass.'

Bryn flashed his pass at the guard, thumb over the photo, not over-polite. He was supposed to be a Managing Director, after all.

'OK, mate. Just a rule.'

Bryn swiped his card through the turnstile and waited for a tiny click to tell him that the barrier had been released. The click came and Bryn pushed. The guard watched, relaxed. First timers always pushed too soon and had to reswipe their card. If Bryn had fumbled the barrier, the guard would have stopped him and rechecked his pass. But no fumble. The guard relapsed into his three-pound-fifty-an-hour coma, as Bryn made his way to the fourth floor, which stood silent, dark and deserted. Excellent.

The layout was open-plan, with a fringe of glass-walled offices around the edge of the large room. Goldfish get more privacy. Not missing his banking days, Bryn walked into the office belonging to the European Head of Credit and booted up the computer. He allowed himself a desk lamp to work by, but otherwise preferred to keep the floor in darkness. The computer yawned, stretched, and groped for its slippers. 'User ID?' it demanded, once awake. 'Password?'

User ID was easy: blistoff, standing for Bernie Listoff, whose office this was. Password was tougher, but Meg had told Bryn that Bernie was famous for his forgetfulness. It was common knowledge, so she said, that his password was always scribbled on a note by his PC. What she hadn't mentioned was that there were about twelve notes stuck there, plus more that had fallen off and were lying beside the monitor. Damn Meg's common knowledge. Bryn began to search through the notes.

'Veba. Euro 400 mm evergreen. Phone Kurt.'

'JP Morgan. Co-agent role. Ericsson. 1 billion. 5 yr. Upfront fee OK?'

'Call Keown at HSBC. Joint pitch to BAA.'

'Get revised spreads from Volkswagen. Covenants are a bloody mess. Müller.'

Bryn leafed through the sheaf of scribbles. None of them said anything like 'Password: carnation'. Hell. Bryn thought of calling Meg for help but remembered she was out tonight, with Cameron of all people. He tried briefly to imagine the two of them together, failed, and looked around for inspiration.

Listoff's desk diary. Worth a try. Berger Scholes obliged all employees to change their passwords every month. Perhaps Listoff kept them in his diary. Lists of business meetings. A corporate entertainment at a football match. A weekend in Paris with his wife. No password. Hell.

Bryn tossed the diary down, sending a heavy glass paperweight flying. He picked it up. A miniature cannon sat like an idiot in the bubbly glass. Football colours and mottos encircled the cannon. Arsenal Football Club. Stupid sport. Stupid toy.

Bryn was about to put it away, when a thought struck him. *Arsenal*. Back to the diary. Ha! The corporate entertainment was at Highbury stadium. Back to Listoff's scribbled notes. Call Keown at HSBC. Ha, again! 'Stupid bloody sport,' said Bryn, and turned back to the computer.

'Password?' it asked.

He typed one word: 'Keown'.

The computer didn't scream hosanna or mutter a sarcastic 'at last'. It didn't comment on Listoff's football obsession or compare Martin Keown with other Arsenal defenders, past and present. It just finished putting on its slippers, splashed some water on its face, ran a comb through its hair and was done. Ready for action.

4

Seated at the keyboard with the bank's systems open to his view, Bryn typed in 'Fulham Clinic' under 'Client name'. The system blinked, then brought up just three notes.

The first, at the start of the week, had been entered by the friend of Bryn's to whom he'd addressed his loan application. The note read, 'Company is a start-up health-care venture, owned by ex-Berger Scholes MD, Bryn Hughes. Proposed loan is very small, but Hughes has suggested there may be opportunity to buy equity. Suggest follow-up, with view to equity participation. Relationship status: under review.'

Ha! Nice guy. Bryn had always liked him.

The second note was from Rudy Saddler, dated two days later. It read: 'Under NO CIRCUMSTANCES engage with Bryn Hughes or Fulham Clinic. Bank is currently seeking to participate in a major financing with Corinth Laboratories of the US. Corinth has made it exceptionally plain that it regards Clinic as fundamentally unethical, and will not do business with any bank that supports it. WE WILL LOSE ROLE ON CURRENT AND ALL FUTURE FINANCINGS IF WE PROCEED.'

The third note, written by the writer of the first, read simply: 'Application refused. Relationship status: closed.'

So that was it. Every bank that received a loan application from Bryn, also received a call from some smirking sod at Corinth. The message would be plain: their business or ours, you can't have both. And the banks chose. They chose the big business, the huge loans, the giant fees. Once again, Bryn cursed Saddler for doing something that, given the same circumstances, he'd have done too.

But what disturbed Bryn more was the timing. Within two days of getting his loan application, Berger Scholes had been warned off by Corinth. Coincidence? Maybe. But if it wasn't, then Corinth was learning about Bryn's applications within hours of them being sent. A mole inside the clinic? A mole who'd known about Bryn's loan applications? It seemed almost impossible, given the precautions Bryn had taken, yet the coincidence was glaring . . .

Deep in thought, Bryn reached out to turn off the PC. His hand had reached as far as the power switch, when an idea struck. He moved his hand again, back to the keyboard, trembling with excitement.

5

Put a pig inside a frock coat, it still looks like a pig. Put a bouncer inside a dinner jacket and the bent nose and bristling hair speak louder than any amount of fancy shirt-front. But the bouncers didn't need to use much of their scarce mental energies to decide about the next two in line. One of the girls was tall, slim and dressed to kill, even if she did come over a bit gawky. The other was shorter, bubbly, a natural party animal.

'On you go, girls. Enjoy your evening.'

'We will,' said Meg, as she and Cameron walked on in.

6

Bryn typed new instructions into the PC, and jumped back to the systems entry menu. On the far right, tucked discreetly away, there was a tab marked 'HNWI'. Just that. Four letters, spelling gold. Excitement flared once again. This was better than a loan, better than a bank. He clicked the tab.

A new dialogue box came up, asking for user ID and password. Bryn tried 'blistoff' and 'keown' again, but was rejected. 'First attempt of three,' commented the computer. Hell.

HNWI stands for High Net Worth Individuals. In the language of Berger Scholes, an HNWI had personal assets of fifty million dollars or more. Mostly more, mostly much more.

Bryn skimmed back through Listoff's diary. In the preceding month, there was a note about a charity do for the Seaman's Defence Fund. Yeah, right. For his second attempt, Bryn entered 'blistoff' and 'seaman', the Arsenal goalkeeper. Another cold pulse of excitement washed through his body, down to his fingertips. One of Berger Scholes' HNWIs could recapitalise the clinic without even noticing the cost. He clicked 'Enter'. No joy. 'Second attempt of three,' said the computer.

Hell and damnation.

He closed the diary, drumming his fingers on the desk. There were other places you could get information about rich people, but nowhere was as good as Berger Scholes. The bank had invested tens of millions of dollars in the system, and spent millions of dollars every year keeping it up to date. It didn't just contain financial information, it contained everything: family, hobbies, friends, charities, politics, health, education, clubs and associations, everything. The database was what MI6 would have had in its files, if the gay Cambridge commies who ran it had ever had the brains, the money and the organisation.

One more try.

Bryn typed 'blistoff' and for password, he entered 'password'. What the hell? Worth a go. The screen blinked for a while, then changed. 'Password refused,' it stated. 'Access denied. Your security code has been frozen, please contact your IT manager for instructions on how to proceed.'

Damn it, damn it, damn it.

The trouble with the 'if at first you don't succeed, then batter it three quarters to death and try, try, try again' philosophy, is it doesn't work nearly as well on computers as it does on people. Bryn was just about to try it anyway, just for the hell of it, when he remembered Mungo. He phoned Mungo's pager with a super-urgent message, and – thank God – got a call back within fifteen minutes.

'Yeah?'

Mungo's dazed voice emerged weakly from a background racket, which could have been music or could have been a new type of warfare based around machine guns and pneumatic drills, with some electronic gizmos wailing away in the distance.

'Mungo, I need a hand. Is there any chance I could pull you away from your party?'

The drills drilled and the machine guns fired, and the gizmos screamed. Then, dimly, Mungo's voice again: 'Yeah?'

'Mungo, it's me, Bryn. Can we talk?'

Another long pause punctuated by some kind of crescendo in the music, and what sounded like somebody dying close at hand and painfully. 'Yeah? . . . I'm not getting you, man.'

'MUNGO! CALL ME, BRYN, NOW. PLEASE! SOMEWHERE QUIET.'

Bryn yelled not his very, very loudest – he wasn't at a rugby match, after all – but quite loud enough to alert a flood of security guards if they felt like being alerted. The line went dead. Five minutes passed. The security guards didn't appear – perhaps lots of MDs spent the small hours shouting their heads off in the bank. Then Bryn's mobile rang. At last: Mungo calling from a quiet line.

'Mungo? It's Bryn. I need you here as soon as possible.' Bryn explained what he wanted.

'Yeah, alright.' Mungo's *yeah, alright* sounded more like

yer-igh, as though he were experimenting with a new kind of language based on two vowel sounds and no consonants. 'No probs. Need to go home first, though.'

Mungo rang off vaguely, then rang back for instructions on where to come, then rang off again. Bryn waited.

And waited.

And waited. It was coming up to four o'clock, and Bryn was beginning to wonder how much longer he dared to occupy Bernie Listoff's office, in the uncertain hope that Mungo would arrive, and not even knowing whether he could help. At one point the lights came on, and a team of maintenance workers began to rip up flooring and dismantle some internal walls. Anyplace else, it would be a strange time to do it, but not at Berger Scholes, where maintenance work was always scheduled for the weekend to avoid disruption. Eventually, Bryn's mobile rang again. It was Mungo, just five minutes away.

'Good man,' said Bryn. 'I'll be down to meet you.'

Mungo was resplendent in his clubbing gear – sweat-smeared orange T-shirt, gold chain with a peace emblem, huge black trousers and a headband made of something which emitted a pale red fluorescent light. His eyes were vast, bulgy and happy, he carried an unopened two-litre bottle of water in his hand, and he smelled like the sort of thing sniffer dogs would pull you out of the queue for at Heathrow.

'W-e-l-c-o-m-e,' said Mungo, opening his arms and swaying. 'Cyber-greetings to you and your tribe.'

'He's with me,' said Bryn to the security guard. 'Believe it or not.'

He frogmarched Mungo through the turnstiles and up to Listoff's office. Mungo rolled his head in disapproval. 'First rule of cyber-trespass. Leave no footprints, take no prisoners. Shouldn't have tried the third time. Look at that.

180

Security code frozen. F-r-o-z-e-n. *Frozen.*' Mungo began to repeat the word in a variety of accents, which a better-educated mind than Bryn's would have recognised as the principal bad-guy accents from Dr Who. '**Frozen**. Frozen.'

'Mungo, can you do anything to help?'

Mungo cocked his head and blinked slowly at Bryn, wagging an authoritative finger. Then, realising he hadn't either said or done anything, he rooted around in his enormous trousers and emerged with a diskette which he slipped into Listoff's disk drive. He rebooted the PC, halting it before the configuration had been completed, then dropped into MS-DOS and began to pull up sheets of program code. '**FROZEN. Frozen**'. After about two hours during which time he managed to drink his entire bottle of water and urinate three times, he began to shake his head disapprovingly.

'Is there a problem?'

'No worries. Be happy,' sang Mungo, making Bryn instantly nostalgic for the days when music had tunes, knowing that old age was when music you'd never stopped listening to had become fashionable once again.

'Have you run into a problem?'

'No, man. It's sorted. It's a bit casual, this place. You'd think with all this money lying about' – here Mungo gestured grandly around the room – 'they'd be a bit more careful, like.'

'It's sorted?'

'Yeah. Buried a sleeper. Wait a coupla days, then dig it up, see what we've got.'

'We need to come back?'

'Coupla days, that's all.'

'What's a sleeper?'

'A sleeper? It's like, you know, buried. A *sleeper*.'

'We can't come back.'

'No com-ee back, no collect-ee sleeper.'

'Mungo. This sleeper, what does it do?'

'This *sleee*-per records all the keystrokes from the keyboard and stores them in memory. When we come back, we have a look in the memory, and just read off the password. Then we're in. What they should have done is build in a memory sweep, which clears –'

'Mungo, focus, please. I nicked a security card to get in here. By Monday, that card will have had its security clearance deleted. I can't go on nicking cards, added to which if we come in here on a weekday, our chances of being caught are way too high. They're high enough as it is.'

'Can't be too high, man.'

'Not you, Mungo, the risks. Focus. We need access tonight, or we need to get access from outside.'

'Can't get it tonight. For one thing it's hardly even night. For another, you're f-r-o-z-e-n, **frozen**, frozen.' Mungo belched for emphasis and looked as much like a disapproving librarian from the 1950s as it is possible for a twenty-year-old ecstasy-popping cyber-head to look.

'Then how about getting in from outside?'

'Remote access?'

'Yes, exactly.'

Mungo's gravely wagging finger came out again.

'That would appear to be our only option.'

It was six fifteen in the morning.

7

Their only option was a desperate one, and the extent of their desperation became apparent as daylight consolidated its grip on the sky outside. The graveyard shift on Saturday was always quiet, but Sunday mornings were actually a popular time to come into the bank. Hell.

At seven ten, Bryn interrupted Mungo's diligent work.

'How's progress?'

'Mm, OK.' Mungo's concentration had returned as his brain punched a way through the chemical fog. 'You don't know how the Gandalf port is configured, do you?'

'I don't know what a Gandalf port is.'

''S OK, I can check.'

More keystrokes. More pages of program code. Bryn's eyes hurt with the glare. As often in Mungo's presence, he felt old. He thought of his dad losing his strength, and felt doubly old; doubly old and with no marriage, no kids to show for it. He thought, randomly, of Cameron. Jesus, that Meg could think he and she should . . . Things weren't that bad, surely. Across the room, more workmen joined the group who had come in a while before, and the floor was now noisy with banter and the sound of power tools as the group began to dismantle and move some internal walls. Seven twenty-five.

'Done,' said Mungo. 'Sweet.'

'Done? We can get out of here?'

'Chill, man. The port's configured, now I just got to check some things, and we're out of here.'

Seven twenty-eight.

Bryn swore that he would be gone by eight, ready or not. An hour previously he'd been swearing he'd be gone by seven. He thought again about the possibility that there was a mole inside the clinic and felt queasy at the idea. The staff was large and rapidly expanding. Virtually any of them could have been bought by Corinth. But how to make certain?

Seven twenty-nine.

8

Just as Bryn checked his watch for the seventh time in twenty minutes, something prompted him to look up. Half a dozen bankers in casual dress were strolling towards him, holding brown paper bags of coffee and pastries. Bryn tumbled to the floor under Listoff's desk, dragging Mungo after him. Even a cursory inspection had revealed that at least three of the new arrivals knew him – not well, but well enough to know he shouldn't be there.

'Bloody hell,' he said. 'Bloody *hell!*'

As they grovelled down amongst the carpet tiles and forgotten pennies, the door to Listoff's office opened and feet, visible to Bryn under the rim of the desk, walked over to within a couple of feet of his nose. Bryn had to restrain Mungo from tickling the banker's ankle with a paperclip.

'Bernie takes it black, no sugar, right?'

A voice outside agreed, and a coffee was dumped on the desk above.

'How come his computer's on? I thought you came in with him.'

'I did. He's just coming.'

Oh shit.

The voices drifted away. Bryn peered out from his hiding place and found nothing to console him. Bernie Listoff had come in and was chatting with a colleague by the main doors, about forty feet away. The group that Bryn had first seen was spreading out at a meeting area about fifteen feet from Bernie's door. Meantime, the workmen were busy on the far side of the floor, so that one way or another, virtually the whole area was under surveillance.

Beneath his breath, Bryn began to use swearwords he hadn't used since his rugby-playing days. If Bernie was coming, then they had to get out, no matter what the consequences.

'Do you need to close what you're doing?' he hissed.

Mungo shrugged, and Bryn yanked the power cord from the PC as Mungo retrieved his diskette. For a couple of seconds he tried to think of a clever way of exiting Bernie's office. There wasn't one. He crouched at the door, peeped out, saw people coming, going, filling the aisle. Opposite him, there was a secretary's cubicle, and to its right another aisle intersecting the floor. 'Follow me. *Quietly.*' Bryn leaped. His leap took him to the cubicle, and a couple of paces swung him round into the aisle, out of sight of the bankers.

He paused briefly to hear if he'd been spotted, but if he had been, they were quietly phoning security and not shouting about it. Mungo followed, an apparition in luminous orange, his fluorescent headband falling off during flight. If anyone saw him, they obviously didn't believe their own eyes.

Followed by Mungo, Bryn raced, panting, along the aisle, keeping his head below the level of the partitions, and crawled into another cubicle away from view. Temporarily they were safe, the way a man on a one-foot-high sand dune is safe, until the tide turns and one-foot-high becomes ten-foot-under.

Think.

They had to leave. The main doors were directly in view of Bernie Listoff and his merry men, and it would be approaching suicide to walk out under their eyes. They could try simply making a run for it – but Bryn was as certain as he could be that their escape would be cut off before they'd even made it downstairs. That only left the fire exits, which Bryn knew to be connected to the building's alarm system.

'Wow. This is like *Escape From Alcatraz*, only without the Germans.'

'Colditz,' muttered Bryn, as the tide notched up a few

more inches until he could feel the cold salt sea sloshing around his ankles.

'How 'bout a tunnel, man? Or didn' one of them Colonel Mustard chappies escape by building a glider out of toilet rolls?'

The workmen's voices grew closer, and at the end of the aisle a couple of men dumped paintpots and ladders, preparing to renovate the wall behind. Bryn and Mungo were crouched down beneath the cubicle's worktop – a certain sign of guilt. A flurry of ideas raced through Bryn's mind, all of them stupid, but one less stupid than the rest.

'You got a light, Mungo?' he asked.

'You want to smoke? Now?' Flapping around in his ballooning pockets, Mungo came away with a cheap disposable lighter and handed it over. 'I don't have any tobacco, but I've got some really good –'

'That's OK.'

Bryn checked the aisle one more time. The paintpots were still at one end, although the workmen were now off in another corner. But at the far end of the aisle two bankers were standing, talking. Damn.

Bryn withdrew back into the cubicle and dug around in the waste bin and desk drawers for supplies. He found a sheet of paper, some cotton wool, a rubber band, and a box of staples. Excellent. Taking a sheet of paper from the bin, he rolled it into a taper and lit it, cradling the flame till it burned strong and steady. Satisfied, Bryn wrenched the top off the lighter, and splashed a bit of lighter fluid over the cotton wool before loosely setting the top back on to the lighter. He wrapped the cotton in the paper, weighting it with the box of staples and securing the bundle with a rubber band. He hefted it for weight and shape. It was good.

He poked his nose out again, careful to keep his burning

taper alight. The bankers were still there, still chatting. He was pinned in the cubicle, water at his knees, paintpots still thirty feet distant. A long way, thirty feet. He took a deep breath, and threw.

First the lighter, which struck the paintpots and over-turned, leaking fuel into the carpet tiles. Next he lit his cotton wool and staple firebomb, and threw that, too. For a moment, he thought he'd missed his aim, then bingo! A blue flame flickered almost invisibly, then climbed to the paintpots and clung there. Don't go out, damn you, don't leave me now.

The blue flame flickered, hung, then disappeared.

It disappeared in a boom of yellow fire, as heat ignited the paint and the paintpots exploded open, splattering walls and ceiling with flame. Already, within a second, the smoke was unbelievable, the fire roaring away like a team of demons on piece rate. Smoke alarms were screaming and the sprinkler system leaped into operation. Fire and water. Shouldn't there be a rainbow?

There was no time to lose. The sprinklers would soon overwhelm the flames. Expanding his lungs like bellows, Bryn drank a bellyful of clean air, took a bodily hold of Mungo, then dived into the path of the fire and out again on the other side. If he was singed he didn't notice. A group of workmen stood like statues as he emerged. If they moved or spoke, he was moving too fast to notice. Next to him, Mungo was tearing along, an ecstatic expression on his face. 'Sod this,' roared Bryn to the workmen, plunging towards the fire exit.

He crashed the door open, causing an extra alarm to sound over the noise of the smoke alarm. A loudspeaker system somewhere was telling people to clear the floor and not to panic. Bryn and Mungo clattered down the stairs into coolness and silence, not stopping until they'd reached street level, bursting the exit door open, crashing out on to the placid silence of Sunday morning London.

'Wicked entertainment,' said Mungo, with bright, delighted eyes.

9

And just a few hours before Bryn and Mungo tumbled head-long into the morning streets, elsewhere in London two women left a nightclub. One, shorter and chestnut-haired, was in the company of a man who held her loosely in the crook of his arm. The other was without a partner, but pink with alcohol and excitement.

'See you Monday, Cammie,' said Meg, climbing into a taxi with her partner for the night.

'Yeah, sure, see you,' said Cameron, sleek-haired and little-black-dressed. Another cab stopped for her, but she waved it away, walking out of the grey heart of London into the living green of St James' Park. It was the first of June, and the grass was cool and inviting. She pulled off her shoes, and walked on the dewy lawn beneath the plane trees. A couple of male joggers assessed her with their eyes as they went past. She smiled at them. As the night had passed, she'd begun to enjoy it. The nightclub wasn't her scene, but, as Meg had said, that was the point. 'Think of it as safe play, Cammie. Flirting for fun, like poufs in a harem.' And so she'd flirted. She'd smiled lots, made eye contact, ran her finger round her lips, and allowed men to buy her drinks. She'd even let herself be lured out on to a dance floor where the very, very best that could be said of her dancing was that it was uninhibited.

And as the grass pressed its cool green into the soles of her feet, one of the songs from the evening floated into her semi-conscious and remained there, playing itself again and again. It was Nina Simone, a husky black voice from a different continent and a different age.

'I'm a woman,' sang Cameron. 'Don't you know what I am?'

SIXTEEN

1

How high can you build a house? Answer: as high as the foundations let you.

How big can you build a business? Answer: as big as your capital permits.

And how do you build a business that encircles the globe, racing a hundred-billion-dollar corporation to the Patent Office, when that same hundred-billion-dollar corporation has its hands round your baby's throat, depriving it of the vital cash it needs to grow? Answer: you can't, it's impossible, forget it.

2

Monday broke hot and heavy over London. In the centre of town, an invisible brown fog collected, fed by a million car exhausts, the waste products of seven million people living one on top of the other with barely a patch of green to interrupt the grey. As the day drew on, the sun baked the toxic stew until nitrogen dioxide levels stood at five times World Health Organisation limits, carbon monoxide at more than four times. In the concrete rat runs, sun and shadow competed for mastery, cars honked at pedestrians, while those famously polite British pedestrians made V-signs right back.

Out in Fulham, beside a sluggish brown river, the air is better, and at least there are smells in the air other than those of a planet killing itself for gain. There are smells of weed and water, smells of rotting wood and rosebay willowherb, smells of elderflower and mud. Even with the doors and windows propped open the boathouse sweltered, and it was with relief that Bryn and Kati burst outside at lunchtime to eat sandwiches on the roof of the barge, shoes and socks off in Bryn's case, shoes and socks never even on in Kati's. At the end of the barge, Tallulah hopped around, practising the vocabulary that Meg had been so carefully teaching her: *'O-shi'*, *'Matey'*, as well as her most recent achievement, *'Uddy ell'*.

'Heard anything from Cameron?' mumbled Bryn, throwing a wedge of what passed for pastrami in Fulham into the water.

'Uh-uh.' Kati shook her head, finishing her mouthful before continuing. 'And how about Meg?'

'They went out clubbing together, believe it or not. Heard nothing since.'

'Clubbing? Does that mean the same thing in London as it does in Vancouver?'

Bryn nodded.

'Wow . . .' Kati paused to contemplate the idea. 'It's hard to picture that somehow.'

'Yeah. You think Meg persuaded her to take off her labcoat?'

Kati laughed. 'Or if her dancing partner got lectures on immune modulation . . . Mind you, that nickname she used to have in Boston, Dr Dynamite – it does sound like a DJ's stage name.'

They both laughed. Kati was wearing a dark-blue

summer dress sprigged with red and white roses. Bryn rubbed her on the back of the leg, pushing her skirt up a few inches. He left his hand there, both of them enjoying the warm sun. A minute passed, then Kati rolled over on to her side, dislodging Bryn's hand. Tallulah came close to pick up any stray crumbs.

'You know my friend's flatmate I was telling you about?' she asked.

'Thierry somebody-or-other of the gorgeous brown eyes? Yes.'

'He's asked me out.'

'Ask as in date, ask?'

'Yeah, ask as in date.'

'And you said sorry, but you were desperately in love with this hunky businessman who lives on a yacht and operates a multi-million-dollar healthcare concern.'

'You know, I totally forgot to mention that.'

'You said yes?'

'Yes.'

'When?'

'Soon.'

'Tonight?'

'Uh-huh.'

Bryn put his hand out again, not on Kati's unattainable brown thigh, but on her back in a spot where good friends are allowed to touch. He gave her a rub and a kiss high up on her temple, a long, long way from her rosebud mouth and cute little seashell ear. Her dark-brown curls tumbled about her head, Bryn's property no longer. Tallulah hopped on to Kati's back, as though to guard her from any more of Bryn's marauding hand.

'I'm really pleased for you. Hope it goes well.'

'Yeah, me too. He's cute.'

Bryn gave her a smile, which was meant to be full of

big-brotherly encouragement, but which ended up a bit more pained than that.

'You're upset?' she said.

'No . . . Well, OK, yes, but go for it, Kati. I *am* pleased for you, it's just there's a bit of me which isn't quite so thrilled. But I'll get over it. And you're probably right that it's time for us to go back to the real world of dates and relationships and all that.'

'Sod the engagement rings, though,' said Kati.

'Yeah, sod 'em.'

'And sod all deceiving bastards of the opposite sex.'

'Yeah, sod 'em all.'

'For now.'

'For now,' agreed Bryn.

Kati appraised her now ex-lover with a warm-hearted gaze. She gave him a big affectionate hug. 'At least Thierry is a bit more my size,' she said. 'I can get my arms round him.'

Bryn smiled again, but it was still wry, still pained. Whichever way you looked at it, he was on the losing side once again.

'You've been a real buddy,' she said.

'Yeah, you too.'

She got up to go, walking barefoot down the length of the barge roof, dark-blue cotton falling down to conceal what Bryn would never again lie next to. He felt lonely and under threat. Tallulah looked at him scornfully and flew with slow wingbeats back to the clinic, the world of winners.

3

That same afternoon, a second revelation.

At four o'clock, as the heat was sinking from the day, the door to the boathouse flew open to reveal a tall slim woman dressed in a cool yellow linen suit, the skirt cut well above the knee, and designer-labelled dark glasses. Her complexion was pale, but no longer pallid, thanks to some lightly applied make-up and a day spent slogging round the shops in Meg's ever-enthusiastic company.

'Wow, *Cameron*!' exclaimed Janine, Meg's recently hired assistant, from the reception desk.

'Hey.' Cameron nodded briefly, uncomfortable with the inspection.

'Wow ... er, Kati's been looking for you all day. I mean, there's nothing wrong, just ...' Janine felt the force of Cameron's discomfort, and her explanation sputtered to a close. 'I love your hair, by the way. And that suit is to kill for.'

'Thanks.'

'Linen?'

'Huh? Oh, yeah, sure.' Cameron crinkled the fabric between her fingers. 'I think so, anyway.'

From the gallery of consulting rooms above the reception area, Dr Rauschenberg and one of his colleagues were discussing one of their patients, when they saw Cameron and broke off.

'New look, Cameron?' Rauschenberg called down. 'It really suits you well.'

Cameron acknowledged the compliment with a quarter-grin, then half-walked, half-ran for the relative shelter of the laboratory. 'Of course they're going to look at you,' Meg had told her. 'That's the whole damn point, if you don't mind me pointing out the bleedin' obvious. It'll feel weird for a day or two, then normal, then you'll be complaining about the number of men you have to fight off. Big purple arse, remember.'

Meg's sloganising encouragement was all very well, but this was the first day of Cameron's experiment with a different kind of womanhood, and she was already half-stunned by the experience. Charging into the sanctuary of her viruses and test-tubes, she dived into a labcoat and threw herself gratefully into her work.

4

Janine and Rauschenberg weren't the only ones to comment on Cameron's make-over. Bryn and Mungo were locked away in Bryn's office, but had seen the cool yellow apparition arrive, and, after some hesitation, had identified it as Cameron.

'Wow, man. This is Babe Control to all units. Stand by on full babe alert. Wo-ah, wo-ah, wo-ah!' Mungo's sirens sputtered to a halt. 'I'm going to get a Coke,' he added.

Going to get a Coke meant, apparently, that he would march straight into the lab, ask Kati and Cameron if they wanted anything, gawp openly and open-mouthed at the new-look Cameron, then go to the vending machine in the reception area and bring himself back a drink.

'Man, she has legs, like, I mean, I knew she had legs, but –'

'For God's sake, Mungo,' snapped Bryn, feeling suddenly angry. 'Have you never seen a woman in a skirt before? She's old enough to be your mother.'

'Yeah, if she'd got pregnant when she was ten.'

'It's none of your bloody business, or mine, what she wears. It's unprofessional to pass that sort of comment. One day you'll have to learn –'.

'I only said she had legs,' said Mungo patiently, 'which technically I think you'll find –'

'We've got work to do. Once we're done, you can go and languish over your Lara Croft pin-ups all you like, but till then . . .'

Bryn's storm of anger trailed away. He knew he was being unreasonable, but didn't feel calm enough to apologise. Mungo muttered as he turned back to work. 'Keep your hair on, man. *Languish*, though, top word. *Languish*. I'm gonna languish me some chick tonight.'

But Mungo's ramblings also died away. The current phase of work was delicate and critical. It was now four thirty, and the day's fifth furtive attempt had revealed that Listoff's clearance had been unfrozen.

'Now-ee time go catch-ee sleeper.'

Mungo typed some instructions into his PC and waited as the modem dialled. A distant modem sent an answering signal. Mungo frowned, then his face cleared and he shook his head, as he nearly always did when considering Berger Scholes security arrangements. More keystrokes brought a slab of program code to the screen, followed by a mass of all-but-unintelligible text.

'Lovely jubbly. Now we jus' need to find the open-cecily –'

'Sesame.'

'Makes me burp, that. Get all the bits between my teeth. Uh-uh-uh,' Mungo mimed eating sand, but all the time he was scrutinising the forest of letters. 'Here's the database entry request . . . dialogue box . . . password: Highbury. Make sense?'

Bryn nodded, but Mungo's fingers had already raced away, requesting permission to enter the precious database. 'Username?' it queried. Blistoff. 'Password?' Highbury. The screen cleared and re-formed. 'Please select HNWI search, by name, country, industry, net worth or d.o.b.' The computer was politeness itself, flinging open its most secret doors like eunuchs bidding welcome to their sultan.

'Select all,' commanded Bryn. 'Print all.'

The printer salaamed and obeyed.

5

And one final event, that hot and turbulent day.

'It'll pass,' said Mervyn Hughes. 'Probably just a bit of flu, I imagine.'

Derek Williams, the vet, a long-time family friend and the first port of call for any question of medicine, stood alone with Mervyn in the dim cow barn. Outside, the fiery sun still sat above the ancient ice-age curves of the Brecon Beacons, but inside, the barn was dark enough to require electric lighting at all times. Steel shades focused the light down on to the straw and dung, the swishing tails, the humped black-and-white mottled backs.

'Don't be daft, man. It hasn't passed, and it's not the bloody flu, as well you know . . . you need to see a doctor, get some tests done and that.'

'Can you do that? Do the tests?'

'No, not even if you were one of your damn cows. You need a doctor.'

Mervyn Hughes leaned an elbow on the tubular metal fencing that penned the cows in. The fencing had once been blue, but long, long ago, when Mervyn was getting the farm shipshape again after his father's slow decline and death. What goes around, comes around, and in Mervyn's current state of health, the farm, once again, was beginning to slide.

'I don't know,' said Mervyn. 'I've never really held with doctors and that. We've all got a time to go.' He spoke quietly, but quietly is a relative term, and Mervyn's voice had been trained calling to sheepdogs on the windswept Beacons, and bellowing support on the terraces at Pontypridd and Cardiff. His voice boomed around the barn, causing a couple of the cows to pause from their munching.

'Bugger that,' said Williams. 'I've never said that about

your cows, and I'm not going to say that about you. You'll see a doctor, if I have to drag you there.'

'I don't know,' said Mervyn, looking along the rows of black-and-white backs, kicking straw into place with his toe, looking anywhere except at Derek Williams. If the light had been brighter, or if any temporary colouring had been able to make its way into the old farmer's weather-beaten face, you might have noticed the red scorch-marks of deep embarrassment. 'You know, these days, so many doctors are just out of college, young ladies some of them.'

Derek Williams laughed. 'And we don't want that, now, do we? I'll make an appointment for you with my own doctor, Ken Hartson. He's an old dog like us, Mervyn. Old, grey and heading for the knacker's yard.'

Mervyn nodded gratefully, a bit too choked to say yes. When he recovered, and his foot was done rearranging straw, he put his hand on Derek Williams' arm. 'Just one thing. I'll go and see your Dr Hartson, but . . . But I think it would be better if you didn't say anything to Gwyneth. Not just yet. I don't want to worry her.'

'No, of course. It's all probably nothing. She doesn't need to know.'

Mervyn's storm clouds of worry cleared away, and he began nodding his head at the rightness of the arrangements. As they left the barn his voice was restored to its normal thundering pitch, and the conversation turned once again to the hoary old subjects that had been good for the last thirty years, and – God willing – would continue to be for many more to come: the sins of government, news from the sheep and cattle markets, weather, rugby, neighbours, kids.

SEVENTEEN

1

Bryn began to grow obsessive. He stayed on the barge and shut himself in, poring over the mounds of data pilfered from Berger Scholes. Every name was followed by six or eight sheets of detailed discussion. Every name belonged to a millionaire.

Bryn sorted through them with tireless patience. He didn't just want any old millionaire. He wanted ones with an entrepreneurial record. He wanted ones with experience of biotech or medical-type investments. He wanted ones who enjoyed bypassing or upsetting the establishment. He wanted those who were sick, or whose wives or children were sick, with illnesses that the clinic could address. Ineligible millionaires dropped like confetti to the floor, but a stack of possibles grew bigger and fatter, until Bryn's hopeless dream even began to seem like a serious possibility.

He kept his door double-locked. He sent Meg out for food. He told no one what he was doing.

2

First thing in the morning, Meg arrived with the daily shopping.

'Latvian-Lithuanian-Polish today,' she announced, setting down her bag. 'The shopkeeper adores me, and I'm going to marry his son.' She flashed Bryn a photo. 'He lives in Riga and his name is Tomasz, but I'm allowed to call him Tomek.'

Bryn prodded morosely inside the bag, which contained some good-smelling sausages, but also far too many jars of pickled cabbage, beetroots, cucumbers and mushrooms. 'What is all this, Meg? Repulsive Foods of the World Week? Or is this just the pickles category?'

'If you won't come to the world, then it's my duty to bring the world to you. At least the world this side of the Talgarth Road.' She produced some coffee, which Bryn inspected carefully before deciding the quality was acceptable.

'Thanks, Meg. Do I owe you money, or do they pay you to remove this stuff?'

'You should respect the dignity of other cultures,' said Meg, picking Bryn's dark moleskin jacket from the arm of his chesterfield, locating his wallet, and helping herself. 'And I spotted this wicked Jamaican place. All dried cuttlefish and pepper sauces. And I just know the proprietor's got a son he's gonna want me to marry. Choices, choices.' She peered with interest at the floor, where millionaires were stacked, categorised, cross-referenced, and annotated. 'The Duke of Devonshire? I've heard of him.'

'You astonish me.'

'Are these all millionaires?' she asked curiously.

Bryn grunted. He hadn't wanted to say anything, but it was hard to scatter detailed notes on millionaires with significant British assets all over your floor and not have anybody notice. 'Yep. All millionaires.'

'Like, with notes on them? Eight pages of notes on this one. Blimey.'

'Yes. Meg, I want you to tell absolutely nobody at all that I've got this stuff, let alone what I'm doing with it.'

'Making a mess of your floor, you mean?'

'I'm serious. I think that somewhere inside the clinic we may have a Corinth spy.'

'You're joking,' said Meg, knowing immediately that he wasn't.

'Corinth found out about our loan applications within a matter of days.'

'Bloody hell.' She paused. The question that hung in the air was so obvious, she hardly needed to ask it. 'Do you have any idea . . .'

Bryn shook his head. It wasn't like he hadn't spent the last few days racking his brains over it. 'Anyone in the clinic could have found out who we were writing to. All they'd have had to do was take a peek into our postbag. From now on, the only people I'm willing to rely on are those people who got here before the Kessler story broke. Until then, we were invisible. Afterwards . . .' Again he shook his head.

'People who got here before Kessler? That was only you, me, Cammie, and Kati.'

'And Mungo. Five of us. Everybody else I distrust. Everyone.'

'Wow. Even Rauschenberg, even Janine . . . Anyone?'

'Yes.'

Meg thought some more, wide-eyed. 'I'll keep my eyes open,' she said, 'find the villain . . . And then there's security. Do you want me to –'

'Taken care of. A security specialist is coming round later. Same firm that did the MI6 building. They're putting in

CCTV, intruder alarms, additional locks, sealed safe for documents, palm-reading devices on my office door and the whole research area. They'll also overhaul our waste disposal arrangements.'

'Bleeding hell. How much does that lot come in at?'

'Don't ask, don't even ask.' Bryn's eyes drifted back to his millionaires, and his thoughts drifted back to the thought of safe money, quiet money, money beyond the reach of Corinth Laboratories. Meg slipped away, excited and a little scared, listening to the door lock and double-lock behind her.

3

Time passed. Bryn drank some coffee and even got hungry enough to eat some of the food Meg had brought. He hadn't wanted visitors, but there was a light tread on the jetty, a spring on to the deck and a rap at his door.

'Who is it?'

'Me,' said Cameron.

Bryn unlocked the door. Cameron, casually dressed in stretch tan capri pants and a sleeveless blue top, ducked her head to enter the barge. She had a newspaper folded under her arm.

'Hi,' she said.

'Hi.'

Already, just a few days into her make-over, Cameron was more confident, less self-conscious, less keen to shrink away from view, and Bryn welcomed her with a flash of irritation. Of course Cameron had the right to wear whatever she wanted, but it bugged him that she should let herself be distracted when really her whole attention should be on racing Corinth. She moved a still-warm pot of espresso from the arm of the chesterfield and sat there, swinging a leg. Bryn was too irritated to notice, but for all her relaxed posture her face was taut and grim.

'Millionaires, huh?' she said.

Bryn nodded.

'You still think we need the money? Rauschenberg was just telling me he's about to hire his fourteenth doctor. Patient flow is massive. I've just hired my third assistant, in addition to Kati, that is. Rick Somebody. Beard. Good PhD from Cambridge. Your Cambridge, I mean. England.'

Bryn's irritation surged again – for no well-explained reason – and he mentally stamped it out, forcing himself to answer civilly. 'Corinth is racing us. They've stuck Anita Morris into a high-tech lab with everything she could ask for, and resources we can only dream of. Meanwhile they've blocked our route to the banks, and we daren't risk venture capital. You tell me. Who's going to win? Our shoestring little operation here, or Corinth? You think Rick the Beard is going to swing it for us?'

Cameron nodded sombrely. 'You're right. We need more staff, more resources, a whole bunch more.' Her admission came in a low tone, and Bryn guessed that it was the first time she'd admitted the fact to herself. 'So how come millionaires?' she added after a pause. 'Why are they any better for us?'

'OK. Point one, unlike venture capitalists, millionaires aren't forced to sell. If they like a company, they can just carry on holding.'

'Fair enough.'

'Point two. If Corinth can bully the banks into refusing to lend, they can probably bully or bribe the venture capital houses. I doubt if it's the same with millionaires. They're a bloody-minded lot, the rich.'

Cameron nodded. 'I guess.'

'Point three, and the most important: Corinth won't be

expecting us to do this. They'll have no way of guessing who we're approaching. No way of getting to them first.'

'They're not expecting it, huh?' Cameron unfolded her newspaper, her face grim but also inscrutable. 'I only hope you're right. This is today's *Herald*. I thought you should see.'

She passed the paper to Bryn, who spread it on the trunk at the page indicated by Cameron, and began to read.

'KESSLER CLINIC CAN'T EVEN RECOGNISE A HANG-OVER,' gloated the headline. 'Special Reporter Luke Hancock put the super-fashionable Fulham Clinic to the test with the simplest of medical problems. Recognise a hangover? We doubt they could recognise their own feet.'

The paper had printed a table showing the clinic's exhaustive analysis of Hancock's immunological deficiencies, captioned, 'My GP just laughed when I told him'.

There was plenty more of the same. 'The Fulham Clinic came to prominence earlier this year when it achieved a so-called miracle cure on ailing pop-goddess Cheryl Kessler. Since then the clinic has attracted sick yuppies like ants to a yoghurt pot. But does it really do anything, except extract large cheques painlessly? I went along to test it. Apart from a crashing hangover, there was nothing wrong with me. Any competent doctor would have laughed me out of the surgery, but that kind of approach wouldn't suit the moneyed hypochondriacs who crowd the clinic. Instead, I was made to fill out a six-page questionnaire, give blood and urine samples, and have a consultation with not one but two doctors, including the clinic's American director of research, Dr Cameron Wilde. And the upshot? They diagnosed Impaired Immune Status and recommended a crash course of intravenous shots plus – I kid you not – a course of counselling.

'Experienced GP Dr Martin Rogers commented, "That's

the trouble with these places. If they charge their kind of money, they don't feel entitled to kick you out for whingeing. As for their inability to spot a hangover when they saw one," Rogers said, "that's General Practice 1.01. It should be the first skill a doctor picks up."'

Bryn lifted his eyes from the paper, to find Cameron watching him. She'd found one of Meg's cucumbers and was biting into it, releasing the crisp scents of Latvian forests, black bread, pine cones, oak leaves. 'There's more,' she said, flipping the pages.

In the opinion section, the paper declared: 'Thank God for the good old-fashioned British doctor. Those who moan about the Health Service should just try forking out for meaningless advice and idiotic errors. What these yuppie whingers need isn't sympathy, it's a boot up the backside. We say: if it's good enough for granny, it's good enough for us.'

Bryn began to fold the paper angrily, but Cameron put out a hand to stop him. Even in his anger, Bryn noted that, of all things, Cameron had got a manicure from somewhere, and, for no reason at all, the fact enraged him. What was she doing painting her nails, when the clinic – the whole enterprise – was in crisis? She flipped the pages again, past the tits, horoscopes, lies and bitching. She stopped at the financial pages.

'Kessler clinic in danger of bankruptcy. Leaked cash flows reveal imminent collapse.' There was a short article – the *Herald*'s readers didn't cope too well with anything longer – which ran through the story: over-rapid expansion, over-burdened cash flows, collapse. The cash flow statements were accurate to the penny. Rubbishy as the article might be, there was nothing wrong with its source material.

Bryn rose to his feet, taking the paper with him. A new addition to the barge was a Swedish-built wood-burning stove. Bryn opened the door of the stove, shoved the newspaper inside and lit a match. With a *woof* of flame, the malevolent half-truths disappeared up the chimney. Black ash fell back and lay glowing red at the edges. Bryn slammed the door shut.

'You really told Hancock to go for counselling?' he asked, anger burning in his voice.

'I didn't know he was a journalist,' retorted Cameron. 'Or that he was on Corinth's payroll. If you knew better, then you forgot to tell me.'

'But counselling? And how come you saw him at all?'

'New doctor. Either Rauschenberg or I sit with all new doctors when they start, to get them used to our treatment methods. Rauschenberg was on vacation, so it was me.'

Bryn nodded and Cameron continued, frowning as she recalled the occasion.

'This guy Hancock turns up. Looks like a wreck, smells like a wreck. Puts down on the form that he's a light social drinker, no drugs. Like hell. The guy was an addict. I was worried enough, just by the look of him, that we ran a full chemistry panel on his blood. His liver was this far from collapse.' Through her finger and thumb, Bryn could see a sliver of light, no more. 'No specific problem at present, but virtually anything could become the matter. The hangover was obvious, but it wasn't his major health problem. We recommended counselling because unless the guy deals with his addictions, he's going to drop dead. Don't know with what. Just know that he will.'

'Fair enough.'

Bryn sighed. He put his hand to the espresso pot. It was cold now, but not empty. He poured the dregs out into a cup and swallowed. On the wall opposite, one of Bryn's deal mementoes was the framed front page of an Austrian newspaper: *Claussen Verkauft*, sang the headline – Claussen sold. The deal had been struck at thirty-one billion dollars, and Bryn had earned twenty-five million dollars in fees for his bank. What the hell was he doing here? His million-pound house in Chelsea sold, his deferred bonuses forfeited, all in exchange for a two-roomed houseboat and a wildly underfunded research project. He was crazy.

'The cash flows?' asked Cameron, gently. 'Real or made up?'

Bryn shook his head and sighed deeply. 'Real, I'm afraid. No idea how they got them.'

'And your millionaires? Is there any chance now . . . ? I suppose –'

'You suppose right,' said Bryn. 'The hangover story may be bullshit, but the story about our finances could kill us. Even the slightest smell of trouble will make any sane investor run a mile. Why invest in a business which you think is desperate?'

'Maybe the story will die,' said Cameron. 'Maybe it'll all blow over.'

'Maybe. Maybe.'

The silence stretched out. A waterfly settled on Cameron's bare arm, and she knocked it away with a hand, continuing to rub long after the fly had gone. Once again, the room was filled with an unspoken question. Eventually, Cameron broke the silence, asked the question.

'Is this just coincidence?' she asked. 'Or is there a mole? First the banks, now this. What's going on?'

Bryn shook his head. 'It looks awful,' he admitted. 'I send a letter to Berger Scholes. Within two days, Corinth has stamped on it. Now, I'm just two or three days away from sending out my first batch of begging letters, and this happens.'

'That's never just coincidence,' whispered Cameron solemnly.

'No, it doesn't look that way. But it's not so simple. Who knew I was writing to millionaires? You. Me. Meg. That's all. Neither of us are moles, and Meg's not a Corinth stooge, never in a million years.'

'Kati, maybe I said something to Kati . . . but –'

'Kati? Come on. She'd sooner betray her own mother.' He shook his head and helped himself to a cucumber. 'But I have to say I don't like it. I don't like it at all.'

4

Mungo, meanwhile, had fallen into an untypically gloomy mood.

He arrived when he woke up, in the clothes he'd woken up in. He stirred the layer of garbage which lay a foot or two thick on his desk, and shovelled a clearing for his keyboard. Then he worked. He kept the company's computer systems up and running. He did little programming errands for Kati and Cameron. But most of all he hit his head against a brick wall. The wall was in Connecticut, and the bricks were cyber-bricks, but they hurt just the same.

Of three or four hundred phone numbers, Mungo had managed to exclude about two hundred and fifty, leaving him with ninety-three numbers, any of which could be the way into the American phone system. Trouble was ninety-three numbers was a hell of a lot. If you were certain of the number, you could use a computer program to automate the job of trying different passwords. Ring, connect, password, password, password, fail, disconnect, ring again, connect again, password, password, password. Even that was dodgy, as even a measly ten-digit password would keep you guessing for ever. But Mungo's problem was worse than that, since ninety-two of his numbers – or at least ninety of them – were bound to have nothing to do with the phone system anyway. He gnashed his teeth with frustration. His mood grew worse.

Once Kati tried to break in to his isolation. She walked up the stairs to the rooftop corner room which was Pod Mungo, treading carefully but not avoiding the distinctive snap-crackle-and-slurp of Mungo's floor décor.

'Here. I thought you might need these,' she said, offering him a Mars Bar and a Coke.

'Brilliant. Wicked. Ta.'

He took the Mars and crumbled it over a carton of toffee popcorn. He shoved the concoction into Pod Mungo's very own microwave and set the timer, with a sigh of satisfaction. 'I ought to get my own TV show, really. *Mungo's Microwave Magic.* All the things you can cook in two minutes, using nothing but the contents of a perfec'ly ordinary vending machine.'

He licked his fingers, then moved back to his keyboard, spreading chocolatey grease all over it. One of Mungo's self-donated perks was a regular supply of new keyboards. That way, when a board gummed up with the junk food shoved into its gaps, he simply threw it away and unwrapped a new one from his stock.

'Co-host Anthea-Turner, pref'rably. That way viewers could sit comfortably at home learning the secret arts of microwave cookery, wondering if Anthea knows she's only got one button done up on her cardie and that one's looking dodgy, an' all the time asking themselves whether the cardie's going to blow before Mungo can complete his two-minute Waggon Wheel Spectacular. All the makings of fine, on-screen entertainment.'

'You need a break.'

The pinger pinged.

'Have a break,' said Mungo. 'Have a chocolate-caramel-toffee-popcorn-surprise.'

Kati shook her head.

'Mistake,' he said, gingerly picking bits of popcorn out of the boiling chocolate.

''S exquisite. See how it goes all foamy on top.'

With his elbow on the enter key, Mungo instructed the computer to dial another number, one he'd tried half a dozen times before. The modems chatted to each other and connected with a click. Mungo listened intently to the sound of the foreign modem on his handset. He'd once had a major breakthrough in his earlier cracker career by realising that a telco modem sounded different to a normal one. That trick didn't seem to be getting him anywhere on this occasion.

'Oh widdle,' he said, as a popcorn blob fell steaming on to his mousemat. He picked the blob up with his mouth, hit the enter key again, and the computer dialled the next number on its list.

'Are you OK, Mungo? This last week or two, you've seemed upset.'

''S nothing.'

'It's your family situation, isn't it? Your sisters? JoJo and . . .'

'JoJo and Dar.' Mungo crunched some more popcorn, his mouth bravely tolerating the near-sun temperatures achievable by even the humblest kitchen microwave. 'It's dicey at the moment, well dicey. You wouldn't understand.'

'May I?' said Kati, reaching out to a photo stuck to one of Mungo's PCs. He nodded permission, and she unglued it and scrutinised it closely. The picture showed an adolescent Mungo with two young girls beside him, both thin and freckled, one fair-haired, the other, older one, with hair of flaming red. A grey-haired parental-looking couple stood behind. In the background was a nice suburban semi, with an orderly and well-trimmed garden. Mungo looked much the same as now: ageless, big-eyed, serious. His two sisters, though well-dressed and properly fed, both had the eyes of street-children – knowing, hard, hungry.

'They look gorgeous,' she said neutrally.

'What? JoJo and Dar? Hardly.' Mungo inspected the photo dispassionately himself before gluing it back on to the PC with a blob of molten toffee-chocolate. 'That was three foster folk ago. Quite nice, only they couldn't manage Dar's tantrums. Two hundred and four days, they lasted.'

'Oh, Mungo. I'm so sorry.'

He shrugged.

'Is that what's upsetting you now? More trouble with foster parents?'

'Yeah, look, Kati, I 'preciate you being bothered and that, but there's always trouble with the foster mob. Law of the universe. Daleks will be daleks. You wouldn't understand.'

Viciously, he stabbed at his keyboard, breaking one connection and dialling another. Kati watched for a while, asking a couple of technical questions as Mungo worked. He muttered answers, at least some of which were intelligible. As Kati began to understand what he was up to, she gave out a low whistle of impressed surprise. 'You're trying to hack the entire US phone system?'

As if in answer, a couple of lines of random characters skittered across Mungo's screen and stopped, the cursor flashing patiently as it waited.

Mungo gripped the side of his chair. 'Do that again,' he said. 'The whistle. Exactly the same. *Exactly*.' He held the handset up so the receiver would catch her whistle more clearly.

Kati repeated her whistle as near exactly as she could. The cursor dived into motion again. Another stream of jumbled characters appeared, then a question mark. 'Login,' typed Mungo. 'Enter'. The cursor clicked down a line, another question mark appeared. 'Show users,' ordered Mungo, and this time the screen filled not with gibberish, not with Mungo's own failed password attempts, not with the constant infuriating question marks, but with a list of user names and the delightful message, 'Welcome to Bell Atlantic'.

'All hail, Canadian Kate, Time Lord and cyber-queen.'

'You've done it?'

'All hail, La-Rousse of the Net-Busters.'

'I didn't do anything.'

'Your whistle. Hangover from the pre-digital days when you sometimes needed sound instead of data to give you access to stuff. Peace be to your planet, earthling.'

Kati said something in response, but Mungo wasn't listening. He was still a long way from Corinth, but he was in the right continent, with his fingers now on the pulse of power. His hands whirled across the keyboard. Somewhere in Connecticut, a massive computer obeyed its new master.

5

And as Mungo worked on cyber-burglary upstairs, the security men moved in downstairs to prevent burglaries of the more conventional sort. Cameras were installed everywhere. Their lenses swept the green sofas of the reception area, the grand timbered entrance, the crowded wet-benches of the bloodwork laboratory, the humming computers and spectroscopy equipment of the upper laboratory. They were everywhere.

Meantime, a one-person-only entrance booth was fitted at the way in to the research area, and only the physical palm-print of authorised staff would give access. Meantime, locks were reinforced with double-locks. Shredders were thrown out in favour of shredder-masher-compactor-destroyers. Staff were drilled on security dos and don'ts.

The boathouse was a boathouse no more. It had become a fortress.

EIGHTEEN

1

'Nah. Not in yet, mate. Try again in 'bout an hour.'

Electric lamps struck white fire into the night, the only cheerful thing on the rainswept street. Beneath the lamps, a thin plastic sheet protected rows of newspapers from the elements.

'What are these, then?'

'This is still the evening papers,' said the man. 'Tomorrow morning's papers come in an hour.'

'Know anywhere I can get coffee?'

The bloke gestured up the street.

'McDonald's. It's where I go.'

Bryn shook his head. Cameron had strong views on healthy eating, and he'd get her into McDonald's only when the Pope got divorced and Bill Clinton took a vow of chastity.

'Anywhere else?'

'Like baked potatoes? There's a place just down the lane behind.'

The place in question was a squalid little hole, flanked by a couple of urinating drunks and a mound of refuse in black plastic bags. The interior, however, was better: an Iranian proprietor talking to a couple of friends while a policeman sipped a cup of steaming coffee, watching the drunks complete their handiwork.

'Hello, my friends. What you want?' asked the Iranian, breaking off his conversation.

'Just coffee. Two coffees, please,' said Bryn, ordering for himself and Meg. 'Cameron, is there anything you want?'

Cameron surveyed the fizzy drinks, the elderly potatoes, the plastic containers of butter, cheese, beans and coleslaw. 'Herbal tea. That's what you like, isn't it, babe?' said Meg. Then, smiling a giant smile at the proprietor as though she could flirt some herbal tea into existence, she asked, 'Do you have any herbal teas?'

'No. I got regular tea – or the lady, she like green tea? I make you real Persian green tea.'

'Sure,' said Cameron. 'Green tea, that'd be great. I had an Iranian roommate once at Harvard. Drank it all the time.'

The green tea came not in a styrofoam beaker like the coffees, but in a china teacup bearing a portrait of Diana, Queen of Hearts. The tea was sweetened with honey and fragrant with hints of cardamom and nutmeg.

'You like?'

Cameron sipped like a connoisseur. 'Perfect. Just what I needed. Thanks.'

'Brilliant, fab, ta very much,' said Meg, as though obliged to translate.

Bryn paid for the coffees, but the proprietor wouldn't accept payment for the tea. 'Persian tea, I no sell, only give,' he explained, before resuming his low conversation with his two friends. The policeman finished his coffee and went reluctantly back out into the rain, his radio chattering on his shoulder like some black technological parrot.

'How long?' asked Cameron.

'Fifty minutes,' said Bryn.

The conversation fell into a quiet mutter. Whatever they talked about, the fate of their research work, the fate of their business, loomed above them, dark and menacing. Corinth was racing them to the mystery of the human peptide codes. The clinic had the talent, but Corinth had the money. Would tomorrow's papers run with the *Herald*'s story, or would they drop it and give the clinic a chance of recovery? Well, they were about to find out.

'How's your dad?' asked Meg.

Bryn shook his head. 'Not well. The doctors are talking a load of rubbish about late-onset neuro-psychiatric disturbance and handing out fifty-seven varieties of antidepressants. If you knew my dad, that's a bit like giving slimming pills to an anorexic. The closest he gets to depression is watching Wales get beaten at rugby.'

'Your dad's sick?' asked Cameron, who hadn't known.

Bryn ran through the symptoms: brain-fog, listlessness, blurred speech, clumsiness.

'His doctor calls that depression?'

'His doctor doesn't have a clue.'

'Honestly. The way these guys hand out pills ... If in doubt, your dad shouldn't take them.'

'He doesn't. He crunched them up and mixed them in with the cow feed to see if it perked them up.'

Cameron laughed. 'Did it?'

'Made 'em fart, apparently, though they fart like Trojans anyway.' Bryn sighed again. 'There's nothing you can do, Cameron, is there? I know this is outside your area, but I'd love it if you could give us a second opinion.'

'It really *isn't* my specialty.'

'I know.'

'Sure, if you want, I'd be happy to see him. Bring him into the clinic, I'll check him out.'

'This is going to sound crazy, but is there anything you can do without seeing him?'

'A physical exam can be real helpful, but ... I guess you could set up a phone consultation.'

216

'He's not great with the phone.'

'You want me to treat someone who I haven't seen and aren't allowed to speak to? Sure. I also resurrect the dead.'

'He won't come to London, Cameron. The only time he's been was for my wedding, and then only because my mother forced him. He'd never come to see a doctor.'

It was true. The day before his wedding, Bryn had taken his dad sightseeing to Piccadilly Circus. Mervyn Hughes, then in his early fifties, had stood there, mouth open, transfixed. 'By damn, Bryn, by damn,' he said. Searching for a comparison huge enough, he added, 'It's like Hereford on a market day.' That once had been enough. He still spoke of it most times Bryn visited, but not even the biggest sheep market in the world would have tempted him back.

'OK, so bring me blood.'

'I'm sorry?'

'Bring me blood, four tubes, stool and urine too. I'll run a full chemistry panel, see what I find.'

'Thanks, Cameron. You're a total star.'

Bryn trailed off into anxious silence, thinking about his dad and the fate of the clinic. If the clinic failed and his dad got worse, then Bryn could always make his mum happy by returning home and managing the farm. Bloody hell, he might even go into business with Dai, coming in as the junior partner. He finished his coffee, terrible though it was. After a silence, Meg and Cameron began to talk about manhunts and make-overs.

'Oh, Bryn, that reminds me. Can you go and take a walk outside?'

'Take a walk? It's pouring.'

'Just take a walk. That's why they invented coats.'

Pushing him out into the rain, Meg turned back to Cameron.

'I've had a brainwave. Look what I've got. Warpaint, the

real McCoy.' She pushed a bottle of hair-dye along the greasy counter to Cameron. 'Blondes have more fun.'

Cameron's face transformed like a mountainside on a changeable day as she considered the bottle. First, puzzlement. Then, a momentary leap back into the past: worried and defensive. But then, even before Meg had opened her mouth to argue, her new confidence had stormed back to take control and she picked up the bottle, ready to consider it squarely, work out what she wanted.

'Hair-dye, huh?'

'It'll really suit you, and this is your shade.'

'I gotta tell you Meg, I've never had a problem with the colour of my hair.'

'To be fair, love, you never had a problem with anything, so long as it meant people didn't look at you.'

Cameron rolled the packet round in her fingers, intrigued by the idea. 'There's a lot of bad stuff in these things.'

'You don't have to drink it.'

'No, it's the transdermal absorption –'

'English, remember. *No hablo medico.*'

'It's absorbed through the skin, Meg. It's a serious carcinogen.'

Meg turned to the Iranian at the counter.

'S'cuse me. Can I ask you a question? Do you think my friend here would look better as a blonde, or should she stay as she is?'

'Your friend? How she look?' One of the Iranian's two friends spoke to him quickly in a low mutter. He nodded his comprehension. 'Is a very beautiful lady. She no need to put on top.' He mimed the action of putting hair-dye on.

Meg, disappointed, was turning away when Cameron butted in. 'But Princess Diana, she was blonde, right?'

'Yes,' said the Iranian. 'Blonde is beautiful too. Princess Diana, she blonde.'

Cameron turned to Meg with an air of triumph, as though it was she who had been arguing in favour of the dye. 'Well, then,' she said, and dropped the packet into her pocket.

Just then, Bryn tumbled in, sopping wet. 'It's absolutely chucking it down. Newspaper bloke says it's still another fifty minutes. Some hold-up. Don't know why.'

The conversation rolled on to other subjects. Bryn spoke about Cecily. He and she were only a few months from being formally divorced now, but her lawyers were getting shrill about the overdue return of her furniture and paintings.

'So return it,' said Cameron. 'It's hers.'

'Not any more it isn't. I've flogged it off. I had to, to get the clinic funded.'

Cameron ignored him. 'When you do return it, careful who you use. When Kati had stuff sent over here, the shippers lost a couple of trunkloads in a fire. Happens surprisingly often, so I've heard. You ought to think about it.'

More coffees, another cup of green tea, another delay in the arrival of the newspapers. The Iranian's friends left, and he joined Bryn and the others in front of the counter, everyone now drinking the famous green tea. They heard his story: a wealthy Persian of the old regime, lucky to escape with his life in the revolution, years of exile, ending up in England, proud as anything of his baked potato franchise, his fanatical pro-British monarchism.

Then there was the rumble of a delivery truck outside and the mild swearing as newspapers were hauled across a wet pavement. Bryn left the others and went to help unload the papers, then returned, carrying one of everything.

It was as bad as could be.

Every paper carried the story in one way or another. Even the *Financial Times* ran a couple of sentences in its Company News section: 'Kessler clinic reported close to collapse'. They went through the papers in silence, even Meg staying quiet in view of the volcano she expected any moment from Bryn. But, for once, he disappointed her.

'Well, at least we know where we stand,' he said, folding the last paper and speaking quietly.

'How bad is it sweetie? What does this mean?'

Bryn rubbed his face. It was now one thirty in the morning, and his chin was rough.

'It's hard to say. If patients desert us, then it's very bad. We rely completely on the clinic to fund the research programme. If the patients stick with us – well, it's still bad, very bad. We won't get any investors if they think we're drowning. And if we don't get some money soon ... So, I don't know, Meg, I don't know. It's anything from bad to lethal.'

2

Early morning.

Bryn at the boathouse, scrutinising the appointment books. Today, they're full. Tomorrow – who knows? Do patients believe the lies that papers print? Or are they smarter than that? Does the clinic's big and growing reputation provide shield enough?

Meg is in charge of the appointments register. She's teaching Tallulah to say 'bunch of tossers' every time she says 'Corinth'.

'Corinth,' says Meg. 'Corinth, Corinth, Corinth.'

'*Uncha gossa,*' squawks Tallulah. '*Uncha gossa.*'

'Good bird!' Meg feeds it more of the birdseed which is fast turning Tallulah into Fulham's fattest parrot.

'Have you taken any calls yet? New appointments?'

'It's not even eight o'clock, matey. How many people phone the doctor at eight o'clock in the morning?'

220

'Well, let me know how it goes. We need those bloody patients.'

'Get some coffee and stop worrying. You're bothering Tallulah.'

Bryn goes off to get more coffee (a silky Hawaiian Kona, too soft for Bryn's taste), but he's still worried, still worrying. In the background he hears Tallulah screeching away, rehearsing her lessons. '*Uncha gossa, uncha gossa, uncha gossa.*'

3

The Park Lane Hotel, London. An Art Deco ballroom crowded with seats, canapés growing warm on sidetables, scrums of people around the doors to the toilets.

A pharmaceutical industry conference is in full swing. Boffins gather to talk about the things that turn them on: molecules, viruses, what you get when you grind up a rat's brain and dunk it in solvent. The chatter in the corridors is scientific, of course, but it's gossipy and jokey, too.

'. . . Ten million quid later, they take their discovery to the Patent Office. You know what? The Staedtler crowd had been in that same morning with the same damn thing! Beat them by three hours. 'Course they sued . . .'

'. . . So the experimenter cuts off the fourth leg, tells the rabbit to jump. Nothing happens. He shouts. Still nothing. So he writes up his conclusions: amputation of legs causes total hearing loss . . .'

'. . . Claimed he was entitled to a one-third share in the patent. He was an asshole but they thought it was worthless, so they agreed. Damn thing turned out to be a goldmine. Two million bucks a year and he's still an asshole.'

Cameron is there. She's blonde. She made the change not because of pressure from Meg, but because Cameron is the sort of person who, if she sets her mind to something, follows it through as completely as possible. She decided she'd look better blonde, decided she'd enjoy the change, and went for it.

And one other change is also complete. Cameron knows Bryn doesn't fancy her. She doesn't pretend that it didn't upset her. It did, for a long time. But she's over him now, almost completely. At long last, for the first time in her unusual life, she's ready to get a grip of her emotional world, ready to go manhunting in her own territory.

She's at this conference to hear the papers, to exchange views, to network with other scientists. But most of all, she's here for another reason completely, a reason that has nothing to do with research: she's here to flirt.

4

Coffee break – only of course Cameron seldom drank coffee and for her this wasn't a break, it was a central purpose in being here. She wore a kingfisher-blue suit which was *her* colour, according to Meg. The blue was in stunning contrast to her sleek pale-blonde hair and coral lips. Her two-and-a-half inch heels left her taller than half the men in the room. She didn't feel as comfortable as she did in jeans and a T-shirt, but she could sense male heads turning wherever she went; male eyes fastening on to her buttocks, breasts, hair, and lips; male conversations suddenly becalmed as she moved into view.

She surveyed the room and selected her target: a tall, dark, handsome man with something priestly about him, something that let you know he was better connected to the Almighty than you. She went up to him, feeling naked.

'Hi, there,' she said. 'Cameron Wilde.'

He extended his hand, his eyes doing what men's eyes

do. Without overstepping the limits of politeness, but directly and thoroughly, he took in the face and figure of the person he was talking to. Usually it was a fault-finding procedure. The person looked nice, but their skin was tired, their figure saggy, or their nose wonky. Not today, not with Cameron. The mental register returned a virtually perfect score. The speaker was surprised, alerted.

'Hello,' he said. 'Allen Green, nice to meet you.'

5

The weekend.

Patient bookings had halved from the week before. They hadn't dried up, existing patients remained rock solid loyal, but the clinic was in trouble. Worse still – much worse – was the fact that every day spent without money meant another day of Corinth's relentless advance on the patents and the clinic's own relative decline.

Bryn and Cameron had agreed to spend a long Sunday brunch discussing tactics and strategy for what Bryn called 'the fightback', but as always, reality intervened.

A hairline crack just below the waterline of the barge had widened enough to allow damp inside, which was threatening to turn into an out-and-out leak. By the time Cameron arrived at eleven o'clock, Bryn had managed to tilt the heavy barge by moving all the furniture to one side of it and ballasting it further with a half-dozen oil drums filled with water. The crack was now exposed, several inches clear of the river, and Bryn was working to plug it with a black tar paint, beginning at the bows. He wore old jogging pants, and his top half was bare and streaked with sweat.

Cameron approached from round the corner of the boat-houses, down the paved steps leading to the jetty. She was wearing her pale-yellow suit with a clean white top under the jacket, and she stood gingerly at the head of the jetty as though worried that the pitch would fly from Bryn's tin and splatter her.

'Problem?' she said.

'Crack,' said Bryn, pointing to it with his brush. 'Solution,' – he waved his tin.

'I'd offer to help, only . . .'

'That's OK.'

'You want to meet some other day?'

'Uh, hell.' Bryn reached in through the barge window to switch off the radio, which was in the middle of some tedious discussion show. He wiped his hands on his old Wales rugby shirt which lay on the deck in front of him. 'No, it's important – critical. I'll be another hour, if you don't mind waiting. Otherwise, I –'

'No, I've got stuff to be getting on with.'

Bryn nodded and picked up his paintbrush again, dropping gobbets of tar into the sultry Thames. Having finished work on the bows, he needed to continue right down the length of the vessel, and that meant wading into the river. The muddy river bed farted noisily as he sank his feet into it, with an uprush of bubbles full of stinking gas.

Instead of going into the boathouse, Cameron continued to watch. 'Do you mind telling me what you're thinking of? The grand fightback, I mean.'

'Now?' Bryn shrugged. 'OK.' He began to talk, painting as he did so, a burst of fish-flavoured bubbles greeting each further step down the side of the boat. The way he saw it, the first step was to 'turn the news flow around'. He was full of plans for meeting with editors, launching libel actions, contacting patients who were 'opinion formers', launching new public relations initiatives.

'PR?' said Cameron, after a time. 'You think we're going to survive with some PR?'

224

Bryn jabbed his brush into the crevices of the planking in annoyance. 'We need visibility. We need positive coverage,' he said. 'I hate the idea of wasting money on stupid public relations types just as much as you do, but we'll never get an investor with the media as hostile as it is. And I don't think we can afford to just wait it out. Corinth are bound to be in fifth gear, while we're crawling along in bottom.'

Cameron shook her head. 'I agree.' She continued to watch her partner, squatting in front of her looking like a cross between a tar-baby and a mud-demon. 'How much do we think we can afford to spend? Total cost of the fightback?'

'Anything.' Bryn wiped his forehead with his pitch-streaked arm, leaving it pitch-streaked too. 'This is life or death. I just don't think we can afford to fail.'

'Twenty grand?' said Cameron. 'Thirty?'

'Of course. Twice that. As much as we have. Cameron, I don't think we –'

'OK. I'll see you later,' she said abruptly, walking back up to the boathouse.

An hour passed. Bryn got to the end of the boat, the great curve of the stern, where the timbers rose in a powerful arch above the waterline. The crack was bigger down at this end, and the river deeper. To an outside observer, Bryn was little more than a mud-stained head bobbing in the water, alongside a filthy arm, a tin of pitch and a paintbrush.

Light footsteps pattered down the roof of the barge, and Cameron, shoes off, leapt lightly on to the short deck at the end. The movement was enough to send a ripple washing into Bryn's mouth. He spat out, trying to avoid a swearword.

'Here,' said Cameron. 'Take the taste away. Some baklava, from that little Greek shop. I bought you a coffee from your Italian place, too. Milk, no sugar, Java bean I think they said. Can't remember. Sorry.'

Bryn, still up to the neck in water, swallowed the baklava, sipped the coffee. 'Yes, Java,' he said. 'I'd have roasted it a little longer myself, but I'm fussy.'

'Damn right. You ought to be gay, you know. Home decoration. Fussy about coffee. I've got some friends back in Boston I could introduce you to.'

'Thanks, Cameron, but somehow –'

'No, you're right,' she said, squinting at him in mock-appraisal. 'Look at you. Gays are well known for their care over personal hygiene.'

'Listen, I'll be another ten or fifteen minutes. Do you want to –'

'No need.'

'No need? What? We still have to –'

'Sorted. It's all sorted. We're paying thirty grand, by the way. Hope that's OK.'

'Sorted? What d'you mean?' Bryn the Head spoke from the depths. 'And I hope you haven't gone and spent –'

'Like I say, I've fixed it. It'll take two months, then – boom – back on track.'

Bryn closed his eyes, in a silent prayer for patience. 'Hang on. I'll stop here. Finish this later.' He began to wade back through the water, rising from the surface like an ill-smelling troll. Cameron kept pace with him, treading lightly along the roof, shoes in hand, spotless in her pale yellow, laughing at him. 'My Boston friends would kill me if they even knew,' she said. 'But I don't know. Isn't there a kind of sweaty boiler-repairman look among some sections of the gay community? Perhaps if you . . .'

But Bryn had reached the bank and Cameron stood her distance, holding her nose.

'Cameron, we have to do this properly. We can't just rush out and spend money thinking that –'

'I know.'

226

'Look,' said Bryn, a little more gently. 'The deal is, I take care of the business, you take care of the science. Now, I do genuinely welcome your help on the business side, that's why I –'

'I know. You're right. I take care of the science.'

'OK. So just tell me you have not gone and spent –'

'I've gone and spent thirty grand on some science. A guy called Professor Hass from St Thomas' med school. An old guy, but real good – you know, really strong on the numbers, excellent reputation. I was very impressed. Anyways, like I said, two months – boom – back on track.'

'Cameron, please, would you mind telling me what's going on?'

'I'd be happy to,' said Cameron.

And she told him.

6

Having obtained entry to Bell Atlantic, it was child's play to connect to Corinth's switchboard computer. 'They're *designed* to connect, see?' explained Mungo. 'We've logged in correctly to Bell Atlantic, so the way Corinth looks at us, we're totally pukka. They're not even trying to keep us out.'

The Corinth PABX gave Mungo a file listing everyone in the firm along with their switchboard extensions. A couple of keystrokes enabled him to listen to any conversation he felt like.

'Wow,' said Kati. 'It's as easy as that?'

''Course. We're like the operator, or one of them old-fashioned party lines.'

'So we can listen in to Huizinga, or Anita Morris, even?'

'That's the idea.'

A few more keystrokes and Brent Huizinga's deep voice

was on the phone, playing from the cruddy little speakers on Mungo's PC. Huizinga was talking about some quarterly report meeting; routine stuff, nothing of interest. 'Suit-alert,' yelped Mungo. 'Money-droids on patrol! Lasers to vaporise!'

'Quiet! Can't he hear you?'

'*Coo*-eeee, *Mister Hooooo*-zing,' shouted Mungo. Nothing happened. Huizinga continued to burble gruffly from the tinny speakers. After a few seconds, Mungo typed in another command and the voice vanished.

'Hey, shouldn't we go on listening? Isn't that the point?'

Mungo shook his head. 'We're not the only kids in the playground. We aren't far enough into the system to cover our tracks and we don't want the cyborgs from Corinth wondering how come Bell Atlantic is listening in to their Supreme Commander.'

'So?'

'So we don't listen.'

'What? You get us within earshot of the enemy, then tell us we mustn't listen?'

Mungo sighed. 'Look, if you were spying on us, which would you rather have: five days solid of listening in to Cam'ron's phone conversations or one single hour spent in her knicker drawer?'

'Knicker drawer?'

'Data files. Like one hour downloading data.'

'You'd take the hour-long download. No contest, really.'

Mungo nodded. ''Course. Any day.' He shrugged, as though what he was about to say was the sort of run-of-the-mill workaday suggestion that hardly needed mentioning. 'So we need to get authorised to read Corinth's data. Pop a back door on to her PC, and we can drop in whenever we like. If she can see it, we can see it.'

Kati's hands flew, to her mouth in astonished surprise. 'Mungo! You're serious?'

Mungo nodded. ''S th'plan,' he admitted, his single-syllable agreement plopping out like a burp.

'You can do that?'

'Yeah,' he said. 'Well, no. Or rather, yes, only you're going to do it.'

'Me?'

Mungo nodded. 'Canadian Kate, cyber-queen.'

7

Bryn could take a hint.

One morning, desperate to escape the gnawing anxiety of running a business which was teetering on the brink, he drove a hired van up to the Portobello Road. There, he bought three large metal trunks, and spent the morning assembling a collection of junk corresponding to the items of Cecily's that he'd sold. He bought cheap framed pictures in place of the etchings, a set of four squalid old rugs costing thirty quid in place of her eighteenth-century Persian carpets, tatty wooden boxes instead of her ebony sewing chests, and a cruddy little sidetable in place of her Venetian chess table. On completing his shopping list he drove back to the boathouse, then waited till evening when the yard was empty.

When the last patients had left, Rauschenberg and all the doctors and nurses had cleared away, Bryn hauled his purchases out of the van, stowed them roughly into the three trunks, and locked them. It was a golden June evening, swallows soaring high in the air over London, enjoying the last of the sun.

Bryn grinned.

He took a crowbar and busted the padlocks, ripping the clasps clean off. Then he wrenched open the trunks, doused the contents with petrol and set them alight. Once it was all burned out, he drenched the smoking remnants with bucketfuls of water mixed with sea salt, until the yard was full of charred debris floating in puddles of brine. He was finished.

He bandaged the ruined trunks back up in corrugated cardboard and shipped them off to Cecily using the most disreputable firm he could find. Meantime, he sent her a letter, sweet as could be, apologising for the delay, giving her the shipment details, hoping all was well in her new life.

'You ought to think about it,' Cameron had said, as she told him how Kati's belongings had been destroyed by fire while in the care of shippers. It had been a subtle hint, but not too subtle. Bryn *had* thought about it. As both he and Cameron had known perfectly well, Kati hadn't lost anything in a fire.

NINETEEN

1

Long Acre, Covent Garden.

A restaurant French enough that the food is good, the wine is excellent, and the waiters are so contemptuous, you'd swear they were royalty. Allen Green and Cameron Wilde. Their first proper date.

Things went OK. At the start, Cameron had been as nervous as a tightrope walker, and her nervousness had made her abrupt and hard-edged, a fiercely rational scientist right down to the tips of her fingers. The first course had passed in a highly technical discussion of Allen's original field of expertise, respiratory disease, during which time Cameron had acted like a bloody-minded research supervisor. She wore a black velvet dress, but might just as well have worn chainmail for all the signals she was sending off. The breakthrough had come after the *moules marinières* had been cleared away.

'Are you nervous?' he asked,

'Nervous? No. Why?' He caught her arm, and the touch made her literally jump in her seat. 'OK. I'm nervous.'

'First big date for a while?'

'Uh-huh.'

'For a long time, maybe?'

'Yes.' Her mouth was dry at the admission.

'That's OK. Can I make a suggestion?'

She nodded.

'Good. When I first started dating and I didn't know what to say or I ran out of things to say, I just stuck some food in my mouth and pretended to chew. First dates are cringy for everybody. No one in the history of the world ever has had a first date they feel proud of.'

'You don't mind?'

Allen smiled at her in his priestly way. Less a smile, it was more a way of giving benediction. 'You're beautiful. You're smart. You think I care if you're nervous?'

She smiled back at him, chock full of relief.

'And maybe one other tip?'

She nodded.

'You are allowed to talk about things other than science, you know.'

She nodded. 'True,' she said, 'sorry.' Then didn't know what else to say. She stuffed some food into her mouth. Too much. She began to chew, but she began to laugh as well. There was a short contest. The laughter won. Mashed-up breadstick spurted out over the tablecloth. She created a homemade *île flotante* in her wine glass and red wine flickered over the white linen. She laughed louder. Her nervousness was over. Conversation flowed.

2

After pudding, Allen asked if she'd like coffee here in the restaurant, or back at his place.

Cameron frowned. The evening had gone well – really well – but the nuts and bolts of dating were far more mysterious to her than the most complex reaches of immunology. She still grasped a breadstick in her hand, as a kind of jokey defence against finding herself short of things to say. This time she opted for the direct approach. 'Do you want to know if I like coffee, or are you asking me if I want to make love?'

Allen was taken aback, but only for as long as it takes a man's mating instinct to overwhelm every other impulse – which is to say, in this case, about the twentieth part of one second. 'If you feel ready to come back home with me,' he began. 'No, sorry, what I mean is, I'd love to make love with you. If that's too soon, then say so, and we'll take things slowly.'

She shook her head. Part of her reason for success in science was an attitude which said that every minute wasted was a minute lost. She didn't see why dating should be any different.

'Sex,' she said. 'I don't drink coffee anyway.'

Back at his flat, they didn't fuss over coffee, tea or other props of the conventional endgame. Cameron trotted round like a puppy exploring its new home. The flat had polished wood floors throughout, bare white walls, modern rugs and an eclectic collection of modern Italian designer furniture – Allen's pride and joy.

'Nice place,' commented Cameron at length, leaning against a sofa of Japanese bamboo with grey suede cushions.

'Thank you,' said Allen, looking around. 'If I hadn't gone into science, I'd have loved to deal in contemporary furniture. Good drugs, good furniture. It's all about clean design, clean action.' To illustrate his point, he tilted the back of an improbable chrome rocking chair with a sliding leather seat. The back rocked, the seat shifted, all in one smooth motion.

Suddenly remembering Meg's commandment that no woman wearing velvet was allowed anywhere near cane or bamboo, Cameron rose hurriedly, shifting her seat from her bamboo perch and wiping the back of her dress in apology.

She was standing a few metres apart from Allen, her bread-stick foolishly left back at the restaurant.

'Just a sec,' she said, darting into the stainless-steel-topped kitchen. There was an opening and closing of cupboard doors, then she emerged, crimson-red, waving a slice of bread. 'OK,' she said. 'I admit. Before I was nervous. Now I'm terrified.'

'You want to leave it?'

She shook her head, still crimson.

'We'll take it slow. Shout if you start to feel uncomfortable.'

'Aaargh!' Cameron pretended to scream, but forced a smile.

He smiled back, absolving her. They were close now, standing straight, just a few inches apart. They kissed, her mouth yielding to his, her body bending to his hands. Cameron was unpolished but natural, responding hungrily to the suggestions of his touch. After a short while kissing, they moved through to his room.

'Are you ready?' he asked. 'Don't go faster than you want to.'

She shook her head.

She put her hand to the zip at the back of her dress, but he stopped her. 'Important ritual,' he said. 'I undress you. You undress me. It's not the fastest way of doing things, but for some reason it's the best.'

She took off his jacket, but had no idea what to do with a tie. She pulled it into a tight knot, then let him sort it out. He bent close to find the clasp of her necklace, figure out the secret of her earrings. She unbuttoned his shirt, hands stopping to explore the broad new territories of his chest, the strong join between arms and shoulder. He found her zip without looking, dropped the dress to the floor, swept his hands up the curve of her hips, the valley of her waist, the thrust of her breasts. She had trouble with his belt, but found the rest of the trousers easy. Faced with visible proof of his excitement, she paused, but at a sign from him allowed herself to touch it. Blood throbbed in response, and he pulled her close, removing her hand. They stood, her belly against his member, her breasts crushed against his chest, her scented head buried in the smell of his neck.

The rest of their clothes fell to the floor. The bed (a stainless-steel frame suspended from four huge pillars of raw oak, a thick mattress and abundant white linen) was large and welcoming. They made love twice that night, once again the following morning. Cameron was uninhibited and openly delighted with the brave new world she'd found her way into.

'I can't believe you preferred coffee to this,' she said, slipping off to sleep against his side, face pressed happily into his arm.

Next morning at work, when Cameron shyly and quietly told Meg the outcome of her evening's adventure, Meg squawked so loud that doctors halted, patients stared, phone conversations fell silent. 'Yo, Cammie! You purple-arsed *man*-bandit!'

Like everyone else, Bryn heard the shriek. He was pleased for her. His medical director was no longer hot on him. Their relations had seemed tense recently, and perhaps they would now be able to relax with each other again, drift back towards normal. He shook his head and went back to work.

3

Getting the samples from his dad had been a nightmare. Mervyn Hughes had been locked in his 'I don't hold with doctors and that, we've all got a time to go' philosophy, and resisted all interference. It was only when Gwyneth arranged a dinner for Derek Williams, the vet, and the three of them – the vet, Gwyneth and Bryn – surrounded the stubborn old man that he relented.

'Bloody hell!' he complained in his usual bellow. 'I've never seen you making this much fuss over one of my sheep.'

Derek Williams unsheathed a needle. 'I could go to prison for this. Unless I can persuade them that you're an animal. Not a sheep, mind. Bloody ass, more like.'

'At least give me some more whisky, Bryn lad. If they're going to have my blood, I want it to smell nice.' A tumbler of whisky, taken with so little water it was a wonder he bothered, disappeared in a trice. 'Knowing that bloody man Williams, he'll stick that damn thing in the wrong place and I'll end up bleeding to death.'

'Hold still, or I'll get Rhys to put you in the bloody sheep pen.'

Rhys, who'd been sleeping, but only the way that an alert collie ever sleeps, leaped up and barked his approval of the scheme.

Derek Williams looked at the bulging veins on the old man's arms and inserted his needle, calm and accurate as you please. Although his was a large animal practice, he was happy to treat the domestic animals of his farming clients, and once you've inserted pins into the thighs of six-week-old kittens or dealt with a blockage in the oesophagus of a four-week-old pup, finding a vein on a human arm isn't too much of a toughie. Four tubes of blood followed. 'Bleeding me dry, as always.' Mervyn bellowed with laughter at his own joke, stopping abruptly once Williams produced his next two containers.

Mervyn looked highly dubious. 'When did you ever get my sheep to piss into a bottle? And if you think I'm going to –'

'Now, dear,' said Gwyneth sharply. 'Mr Williams' – she still, after thirty years, called him that – 'Mr Williams is only trying to do what's best for you, so go now –'

But Mervyn had surrendered, and when Bryn turned back for London the following night, six tubes clicked in his overnight bag: four red, one earth, one straw; the colours of life; secret keys to the ultimate riddle.

4

Meg, of course, demanded a detailed account of Cameron's newest conquest.

'Give me a blow-by-blow account, love. Not a detail missed.'

They were upstairs in Cameron's tower office, windows open in every direction, blazing sunshine outside, a light breeze stirring the chaos of paper. Meg fanned herself with photocopied extracts from *The Clinician's Handbook of Environmental Medicine*, and Tallulah sat on the window sill facing the river, cleaning her wing and every now and then expressing opinions as they came to her.

Cameron, shyly at first, but later with genuine enthusiasm, began to relate every detail, under Meg's interrogation: clothes, hair, flirting, Allen's appearance, his pluses, his minuses, his flat, the dinner, the kissing, the sex.

'And?' said Meg.

'And what?'

'Do you still think sex isn't what it's cracked up to be?'

Cameron laughed, reddening. 'I never said –'

'You did.'

'Alright, well, anyway . . .' She laughed again. 'It was nice. Maybe I'll do it again sometime.' In her lap, Cameron held one of those plastic models of chemical molecules, built out of coloured balls and black plastic joining-rods. She fiddled busily with it in embarrassment, before her face changed.

'You know, Meg. There is something I didn't know about Allen . . . I don't think there's a problem, but I just wanted to get your reaction.'

Meg's face grew serious too. 'He's got a compulsive S & M habit, and he needs you to –'

'No, seriously . . . Look, he trained in respiratory disease, which is what he truly loves, but then got made redundant and ended up working for this specialist chemo outfit.'

'I wouldn't say that was a problem.'

'No, but he's thinking of moving on again, back into respiratory. The thing is, he's thinking of applying to Corinth.'

Meg's jaw dropped. *'Corinth?'*

On the window sill, Tallulah perked up from her lethargy shrieking, 'Uncha gossa,' and flapped her wings vigorously as though to prove she still knew how to use them.

'Yes. I mean, he *hasn't* yet applied. I told him I had serious reservations about the company, but, as far as I know Corinth's respiratory wing is about the only part of it which produces drugs fit for human consumption. It's not like there's any good *medical* reason why he shouldn't go there.'

'Yes.' Meg's voice was deeply uncertain.

'He said to me . . . Hell, he said all the right things. How he'd never let loyalty to a company override loyalty to a – well, to a lover, I guess.' Cameron hesitated before realising that the word 'lover' applied to herself now. 'He said, if I had a big problem, he wouldn't do anything right away, let me think it over.'

'That's good,' said Meg. 'To be honest, I can't see that it's a good idea.'

'Look, you need to remember that Corinth has around twenty-five thousand employees. It's not like they're all bent

238

on our destruction. In fact, probably only about five of them even give a damn about us. And Allen, hell, he's a bench scientist, a researcher. Corinth's share price matters about as much to him as it does to me.'

'Mmm, but still *you* might not see a problem, and *I* might not see a problem, but we both know one paranoid Welshman who'd see a big problem.'

A gust of wind caused Cameron's Post-it notes to rustle, fluttering and multi-coloured like the plumage of a giant parrot. Tallulah looked round suspiciously, before getting back to her under-wing hygiene programme.

'Look, for now it isn't even an issue. Allen doesn't work for Corinth, and isn't applying to them. But in the end, Meg, this is about more than just Bryn's paranoias. I'm not having him tell me who I can and can't date.' Cameron spoke defiantly, feeling guilty as she did so, but also too embarrassed to face raising the matter with Bryn.

'Quite right, we all know what taste he's got.' Meg cackled with laughter. 'But seriously, don't you think you ought to tell him at least?'

'Sure. If he ever asks me, sure.'

'That's not exactly a resounding yes, now, is it?'

'He's been kind of weird with me lately. Kind of stiff, irritable, I don't know. It's like I bug him a lot at the moment, even when I'm not doing anything. At least I used to know *why* I annoyed him.'

'Men,' said Meg, solving the emotional mystery at a stroke, and summoning Tallulah with an outstretched hand. 'Testosterone addles the brain. Well-known fact. Big chap like Bryn, big goolies, little brain. Fact is, it's a miracle he even talks.'

5

And one day, at last, Mungo came to Kati, saying, 'Think it's alright to go.'

She came up into the dark secrecy of Pod Mungo, its clutter everywhere, its three magic windows on to a world as vast and mysterious as anything Kati had ever explored. It was a warm day outside and the sun blazed down on the boathouse roof right above Mungo's head. Meantime, everything in his stacked-up electrical empire was all on, all hot, and a stupid little white fan pushed the boiling air round in circles as though that was a solution to anything.

Mungo gestured at his middle screen. 'Corinth PABX shows no outies from her phone. So either she's gone *stumm*, or more likely she's away.'

'No outgoing calls, huh?' Kati swallowed.

''S right. And she's a big phone yakker, like my sister, Dar. Give Dar a big red phone and a bag full of pennies and she's a happy camper till the pennies run out.'

'So you think Anita Morris is away? Is everything else ready?'

'Done and dusted. All ready for Canadian Kate.'

Kati was shockingly nervous. This was stage fright mixed with fear of capture; what you'd get if you planned a hold-up in the middle of performing *Hamlet*. 'OK,' she said. 'Ready, I guess.'

'Remember to switch voices,' said Mungo.

Kati nodded.

'And you've got your handsets sorted?'

Kati nodded again.

'Want a drink first? Don't want you doin' a dead man's croak in the middle of everything.' He offered her some Tango cherry drink, in a can that had been opened yesterday and had been simmering gently in the dust on top of Mungo's banked PCs ever since.

'No thanks.'

'OK then.'

Taking the phone to the left of his computer, the only one that was simply a phone and was not also plugged into a computer, Mungo dialled a number and handed the receiver, ringing, to Kati. The scientist took it as though it was a ticking bomb. The rings stopped. An American voice said, 'IT Help Desk, Mike speaking, how can I help?'

Speaking with brisk authority, and an accent from the north-east seaboard, Kati replied, 'Anita Morris here. I've forgotten my password. Can you remind me what it is, please?'

'We can't read your password. What we have to do is issue you with a new one.'

'Fine.'

'I'll send someone to your workstation right away.'

Kati glanced at Mungo. He'd told her the help desk would say that. ''S like security one-oh-one.'

But she was prepared. 'That's not possible,' she said. 'I'm out of the office. I need access right away.' Kati remembered her brief: she was Anita Morris, a top banana, impatient and authoritative. She still felt nervous, but her nerves weren't affecting her performance.

Mike the IT guy put Kati on hold as he spoke with his supervisor. 'I'll need to run through some security questions. Let's see ...'

'Look,' snapped Kati. 'Just dial my extension, 4812. My assistant Pat can transfer your call to my cellphone. That way, you know it's me.'

'Oh, sure, OK. Let me just check the directory ... 4812, Anita Morris. Right, OK.' Mike liked the suggestion. Kati replaced the handset.

'Wicked,' said Mungo, eyes glued to the monitor. For just a couple of minutes he had placed a line-divert instruction in the Corinth PABX. If all went well, the handset connected to his phone would ring, and Mike the IT guy would believe he'd come through on a regular in-house extension.

It rang.

Kati reached for it instantly, but Mungo knocked her hand away. 'Leave it a coupla rings. Patsy Duke, remember.'

She let the phone ring a couple of times then picked up.

'This is Anita Morris's office, Patsy Duke speaking.' Kati's voice was now soft and unhurried, with hints of the south. Over the last few days, Kati had called Duke on different pretexts simply to hear and study her voice. There wasn't a big chance that Mike the IT guy would know Duke, but Mungo's strategy was to eliminate the possibility of error.

'Uh, hi. This is Mike from the help desk. I got a call from Anita Morris. She's forgotten her password, apparently . . .'

'Oh, *right*, absolutely. She's out of the office and she's been getting real frustrated.' Kati's voice was loaded with sympathy, and the desire to talk about it. During her telephone reconnaissance, Duke had been willing to chat with a wrong-number dialler, so an IT guy would definitely get the full treatment. 'Are you going to be able to help?'

'Sure. If you can just transfer me.'

'Oh . . . That's all you need? Sure.' Kati nodded to Mungo, who put the IT guy on hold for a few moments, then released the hold button and nodded back at Kati. 'Morris,' she snapped.

'Hi, Mike from the help desk. That's fine, I just needed confirmation of ID. Your new password is . . .' He read some numbers and digits from the screen in front of him. 'You shouldn't have any more trouble.'

And he was right, they didn't.

6

In the meantime, Cameron's plan was creeping to fruition. As June turned into July, and July tipped over into August, the computers were busy at St Thomas' Medical School. Professor Hass – one of the most distinguished medical statisticians of the last thirty years – led a small team through a forest of numbers.

Statistics is a strange subject. Piles of data, sorted and categorised this way, that way, computed, reshuffled and recomputed. 'Lies, damned lies, and statistics'? – that's not fair, really; at least, it's not fair to men like Hass, men who have spent their entire professional lives in search of truth and only truth. He's receiving thirty grand for this work, but the money won't sway him one iota. When he comes to report, he'll speak the truth as he finds it, speak it clearly, speak it straight.

TWENTY

1

Cables everywhere set traps for the feet. The unnecessary brilliance of TV lamps crowded the room with heat and light. The room filled with lightmen, soundmen, cameramen, photographers, journalists. Shorthand notebooks were open, crammed with the news of the week before, blank pages ready for the days to come: murders, scandals, health scares, earthquake, tragedy, and death. Mobile phones chirruped, adding their own microwave toxins to the room's thick electromagnetic stew. Conversation buzzed with the cynicism of the trade.

'Were you there for the Macavity verdict?'

'No. Madonna-hunting in Knightsbridge. Scottie from the *Sun* caught up with her, swearing like fury because he'd caught his foot in the door. She thought he was swearing at her, gave as good as she got, made a face, snap, snap, snap, thank you sweetheart, picture of the year. Bastard's not syndicating, though.'

'Bastard . . .'

Up on the podium, Meg fussed around. She'd spent half an hour rebuilding Cameron's make-up to cope with the lights and a further half-hour begging Bryn to let her put some powder on him. He'd refused completely, but now things were held up as two journalists were stuck in traffic, and he was sweating like a donkey in jacket and tie. 'It'll only take a moment,' badgered Meg. 'No one'll notice.'

'No way. I'd kill for some water, though.'

'Only if I can sit at the podium. I've never been on telly.'

'Jesus, Meg, OK.'

Meg, already dolled up to the nines, produced a jug of iced water and a fourth seat at the podium. She grinned at the cameras, as though rehearsing for a hot date, then leaned behind Bryn and poked Cameron, who was wearing a smart blue dress for the occasion.

'Looking good, Cammie.'

Cameron looked up distractedly from her conversation with the professor. 'Uh, thanks Meg, oh, water, great.' She and Professor Hass were getting on splendidly. 'A most impressive achievement, my dear,' he'd kept saying. 'Most impressive indeed, and such a young girl too.'

For her part, she'd developed an immediate respect for him. 'Very careful work,' she said. 'Real thorough for an old guy.'

Cameron and the professor resumed their conversation. Bryn sat silent, still sweating; Meg perched, unruffled, wondering whether she'd make it into the camera's view and thanking heaven for widescreen TV. Eventually, the missing journalists turned up, Bryn began to speak, a couple of microphones screeched with feedback, and the room fell silent.

'On behalf of the Fulham Clinic,' said Bryn, 'I'd like to welcome you all. As you know there has been substantial controversy recently over the medical effectiveness of the treatments we offer.' That was an understatement. Since the original *Herald* article, there had been a surge of knocking copy from the national press. The Fulham Clinic was in danger of becoming a byword for quackery in medicine, and

Bryn's hopes of finding an investor had fallen to less than zero. 'Since our effectiveness has been called into question, we believed it was only fair to invite the strictest possible test of our techniques and to release the results of that test to the public. So to that end, we contacted Professor Hass of St Thomas' Medical School in London . . .'

Bryn introduced the professor and outlined the tests he had been invited to perform. The assembled journalists all had a copy of Hass's resumé, which was deeply impressive. A former president of the Royal Statistical Society and author of more than forty papers in the medical literature, there was probably no better man in Britain to undertake the tests in question. 'Perhaps, Professor, you would like to announce your results?'

'Yes, indeed.' The professor blinked in the glare of the lamps and the unmerciful gaze of the assembled reporters. A battery of flashes signalled the first salvo of photo-taking. The professor removed his glasses, put them on again, and took them off. 'All this terrible light,' he said. 'Is it really necessary? I wonder if we could have it off, perhaps.'

'You want to have it off, Professor?' called a hack from the back of the room, to laughter.

Bryn leaned across. 'I'm afraid they need the lights for the TV. Perhaps if you could manage . . . I know it's bright.'

'Oh, yes, the television, I do see. I'm surprised, I've never known them to be interested in this type of thing. Still . . .' He began a meticulous report of his results, reading from a prepared script, not once looking up into the besieging cameras. 'So in conclusion, I would state that for eight of the fourteen disease groups analysed, there is extremely strong evidence to support the hypothesis of an outstanding clinical performance as compared with conventional standards. For the remaining six subgroups, the data support the hypothesis of a superior clinical performance.'

246

The professor removed his glasses and pinched the bridge of his nose, frowning down at the notes which had dissolved into a dazzling blur. Alone with his computers, Professor Hass had felt a sense of gathering excitement. He wasn't a fan of Immune Reprogramming as such. He knew nothing of it, was too old to learn. But he was absolutely fair-minded – the first and overriding qualification for a statistician. And being fair-minded, his conclusions had been unavoidable. For the first time in modern medical history, a revolutionary model of patient treatment reaching right across the spectrum of disease had been tested with the most rigorous tools known to science – and the revolution had been triumphantly endorsed. The professor was a humble man, but felt a duty to share the excitement of his discovery with the world at large. He rubbed his nose and blinked again, brain addled by the glare.

'On a personal note, I wish to add that I have never in all my years as a scientist seen such a comprehensive . . . such an overwhelming . . . validation of a new technology. It is quite remarkable . . . astounding. The two young people here, Mr Hughes and Dr Wilde – such a nice pair, actually – have a most extraordinary achievement to their credit. Yes, indeed. Quite remarkable. Er . . . Thank you all very much.'

His last word barely made it beyond his tonsils before the journalists trampled in with their questions, as though worried that Hass was about to make a run for it.

'Professor, Professor . . .'

'Are you claiming that traditional pharmaceutical approaches are ineffective?'

'Can you offer any comment on Cheryl Kessler's cure?'

'D'you have any health tips for our readers?'

'May I ask . . .'

There was a frenzy of snapping. Flash lights. Sound

booms lowered as the cameras moved in. Swearing *sotto voce* at the back of the room as a power cord snagged. Silent swearing from the sound crew who didn't want to snarl up their tape. Howls of feedback as rival electrical teams fought to get their equipment in closer.

'. . . Take vitamin pills?'

'. . . how old . . .'

'. . . what form of exercise, if any . . .'

'. . . married . . .'

'. . . do you recommend?'

'. . . your opposition to the drugs industry?'

'Please,' begged the professor, 'please,' as Bryn tried to regain command over the room. 'Please,' he murmured once again, as the barrage of questions continued to fly, one at a time now, but still overwhelming. The press conference ended half an hour later. Bryn, on a tide of triumph, wrapped up the session.

'Professor Hass has been very generous, but my colleague, Dr Wilde, and myself are still not satisfied. In an earlier generation of animal experiments, Dr Wilde was able to provide a complete cure for viral disease in rats. Despite the huge advances in treatment that Professor Hass has described, we are still a long way from that goal in human beings. In order to get there, we are currently looking for some outside investment. It is our firm belief that a relatively modest further investment will allow us to provide a permanent and complete cure for an enormous range of human disease. Thank you.'

There was a swift tak-tak-tak of further questions. Then, looking around the room for Luke Hancock, author of the original nasty article in the *Herald*, Bryn said, 'Time for one last question. Maybe Luke Hancock? Is he here?' There was some laughter and joshing, words Bryn was unable to catch. 'Is he here anywhere? Anyone from the *Herald*?'

'Tell him, George, tell him.' A scarlet-faced man raised a nicotine-painted hand.

'Greg Wilson from the *Herald*,' he said, introducing himself. 'Luke was unable to be here.'

He wasn't allowed to leave it there. From round the room, voices continued to call, 'Why, Greg, tell him why.' The man from the *Herald* coughed and admitted what the others all knew.

'Yeah, Luke, his liver collapsed. He's in hospital right now. Intensive care.'

The conference broke up. A few journalists stayed on to chat, but most were already yanking plugs from sockets, shouting their stories down the phone lines to waiting copyists, taking instructions for the next story to run to. Cameron stood with Hass, her face ablaze with unconcealed delight. For her, this wasn't simply good news for the clinic, this was the scientific vindication she'd been missing ever since her paper on rats had been so hurtfully rejected. Bryn bore down on the pair of scientists, and gave Cameron a bear-hug of congratulation which lifted her feet from the ground. 'Bloody genius, woman!' he cried, his Welsh accent re-emerging in his excitement.

The clinic had defeated the *Herald*. The money would come. Bryn was too experienced to believe that this was a decisive victory. In capitalism, as in the jungle, victory is a passing thing: a fight won, a belly filled, a day survived. Bryn knew this. Often enough, he'd seen businesses beat off one attack to fall victim to another. He didn't care. Right now, the fight was running his way and he was happy.

2

The mood lasted all of a minute or two. As Bryn and Cameron raced upstairs to bring Kati the good news of how it had gone, they met her coming down, in tears.

'Kati, what . . . ? It went great. Are you OK?'

Wordlessly, Kati took them into the researchers' computer room. Rick the Beard was in there, working on another PC, but Bryn quickly shooed him away. Tallulah was also there, perched on a rafter, scratching the paint off and causing a little shower of white flakes to fall like confetti. She worked busily, and looked disapproving.

'The download,' said Kati in a tear-laden voice. 'The one Mungo got from Anita Morris. I've been going through it. Look at it. Look. They're way ahead. Yesterday, they got their very first HIV peptide. They're just getting the data in order, apparently, but they aim to be at the Patent Office within two or three days.'

Cameron and Bryn looked at the screen. It was an e-mail from Anita Morris to Brent Huizinga, no less, reporting progress on 'Project Champion'. There were a couple of dozen viral illnesses listed, with terse comments on developments in each area. On some diseases, they were no further ahead than Cameron. On most of them, they were literally months ahead. And, as Kati said, they seemed to have obtained their very first HIV peptide yesterday.

'They've got the HIV peptide?' said Bryn in shock. 'HIV as in AIDS? They can cure AIDS?'

Cameron shook her head impatiently. 'No. There are several critical peptides at work in AIDS. They've got the first, most minor one. We're only a few weeks away from it ourselves.'

'No,' said Kati. 'We've just got it.' She opened another file downloaded from Corinth, and stepped back to let Cameron view the screen. The file contained the full specifications of the peptide, and Cameron leaned forward to inspect it closely.

'This seems to be in order,' she said. 'Have you checked it against our data?'

Kati nodded, then, her voice absolutely breaking with tears, added, 'Oh my God, it's so heart-breaking. You know that stupid joke? About the Newfies – you know, Newfoundlanders – who tried to climb Everest. They had to stop because they ran out of scaffolding. I thought it would be like that. I didn't think you could just hire an OK scientist and chuck money around and come up with the goods. I didn't –' Kati was sobbing now. 'I honestly thought we were going to win.'

Bryn rubbed Kati's back with his big bear-paw, as Cameron massaged her hands and stroked her hair. None of them said anything. None of them had anything to say.

3

It was then that Mungo entered. 'Lighten up,' he said. 'Old Hassie Baby kicked butt, didn't he? Crack open the cherryade and let the rave commence.'

'Professor Hass may have kicked butt, but Corinth is kicking ours,' said Bryn roughly. Up in the rafters, Tallulah chorused her thoughts: 'O-shi, matey,' and let another shower of paint fall to the floor. In a few gruff sentences, Bryn explained the problem, with Mungo nodding and grinning like a halfwit.

'They're one day ahead? Just one?' he asked. ''S no biggie.'

'No, Mungo. This is serious.'

'Lighten up. We can sort it.'

'Now's not the time,' said Kati, still grief-stricken. 'This is horrible news.'

'Well, pardon me,' said Mungo, 'I know how upsettin' it is. Bleeding funeral, everything pukka, everyone's got a long face an' a cup of tea that tastes like the cat widdled in it, then some nitwit starts handing out the happy juice. One minute, everything's boo-hoo. Next minute, everything's tee-hee, an' the front parlour's swarming with maiden aunties pecking away at the grass cookies and doing the foxtrot till their knickers show.' He peered around the room, blinking, as though he might get into trouble for speaking. 'What I'm trying to say is, wouldn' it be a good idea to stop Corinth? I mean, I know all about the sacred nature of the prop'ty relationship an' everything, but we could always say a couple of Hail-Marys an' light a few joss sticks.'

Bryn stared hard at Mungo. 'You're serious? You can stop them?'

'Not for long. I don't mean I can do it for long.'

'We'd only need a day or two. We can get to the Patent Office every bit as fast as they can.'

'Day or two, man. 'S no prob.'

'What are you going to do?'

Tension caused Bryn's voice to grate as he asked the question, and both Kati and Cameron were by now staring at Mungo.

Mungo wiggled his eyebrows at them and rushed, galumphing, upstairs to Pod Mungo. He came down again with a floppy disk and a mouth full of Waggon Wheel. He slipped the disk into Cameron's PC and brought up a list of files. 'LOVEBUG2, MAYDAY, PACMAN, AMDSPLAT, CONANZZZ, FATLADY, CORSAIR, MOUSE, MS-KILL.'

'Pick a virus,' he said, jabbing his Waggon Wheel at the screen, 'any virus.'

Tallulah, scenting marshmallow filling, dropped down

from the rafters and sat on the PC monitor, shaking white paint from her talons and pecking bits of Waggon Wheel from Mungo's sticky fingers.

'Mungo, what's the idea?'

'The i-*dee*-a, man, is we wipe out their computer system. Not for long, obviously. They'll have pretty much everything archived an' retrievable. But even a really top outfit's gonna be knocked out for a day or two. That's the i-*dee*-a.'

'How do you get the virus into their system?'

'First up, select your badster.'

Bryn looked at Kati, whose face was still pained and tearful. 'Kati,' he said, 'you want to choose?'

She wiped her face on her shoulder. 'I don't mind. Something nasty.'

'They're all nasty,' said Mungo.

'CORSAIR?' said Bryn. 'Sounds OK to me.'

Cameron nodded. 'CORSAIR it is, guv, an' CORSAIR for the lady.' Mungo paused to gaze at Kati. 'You alright? I've got some wet wipes up in the Pod, all nice an' toasty on the laptop transformers.' He mimed the wiping action for her, in case she didn't know how to do it.

She shook her head, and Mungo turned his serious eyes back to the monitor. Dialling in through a now-familiar modem sequence, Mungo brought up Anita Morris's own log-on screen, and logged on using her name and password. 'Welcome to Corinth Laboratories Data and Computing Services.'

'Suits,' commented Mungo. 'Welcome to suit city.' (His own log-on procedure at the clinic welcomed each user with a blaze of psychedelic colour and an uplifting message that turned cartwheels round the lurid pink-and-green screen. 'Doctor Ganja's Magic Smoke' was today's offering, with fluffy white clouds puffing out of the 'i' in Magic.)

He entered Morris's e-mail package and opened a new

message addressed to 'Corinth Norwalk – all employees'. In the message box he simply wrote, 'Please see attached ASAP,' then saved the virus as an attachment under the innocuous name 'AM_0902'.

'That's it?' said Bryn, astonished. 'That's all?'

'Yep, 'cept for fusin' and pretties.'

'Which in English would be?'

'Fusing. Gotta choose a time when the virus goes off. Far enough away so enough people have opened the file, near enough that they haven't finished all their patent blah-de-blah.'

'OK. Midnight tonight. East Coast Standard time. That's five a.m. our time.'

'You think Mr Corsair Virus-Man is gonna adjust his watch as he zooms across the Atlantic on a lil' bit of cable?'

'OK. Just midnight then.'

'Midnight it is, okie-doke.'

'And pretties?'

'Don' want people all knickers-in-a-twist over the message we send. I usually just make the attachment a blank page with some random ASCII symbols on it. That way everyone assumes it's an error and waits for the proper message. Even if 'Nita Morris gets asked about it, she'll be a bit puzzled, but it's not the sort of thing anyone gets frazzled by. 'Course, if it ever happens to you, you should get frazzled big-time. *Hurry up, Flash, we've only got an hour to save the world,*' he said, yelping the last bit in falsetto.

'And that's it? That's all?'

'Yep. 'Course, it takes time to build up a really good virus collection.'

Cameron shook her head and laughed. 'Tell me about it.'

4

They'd all intended to stay up to watch the fireworks, but come about eleven o'clock, Kati's big brown spaniel eyes drooped with sleepiness, and Bryn sent her to sleep in his double bed in the barge's grand stern gallery. Even Mungo, essentially a nocturnal creature, disappeared off at about three a.m. and was found snoring amongst the junk food sediments on the floor of the Pod.

Cameron worked on her own, in her tower, with an apparently invincible ability to work at top pressure all hours of the day and night. At a quarter to five, as dawn was beginning to get its act together on London's eastern horizon, Bryn arrived with a pot of coffee, a mug of peppermint tea, and a couple of sheets of paper. The scene reminded him of their first meeting: the cluttered office, the anglepoise lamps, the fluttering Post-it notes, the strange, attractive doctor – better-dressed now, better-looking, but still the same. He felt fond of her, warm. And as always, he was excited and alerted by the mood, the sense that, in her company, he was standing close to the edge of knowledge, perhaps only inches away from Nobel Prizes and the thanks of history.

'Coffee for me,' he said. 'Wet hay for you.'

'Liver support for me,' she said. 'Acid-forming, liver-trashing, adrenal gland destruction for you.'

They sipped their drinks and Cameron examined her counterpart, this battered-seeming man who looked like he'd been put together by bulldozer and mechanical-shovel. She felt somehow reassured and comforted. It still seemed odd to her the way this man had come crashing into her life. Back in the New England winter, on that snowy night in Boston, was it really only money that had brought him to her? Had that really been his only motive? Cameron

255

sighed. Those were questions for another day. She glanced up and realised that Bryn was smiling broadly, had been ever since coming upstairs.

'What's up?'

'Good news,' he said. 'Fax. It came in just now.' He handed Cameron the sheets of paper and she read them, perplexed.

'Max Altmeyer? Am I meant to know him?' She went on reading. 'He wants to invest? In the clinic? You've found some money?' Her voice rose in mounting surprise and delight.

Bryn nodded. 'Altmeyer heard Hass on the six o'clock news. He calls me up, we have a chat, and he sounds interested. He promised to send a proposal. This is it. He must have cranked right through the night. Twenty million pounds. We could have it within ten days.'

5

They spoke for a while about the money. 'Twenty million pounds . . . Whew! We can go buy the mother of all peptide fractionation machines and really blast away. Hell, we can have two machines, three. Rick and Kati can each head up a research unit, and we could go out on a hiring spree. Wow! We'll really begin to motor, especially with Mungo giving us access to their data.'

Cameron laughed, hope once again glittering in her eyes. Bryn watched her excitement with delighted pleasure. Cameron was a wonderful scientist and a wonderful woman. For too long, he'd been obsessed only by her science part – the bit which would end up (he hoped) making him rich. He hadn't just ignored her woman part, he'd been actively annoyed by it – a distraction he just didn't need. That was gone. He understood that the woman and scientist didn't have to be in conflict. He admired and liked her.

256

'So. Tell me about Altmeyer,' she said.

'He was one of my A-list millionaires,' said Bryn. 'I was literally on the point of writing to him anyway. What else d'you need to know? He's loaded. He likes us.'

In fact, the Berger Scholes notes had been highly detailed. In his early twenties, Altmeyer had managed to persuade a small Italian pharma company to let him be the distributor of their product in the UK and the US. He'd had no capital, no organisation, no sales team. Despite that, through sheer force of character, he'd bombarded doctors into believing his product was one of the leading drugs in its category. Although the range of uses was small – at its peak the drug never did more than fifteen or twenty million pounds in revenues – Altmeyer had managed to negotiate himself a remarkable thirty-three per cent cut of sales. By the age of thirty, he had got through his first wife, his first yacht, was worth upwards of thirty million and his annual royalties were still several million a year. He'd ploughed most of the money back into developing his own research operation and much of the rest of it into building up a salesforce. He continued to license drugs from research companies too small to market them effectively themselves, and had a nice business earning royalties from other people's innovations.

'Can we trust him?' asked Cameron. 'Are we sure he's not just a stooge for Corinth?'

'I doubt it. It was only a few hours after Hass's conference that Altmeyer faxed his offer. That'd be pretty fast work, even by Corinth's standards.'

'But still . . . it's possible, isn't it? If they had some prior relationship?'

'True. Not likely, but possible. On the other hand, I'm not sure I even care.'

'What?'

Bryn nodded. 'Thanks to the excitement you and Hass

257

generated, I reckon we can get all the money we need by selling just forty per cent of the company. That way I'd retain total control.'

'Because your sixty per cent can outvote the other forty per cent?'

'Yep.'

'But, like, every time?'

'Yep.'

'That's democratic?'

Bryn smiled.

'That's business.'

6

They smiled, and their eyes met. The moment lasted for a second or two longer than was normal.

Then Cameron looked away, and Bryn glanced at his watch. It was gone five. Over in Norwalk, Connecticut, Mungo's virus had either gone into action or been located and disabled. It was time to check.

Watched in solemn silence by Cameron, Bryn logged in to Anita Morris's machine. Or rather, tried to. 'Dialup sequence aborted', it commented. 'Remote modem not responding'.

For a brief moment, Bryn felt a flash of annoyance. Why was it that systems always failed when you needed them? Then it clicked. That was the point. The system had failed. Not when he needed it, but when Anita Morris did.

He turned to Cameron. Her eyes, like his, were shining in triumph.

7

That night – or morning, rather – Cameron got to Allen's flat just as he was getting up.

He raised an eyebrow. 'When you said you'd be working late, I didn't think ... *Were* you working?'

'Uh-huh,' said Cameron airily. 'Partly working. Partly not.'

'And the partly not part?'

'Oh, you know, this and that. Industrial espionage, blowing up computer systems, that kind of thing.'

'The big bad wolf at Corinth, I hope.'

'You bet.'

Allen's getting up had progressed as far as a shower, a shave and a pair of clean underpants. Cameron swung coquettishly from one of the rough oak pillars of the bed frame, playing with her hair. 'I see you're all ready for me,' she said.

'Ready ... ?'

Cameron explained herself by slipping out of her dark-blue dress and underwear. She stood in front of him, naked, leaning against the wooden bedpost with her arm around it.

'It's seven o'clock in the morning,' he said. 'I've an early meeting.'

Cameron slipped into bed, tugging at his elbow. 'Aren't you even going to tuck me in?' Her lips began fluttering in small circles round his back, heading towards his waist.

'You know what day it is today? It's the eighteenth of August.'

'So?' Her monosyllabic reply wasn't meant to be curt, it was just that her mouth was busy doing other things.

'So, the big bad wolf needs to know if I'm applying to them for a job or not. Remember? We did talk about it. We agreed to make up our minds by today.'

'Oh.' Cameron was disappointed. They *had* talked about it, but Cameron had been sticking her head in the sand, hoping the problem would go away. Allen simply didn't believe Cameron's 'conspiracy theories', and laughed at the idea that there was anything other than healthy competition between Corinth and the clinic. He genuinely wanted the job – not for sinister reasons, but just because it was a good job, with a great salary, in a research field which was Allen's particular favourite. 'You still want to go ahead?'

Allen pulled away from Cameron and spoke seriously. 'Look, of course I'm still keen. You said you'd think about it and let me know.'

'And if I said no?'

'If you said no, I'd think you were being very silly. I'm not suddenly going to turn into a vampire just because I've got a new employer.'

'But Corinth . . . I know you don't think they're so evil, but believe me, they fight dirty. And their anti-viral drugs are just the worst.'

'Yes, we've been through that. I wouldn't be working on the anti-viral side. You said yourself that their respiratory work is first-rate.'

'I know.'

Cameron cuddled into Allen's tall, unyielding frame, trying to soften him, as though a bit of foreplay would make the issue melt away.

'We need to resolve this,' he said.

Cameron sat up, holding the sheet over her breasts. 'OK, two questions. One, if I said no, would you apply to them? If it was that important to me?'

He considered. He had a beautiful intelligent girlfriend, sitting naked in his bed. She had cranky views about one of the world's leading pharmaceutical companies, but that was OK. If he applied to Corinth, he mightn't even get the job anyway. The choice wasn't hard. 'If you said no, I'd be disappointed, but I wouldn't apply.'

'And two, if you did work there, could you swear – like, totally, absolutely on-your-mother's-grave swear – that you'd stay loyal to me, not them, come what may?'

Allen smiled benevolently, already guessing how this conversation would end. He kissed her lingeringly on the lips. 'My mother is alive and well and living in Brighton. Apart from that, I swear.'

'Whatever happened?'

'Come hell or high water.' It was an easy promise to make. After all, he was certain that it would never be tested, certain that the supposed conflict would remain a part of Cameron's fantasy life and nothing more.

'Well, then,' she said. What with the success of the press conference, Mungo's sabotage, the offer from Altmeyer, she was feeling light-headed – eager to trust this man she thought she was starting to love. She snuggled down into bed and wiggled her hips. 'My answer will depend on how happy I become over the next half-hour or so.'

Allen laughed. 'I have an early meeting,' he said. 'Remember?'

But his underpants came off, his lips got busy, and his chances of making a speedy departure for work tumbled to round about zero.

TWENTY-ONE

1

'Bryn?'

'Yes?'

Bryn was wearing dark glasses to drive. With a light-weight navy jacket over a sky-blue linen shirt, he looked 'almost fashionable', as Meg had put it – 'You can hardly even tell you're Welsh.' Cameron too was dressed for the Riviera heat, in a pale-pink shift dress and strappy brown sandals. ('Absolutely gorgeous, babe, total knock-out.')

'Listen, I've got something to tell you. I was going to wait . . . Only I figure you'd prefer to know sooner rather than later.'

Bryn stole a glance across at his driving companion. He guessed what she was about to bring up, and he was suddenly, violently anxious about what she might have to say. 'Yes?' His voice was hoarse and cracked, and he dropped his speed as a lunatic French driver cut him up at a hundred and thirty kilometres an hour.

'Your father,' she said gently.

'Yes.'

'I've been taking a good long look at his blood.'

'Uh-huh.'

'Now, you know I'm an immunologist. My doctoring skills in other areas aren't everything they should be.'

'That's not what Kati says. That's not what Rauschenberg says. That's not what Rick the Beard says.'

Cameron shook her head. She wasn't going to argue. 'I'm getting a pretty clear reading from the samples he gave us.' Her tone was concerned and careful. 'He's a sheep farmer, right?'

Bryn nodded. 'Sheep and cows, mostly sheep.'

'Sheep dip and all that?'

He nodded again, eyes fixed on the dazzling tarmac in front of him.

Cameron dropped her voice. 'His blood is swimming in organophosphates. Given his job, that's not surprising. What matters is whether he's susceptible. Not everyone is.'

'And he is, right? Susceptible?'

'Yes. He is now. I guess he usen't to be, or you'd have known about it. Maybe he was over-exposed one day, and that sensitised him. Who knows? The point is, he's got a serious toxic load, and he won't get better till that resolves.'

'Is there anything . . .' Bryn's voice croaked out and disappeared. An effort of will brought it back. 'Is there anything we can do?'

'Uh. You do understand it's not my area? If you wanted me to refer you to someone, I'd be really happy to locate someone you could trust.'

'I trust you, Cameron. I don't want anyone else.'

'OK.' She looked at him with her huge eyes, unblinking like an owl, a beautiful grey-eyed owl. 'The first thing is to strengthen his own detox pathways in the liver, mostly the cytochrome P450 pathway. I guess there's no chance of your dad taking an injection? 3cc daily. A one-inch needle right into the backside. He could do it himself if I showed him how. It hurts though, I'm afraid.'

Bryn shook his head. 'Never in a million years. It's not the pain, it's just . . . Oh, hell, Cameron, he's a stubborn old fool. I'm sorry.'

'I thought you'd say that. Look.' She reached into her bag in the back of the car and dug out a cardboard box which was rattling with pills. As she gave it to him, she placed her hand on his arm, only for a moment, but it was a mark of warmth, solidarity in times of trouble. 'This is the best I can do with oral supplements. It's a lot to take, but – well, it's a serious problem. You can't just take out the crap. You have to replenish all the good stuff he's lost.'

'I understand.'

Bryn took the box on to his lap and opened it. There were half a dozen pill bottles inside, with instructions on how and when to take them pasted to the inside flap.

'He's treatment-resistant, I know. I've really squeezed down hard on supplements. I'd say this was the bare minimum.' She shrugged. 'If he even wants to go this route. Not everyone does.'

Bryn rattled the box. It *was* a lot of pills. 'Thanks, anyway.'

Cameron paused. 'That's only half of it. The other part is he has to avoid all OPs from now on. Completely. New exposure could push him down to a new level.'

Bryn nodded again. He'd take the box and explain things to his dad, who'd ignore it, like he ignored anything he didn't want to hear. And who could blame him, in a way? Mervyn Hughes was a sheep farmer, like his father and like his grandfather. He'd go on farming, and go on sickening, till he couldn't go on any more. Maybe that wasn't the worst thing. Everyone had to die. Perhaps dying in your own way, in your own pig-headed fashion, was as good as you could expect. 'Thanks, Cameron. You're a total star.'

'It's nothing, really.'

'I'm sorry your patient's such a difficult so-and-so.'

'That's OK. I'm difficult myself. I've even known you to be a tad difficult on occasion.'

Their eyes met, smiled, and looked away.

2

The launch skimmed across the harbour and out on to the sparkling sea. Veering right in a long sweep of foam, they headed down the coast to Altmeyer's yacht, the *Sally Jane*. Its gleaming white walls climbed from the sea like a castle in a fairy-tale, and its proud proprietor, dressed in a blue blazer and open-necked shirt, was at the rail to greet them.

'Bryn Hughes? Dr Wilde? I'm Max Altmeyer. Welcome aboard.'

Altmeyer had a pudgy, cherubic face and the suffering pink complexion of an Englishman on holiday. He pumped their hands and led them to a mahogany-panelled seating area sunk into the main deck beneath a white canvas awning. Cushioned benches let them see north into the dusty clutter of Cannes, or south across the dazzling ocean itself.

'Drinks? What can I get you? I'm on gin myself.'

Altmeyer waved a huge tumbler of gin and tonic at them.

'Thanks, no, just lemonade,' said Bryn, wondering if his host always did business on a float of forty per cent alcohol. Then, after Cameron had echoed his request and a steward had disappeared into the cool interior for the drinks, he added, 'Nice boat, this. Have you had her long?'

'The *Sally Jane*? She's the first yacht I've had that's outlasted my marriage. Usually, I get a wife, get a yacht, then, *pouf*. The wife goes and I have to sell the yacht to pay the wife. But I've improved my technique now.'

'Uh?' grunted Bryn, unwilling to show interest but not wanting to offend.

'You want to know what I do now? Evening before the

wedding, I send my lovely bride a gift. Something nice, car, diamond, whatever. Along with it I send a pre-nup. Divorce – bang – half a million quid, get out of my life. They can sign the agreement, or they can call up their mum and dad and all their friends and tell them the wedding's off. Tried it out with Sally Jane, wife number three, got the pre-nup back no problems, big thank you for the diamond. Two years later divorce – bang – here's your cheque, now sod off. And here's the yacht to prove me right.'

'So I see,' said Bryn.

The Berger Scholes notes had commented, 'Not sensitive to issues of gender/culture diversity. Likely to give offence to minority groups and women. Takes significant pride in financial and commercial achievements.' Bryn might have phrased it differently, but he didn't have to like Altmeyer, just his money.

'Right, right,' said the host. 'Now, what about you? Bryn, you have a business I'm pretty interested in. Immune Reprogramming, eh?'

'That's correct. We –'

'Love the name. Blind 'em with science, eh? Medicine without drugs. About as interesting as alcohol-free beer, but if people are dumb enough to pay for it . . . Right?'

'No, no. Not at all,' said Bryn. 'We totally believe in our medicine. As Professor Hass mentioned in his report –'

'Yeah, yeah, of course,' said Altmeyer. The steward had brought a bowl of salted pistachios with the drinks, and Altmeyer's hand was closed over the bowl, spooning the nuts into his mouth. 'Whatever. It's all in the set-up, right, Cameron love?'

'I'm sorry? The set-up?'

'Yeah. There was this dumb-ass German migraine product, stupid name, Keraplek. The thing was going nowhere. I arrive. Buy up the rights. Cost nothing. The product was shite and everyone knew it. Time for some science. Hired some scientists to run some tests. If I liked the results, I said I'd buy them each a top of the range Mercedes with the glove box stuffed with fifty-pound notes. Big glove compartments, too. You know, Bryn. Those E-class Mercs. Big sods. Anyway. Scientists trot off to their labs. Ran some tests. Totally independent, impartial science, blah blah. What d'you know? Pills were amazing. Best migraine product on the market. Outperform this, that, blah, blah, all the rest of it. Mercs all round, ladies. Then I get going. Salesmanship. If in doubt, make it up. Ad campaign. Freebies. Telesales. Boom. Product through the roof. Sales out of sight. Poor sods in Germany ringing up and asking for a cut of royalties. Piss off, Fritz. *Donner und blitzen*. No chance.'

Altmeyer stopped for applause. Bryn and Cameron stared open-mouthed, hardly able to believe their ears. Bryn was first to recover.

'Cameron, why don't you do your bit? Run through the science. We can have a look at the business plan numbers later.' Cameron had brought her laptop, and she swivelled the screen so Altmeyer could see it. She began to run through her lecture. The importance of the immune system. The role of peptides and Immune Reprogramming. Experience with rats. The clinic. The clinic's success rates. Hopes for the future. She said nothing about Corinth, nothing about Anita Morris, nothing about the HIV peptides they had patented by the skin of their teeth, and only thanks to Mungo's trickery.

It was a masterful lecture by one of the world's great scientists, but Altmeyer wasn't interested. He yawned frequently, gazed out to sea, went inside to fetch himself another tumbler of gin.

'Yes, yes,' he said, cutting in. 'Cameron, sweetheart,' he said, reaching out to pat her hand, 'I'm sure you're very brainy and I can see you're very pretty, but I want to talk business with Bryn here. Boring money stuff. Maybe you'd like to lie out on the sundeck and get yourself a tan, eh? No need for a bikini. The boat crew won't ogle you.' Altmeyer's mouth worked hard, eyes soliciting Bryn's applause as he spat out his punchline: 'They know they've got to leave that to me.'

Cameron gasped, momentarily at a loss for a reply violent enough. Bryn was faster, leaping out of his seat.

'Max, that's completely inappropriate and you know it. Do that again, and we're out of here.'

'OK, OK. It was a joke.' If Altmeyer was abashed, you wouldn't have guessed it from his face.

'Sit down,' said Cameron to Bryn. 'Get his money, then get out.'

Bryn sat back down, only half-pacified. He pulled management accounts from his case and passed them over.

Altmeyer seized the numbers and devoured them greedily. He was offensive, he was childish, and, given the way he was getting through gin, he ought to be drunk as well. But you don't make as many millions as Max Altmeyer had unless you've got something sliding around your brain pan, and Bryn could quickly tell that his eye for business was excellent.

With a brisk snapping fire, he directed questions at Bryn, the right ones, the ones Bryn would have asked if the roles had been reversed. They moved from a discussion about the clinic to the business plan for the research wing. The heat and the sun caused Bryn to feel muzzy, but he easily handled Altmeyer's interrogation. At Berger Scholes, Bryn had overseen transactions worth more than a hundred billion dollars. He'd been a heavy hitter in the biggest leagues of all, and there was no way he was going to let some pre-schooler spoil his game. After a couple of hours, Altmeyer pushed back the papers.

'These are only internal accounts, right? You've got nothing audited?'

'Correct. Naturally, you'll want audited accounts –'

'Using my auditors, not yours. Set a thief to catch a thief, eh?'

'Use whoever you want, but I –'

'Plus I'll need to inspect the building freehold, qualifications of medical personnel, ownership of intellectual property, an audit of patient records, tax returns, articles of association, and all other company documents.'

'Of course. Some of that material I have with me. For the rest, we'll need –'

'What's the price, Bryn? What are you asking?'

'I'm selling forty per cent of the company for twenty million pounds.'

'That's a lot for a company I don't control.'

'That's cheap for a stake in the future of medicine.'

Altmeyer paused, scrutinising Bryn through narrow eyes. 'Twenty mill is fine, but I'm going to need fifty-one per cent.'

'Get real, Max.'

Altmeyer's mouth stopped working briefly, its cargo of mashed-up pistachio pouched away in a cheek. His eyes were suddenly malevolent. If he was a child, he was the sort to cut legs off frogs and set fire to mice. Feeling woozy, Bryn ordered himself to remain in control. He shifted in his seat to get further into the shade and took another long drink to keep himself hydrated.

'I'll go up to twenty-five mill. Thirty. Forty. Double your money.'

'Forget it, Max. No chance.'

Altmeyer sucked his lip. Gobbets of greenish pistachio gunk adorned the corners of his mouth. 'I'd still need to have my people go over the business. Strip search, knickers down, fingers in the naughty bits.'

Altmeyer paused, his greedy little eyes roving, mouth busy with the pistachios he hadn't bothered to offer his guests. Bryn, on the other hand, sat like a statue, waiting. This was the moment of truth. The sun burned fiercely on to the awning above. A mild breeze barely stirred the papers on the table. Distant seagulls fought over invisible prizes. The world fell still.

Then Altmeyer stretched out his hand. 'It's a deal,' he said.

3

That was it for the day. Bryn could take no more. Altmeyer handed over a draft investment contract, and Bryn promised to review it overnight before returning to negotiate it the next day. As they stood on the gangway leading down to the launch, Altmeyer was suddenly struck by a thought.

'What about the clinic, Bryn? Cameron tells me the twenty mill's all going on research. Where does that leave the clinic itself, the patients?'

Bryn glanced at Cameron. It was a critical question. He was burning with impatience to expand the clinic. At present, they had patients travelling from Scotland, even America, just to see Rauschenberg and his team. Their market research had told them that there was strong demand for satellite clinics in Birmingham, Glasgow, Manchester – and even overseas, in Paris and Amsterdam, Frankfurt and New York. On the other hand, however profitable it might become, any expansion would need money to get it going. But it was Cameron's call.

She shook her head. 'I need every dime of that twenty million. The more I look at my research strategy, the more I figure I need.'

'You can have more. Fifty-one per cent is all I ask.'

'Forget it, Max.'

Altmeyer paused, clutching a document to his heart like a miser with his last gold coin. At last he relented, and unglued the document from his chest.

'Let's do both,' he said. 'Fund the research and build the clinic.'

'It's a nice idea, Max. I'd love to, but –'

'But nothing.' Altmeyer flipped the document over and handed it to Bryn, who looked at it, startled. 'This is a loan agreement. I'll lend you the money. Ten million quid. If you need more, I'll find it.'

4

In the launch going back to Cannes, Bryn and Cameron let the ocean breeze sweep over them, finding the air refreshing in the last heat of the afternoon.

'Another few hours with Max and I'd've been thumping him instead of negotiating.'

'Another few hours, and you'd have been too soused to thump him.'

'Soused? I didn't drink a drop. He was the one –'

'Drinking the gin-free gin and tonics, right. You were the one guzzling the spiked lemonade.'

'Bloody hell, I do feel muzzy. Little runt.' Bryn dipped his hands into the racing water and rinsed his face in the stinging brine. He remembered that Cameron hadn't touched her lemonade after the first few sips. 'Thanks for warning me.'

She shrugged. 'I assumed you knew. Jerk like Altmeyer, what do you expect?' She paused as the launch rocked heavily over a particularly full swell, before its motion evened out once again. 'You did fine, anyway . . . Strange though, him offering to lend us money. It almost looked generous, and he didn't strike me as the generous type.'

Bryn shook his head. 'It surprised me, till I took a peek at his interest rate. Four per cent over base. It's criminal, really, but we'll probably take it.'

Back at the hotel, they showered and regrouped, sitting out in a little courtyard at the back of the hotel on rickety white metal chairs which screeched every time they scraped across the cobbles. In the centre of the stone yard, a couple of aged orange trees struggled to grow upright, while somewhere in the rooms above an argument between a couple of hundred-and-fifty-year-old neighbours ricocheted around the old walls. But it was a golden evening, and they were in the mood to relax. They agreed to work for a couple of hours – Bryn on the two agreements, Cameron on her new twenty million pound research plan – before breaking for dinner. Two hours stretched to three, then three to three and a half, but eventually, at around nine in the evening, Bryn was finished.

'Done,' he announced, throwing down his pencil.

'Lucky you.'

'I'm famished.'

'Uh, they do sandwiches at the bar,' said Cameron vaguely, still wrapped up in her research plans. 'How were the contracts?'

'Which one? The investment contract was professional, well-drafted, totally one-sided.'

'Is that a problem?'

'I'm making three lists of comments. There are my got-to-haves, my like-to-haves, and my pretend-to-wants. I'll make sure I get everything from the first list and as much as I can from the second. Stuff on the third list, I'll scream about, but concede. That way he thinks he's getting the better of me.'

272

Cameron shook her head. 'Children, honestly,' she muttered. 'How about the loan?'

'Strange. It's a pretty standard loan contract. The interest rate is ridiculous, but the rest of it . . . Well, it's pretty loose. From our point of view, it's a good contract.'

Cameron nodded. 'That's kind of odd, isn't it?' she said, flipping through the agreement. 'He may be a jerk, but he strikes me as a thorough one . . . What's this all about, then? "Suspension of business"? I don't like the sound of that.'

Bryn glanced back at the agreement, where Cameron's pencil wavered over one of the black printed paragraphs. 'Suspension of business', it said. 'Lender is permitted to call the Loan due for Repayment or Conversion if the operations of the Business are suspended or under investigation for possible suspension by any governmental or regulatory authority who is empowered so to act.'

'It's true,' he said. 'It looked totally weird, until I realised. He's most likely given us an old loan agreement, picked off the word processor. My guess is he used this agreement with a pharma company once. And since pharma companies need a licence to manufacture, you have to have a clause like this to protect you We don't need any kind of licence, so the clause is pretty much meaningless in our case.'

'So we ought to delete the clause?'

Bryn pursed his lips and shook his head. 'Not really. The point is, this agreement is actually favourable to us. The less we look at it the better, in case he has second thoughts . . .' He hesitated. He didn't like pointless clauses wandering round an agreement. It was unworkmanlike, unprofessional, unsightly. But his mind was made up. One stupid clause in exchange for a favourable agreement? No contest. 'Yes, that's what we'll do. We'll complain like hell about the interest rate, then sign. Leave him thinking he's God's gift.'

Cameron paused a moment longer. She didn't like it,

and she sensed Bryn didn't either. Her pencil continued to hover over the clause – then moved away. She tossed the contract back on to the table.

'*Coquilles St Jacques* to start with, I think,' said Bryn, scraping his chair back across the cobbles. 'And somewhere in Cannes there's a lobster with my name on it.'

'You're going out?'

'Nope,' said Bryn, deftly tucking his thumbs under her arms and rocketing her upwards. 'We are.'

5

Except for one thing, the evening was a delight. They found a waterfront restaurant, with big plate-glass doors wide open to let in the cool evening air, and that happiest of signs, a Michelin star, which guaranteed them food of exceptional quality. Bryn succeeded in his campaign to persuade Cameron to share the two-person *assiette des fruits de mer* as a starter.

'*Fruits de mer*? The French think shellfish are fruits? They can't be up to much as zoologists,' said Cameron, up to the elbow in brine, lemon juice, and the assorted oozings of a dozen different sorts of sea creature.

'Not up to anything much,' agreed Bryn. 'Except in the kitchen where they belong. I don't think we'll manage with one measly bottle of wine, though.' He signalled to the waiter for another bottle.

Wine came, the meal went. One lobster died a grisly death, but not in vain, as two people covered themselves with hollandaise sauce and ended up with chins dripping and eyes sparkling.

'So tell me about your man,' he said, switching topics. 'The mysterious Allen Green.'

'Allen? He's a good guy. We're getting on well. I'm

274

thinking of moving in with him. Properly, that is. I mostly already have.'

'You have? You are?' Bryn was momentarily taken aback, then annoyed, then simply glad for her. A happy research director made for a prosperous business. He should be pleased. He was pleased. Certainly he was. 'So. What d'you see in each other, then? Don't tell me, he loves you for your tidiness and ability to keep house.'

Cameron laughed. 'Yeah, right. I caused so much mess, he had to sign over the spare room to me.'

'He's a scientist, you say? So you discuss blood cells with your cornflakes, and viruses with your Ovaltine?'

'Yes, absolutely,' said Cameron without conviction. 'It's great.'

'He's in research, like you? An immunologist?'

Cameron fell silent, a lobster claw motionless in her fist. She realised that Bryn knew virtually nothing about Allen. 'No. He trained in respiratory, but he's been working in chemotherapy these past few years. His immunology is probably worse than yours.'

'I hope not.'

'But he's hoping to get back into respiratory.'

'Great.'

'He's been applying around for jobs.'

'Good for him.'

'Maybe he'll end up working for Corinth.' There was a pause wider and deeper than the ocean outside. 'Corinth Respiratory. Headquartered on the Marylebone Road.'

Bryn had given up on the little fish forks and mallets for getting meat from the lobster. He had a full half-shell in one hand and had been ripping flesh out with the other. He put the shell down, rinsed his hands in his finger bowl and wiped then carefully on his napkin, first his left and then his right. He took a sip of wine, poured some more, refilled Cameron's glass, and set the bottle back in its ice-bucket.

'He's going to go and work for Corinth,' he said. His voice was quiet and calm, like the ocean on a still blue day.

'Right. Corinth Respiratory.'

Bryn picked up the bowl of hollandaise and put another dollop on his plate.

'The lobster is good,' he said.

'Uh-huh. Great.'

'More hollandaise?'

'I'm fine.'

'I believe you said he's intending to work for Corinth.' Still calm. Still quiet. Still ever so pleasant. Any wind on the sea was just enough to ruffle the water, make it look frilly and fun.

'Right.'

Bryn took another drink of wine. 'Now, correct me if I'm wrong,' he said, settling the glass back on to the tablecloth and still sounding pleasant if not maybe quite so relaxed, 'but isn't Corinth trying to destroy our company and steal our research?'

'Brent Huizinga might be. Allen Green isn't.'

'Forgive me if I'm in error,' said Bryn, in a voice which was growing louder and distinctly less pleasant with every word, 'but aren't there approximately one million males of marriageable age in London, and you had to go and pick someone who's about to start working for Corinth?'

'I'll go out with who I damn well please.'

'So I can bloody well see. I can't believe –'

' – *I* can't believe –'

' – that you'd choose to share your life and work –'

' – that you'd have the nerve –'

' – with someone whose primary loyalty is to bloody Corinth!'

' – to tell me who the hell I see! And Allen's loyalty is to me, and not to Corinth, and not to Huizinga, and not to anyone who wishes me harm.'

Bryn's voice had risen to a thunderous pitch, rolling round the walls of the restaurant and out on to the street like the ocean running before a gale, grey and violent. It boomed like artillery fire. Diners fell silent. Passers-by on the street outside stopped and stared. Waiters stood stock-still and open-mouthed. Cameron, too, did her share. Her voice lacked the resounding force of Bryn's wide-chested roar, but what she lacked in volume she made up for in passion, and they were evenly matched, indifferent to the watching world.

And that was that.

Cameron stormed out. Bryn ripped his lobster into tiny fragments, then did the same with whatever was left of hers. He ordered another bottle of wine, followed by coffee, brandy, more coffee and more brandy. He went to bed drunk, angry, and confused.

TWENTY-TWO

1

The next day dawned hotter and fiercer than the one before, though a weather forecast in the hotel lobby warned of more unsettled weather coming in later.

'Sorry for jumping down your throat last night,' said Bryn. 'I overdid it.'

'Overdid it? I've met quieter volcanoes.'

'You go out with whoever the hell you want.'

'I will.'

'But, all the same, I do think that –'

'That's OK. I've been thinking about it. I think you're right. Allen did put in a job application, but I think I'm going to have to ask him to withdraw it. I can't see that it'd be a problem but I don't want to chance it.'

Bryn nodded. 'Good. I'm happy to hear it.'

Friends again, they had time for an excellent breakfast of coffee and croissants, before the launch was due at nine. The day had started well.

2

'Bryn! How did the fleshpots of Cannes suit your taste? I should have shown you round. *Spanking* good fun, I assure you. And Cameron, my dear, even lovelier than yesterday. The sun deck still very free. Anytime you like, my love, just say the word.'

'Go to hell,' said Cameron pleasantly. After getting the measure of Altmeyer yesterday, she had taken care to dress down today: casual denims and a crisp white shirt that revealed nothing.

'Careful, Max,' said Bryn. 'Let's just negotiate, shall we?'

'Certainly, certainly.'

They sat down, as before, under the gleaming white awnings in the seating area sunk into the deck. It was already warm, and in the absence of any breeze the heat would ratchet up to intolerable levels before too long. There was a jug of ice-cold, freshly squeezed lemonade on the table in front of them, which Bryn smelled carefully before tossing overboard.

'Not funny. Water this time, no alcohol, thanks very much.'

If Altmeyer was embarrassed at being found out, you'd never have guessed it. 'You enjoyed my little joke?' he tittered.

'Idiot.'

Altmeyer called a steward, who supplied two glasses and a tiny little jug of water, mostly full of ice. Bryn poured the water out for Cameron.

'Let's get going.'

They began to negotiate – a nightmare. Normally, negotiations proceed because there is some mutual recognition of what is fair or, failing that, of where the balance of power lies. Both sides have a reasonable idea of where things ought to settle and the process of negotiation is to make sure that the balance is as optimal as possible, the compromises neatly worked through. Altmeyer would have none of that. Every issue was a wrestling match. Altmeyer didn't argue, he just resisted. Bryn attempted intelligent negotiation, he attempted flattery, he attempted threats. In the end, all that was left was attrition: cannon fire trained on a massive stone rampart, chipping bits off, time after time after time. Bryn mostly swung the punches, then, when his mouth dried up with thirst and irritation, Cameron stepped in to continue the barrage, using her flashing incisive mind to win concessions that had so far eluded Bryn's constant battery. The hot day drew on as the cannon fire continued to boom, and point after point was wrested from Altmeyer's grip.

Meantime, the air changed, and a heavy ocean swell warned of a change in weather to windward. Cameron's gaze turned inward, and her stomach began to mutter rebellion. Bryn resolutely continued his campaign until he'd obtained all of what he needed and most of what he wanted. Only the loan agreement remained unchanged, Altmeyer tittering over the high interest rate but refusing to drop it even an inch.

Eventually – hot, thirsty, and angry – Bryn was done.

'OK,' he said. 'Bugger it. Let's go. Both contracts. Type and sign.'

Altmeyer rocked to and fro in his seat, hugging himself. He looked like a smug little brat, the sort to give smacking a good name. 'Type and sign, *partner*,' he said. 'From this day on, we're partners, remember.'

Bryn muttered something under his breath, and supervised Altmeyer as he instructed a secretary on correcting the two agreements. Now that the purpose of starving his guests was completed, Altmeyer proved a suddenly generous host with a table spread with oysters and champagne, brown bread and butter.

'Cameron, my dear, nothing gets you in the mood quite like oysters, eh?'

'Leave it,' growled Bryn.

Whether or not the idea of eating oysters with Max Altmeyer was her idea of fun, Cameron took one look at the food and ran. Her seasickness was mounting by the minute, and Bryn was desperate to get the contracts signed so they could get out of there. As the secretary worked, Altmeyer was like a four-year-old wanting Bryn to admire his yacht: the mahogany panelled stateroom with its black leather sofas, the bathroom and its taps plated in real gold, the bedroom with a ceiling painted with naked angels, the radio room, the engine room . . .

'What d'you think, Bryn?'

'Vulgar as a horse's arse, Max. I'm going back to check the documents.'

Altmeyer sprang after him, chortling.

'*Race*horse's arse, you mean, *race*horse's arse. It's very expensive.'

They passed through the dining room (gold statuettes in each corner holding lamps, naked bodies with tits out of *Baywatch*). Cameron sipped a glass of water, holding her eyes away from the food and looking awful.

'Not long now, Cameron. I appreciate this.'

She lifted her eyes miserably as they passed. They arrived to find the last of the documents spilling out of the printer. Bryn took each page as it came, proof-reading carefully, spotting and correcting a small handful of typos. The new pages were run off. At one point, Altmeyer rudely pushed his secretary from the keyboard and made some adjustments himself. The new page ran off with fifty-one per cent of the shares printed where forty per cent should have been.

'Don't be a jerk.'

'Give me fifty-one per cent and I'll throw in the yacht for free.'

'Give me this pimp's palace and you get thirty per cent.'

Altmeyer roared with laughter, pounding Bryn on the back. Bryn waved the secretary back to her post and instructed her to reverse the change. Eventually, they got there. 'OK. This looks OK.'

Altmeyer tittered. 'We'll sign, then, shall we?' He produced a pen, rolled-gold, Swiss-made, laughing at Bryn's disposable biro. 'Racehorse's arse, Bryn, not donkey's arse.'

Two copies of each contract came off the printer. Bryn signed the back page of each, checking that Altmeyer did the same, then initialled every page in turn.

'Initialling pages, Bryn? You don't trust me?'

'Not an inch.'

Altmeyer initialled in the spaces after Bryn. His handwriting was childish and vain at the same time, combining look-at-me-flourishes with schoolboy care over his letter formation. At last they were done. 'Investment agreement, loan agreement,' said Bryn, helping himself to one of each. 'You can get going on the due diligence right away. Money in ten days.'

When they came out on deck, it was night. The coastal hills were lit up by strings of fairy-lights, while to the south only the lights of big ships passing lightened the black edges of the sea. Bryn had hoped that open air would help Cameron's stomach, but the opposite was true. The sight of a fixed horizon exacerbated the plunging sensation and the first dry retch came to her lips.

'Cameron, my dear, perhaps you'd better stay the night. Bryn's seen the bedroom. I'm sure it'll be to your taste.'

Enough was enough.

Bryn grabbed Altmeyer by the top of his shirt and threw

him against the rail, bending him back over the voracious sea, further, much further, than could be explained by a joke. Beneath Altmeyer's pale face, the black waves foamed strong and insatiable. The slapping of water against the hull sounded like a giant mouth preparing to feed.

'One more crack like that, you little fool, and I'm shoving you overboard!'

'Bryn, honestly, Bryn. Can't you take a joke?'

Altmeyer's words belied his face, which whitened against the darkness below. Bryn pulled him out another couple of inches over the rail, holding him there longer than he needed to, not as long as he wanted to. Now that the contract was signed, Altmeyer couldn't withhold the money, however much he might want to. Bryn lowered his hand, moving his victim another inch or two towards the sea.

'Bryn!' said Cameron weakly. 'For God's sake.'

Bryn pulled Altmeyer slowly back to the safe side of the rail and released his grip.

The journey back into Cannes went slowly. For some reason, the smaller boat was easier than the larger one, and though Cameron was still ill, her discomfort didn't tip over into full-scale seasickness. The night air was cool and the wind mixing with spray from the bows picked at her cotton shirt and whipped the hair back from her face. Bryn put his jacket round Cameron and sat with his arm around her, quiet and companionable. Her body was warm beneath his touch, surprisingly slender and feminine. He suddenly felt acutely fond of her.

As they entered the harbour, Cameron's incipient nausea dropped away like a cloak, and she moved away from his arms. The air smelled good. Restaurant lights twinkled in promise of good things. And in their hands were a pair of contracts, promising money, promising peace.

3

That night, Bryn was racked by an odd feeling. It should have been elation at securing the clinic's future, but this was the opposite: a kind of vomity dread, a dreadful foreboding of failure. Bryn sat alone, drinking the muck which passes for beer in France. In the corner of the bar, a gaggle of tourists sheltered from the rain. What was it, this feeling?

He reviewed the day. Breakfast with Cameron had been a pleasure. There had followed the ride out to Altmeyer's yacht, the long trawl through the documents, the agonising negotiation. The only brightness there had been the joy of hearing Cameron's incisive interventions, cutting straight through Altmeyer's bullshit, destroying his opposition. What a woman! Then the oysters and bread, the secretary labouring to put the contract changes through, Altmeyer's antics, the boat ride back. Bryn remembered Altmeyer's white face, Cameron's seasickness, her body tense but grateful beneath his hands. What was so awful that his stomach clenched and his heart felt weak?

It had been a good day, a successful day, a day when he'd really enjoyed being with Cameron, and ... But his train of thought lurched abruptly to a halt. Cameron, by God, it was something to do with Cameron. His stomach actually lurched at the thought of her. The feeling of dread doubled in intensity. But why? Why this feeling of horror? On the whole, they got on so well these days, he admired her, liked her, he believed she liked him too ... And then in the launch coming back tonight, with her body nestling into his, her hair damp beneath his cheek, it had reminded him of the very earliest days with Cecily, back in the days when they were still in love.

The word brought him up short. In *love*. Not with Cecily,

with Cameron. He was in love with Cameron, head over heels; truly, madly, deeply.

The sick foreboding fell away with a thump, and in its place came a cold horror, the appalled recognition of calamity. He loved her. He loved her beauty and her strength. He loved her fire, the white heat of her passion, her strong, true heart.

Just a few yards away, in a room above his head, she was asleep. There had been a time when a tap at her door would have been everything necessary to bring them together. One tiny tap. But he'd fluffed it, had his chance and blown it. She was another man's now, happy with him, about to move in with him.

Leaving his beer and the gaggle of tourists, he burst out on to the harbour front. Winds from the west brought angry squalls of rain. He opened himself to the elements, soaking himself, caring for nothing. He loved her and had lost her, loved and lost. Stumbling out on to the beach, he waded into the midnight sea, knee high, waist high, shoulder high, burning with love.

TWENTY-THREE

1

Time passed.

Summer faded into autumn. Trees dropped their leaves. On the King's Road, shop windows emptied of sexy little cotton numbers and began to fill with fake furs, leather boots, cashmere scarves. On the river, the first sharp winds sliced upstream, eddying round the barge and boathouse, making people hurry to get back inside. Late autumn became early winter.

Money poured into the twin companies like a flood after drought. Bryn acquired the dingy offices in the wharf next to the boathouse, and Cameron quickly filled them with research staff, computers and lab equipment costing half a million dollars a throw.

Meanwhile the clinic raced ahead. Altmeyer used his organisation to run property searches and found leases in Glasgow, Manchester, Birmingham and Paris. The leases were big, expensive ones for major city centre properties, but Bryn was happy to commit. He wanted to expand the clinic fast and far. The Fulham Clinic was already one of the world's leading centres for the treatment of viral disease, but the satellite clinics would promote the brand ever more widely. In pursuit of Bryn's aggressive business plan,

Rauschenberg stepped down as London medical director and began to spend his whole time in the other cities, getting the new centres off the ground.

And yet despite the huge surge of acceleration provided by Altmeyer's money, Corinth remained powerful contenders. On some counts, Cameron was ahead; on other counts it was Corinth. Bryn had completed the patent application for the HIV-related peptide sequence in record time and slammed it into the Patent Office, beating Corinth by just fourteen hours.

Since then, on two minor viral diseases, Corinth had submitted a patent application well ahead of the clinic. On one other disease, the clinic had beaten Corinth, again by a matter of days, and again only thanks to their ability to intercept enemy communications. Meantime, all the indications remained that Huizinga was as committed as ever to winning the race at all costs.

'It makes sense,' said Bryn. 'With his latest slew of acquisitions, Huizinga is getting into a position of more or less unchallenged dominance of the really heavy duty drug market. Everyone else is going all kinder-gentler, except Corinth. For all those doctors who want a pill which will kill either the disease or the patient, Corinth is the only place to shop. And meanwhile they're inching prices up and up, making a bloody killing in doing so.'

'Bloody killing is right,' said Cameron. 'You know, you always sound like you admire him, but in the end Huizinga is just killing people for money.'

Bryn shrugged. In a way he *did* admire Huizinga – as a banker it was difficult not to – but that wasn't an argument he wanted to have. 'All I'm saying is that an effective immune-supportive technology is a knockout blow. It could cost Corinth a hundred billion dollars. Of course they're going to chuck money at this problem. They'd be crazy not to.'

'Crazy. Uh-huh. Or ethical. Or caring. It is just possible they might believe it was more important to save lives than make money.'

Bryn laughed incredulously and shook his head. What would happen to the arms companies if they got all dainty about who bought their bombs? What would happen to the drugs companies if they put their patients' interests over the need for profit?

Cameron had always worked hard, but her hours grew longer, her intensity greater. She had moved in with Allen Green, and, when her duties were over at the office, she rushed back to be with him or to get on with her work in peace and quiet. At Cameron's passionate request, he had withdrawn his job application to Corinth, only to receive a very warm lunch invitation from some of the senior guys at Corinth Respiratory. Over lunch, he was told that they'd been thinking of headhunting Allen anyway. Anytime he changed his mind about working for them, he should give them a call first thing. Allen never told Cameron about the lunch. Why should he? It would only double her paranoia.

Kati, too, worked harder and became ever more involved with Thierry Doo-dah, while Bryn's life became increasingly hard-working and lonely. He missed Cameron with a passion, sometimes feeling quite literally dizzy with the sense of loss.

He did what he could to continue with a sort of life. He worked hard during the week, and at weekends he headed down to the farm, helped his dad out on the land, got shit-faced at the pub with Dai, and watched his father sinking further into a foggy, lethargic stupor. Cameron's box of pills lay unopened on a kitchen shelf, after Mervyn had stubbornly refused to let a single one enter his mouth. He was growing listless, giving up, surrendering.

2

'Have you noticed,' said Meg to Janine, 'how our Mungo pops out every Thursday lunchtime and comes back looking like the cat sicked him up?'

'Can't say I have.'

'Every Thursday – I've been watching him for weeks.'

Janine shrugged. 'It's a free country.'

'He's weird,' said Meg. 'What do you think, Tallulah?'

Beside the reception desk, Tallulah scratched at her perch. A pampered bird, she had become fat and flew only when she had to. 'O-shi,' she said, '*uddy ell, matey.*'

'Good parrot,' said Meg, absent-mindedly. 'You know what? I'm going to follow him.' And she did.

3

Cyberspace is a place where the sun don't shine, and Mungo was paler than the moon. All the same, perhaps Meg was right and today he was paler still. He hurried up the back streets towards Hammersmith, gigantic trainers squelching and huge trousers ballooning and flapping around him, Meg following fifty yards behind.

Reaching the Fulham Palace Road, he crossed through a gap in the traffic and continued along the far pavement. He passed a short row of shops, then stopped at the last one, a travel agent, and entered through a graffiti-spattered grey side-door leading upstairs.

'Gotcha,' said Meg to herself.

For a moment, she wondered whether to follow her quarry up the stairs, but, thinking better of it, went into the travel agent and asked an incredibly complicated question about flight connections between New Orleans and Manchester International. The baffled clerk invited her to take a seat, and Meg sat, wishing she'd bought a sandwich, but with a clear view out on to the street. Half an hour passed.

Then: 'I think we've got something,' said the travel agent. 'It was economy you wanted?'

'Economy?' said Meg. 'With my mother's hip?' But Mungo had emerged from his lair and was standing chalk-faced in the street. 'Actually, hang on, I need to go.'

'I've got an itinerary . . .'

But Meg was gone, out on to the street, catching Mungo in a couple of steps.

'Well, well, well, fancy meeting you here!'

Mungo whirled round unsteadily, and had to catch at the aerosol-adorned doorway for support. 'Wow, right, Meg.' He attempted a half-hearted grin, though his cheek muscles barely twitched.

'I've watched you, you know. Going up them stairs. You want to tell me what's going on?'

'Going on? Man! What . . . ? Nothing.'

'You been seeing your dealer? Getting kippered? I don't care what you do at the weekend, matey, but you better not –'

'No, 's nuffin' like that.' Mungo almost laughed in relief, but his voice was high and brittle. 'My dealer? Yeah, if only.'

'Well, either you're telling me, or I'm going up to find out. And either way Bryn's going to know all about it.'

'No. You don't want to know. Straight-up, it's . . .' But even as he spoke, his protest faded and something approaching resolution made its way into his face. 'Wish I was kippered. Look, come in here.'

He pulled her impulsively through a door to their left: the Oak Tree Café, a greasy spoon. Mungo tumbled into the first empty seat, plastic chairs, formica-topped tables, vinegar and ketchup bottles, a bunch of workmen and a ruined-looking pensioner the only customers. A waitress, perm half grown out and a hair-dye job you could sue over, approached listlessly.

'Two teas,' said Meg. 'And I'd kill for a bacon sarny.'

'Him?' asked the waitress, not even bothering to address Mungo directly.

'Nothing else, thanks, just that.'

Mungo sat impatiently. The teas came, the sandwich came, Meg added sugar to one and brown sauce to the other, and stuck Mungo's mug where he could reach it.

'OK then, shoot.'

He stared at her. 'I'm stuffed,' he said, 'whanged, noodled, walloped, cracked.'

'You're well busted, matey.'

'I'm a waster. I should of just gone.'

The way he said 'gone', you couldn't quite be sure if he was talking about leaving or dying. For the first time since trapping him, Meg felt a brief wave of compassion. His submission was so total, he was like a seal pup: you could either club him to death or feel sorry for him.

'Go on,' she said, her voice still tight, trying to hold fast to the clubbing option.

He began to talk.

It was all true. Ages back, right at the start of the clinic, he'd been approached by 'the Darth Vader, Meg, like a cyberman, only with this unreal face, really gnarly – scary, you know – it literally doesn't move, like it's plastic or something.' This character, called Janssen apparently, had forced Mungo to apply for the job with Bryn.

'Like *made* me, man, only not that I cared, I mean, right, I'm not a loafer.'

'He made you? How?'

'That's the shit bit. Jesus, if I tell you, he . . .' Mungo attempted to swig his tea, he burned his tongue and upset the mug in putting it down. 'Oh, shite, shite. I need to get mashed.'

'Not until you tell me.'

'Meg . . . It's my sisters. I mean, this guy, freako, knew about my spliffs and my E and stuff, but I didn't care about that. I mean, he was just another stiff, y'know, world's full of 'em. But he knew stuff about JoJo, said he'd get her nicked. Even if he didn't, it'd be back to care. And Dar. She's only twelve. They'd've been split up, and, Christ, she needs JoJo. I mean they're, like, *sisters*. Well, I mean, they *are* sisters. They're like –'

Words failed him. Meg put her hand on his arm, the clubbing option temporarily ruled out.

'You're close. You were trying to protect them. I understand.' Tears squeezed from Mungo's eyes, and he batted them away with a grubby hand. 'That's not the worst. The worst is he always wanted to know stuff about the company. Lil' stuff, mostly. Who worked there, what Cameron was working on, was she up or down, y'know. How was the wonga. Where was it comin' from.'

'And you told him?' Meg removed her hand, and her voice had tautened once again. She knew perfectly well that Bryn was worried about an internal security leak, and she burned inside with anger – as well as a kind of excitement. *The mole.* She'd caught the mole.

'Yeah, only no, if you get me. I had to tell him some stuff, obviously. Mostly I kind of mixed things up, so he wouldn't know what was what. But I couldn't totally keep him off. I mean, JoJo, she's a good girl, really, but she takes stuff. I tell her to only take stuff from the big shops, y'know. I mean they nick from us, right? Like them big bags of chocolate peanuts for two quid. Rip-off city, if you ask me.' He shrugged. 'But, JoJo, she's not the type to nick from one of them corner shops, but to be perfectly honest with you, if I was some robo-suit patrolling my esteemed Pik-n-Mix confection'ry selection, I wouldn't want JoJo in a hundred miles. Freako knows this. I dunno how, but he does. So I did tell him stuff. Stuff I wish I hadn't.'

'What did you tell him?'

'Second worst thing I said was about banks. He kept wanting to know which banks Bryn was going to. Couldn't see the harm in saying. I mean, I couldn't see how freako could do anything about it. What was he gonna do? Walk in to Lloyds Bank – pardon me, Lloyds *Tee Yess-Beeee* – and say one false move and your black horse thingy gets it. I thought he just wanted to know what was shaking, but –' Mungo shook his head. He was desperately worried, and all his wittering couldn't conceal the fact that his face was drawn and white, his hand shaking.

'You bloody well stitched us up!' cried Meg. 'We were that close to not getting the money 'cos of you.' Her lips were thin and pale beneath her lipstick. Blood spots burned angrily, high up, on her cheeks. If Mungo was a seal pup, he'd have done well to prepare himself for the club.

'I know, I know. But that wasn't the worst. Worst was a real blooper. I was off my chump after a heavy weekend. Boasted that he could stick his banks up his ol' rectal ejection chute. He was, like, what, what, what? Gave me a bad time, like I mean, a *real* bad time. Hitting, slapping, shouting.' Mungo swallowed. 'I mean my dad was bad, but at least he wasn't around much. This was the Death Star, man, the prison planet. And all that stuff he said about JoJo, an' what they'd do to Dar … So I told him about the zillionaire database we'd ripped off from Berger Scholes. How Bryn was going to have enough wonga to swim in. He went ape-shit. Two days later that article came out, in the *Herald*, you know. And Janssen was all like, he'll give Bryn a bleedin' millionaire. I was going to tell you guys, but then Hassie

293

Baby goes on the telly, Bryn is all smiles, an' old Max Moneybags phones up with a sackload of moolah. So I reckoned everything's sorted. And, t'be honest, I was too scared. I mean freako would murder me, if I told.' He paused. 'Which I have now. Obviously.'

There was a long pause. There was no one else in the café. From behind the counter, the greasy-haired waitress let out a long hiss of steam from the coffee machine. It sounded like a whistle of the damned. Mungo stared down at his hands and hated himself. Meg breathed in and out, short sharp breaths drawn through her open mouth. She was angry, alarmed, and – somewhere – terribly sorry for the poor kid opposite her who'd been put under such odious pressure.

'You're coming back with me, Mungo m'boy,' she said. 'Straight in to Bryn, and tell him everything you've just told me. Or I'll tell him.'

Mungo looked up. 'I'll tell him,' he said hollowly. 'Introducing Mungo, the ferret in your PJs.'

'Now.'

Meg dropped some coins on the formica and got up to go. The waitress hurried over suspiciously, waving a bill scribbled out on a bit of war-quality paper. The waitress's look of distrust didn't vanish on seeing the coins, she just scooped them up and examined them as though they were certain to be phoneys or foreign. Under her breath, Meg muttered something about hairstyles.

'Wait.'

Mungo snatched Meg's arms and clamped her back into her seat. Through her thin Lycra top, she could feel the sudden energy of his grip.

'Get off me,' she said. 'I'll tell him if you won't.'

'No, wait.' Mungo let go his hold. 'Look . . . there's something we can do. I mean, if you dare. Get our own back, sort of thing. To be honest, I've been praying someone would catch me. Knew it'd be you, actually. Bit of a snooper, I reckon.'

Mungo poured sugar into his tea, stirred it and slurped. His hand was shaking. He was scared.

'What is it?' said Meg.

'OK. Plan is I go an' get Janssen. Get him out of his hole, for maybe an hour. While he's out, you get in. Should be easy. There's one of them metal fire thingies out the back. Escape, y'know, fire escape. Weird, when you think about it. Like why would a fire need to escape? *Help me, help me, I'm a fire.*' Mungo flung his arms into the air, squawking. It was almost as though the closer he drew to the centre of his terror, the more he felt obliged to cover it in a cloak of babble. 'Don't think so. Anyway. His window backs right on to it, second floor. He never locks it. I mean, there's crap all to steal, unless you know what he's up to, and if you do . . . Shite, Meg, promise me you'll be out of there in an hour. He's a psycho.' Mungo thought about it, and with hands still shaking began to make himself a cigarette, at least part of which contained tobacco. 'Moroccan black. Been saving it. Last cigarettesville.' He sewed together the Rizla paper with a thread of spit, and began to arrange leaves and resin in a line down the middle. 'You think they used to spliff up in them war movies, like before the firing squad? All the music's going da-ra-ra-ra, sad an' stuff, and all the David Niven types are twiddling their moustaches and saying, "Just tell Bess I love her," and looking all top-hole-old-bean, but all the time they're thinking, hey, man, take it easy, wow, love those rifles, for real.' Mungo finished his spliff and waved it around, David Niven on dope.

Meg burst his bubble. 'When I get in there, what should I take?'

Mungo came sharply back to earth, fear once again

emptying out expression from his face. 'He's got a filing cabinet. Keys in the desk drawer . . . Oh, shite, Meg.'

Faced with the hideous reality of what he was about to do, Mungo's nerve began to fail again, but it was too late for second thoughts. Meg was motoring.

'Fire escape. Second-floor window. Keys in the desk drawer. Got it.'

Mungo swallowed. He knew what Janssen was like, and he was terrified. Meg knew nothing, and was desperate for adventure. Mungo tried to make her safe.

'And you got an hour, right? Like, an hour max. And don't take anything, just copy it. There's a copier right there. And, Meg, please, for God's sake, don't what's-it-called, don't linger. In and out. OK?'

Experience spoke to innocence and innocence nodded her head. Experience always spoke like that. Experience was a fool. Meg finished her tea.

'Let's rock.'

4

Over the Brecon Beacons, a long-threatened November storm broke in curtains of rain and the bellow of thunder. Lightning crackled over the mountain tops and Rhys, in his kennel, barked his disapproval. Up at the Quarry End, the sheep would be huddled into the shelter that Mervyn Hughes had built for them, frightened but safe. Once, he'd have gone up there to check. There wouldn't likely be any problems, but you could never be sure. Mountain streams filled so fast that an animal which was drinking one moment could be half-drowned the next. Gwyneth stood in the hall, looking into the living room where the telly flickered.

'You'll be needing your long coat if you go out now. I've put it out for you.'

'That's alright. Sheep'll be fine. No use going out in this.'

'Are you feeling OK?'

'Honestly, woman! It's not long since you'd have been telling me not to go out. There's no pleasing you.'

She came to sit on the arm of his chair, hand on his shoulder, worrying. Her husband was listless, brain-fogged. The TV programme, whatever it was, paused and the ads came on. There was a McDonald's ad, which constructed some hard-to-fathom connection between skimpily dressed women on a beach and McDonald's milkshakes. Mervyn watched the thick liquid snaking its way into a waxed paper cup.

'By God,' he said, 'that doesn't look too bad now, does it?'

The ad changed. Cosmetics, cars, washing powder, shampoo. In the world outside, rain beat down on the stone courtyard, the mountains above lost in cloud. Inside, in the bright and happy world of daytime TV, the programme restarted. Gwyneth squeezed her husband's shoulder and walked back through into the kitchen. Fifteen minutes later she returned holding a beer glass filled with viscous pink liquid.

'No straws, I'm afraid, sorry.'

'What's this, then?'

'Strawberry milkshake, strawberry jam milkshake, anyway. I think it's alright.'

She set it down like a grand cru vintage before a wine expert. Mervyn Hughes sipped it, swigged it, drained the glass.

'Not bad, at that. What's come over you, then, giving me milkshakes?'

She shrugged. 'You said you liked them.' She walked back into the kitchen, wiped up. Jam back in the cupboard. Milk in the fridge. Mental note to get more ice cream. Pills.

Cameron's note had included complex instructions on dosage, times of day, whether to take them with food or away from food. Gwyneth couldn't be doing with that. She threw the note away. She'd given Mervyn two of everything, capsules emptied out into the creamy pink gunge. If he stayed keen on milkshakes, he'd have two more of everything the next day. And the next and the next and the next, until the pills were finished. She put the pills back into the cupboard and washed the glass. She liked a tidy kitchen, did Gwyneth Hughes.

5

'Bryn, m'darling, tell me I'm a genius.'

'You're a genius, Meg. What's it this time?'

'Evidence.' She dropped a huge cardboard box loaded with papers on to the floor. 'Tons of it. My arms are killing me.'

She began to rub her arms, but her face was sparkling with joy and excitement. Bryn picked a sheet of paper from the top of the stack: a memo from someone he didn't know to someone he didn't know concerning a company he'd never heard of.

'This is just great, Meg.'

'No, go on, get stuck in.'

Kneeling on the floor, they began to unpack the box. Most of it concerned other companies or other individuals, but as Bryn began to read, a theme became evident. Every company or individual had a product which directly rivalled one of Corinth's. Though there was no direct mention of Corinth's response, there were newspaper cuttings mentioning mysterious fires, rogue scientists under investigation, promising young companies dying for no well-explained reason. A few times a bundle was tied in string, with a cover note saying simply 'closed'. The case was closed, presumably, but so too, Bryn noticed, were the companies.

'Where the hell did you get this?'

'Go on, sweetheart. The best stuff's at the bottom.'

'Well, Jesus. This stuff is pretty potent. I can think of a couple of journalists who'd love to get their teeth into it.'

'Stop faffing, will you? Look at this.'

Meg hauled out a bundle with the clinic's name prominently marked.

'Staffing diagrams. Financial stuff. Progress reports on Cammie's research.'

Bryn grabbed the papers from her hands. 'Bloody hell, Meg. How did they get this? How did *you* get hold of it, if it comes to that?'

So Meg told him. Her suspicions of Mungo. The pursuit. Mungo's confession. His suggestion that they burgle Janssen, see what he had. Her waiting downstairs to check when Mungo came out. Her first sight of Janssen: white-faced, motionless, terrifying. Then the burglary itself, Meg's personal triumph.

'He told me to copy stuff, but there was way more than I could copy, so I just went down the fire escape again, got the greengrocer round the corner to give me a box. Took the whole lot, even if my arms have grown by about a foot.'

'You're serious? Mungo sold us out?'

'I always told you. Never trust a weirdo.'

'I don't believe it.' Bryn was absolutely rocked by the news. He'd become very attached to Mungo, in a father – son, generation-gappy sort of way, and he was angry, hurt and – perhaps most of all – confused by the idea that Mungo had been the mole. 'Mungo . . . I mean, *Mungo*, of all people. I can't believe it. Jesus!'

'He didn't want to. Janssen was threatening Jojo with jail, with all that would imply for Dar. Mungo was only trying to protect them. He is really upset about it, even if I wanted to kill him for the first half-hour.'

'I swore I'd murder whoever it was, if I ever caught them, but *Mungo*.' He shook his head. 'I don't understand.' He twitched one of the cash flows towards him, eyes narrowing as he scrutinised it. 'He was trying to protect us too, Meg. This cash flow is complete bollocks.'

'Yeah. He said he messed around with things as much as he could. But he did some really bad stuff too.'

Bryn raised his eyebrows, his face locked and hard. Meg told him about the banks, and about Janssen's claim that Corinth would provide Bryn with a millionaire.

'Oh, hell. You mean, Altmeyer might be in on this?'

It all made a miserable sort of sense. Mungo would have told Janssen about their escapade at Berger Scholes. Janssen had clearly planted the story in the *Herald* as soon as possible afterwards, using cash flow data supplied by Mungo for the financial part of the story. And then . . . what? Either Altmeyer was genuinely interested in buying a piece of the business, and had nothing whatever to do with Janssen or Huizinga or Corinth . . . Or Altmeyer was thrown into action by Janssen, who panicked at the thought that Hass's rousing endorsement of the clinic might actually bring genuine investors scuttling out of the woodwork. At the time, Altmeyer's offer had seemed wonderful. Right now, it looked darkly sinister.

'What are you going to do about Mungo?' said Meg.

'I don't know, Meg. I'd like to murder him, but at the same time I feel sorry for the poor little bugger. It must have taken balls to lie to Janssen as much as he did.'

'He lied to us too.'

'Yes. He certainly did.' Bryn looked at some more of the papers, his head still spinning with the shocking news. 'Where is he now? He should be back, shouldn't he?'

'Don't know. Maybe still out with Janssen.'

'Janssen. If that's really his name.'

'Must be. I found a credit card slip that called him Elijah Janssen. You'd have to be a total dork to call yourself that if it wasn't your real name.'

Bryn stared down at the pile of traitor's gold on the floor. He felt unspeakable fury at the betrayal, yet the guy was just a young kid trying to do right by his sisters, while shielding the clinic as best he could. In Bryn's heart, anger and pity clashed for supremacy.

'Did Mungo say when he expected to be back?'

'About an hour ago. But he's probably buggered off home. I would if I were him.'

'Mmm . . . But call him, will you? We ought to know.'

Bryn went back to the stacks of paper as Meg dialled.

'No answer. I'll leave a message, tell him to call.'

Bryn was lost again. Mungo's handiwork lay spread across the floor, and Bryn and Meg bent over it, sorting it into piles, separating the stuff which Mungo had scrambled from the stuff he'd been forced to hand over just as it was. It was obvious from the process that Mungo had fought hard to protect his employer. It was equally clear that he hadn't always succeeded, Janssen's threats and violence extorting real secrets from his mole. After a long afternoon, Meg straightened up.

'I'll call Mungo again,' she said.

'Yeah . . . what's the time now?'

'Six o'clock. He should have phoned in by now.'

'Yeah.'

Meg dialled again, as Bryn stood gazing down at the spoils of Meg's raid.

'No reply. I've left messages.'

Bryn listened slowly to her answer, his brain travelling back from a distant world. He nodded his head in decision. 'OK. Where's Janssen's hang-out? It's time I paid a visit.'

6

Head down, jaw set, Bryn torpedoed through the crowded waiting room, bursting open the big wooden doors at the end and hurtling out into the tarmac yard, past the wharves, through the residential streets towards Fulham Palace Road. Meg scurried along in his wake.

Bryn was boiling with suppressed energy. If you're a healthy thirty-something, built like a brick outhouse and working in a mostly sedentary job, then there's more strength and energy running through your veins than you can find a use for most days. Then, finally, when your adrenal gland starts to signal the approach of action, there's not a nerve cell which isn't humming, not a muscle fibre which isn't rich with blood and ready to go.

Reaching the main road, Bryn whirled round, silently demanding directions from his companion. Silent now, and scared, she pointed to the paint-spattered stairway next to the travel agent. Invulnerable to cars, Bryn barged across the street. Dodging and darting after him, Meg collected the insults that he'd provoked.

'Round the back. Fire escape,' said Meg, but Bryn was already pushing through the tatty grey front door, heading upstairs three at a time. He reached the second-floor landing.

'Here?' he asked.

Meg nodded. Bryn knocked once, waited about a second for an answer, then crashed against the wooden door. It groaned unhappily, but stayed in place. Bryn collected himself, brain, nerves and muscles all now in sync, then crashed against it, all his weight, all his strength, all his energy. The door flew away like a thing of tissue and balsa wood. Bryn smacked the lights on and found what he was looking for. Mungo.

Mungo in a pool of blood. Mungo with his face smashed, body crumpled, blood flowing from ear, eye, lip. Blood darkening his baggy khaki trousers, collecting in the folds at elbow, knee and belly.

7

The hospital was as grim as hospitals always are: white-painted scrapyards for the human machine. If ever you need encouragement to quit smoking, or take up jogging, or eat more greens, then take a stroll round your nearest hospital. Look at the beds. Look at the faces. Abandon hope, you who enter here.

Cameron arrived late. Squelching around in her handbag was a plastic bag full of fluid. Pulling the curtains round Mungo's bed, she unhooked the drip that stood there and hooked her own up instead. 'I happened to have a blood sample from him in the fridge. I've made up his very own trauma support solution.'

Bryn smiled. 'Excellent.'

'Any breaks?' she asked. 'Internal damage?'

Bryn shook his head. 'The vicious sod who did this knew what he was doing. If I ever get my hands on him, I'll kill him.'

Cameron nodded. She pulled the sheets down off Mungo's body as far as his waist and looked aghast at the marks of violence. She pulled the sheets up, very gently, and settled them round his skinny frame. 'He's young. He'll be absolutely fine, I guess.'

'Some scarring. The doctors here thought that would be all. Poor kid.'

'His sisters? Meg said Mungo's sisters were in some kind of trouble?'

'Yeah. Trouble with their foster parents, and one of them

can't stop herself shoplifting. I've phoned them to let them know about this, and they'll be along . . .' Bryn took a deep breath. 'I promised to take them in, if they get any hassle from their foster parents. I'll be buggered if I let Corinth hurt them or Mungo ever again.'

'Sure, right, or me,' said Cameron. 'I'm sure that Allen . . .' She trailed off. Allen, she knew, would run a mile rather than have a pair of teenage shoplifters ruining his flat, but she wasn't going to admit his limitations in front of Bryn. She put her hand on Mungo's forehead, stroked for a while, and then just sat, hand outstretched.

'Just one thing still puzzles me,' said Bryn, after a while. 'According to Mungo, Janssen made him apply to us for a job. That means that Corinth knew about us even before Kessler. It also means one of the people I thought was guaranteed to be safe, wasn't. That's how come I let Mungo have all the access he did.'

Cameron raised her eyebrows without much interest. A cut below Mungo's eye had begun to bleed under its dressing and she rinsed a piece of cotton wool in water and dabbed away the blood. As she worked a thought struck her.

'I think it must have been me,' she said, with a sudden jolt. 'I mailed a birthday gift to my dad, those Lewis Carroll books. The package had a return address on. Dad never received it.'

'Ah, sod it.' Bryn sighed as the last jigsaw piece slotted home. 'I wish you'd told me.'

'Sorry.'

He shook his head, pardoning her.

'I was a bit more defensive back then, didn't want to goof up in front of you. I was . . . Well, I guess I was concerned about your good opinion.'

This was as close as she'd ever come to admitting her

304

former feelings to Bryn. 'Silly,' he said. 'You always had my good opinion. Always will.'

'That's nice. You're nice to say that.' Mungo's face began to bleed some more, and she wiped it clean again. For a senior doctor, she was astonishingly gentle, completely absorbed in the humble act of cleaning a wound as carefully and painlessly as possible. She finished her job and threw away the cotton wool with one hand, leaving the other resting on Mungo's forehead. 'One reason I always knew I'd go into research,' she said. 'I could never take all this kind of thing. Casualty's bad, the cancer wards are worse, the geriatric stuff's just unthinkable. You either have to cut off from the fact that they're people, or else you go crazy. It's a risk I wasn't going to take. Neither the cutting off, nor the going crazy.'

Bryn nodded dumbly. It was absurd, he knew, but he ached with jealousy at the sight of Cameron's hand on Mungo's head. Bryn would have beaten himself into a pulp on the spot, if only that would grant him the same delicious touch. Idiot. He kicked himself. It wasn't Mungo that lay between them, it was Allen Green. Idiot. Idiot. Idiot.

8

Back on the barge, the lights burned late.

Alone with a bottle of wine, the flickering candles and the dark silences of life afloat, Bryn sat with the stolen material. In the corner, his Swedish stove burned fiercely to ward off the surrounding chills. Despite Mungo's bravest efforts, Janssen had obtained access to a rich seam of information. Nevertheless – and thanks entirely to Mungo's heroism – nothing actually fatal appeared to have been transmitted . . .

Nothing fatal, that is, unless Altmeyer was in on

Corinth's plans. Nothing fatal, unless there was more going on here than met the eye – and if so, what? What could it be? The clinic was bursting with health, the research side never healthier, and Altmeyer himself had actually been extremely helpful since joining the company as shareholder, notably by securing the clinic's property leases in double-quick time . . .

But then again, Huizinga was a subtle man, Janssen a ruthless one, and Altmeyer, whatever side he was on, would be willing to do virtually anything for cash . . .

The lights burned late as Bryn pondered.

TWENTY-FOUR

1

Movements in the dark.

Somewhere in the night outside a powerful enemy is manoeuvring. Bryn commands a frigate, knowing that the seas around him swarm with hostile battleships. Decks are cleared for action, the guns run out, men on standby, mess-room emptied to make space for the hospital it's about to become. High up in the crow's-nest there's a boy with a telescope, eyes aching as he searches the black horizon, waiting for first light.

He won't wait long. Out at sea, dawn comes quickly. It won't be long before he knows just how bad it really is.

2

Mungo was a true child of the Information Age, but even an old dog like Bryn had a trick or two still to play.

Once upon a time, when Bryn was an underpaid and overworked analyst at Berger Scholes, Companies House used to store its data on microfilm. If you wanted to examine it, they sent you a packet of transparencies about half the size of a postcard, and you wiggled them about under a fiche-reader – basically a cross between a giant magnifying glass and an overhead projector – until you found what you wanted. To print them off, you had to manoeuvre your transparency round, page by page, under the glass, hitting a clunky print-key each time you had the sheet you wanted. The pages came off the printer hot and crispy, covering your fingers in black toner ink and smelling of the old days.

All that's gone now, not that it matters. These days it's all PCs and modems and bland little cubicles with too much air conditioning, and government-paid staff who've been sent on courses about how to build relationships with the customer. Bugger that. Bryn set down his illegally smuggled cup of coffee (a large latte, dark roast, Kenyan bean) by the keyboard. He wasn't here to reminisce. He was here to dig.

Step one – start from the bottom.

Sitting at a PC, Bryn entered the name of the property company which had produced his leases for the satellite clinics: Scots Metropolitan Commercial Property Ltd. A handful of names came up, including the right one. He selected it and brought the required accounts to screen. With practised fingers, he cut through the blurb and located the list of directors. He printed off. No inky fingers, no smell, no satisfying clunk from the print-key. Just a prim little beep to tell him his print job was done.

Next item. Major shareholders. Who owned Scots Metropolitan? A note recorded the answer: Scots Metropolitan Investments, a Jersey-registered company.

Damn. Bryn swore softly. People don't just go to Jersey to dodge taxes and guzzle cream. They go there for secrecy, too. Jersey-registered companies don't need to file accounts, they don't need to list their directors, they don't need to give you the time of day.

That's the downside. The upside is that, even in Jersey, a company has to reveal who owns it. Bryn called the Jersey Financial Services Commission, who gave him the answer he was expecting. The sole owner of Scots Metropolitan Investments was De Kreuw Holdings SA, a Luxembourg company.

Damn and blast. The trail had run as cold as an Eskimo outhouse. 'SA' stands for Société Anonyme, which literally means an anonymous company, and in Luxembourg, where the stones are more talkative than the bankers, they take that meaning very literally indeed. Bryn swigged his coffee gratefully, knowing his day was about to get a whole lot longer. He settled the plastic lid back on his cup and rolled up his sleeves. A passing bureaucrat saw Bryn's illegal coffee and tutted. Bryn ignored her.

Step two – begin again from the top.

From his briefcase, Bryn pulled out a list of Corinth's subsidiaries, drawn from its compulsory annual filing with the US Securities and Exchange Commission. A quick scan of the list revealed no overlap with any of the names Bryn had identified so far. No problem. Bryn didn't need to win easy, he just needed to win.

He began to dig.

He used the Dun & Bradstreet credit database. He used Companies House. He used online phone directories for companies registered in the Cayman Islands and the Netherlands Antilles. He used a contact of his in the Paris office of Berger Scholes, who knew his way around the Luxembourg system better than most after a life spent helping the rich to dodge taxes.

Down and down through the layers of corporate hierarchy, Bryn probed. Despite the theory, searches of this kind are never simple. Like a Russian doll re-engineered by Kafka, a global company today has companies which own companies which own companies which own companies. Muddled in there at random are dormant companies, shell companies, holding companies, companies which change their names, companies which change their location, companies which bury their paper trail underneath a mountain of dead ends, false leads and red herrings. For six hours, Bryn sifted through dirt, panning for gold.

Then he found it.

Scots Metropolitan – Bryn's property company – had a director rejoicing in the name of Dougal P. Moretti. Theoretically, Moretti had nothing at all to do with pharmaceuticals, and everything to do with property.

But here he was again: D. P. Moretti, listed as an officer of one of Corinth's countless European subsidiaries. It could be a coincidence, but Bryn doubted it. In any event, he proposed to find out.

He called Moretti on the Corinth number and was put straight through. 'Good afternoon, Mr Moretti. I apologise for disturbing you, but I had an urgent enquiry regarding the Scots Metropolitan lease portfolio.'

'Scots Metropolitan? Yes. Certainly. I'm afraid I don't have any of my papers with me at this office. But if I can help –'

'I'm sure you can. Perhaps you could stick your leases up your bum?'

There was a terse pause. Then, nastily, 'Who is speaking, please?'

'My name? My name is Jonah Jackass, of Hogspew, Dogbreath and Wind . . .'

He hung up.

The night before he had been uncertain. No longer. Max Altmeyer – their kind, generous ever-so-helpful new shareholder – had come up with a handful of leases, all of which were ultimately controlled by Corinth.

The man who owned two fifths of the clinic and was the clinic's largest creditor wasn't a friend, and wasn't a supporter. In fact, he was in league with the clinic's deadliest enemy.

3

'Uh, 's good,' mumbled Cameron, through a mouthful of poppadom and lime pickle. She shuffled hot metal dishes between the burners, swapping dishes with Bryn. Kati watched them like they were aliens. What did she know? She ate naan bread with a knife and fork. She had a salad, for God's sake. 'Are we celebrating something?' asked Cameron after a while.

'No. Definitely not. Far from it.' A mouthful of badly advised vindaloo caused Bryn's eyes to prick and water, and he quickly took some yoghurt, pretending he was unconcerned.

'Corinth,' he said. 'They're moving in for the kill.'

Kati and Cameron stopped chewing, stopped breathing.

'Altmeyer is on their side. He's been working for them all this time.'

The two women wore masks for faces: anxiety writ large on Kati's, determination on Cameron's. 'Excuse me?' said Cameron.

Bryn took a nervous swallow of Kingfisher lager. 'The leases,' he said. 'Altmeyer secured them for us. I was grateful, thought he was doing us a favour . . . Turns out I was wrong.'

'Uh-huh?' Cameron prompted him.

'Turns out the leases come from Corinth.'

'Woah! You took out leases from *Corinth*?'

'Altmeyer is about to ask us to repay his loan,' Bryn continued. 'I don't know how he's going to do it, I just know he will.'

Silence followed this statement, which Cameron was the first to break. 'So?' she whispered. 'He wants his money back. We give it to him and tell him to get screwed.' She waved her bread in the air, demonstrating the simplicity

311

of it all. A couple of sultanas pinged out of the dough and landed near Kati. She tidied them silently away with her napkin. The silence settled back again, breathless, expectant.

'That's the whole point,' said Bryn. 'We've spent most of the loan money taking out these bloody leases. I thought we could always sell up or sublet if we needed the money, but –' He sighed heavily. 'Corinth won't let us. They won't let us renegotiate. They won't let us sell.'

Cameron took this in. 'OK. So let me get this straight. You get us an investor. He comes from Corinth. You get us a loan. It comes from Corinth. You get us some new properties. They come from Corinth.'

Like troops patrolling a remote and contested border, Cameron's words signalled a flare-up, an incident which could either dissolve into nothing, or escalate into violence. The oily green fluid at the bottom of the sag aloo dish began to boil and smoke, a sign of trouble.

'That's what I said,' said Bryn, shifting the dish with an asbestos finger.

'There wasn't enough property in England, so you had to go to Corinth?'

'Oh, there weren't enough males in England, so you had to get your boyfriend from Corinth?'

'Don't go there. Don't you even dare go there.'

Bryn breathed out, trying to keep calm. Spread out along the border, his troops were wired, tense, ready. 'The leases didn't look like they came from Corinth. They did a good job at hiding things.'

'And if he asks for his money back,' asked Kati, trying to defuse the situation, 'and we can't pay, then what?'

'He takes shares instead of money. He takes control of the clinic. He sells it to Corinth. I'm sure they've even pre-agreed a price.'

312

Cameron listened, mouth open. Anything she said in this mood would be barbed and dangerous. She moved her lips. Words hesitated on the tip of her tongue. A blazing row was only a couple of syllables away. She licked her lips. She closed her mouth. The moment passed. 'Jesus Christ,' she said. 'That is big news.'

'How come he can just ask for his money back?' said Kati. 'Doesn't he need some kind of reason?'

'That's the weird thing,' said Bryn. 'Of course he needs a reason, like if we were running into default, getting into financial trouble or whatever. But we're a million miles from that. It's as though the leases give him explosive, but he doesn't have a detonator . . .'

He trailed off, beating his brains to find the answer. 'He must have something planned, otherwise why build a bomb? Why go to all the effort? But I don't know what it could be. I've thought of everything, and I still can't fathom it.'

'Well, that's reassuring,' said Cameron, 'coming from the man who buys his property from Brent Huizinga.' She emptied a chicken bhuna and the last of the biryani on to her plate, leaving the empty dishes on the flame to sputter and smoke.

'And why have they waited?' said Kati. 'You guys signed the contract months ago, back in August. Why have they waited so long before striking?'

Bryn shook his head. 'They're smart. The more time goes by, the more money we spend, so we become ever more unable to repay them their money. It's like we've had our head in a noose and haven't even noticed that the rope's been tightening.'

'But now,' said Cameron, 'after Janssen and Mungo and everything, they'll guess that we know –'

'Exactly, they'll guess that we know and they'll put their

313

plan into action, whatever it is. Of course, if it really comes to it, we can always find money from elsewhere, but . . .'

'Elsewhere?' said Cameron. 'You mean the research side?'

Bryn nodded unhappily.

'How bad is it? How much money would we have to find?'

'Ten million. We'd have to close our new office space, lay off, say, thirty staff, and cancel all future hires, and then we'd also need to sell all our new equipment, the big fractionation machines and everything.'

Cameron shook her head, sadly, but emphatically. 'No point. We might as well just give up right now. Even as things stand, we need to add resources rather than cut them. Any less, and we'd lose the rest of the patents to Corinth. We'd lose all the really serious AIDS peptides. And hepatitis. And the whole flu group. Even as it is . . .'

She dug savagely into Bryn's vindaloo and took a mouthful of fiercely spiced chicken. It was the first time she'd ventured that far up the heat-scale, and the experience temporarily seared her. 'Jesus! That's not food, that's a neurotoxin.' The heat gathered and bit. Her eyes swam, her face reddened, her nose poured. 'Jesus. *Jesus!* You eat that for fun?'

'You get used to it.'

'You'd get used to hydrochloric acid. It's legal?'

Bryn handed her the raita, and the yoghurt disappeared in a flash. Bryn beckoned for more.

'I know,' he said. 'It looks horrendous whichever way round you look at it.'

'Vindaloo?'

'The Altmeyer situation.'

'Send him a curry.'

'Seriously. Things look black. I'm not sure I have a solution.'

314

Cameron's mouth calmed down and she focused on what Bryn was saying. A pint of ice-cold water disappeared down her chilli-devastated gullet.

'You're going to give up?' she asked. 'Without a fight?'

Bryn laughed. Cameron had asked tough questions in her time, but this was a cinch. Bryn was a battle tank, rescued from Dunkirk, sent out to North Africa, brought back to storm the Normandy beaches and left to pummel its way eastwards to Berlin. Over the years, he'd been battered, bruised, dented, patched, broken, fixed. He wasn't new, he wasn't fresh, he wasn't young. But his scars had brought experience, and by God, he'd go on fighting, for as long as he had punch left in him.

He picked up the remaining vindaloo, displayed it like a conjuror to Cameron, and swallowed the lot. No yoghurt, no water, no beer. He breathed out: fire and smoke. 'Oh no,' he whispered, 'we'll fight. I promise you we'll fight.'

4

Instead of heading straight home, they wandered out into the night and strolled the chilly streets, anxious about the future, wondering about the past. While they were in the restaurant it had been raining hard, and, though the skies had cleared, the world was still wet and fresh and darkly gleaming. Their stroll took them to Bishop's Park, a small urban park downstream from the boathouse. Cameron found a gate that hadn't been properly locked and they wandered the silent paths, beneath the leafless trees, listening to the rumble of traffic from Putney Bridge and the surreptitious glide of the Thames.

Leaning over the embankment and flicking bits of twig down into the water, Bryn said, 'As a matter of fact, I've been looking into an alternative. It's a long shot . . .

Well, OK, it's born of desperation, but you never know.'

Cameron's previous flash of anger had disappeared. She had a temper on her, but she never held grudges. Cecily had never had much of a visible temper, but grudges grew on her like spikes on a ,cactus, hardening and sharpening in the sterile desert heat.

'I'm sorry for yelling earlier,' she said. 'In the restaurant. I guess I was upset, that's all.'

'That's OK. I'd have yelled too.'

'What's your plan?'

Bryn hesitated. More wood followed the earlier twigs into the Thames as he thought. 'Let me ask you this,' he said. 'How are you on respiratory disease? Are you up to speed with latest developments?'

Cameron shook her head. 'Nope. Not at all.'

Kati interrupted. 'Uh-uh. She knows plenty,' she said. 'I've never found a part of medicine where Cameron wasn't frighteningly well informed. And besides . . .' She looked at Cameron, who looked back at her.

'Besides what?' demanded Bryn.

'My boyfriend, Allen,' admitted Cameron. 'Before he got into chemo, respiratory disease was his research field – and it's still the thing he loves the most. Remember? I did try to tell you once? Anyway, I guess I could ask him for help. But I don't know. He's a pretty straight guy. I'm not sure he'd be OK about anything – uh, anything . . .'

'. . . Anything wildly illegal and improper?' said Bryn.

'Right.'

There was a pause, during which each one of them also thought of the fact that Allen had applied to Corinth for a job. He'd withdrawn his application and now had nothing to do with the company. And yet, none of the three of them standing there under the leafless trees could quite forget the connection. Feeling defensive, Cameron was first to break the silence. 'So?' she said. 'What's the big idea?'

And by the midnight river, amongst the wet and sighing trees, Bryn told them.

5

Somewhere in Cambridgeshire, a biotechnology business.

An ugly Victorian pile houses the admin side, while behind, a purpose-built block of glass and steel rises like a fang from the flat countryside. Winter sunlight flashes blue from tinted glass, while the lawns surrounding it are cropped and bare. The perimeter wall has been brightened up with loops of razor wire, searchlights, notices about dogs. Almost hidden in the rhododendron bushes, there are some long low sheds, cheap affairs with thin metal walls and roofs which must rattle like the devil in the rain. A heap of dung steams gently outside.

Inside the red-brick manor, a secretary is being interviewed. Her CV is impeccable, her computer skills up to the minute. Because it's an interview, the applicant struggles to remain serious, but you can tell she'll be a laugh to work with: one of the girls. The interview is a formality. The new girl is a Londoner, moving out to live nearer her boyfriend. Her last job was PA to a chief executive of a big London investment house, who gave her an outstanding reference. 'He offered me five K to stay on, but I told him my mind was made up,' she says. 'Love before money?' asks the interviewer. 'You're crazy.' Everybody laughs.

Meg smiles, shakes hands, leaves. She drives a short way beyond the main gates, stops, and makes a call. Bryn's out, but she leaves him a voice mail.

'It's me, babe. They haven't actually said so yet, but they're going to give me the job, I'm certain. That reference you gave me was awesome. One of the guys said he'd never seen anything like it. Only trouble was, I nearly forgot what company I was meant to have worked for.'

Meg chatters on, happy and excited, pleased to be involved in Bryn's scheme for the clinic's survival. Despite what happened to Mungo, Meg still lacks a fully developed sense of danger. Over her shoulder, as she completes her call, you can see the red-brick wall that guards the complex. Waxy black rhododendron leaves carve the air like knife-blades, while the looping razor wire flashes silver in the sunlight. There's a sign too: 'MA Research Associates – Bio-technology for the 21st century'. The name and slogan are meaningless, the kind of corporate drivel which someone somewhere should have patented, made a killing from. And beneath the slogan is a byline: 'MARA Ltd – a Max Altmeyer company'.

Meg puts her phone on the seat beside her and winds the window down, ready for the journey back into town. Her mind is elsewhere and she doesn't notice it, but through the window comes a smell. It's a strong smell, a smell of animals.

6

Up in the flickering gloom of Pod Mungo, its proprietor rocked back on his chair, crunching toffee popcorn and shaking crumbs from his keyboard. In Meg's absence, Tallulah had decided that Mungo was her best bet for food and company, and her presence stimulated Mungo to new heights of microwave inventiveness. Tallulah was now, frankly, obese. If she flew at all, her breath was laboured and heavy. Right now, she was down amongst the nest of wires on the floor, lethargically eating the last of the popcorn.

Behind Mungo, Bryn brooded anxiously: knowing he was

318

a distraction, but unable to stay away. Of the three grey windows on to cyberspace, only one was live. Mungo hit a key and the screen beeped again. 'MARA Login Procedure – Access Denied'.

'Oh, widdle. 'S gone Egyptian.'

'Egyptian?'

'Yeah. As in crocodile.' Bryn shook his head blankly and Mungo spoke again, stretching out his words as though speaking to a halfwit. 'Egyptian crocodile. It's in de-nial.'

Bryn's nerves weren't soothed. He was living in a thick fog of anxiety. 'Anything we can do to speed this up? Anything at all?'

Mungo shook his head, grey and sinister in the cyber-twilight.

'Nothing,' he said. 'Absolutely nothing.'

TWENTY-FIVE

1

A crow's-nest at the masthead is a scary place to be. Even a modest ocean swell, amplified through sixty feet of wooden mast, will sweep you through huge circles in space, over the ship, out above the sea, then racing back over black and silent decks to the sea on the other side. A giant's pendulum, balanced between the devil and the deep blue sea.

Meantime, there's a job to do. Over in the east, has the blackness thinned? It's hard to tell. Up here, your eyes play tricks.

Eyes aching, you scan the horizon. Will the sea be empty or crowded with the enemy? Do you have a chance of escape, or no chance at all? There's not enough light to be sure, and you mustn't speak too soon.

Once again you lift the telescope. Out in the black and silent west, stains encroach upon the darkness, dark patches where night thickens and clots. You'll wait a minute, another minute, but already you know the answer. You haven't escaped. The miracle hasn't happened. Out there, lying to windward, is the enemy fleet, massive, ready, and, like you, waiting for dawn.

2

A letter arrives, bland, official and dull.

Bryn – coffee addict that he is – opens his mail with a steaming cafétière by his right elbow (mild roast, Mysore bean, perked up with a dash of dark Jamaican). He rips open the envelope with a blunt thumb, unfolding the letter with his left hand as he reaches for coffee with the right. The right hand never makes it. The left hand brings the letter close, and as he reads the colour drains from his face.

At long last, he's found it – the missing detonator. In thirty days, barring a miracle, the clinic will be dead.

3

White-faced, Cameron looked at the letter. 'You're sure?' she said. 'This seems like no big deal. They can investigate all they want. All they're going to find is a first-rate medical practice.'

'Of course they will. That's not the point.'

'So the point is?'

'The General Medical Council is the body which author- ises all doctors in the United Kingdom. They could strike you off the register. They could close the clinic down.'

'On what grounds? These supposed complaints come from Corinth. You know that. They have no substance whatever.'

Bryn nodded. He did know it. 'True, but you're still miss- ing the point,' he said. 'I haven't explained myself very well. This is the point. Right here, this is the point.'

He directed her attention to the second document he had with him, the loan agreement signed with Altmeyer. Ringed in black was the clause that had concerned them out on the yacht, beneath the blazing heat of the midday sun.

'Suspension of business,' it said. 'Lender is permitted to call the Loan due for Repayment or Conversion if the operations of the Business are suspended or under investigation for possible suspension by any governmental or regulatory authority who is empowered so to act.'

'Damn, I remember this.' Cameron reread it, frowning, puzzling through the complicated English. 'So, according to this, Altmeyer's allowed to ask for his money back, if . . . goddamn, if the General Medical Congress, or whatever you guys call it, comes poking around.'

'Exactly. The GMC *won't* close us down, but the point is they *can*. They're *empowered* to do so. That's all Altmeyer needs. He's got his explosive. He's got his detonator. This is his bomb. Theoretically those GMC investigations are confidential, but I'll bet anything you like that we get a fax from Altmeyer within the next half-hour demanding that we repay his loan.'

'So then we'll either have to find ten million pounds, in – how long?'

'Thirty days.'

'Or watch ourselves being sold to Corinth.'

Bryn nodded.

'And ten million pounds – there's no chance, I suppose . . . ?'

Bryn shook his head. 'No chance. We could fire everyone on the payroll. Sell all our equipment. Sell the buildings. Sell the barge. Then,' he shrugged, 'then of course we could pay it, but what would be the point? We'd hardly beat Corinth, if it was just you, me and a cardboard box.' He paused, aware suddenly of a burning anger towards Corinth, a smouldering, intense fury that the company should play with people's lives for the sake of corporate profit and

Huizinga's pay packet. 'And, sod it, Cameron, sod it. We've got to beat the buggers, we've just got to!'

Cameron barely heard him. Though this moment had been looming for a while, the shock was still staggering when it came. She looked like someone forced to watch a son or daughter be killed in a car accident. Her face, like Bryn's, was taut and white. The only sign of motion in the room was her hand, drumming tak-tak-tak on the table, faster than a humming bird's wing. Outside, through the glass pane in her office door, Bryn could see Rick the Beard and the others moving about, careful with their lab equipment, noting results, collating data, inching closer to the ever more pointless goal. Cameron's hand stopped its drumming.

'Mungo?' she asked. 'I don't suppose he's . . .'

'He's got nowhere. I've just checked.'

Cameron's hand drummed briefly again. Then she stopped, grey eyes the colour of smoke. 'If Mungo can't make it through cyberspace, I guess we'll just have to do it in real space,' she said.

Bryn's head jolted up in surprise.

'Real space?' he asked. 'You mean –'

'Burglary,' said Cameron. 'A good old-fashioned, honest-to-God break-in.'

A slow smile spread across Bryn's face. By God, he loved this woman. She didn't want to be in a fix, but since she was, she'd enjoy – she'd actually *enjoy* – the effort to smash a way out of it. But his reflections were interrupted by the chatter of a fax machine outside. Grimly, Bryn went out and returned with a single sheet of paper.

'Altmeyer?' said Cameron.

Bryn nodded.

'Thirty days from now, huh?'

He nodded again. 'Thirty days.'

She smiled. 'I've always wanted to burgle someone.'

'Me too,' added Bryn. Then, recalling General Patton's philosophy of battle, he quoted, 'Have a plan.'

'Execute it violently,' she responded.

'And do it today.'

Simultaneously, they looked at their watches. There was no time to be lost.

4

Five thirty, the same afternoon. Both buildings empty fast, but the Manor, the red-brick gothic monstrosity, empties faster. As the minute hand clicks from almost-down to straight-down, people drop their pens mid-sentence, grab for coats and scarves, form knots at the doorway leading out. Max Altmeyer has a knack for making money, but getting his employees to love him is a skill he's never mastered. A regular employee now, Meg heads out with the rush.

'Hey, Megsy! You coming down the pub?'

She makes friends fast, does Meg, and one of them is calling her now.

'Yeah, maybe, later. I've got a couple of things to do first,' she says.

A brick pavement connects the two buildings: the Victorian admin block and the sleek, sinister science block. She wanders down towards the science offices, sheeted in their impenetrable glass. She doesn't have a plan, but like Bryn she has instincts. The front entrance is a no-no. Too public, too on-display. She saunters round the back, to the loading bay. Just one-person there: a stringy bloke, Meg's age roughly, wearing the uniform of a security guard. Right now, he's guarding nothing. He's having a fag.

'Alright, gorgeous?'

They recognise each other vaguely, having seen each

other in the canteen at lunchtimes occasionally. The guard, supposedly alert for intruders, switches his mental alarm signals off. Meg is no intruder. She sizes him up, approaches.

'Got a fag?'

He produces one silently, lights it. She closes her lips around the filter in a pout. (Her second best feature, lips.) She inhales – not too deeply, she's not too used to smoking tobacco – and breathes out a tube of smoke. After exhaling, she doesn't quite close her lips. The stringy youth smirks at her. He inhales, gathers concentration, blows a smoke ring. The ring isn't brilliant, but OK. Meg blows a jet of smoke into his ring, like trying to thread a needle. It doesn't work, the smoke just billows out into a mess, but it's not a competition. The youth nods at her.

'Working up at the Manor, then?'

Lots of conversational gambits are open to Meg at this point. For instance, even quite an unimaginative person might think of saying, 'Yes', but decision has come to Meg. She drops her cigarette on the ground, tweaks his cigarette from his mouth and drops it too. Putting both hands behind his head, she kisses him, her tongue drilling deep into his mouth. He tastes of smoke and salted peanuts, but behind those tastes there's something softer, like milk maybe. His head gets the idea pretty quickly, and she doesn't need her hands there any longer. She drops them to his waist and pulls him against her. There is no ambiguity in the movement of her hips. They lock together in silence for a short time, punctuated by little snorts of air when it has become essential to breathe. They kiss like oilmen drilling, Casanova given an hour to live.

She pulls away.

He makes to come forward again, but she steps back, shaking her head, her mouth still open, breathing in rapid pants. He too is open-mouthed, breathing hard.

'It's private here,' he says. 'No one'll come here now, just me.'

Meg looks round at the oil-stained floor and the litter of discarded packaging. She shakes her head, but her face is tilting slightly down, she's looking at him from under her eyebrows, and hunger is written all over her mouth.

The stringy youth is in a dream, a situation he's only ever seen in films. He doesn't know how come he arrived here, but doesn't want to screw things up. He checks his watch.

'I'm on patrol here tonight. Give me till half six to lock up, then I'll be back.'

Meg nods.

He looks doubtful. Nothing like this has ever, ever happened to him. Meg sees his doubt, grabs his belt at the buckle and yanks him over. They kiss again. Her hands are at waist level, but not round the back this time, round the front. He leaves, shaking.

5

Six thirty. Footsteps come running down a concrete corridor. The stringy youth bursts through a steel door. Empty. The loading bay is empty. He sees nothing. Disappointment breaks over him like a cold Atlantic wave. Of course the bay would be empty, what the hell did he expect? Still breathing hard from his run, his desire, his disappointment, he walks along the grimy loading ramp, looking out at the deserted lawns.

Wrong way, he's looking the wrong way. He falls into an ambush. One hand grabs him over his mouth, another hand reaches for his groin. Meg pulls him towards her, and in a moment they are joined to one another again, locked in place like a pair of suction pumps. They kiss as though

326

kissing were oxygen, but in the end their lungs demand the real thing and they pull away as before, panting heavily.

'Gotcha,' says Meg.

The stringy youth is pleased to have been got.

'All clear. No one left.' He jangles some keys. 'And no one can get in, either.'

'Lead on then, tiger.'

He leads on. As promised, the building is deserted. There are laboratories, briefly glimpsed though glass doors: labcoats, test-tubes, racks of chemicals locked and labelled, big white German-made machines promising insight into the most tightly held secrets of life. Meg is impressed, but doesn't say so.

Her companion says, 'There's a common room along here. It's got sofas and everything.'

Before he's finished speaking, they've arrived. It takes them a handful of microseconds to rip cushions off the sofas and scatter them over the floor, but any hope of constructing anything resembling a bed is soon shot to pieces as they grapple again, somehow managing to pull their clothes off as they clinch.

It's quickly over, Meg's choice as much as her lover's haste. She's surprised herself. She'd expected not to let it go any further than some more heavy duty snogs, but perhaps the act of miming passion made her feel it. Whatever the reason, when her newest conquest goes hunting his packet of cigarettes, Meg is feeling happy and excited, and not only because she's inside the building Bryn told her to check out.

'Fag?' he asks, handing her a lighted fag.

'Ta.'

He lights one for himself, using his other hand to thump his chest.

'Degsy,' he says.

'I'm Meg.'

6

He looked her up and down, in a kindly way, not possessively. He stroked away a strand of chestnut hair which had become sweat-glued to her damp cheek. With his clothes on he looked stringy. Clothes off and he looked a bit hunkier than that. Sinewy, thought Meg, strong; like a distance runner, even though she'd always had more of a thing for swimmers. Apart from his fairly rapid execution – and Meg knew she was partly responsible for that – Degsy had been a considerate lover, if considerate is the right word for someone literally quivering with desire.

'Nice to meet you, Meg.'

'Nice to meet you too, Degsy,' she said, running her hand across his chest, up on to his arms and shoulders, then back down again and round.

'You always introduce yourself like that?'

Meg smiled, but her mind was elsewhere, in two places at once. The first spot was in her hand, which lay on his belly, rising and falling with his breaths exactly in sync with her own. She stroked it, round and round, meditatively. The second place was with Bryn. He'd asked her to snoop around a bit, find out what she could about the security arrangements. On balance, Meg felt, she had 'exceeded expectations', as the Berger Scholes performance appraisals used to put it – especially since the most significant element of the security arrangements was currently up on one arm, nibbling her bosom.

'Degsy?' she said.

'Yeah?'

She nudged him away from her breast, but kept him close, so his side stayed pressed up against her. 'D'you like your job?'

'Like my job? What d'you mean?'

'I'm saying do you like your job? Are you committed and all that?'

Degsy's attention moved away from Meg's nipple to her face. 'Look, nobody in the entire universe – least no one with a brain in the entire universe – would get a kick out of watching a wall of TV screens all night, and wandering round with a torch, going, "Is anybody there?" I do it because I get paid, alright?'

His attention wandered back to pleasanter things. Meg let him do as he wanted, cradling his head in her arm. She pondered. The low-risk strategy was to get Degsy to show her around, remember as much as she could, report it on to Bryn; but her pulse was racing, one-twenty beats to the minute, and Bryn himself had never been one for the cautious approach.

'Degsy?'

'Mmm.'

'I've got a favour to ask you.'

He pulled his lips away with a small smacking sound. 'Be my guest.'

'I've got some friends who want to burgle the building.'

He sat upright, pulling himself away from her. There wasn't a single point now where their two bodies touched. 'That's why you jumped all over me? Jesus. Only in my bloody dreams . . .' He reached for his underpants and began to pull them on. Meg grabbed at them before he'd pulled them higher than his knees, and twisted them so he couldn't move them higher.

'I wouldn't have gone all the way if I hadn't liked you. I don't even know why I did go all the way.'

He shook her hand free. 'I'll be crucified if any of the gear goes missing. Some of them machines cost a million quid, apparently.'

Meg shook her head. 'They don't want anything like that.

Just papers. They'll copy them, not take them. You can stick around and check they don't swipe anything.'

'It's not the job, Meg. The job sucks. But there's a principle thing, I suppose. And anyway, there are dogs and stuff. You wouldn't want to mess with them. I'm sorry, Meg. I do like you.'

'Yeah, I think I like you too. I'm not just saying that.'

He pulled his pants up and reached for his trousers, simultaneously giving her a full-on kiss on the mouth. 'The answer's no, though, Meg. Sorry.'

'I'm sorry too . . . Don't you even want to know why my friends want to burgle the place?'

'No, not really, no. I wish you hadn't even –'

'Look, I want to tell you, OK?'

Degsy had his trousers on now, though not his shoes. He was halfway between leaving and staying. He looked down at Meg, who was still naked, stretched out on the scattered sofa cushions. 'Yeah. Alright then,' he said, accepting her plea. 'Why?'

So Meg told him. The whole story, pretty much. The big bad corporation, the science they wanted to crush, Altmeyer's treacherous role in the whole game. Degsy listened without interruption, lighting cigarettes for them both and planting one in Meg's mouth as she spoke.

At the end of it, he was thoughtful. 'I had a mate once, gay bloke, died of AIDS. Just got thinner and thinner, weaker and weaker, until he was gone. Used to be a right laugh, too.'

Meg nodded. She'd told him about the rats that Cameron had saved, the promise that she could repeat the trick with humans.

'When were your friends thinking of coming?'

'Put it this way, they're down at the Fox and Hounds right now, waiting for a call.'

330

'Bloody hell, Meg. Not that you're pushy or anything.' He sat amidst the shower of cushions, in his trousers, belt in his hand, shirt in a screwed-up ball at his feet. He dragged at his cigarette, as though asking it for an answer. 'It would need to be after midnight. And there's nothing I can do about the dogs. And there's a couple of perimeter guards, who spend most of their time watching telly, far as I can tell, but they prowl around a bit too. Plus there's a real more-than-my-job's-worth type over at the Manor. And mobile patrols as well, and not even I know when they're coming ... It's dead chancy, but if you want to ...' He shrugged his acceptance.

Meg grinned at him. 'You're a star.'

Rolling over so that she straddled him with her still-naked legs, she flicked her cigarette and his away into a nearby bin. 'You a one-shot man, Degsy, or've you got a second barrel down there?'

TWENTY-SIX

1

In an upstairs room at the Fox and Hounds, the raiders assembled. Cameron was obviously modelling herself on Purdy in *The Avengers*: long black boots, black leggings, black gloves, a black cotton rollneck, and a black silk scarf which she wore in loops and swags around her neck. Except maybe in the heel of her boot, you wouldn't have been able to place a fifty pence piece anywhere in her clothing and hope to have it pass detection.

Bryn, too, was dressed in dark clothes, with a tool bag and torch at his waist. At Bryn's invitation, his brother Dai was there as well, ready to bring a bit of extra muscle to the proceedings. Despite Meg's blithe confidence that everything would run according to plan, Bryn had never heard of a strategy failing because too much force had been deployed and when it came to delivering force, few people were more reliable than Dai.

Mungo was there too, in ballooning khaki trousers and a grubby black T-shirt. His luminous trainers had caused some concern to Dai, but a more immediate problem was emerging.

'Dogs?' said Mungo.

'Uh-huh.'

'Like, presum'bly we're talking big slavering wolfhounds that've been fed, like, just one yoghurt in the last century, or maybe one of them cream cheese an' celery dip things which girls eat.'

'They're guard dogs, Mungo. German shepherds. They'll attack, but they won't eat you. And we're taking every possible precaution.' Bryn indicated his brother: sixteen stone of thorough-going precaution.

'I don't mind terriers too much, 'cept for the barky ones. Or what are those things with droopy ears and big eyes, going, like, *give me a cuddle?*'

'They're not going to guard the premises with cocker spaniels, Mungo, sorry.'

''S just I've only got two arms, an' I'm not massively keen to donate one of them to the save-a-starving-wolfhound-of-terror appeal, specially as when you think of all the drugs I do and all the crap food I eat, I doubt if my arm would be, like, incredibly healthy.'

'You're bailing out?'

'Sorry, man. Dogs give me the jumpin' heebie-jeebies. Always have.'

'Well, you'd better stay then.' Bryn's voice hardened, not from anger but from worry. Mungo was the only one qualified to recognise the critical clues which might enable him to get access to the IT system. Without Mungo, the whole burglary might prove purposeless.

'That's OK, don't worry,' said Cameron gently in deliberate counterpoint to Bryn's hardness. 'I used to be terrified of dogs. And with a bit of luck we'll find enough paperwork to give me what I need.'

'No worries,' said Mungo blithely. He fished around in a bag he'd brought with him and took out a video camera, a laptop, and a couple of lengths of flex. 'Thought it might be a case of canine calamity, so I brought this. Video hooks into the laptop. Hook the laptop up to a phone jack, an' I've got internet access to the pictures. Take a poke round, an' I can tell you if there's anything worth snitching. Virtual burglary.'

'Bloody hell,' said Dai, not for the first time that evening and most certainly not the last. 'Clever, that.'

Bryn nodded, somewhat relieved, but keen to get going. He repeated his instructions for the last time to Kati and Meg.

'OK, you two, I need you to guard the gate. Kati, I want you five hundred yards to the east, Meg five hundred yards to the west. Any time a car goes past you, call me, one ring only, I've damped down the sound so it won't reach much further than me. If I get two rings, one from each of you, then I know the car's gone right on past. If I only get one ring, then we've got a problem, because the car's gone in through the gate. OK?' Kati and Meg nodded. 'Meantime, Mungo, I guess you'd best stay here, where we can reach you.'

'No, I'll come with Meg. I'm not missing out.' Since Mungo's beating, Meg had forgiven him his weirdness and they were well on their way to becoming friends.

'But you need to be by a phone. You just said you needed internet access.'

'*Whoooh!* You don't need to get all twentieth century with me.' From his bag, he pulled out another laptop with a mobile phone taped to it with black insulating tape, like a piece of hi-tech battlefield equipment made combat-ready by its squaddie proprietor. 'Virtual and mobile, alright?'

Bryn nodded approval. He turned to Cameron and Dai.

Airy assent from Cameron, for whom a little burglary appeared to be the most natural thing in the world; a heavy grunt of assent from Dai.

'Then let's go.'

2

Dai put his hands together to make a platform. Bryn stood on it and reached for the top of the wall as his brother heaved. Making himself secure, he withdrew a pair of wire-cutters from his tool belt and began to snip the razor wire. Three rolls of the vicious stuff hung along the wall. Bryn had got through the first two rolls, and was well into the third when a muffled bleat came from his phone.

'Down,' he snapped.

He dropped from the wall, flung himself to the ground, checking to see that the others had followed suit. For thirty seconds they lay, cheeks pressed to the freezing mud and damp grass. A car swept by, headlights breaking the darkness harmlessly above their heads. Bryn waited until a second ring from Meg's end of the road told him that the car had driven on by.

'OK,' he said, stepping back into position on his brother's hands.

In another minute the last roll of wire was cut through, and the whole entangled section flopped to the ground on the far side of the wall. Bryn probed the ground below with his torch, shutting the beam off as soon as he had found a safe place to jump away from the dangerous coils. He jumped down and used a stick to tow the wire away into the safety of the rhododendrons. He hauled himself quickly back on to the wall, nervous of the dogs.

'OK. Cameron.'

Dai took Cameron's boot in his hands and shot her upwards. She was still ascending fast as Bryn grabbed her, bundling her on to the wall, then over on to the ground. He reached down again, and muscle tugged against muscle as Dai heaved his way up.

'Guys, I think . . .' Cameron's warning ended abruptly.

In the blackness, a grey shape moved with frightening speed. A low growl, the dangerous sort, was audible. Cameron backed against the wall, very scared. The growl intensified, winding up into a spring.

'Good boy,' said Dai. 'Good lad.'

He was good with dogs, always had been. He'd taken over sheepdog training from his father aged fourteen, and if he'd ever trained one to respond to anything other than swear-words and blasphemies, he'd have stood a fair chance in competition. But those weren't the skills he called on now. 'Good dog,' he said again as he tumbled off the wall and crashed down on to the dog's chest and shoulder, knocking the breath from its body and leaving it three-quarters stunned. He wrestled the animal's front half into his jacket, from which it already began to stir in an attempt to escape. It was Dai's turn now to speak with a kind of nervous urgency.

'Cameron, love, would you mind . . . ?'

Cameron didn't need to be told. She moved fast, sweeping her veterinary syringe into the dog's side and ramming the plunger home all in one practised motion. The German shepherd crumpled and fell.

'Bloody hell,' said Dai, dropping it. 'Never seen one go like that before.'

'Triple dose,' said Cameron. 'I figure my Hippocratic oath doesn't apply to animals. I wasn't kidding when I said I was terrified of the things.'

The raiding party beat its way through the bushes, scattering chunks of stewing steak, each spiked with a tablet of high-dose anaesthetic. Degsy had said there were four dogs on patrol, vicious brutes every one of them.

At the edge of the lawn, they paused briefly. A ground frost glittered from the grass, and a thin mist lay, not more than six foot deep, in long wreaths over the ground. Nothing and no one was visible, but there was always the

336

possibility that their movement in the moonlight would attract the attention of either guards or dogs, so they ran together across the lawn, boots crunching on the hard surface, assembling again in the shadow of the loading bay. A low voice greeted them.

'How's the A-team? Alright?'

'Degsy, hi. I'm Bryn.'

Introductions were swiftly made. Degsy produced a roll of duct tape and let himself be bound at ankles, knees, wrists and elbows.

'That should do it,' he said, once he was trussed like a chicken. 'Overpowered by intruders after gallant resistance, Degsy "Hammerfist" Parlour was commended for outstanding bravery.' Then, as Dai tossed him over his shoulder like a sack of grain, he added, 'Go easy, mate. And remember to stuff something in my mouth if anyone comes snooping. I ought to be yelling, remember. I'm a trained professional.'

They set off into the science block, following the route that Degsy and Meg had taken a few hours earlier. The plan was to leave no trace of their visit inside the science area and, if possible, to leave Degsy with an unbesmirched record. The break-in through the razor wire would be discovered come the morning, but Bryn intended to give the investigators plenty of reasons for looking elsewhere. It would be a busy night. He looked at Cameron. From here on, she was in control.

'Systems or papers? What's your first priority?'

'Papers,' she said. 'Degsy mentioned a safe.'

Degsy nodded, and, with Dai carrying him, he led them upstairs to an unprepossessing safe, manufactured back when burgundy was still a fashionable colour.

'You've got the combination?' she asked.

'Yeah. Right-hand pocket,' he said, adding, 'pardon,' as Cameron's hands thrust further than expected.

She withdrew the slip and calmly began to twist the dial on the safe, forwards and back, as though she did this kind of thing for a living. She reached the last number, then twirled the dial back round until it locked into position. She opened the safe.

3

Inside there were half a dozen buff folders and a box of petty cash. Nothing else.

'That's it?' said Dai.

'That's it,' said Bryn, passing the folders to Cameron.

The front page of the first file was marked in big letters: 'Respiritron – the next step in respiratory disorders'. She quickly assessed the files' contents and looked up with a quick smile. 'Oh, this is it, alright. You may as well go do Mungo's stuff. I'm going to be a while.'

Bryn nodded and left. Degsy pointed out the IT administration bay and as Dai acted as internet-cameraman, Bryn hung on the phone to his young assistant. Mungo was silent to begin with as he watched the pictures coming through on his laptop. 'Droid-city,' he commented. 'Clean desk nightmaresville.'

'Any of the folders help, any of the papers?' said Dai, sweeping the camera along a rack of coloured files, clearly in common use.

'Yeah, maybe. Let's have a look-see.'

Dai held the camera vertically down as Bryn turned pages under the lens.

'Network traffic by department . . . by date . . . by security code . . . by server. Wow-ee. This guy's *ay*-nal. Network traffic alphabetically by employee number. This is a very sad person, man. You should put some drugs in his OJ or something. How 'bout the red folder?'

For a full hour, Mungo examined the papers available in the IT area, but the site was a model of IT security. There were no passwords recorded, nothing on paper describing security procedures or countermeasures. Mungo did manage to glean some information on the overall network architecture. 'But it's not good news, man. It's things like they use packet switching everywhere. They've got armageddon firewalls round their internet ports, and their password construction requirements are top end, man; seven-digit, mixed character set, regular change. That's not good news, not good news at all.'

'Pity I can't stay here all night,' said Dai. 'Film the bugger typing his password.'

A voice at the doorway startled them.

'Why not?'

Bryn and Dai leapt with tension. Whirling round, braced for action, they saw Cameron lounging against the doorpost.

'Bloody hell,' said Dai. 'You gave me a shock.'

'Why not do just that?' said Cameron again. 'They've already installed the camera.' She nodded upwards at the ceiling, where one of Altmeyer's ever-present security cameras winked at them. 'It's even pointing at his desk.'

Bryn followed her gaze with his eye. 'Bloody brilliant, woman,' he said, his Welsh accent and vocabulary always more noticeable in his brother's presence. 'Fantastic idea.'

Degsy nodded. 'Getting the tapes is no problem. I can just go in and get them.'

This time it was Bryn's turn to haul Degsy around. He took him downstairs to the deserted security booth, where a row of monitors switched images between the different cameras. Degsy, still taped up like the victim of a jewel heist, told Bryn how to use the security console to bring one of the cameras to screen and hold it there. Having done so, Bryn phoned upstairs.

'We've got you in view. Cameron, you be the IT guy. Dai, can you get the camera to zoom in a bit more?'

Cameron sat at the keyboard, typing nonsense, as Dai manually zoomed the camera in. 'Not too far,' said Bryn. 'We don't want to give the game away. That's OK. And up a bit. Left.' Dai fiddled until Bryn was satisfied. 'OK, Cameron. Type some more. Slowly.'

She typed. The camera angle wasn't perfect, but it wasn't bad. Her left shoulder obscured the bottom right-hand corner of the keyboard, and if the IT guy was broader-shouldered than she was – and though Cameron was tall, she was enviably slim – then more of the keyboard would fall into shadow. No matter. Bryn studied the picture closely. Like most Americans, Cameron was a touch typist. Her eight fingers rested on the home keys, her thumbs on the space bar. When she hit a key, only one of her fingers moved; up, down, occasionally left or right to reach the keys in the centre or on the edges of the pad. Bryn watched intently for a while. 'Do it slowly,' he said. 'When we have it on tape, we can play it slow motion, but right now I just want to check to see if it works at all.'

Cameron moved her fingers, absent-mindedly, slow-motion across the keyboard. Bryn studied her intently. Right hand, middle finger, up. Right hand, ring finger, no movement from the home key, just a quick downstroke to depress the key. Right hand again. Ring finger again. Up one key and depress. Bryn figured out the letters in triplets. ILO VEA LLE NIL OVE ALL ENI. He wrote them down, staring at them as Cameron's long fingers went on playing, dreamy, unregarded. There was something funny about the letters she chose. They weren't random, there was a pattern there. Then he saw it: *I love Allen, I love Allen, I love Allen.* Feeling sick, he screwed up his sheet of paper and threw it in the bin. Why the hell shouldn't she love her boyfriend? Why wouldn't she? All the same, blind with the blackness of jealousy, he could bear no more. He blundered up, jabbing the monitors back to their pre-set position, grabbing Degsy roughly for the trudge back upstairs.

A shame.

Unseen by anyone, the rhythm of Cameron's fingers began to change. Right hand, ring finger, up and depress. Index finger, left hand, up and depress. Thumb. Left hand, middle finger, depress. Right hand, ring finger, up and depress. Thumb. Right hand, middle finger, up and depress. Repeated again, and again, and again. *Or do I, or do I, or do I?*

4

Back to the safe, and Cameron's six buff folders.

They had brought with them a high-resolution digital camera with a tripod designed for document work, but Bryn decided the copier would run faster. He was probably right, but even so the copier took fifteen minutes to warm up (Dai's comment: 'Bloody hell, even I used to warm up faster than that') then it was low on toner, then out of paper. Bryn found the stationery cupboard and searched for what he needed. Stacked on the floor was a heap of old marketing junk, ancient history. On the shelves above there was every-thing they needed. Bryn took the toner, took the paper, fed the copier, set Dai to work copying. ('Bloody hell, Bryn, I thought you wanted me as a burglar, not a bloody secretary.')

When Bryn got back to Cameron, he found her on the floor, lighting the remaining documents with a torch hooded by her black silk headscarf. With her long booted legs stretched out around the torchlight, and her eyes absorbed with scientific papers of incomprehensible density and subtlety, she looked dangerous and intelligent, Catwoman meets Einstein. She was frowning.

'Is there a problem?' Bryn's voice was taut and strained, not from the tension of the break-in but from the bottomless nightmare of the three words he'd watched her type.

She answered coolly. 'No problem.' She tugged a strand of hair across her face and began to play with it, a familiar gesture in the old days, but now only a sign of deep thought. Eventually, she looked up with a smile. 'I'm just beginning to wish I'd spent more time in the past studying respiratory disease. Like a *lot* more time.'

'Do you think you'll be able to . . . ?'

'In thirty days?'

'Twenty-nine days, more like.'

She shook her head, and her eyes travelled back to the papers in front of her. 'I don't know, Bryn . . . I'll do my best, of course, but, I gotta say, I don't know . . .'

As she spoke, she was interrupted by footsteps coming down the corridor outside. Acting on instinct, Bryn bundled Cameron behind a green metal filing cabinet, and extinguished her torch. He crouched on the floor by the door, ready to burst upwards with a punch if the need arose. The phone in his pocket bleeped once, ignored.

The moment passed. Dai and Degsy came in, Dai carrying his cargo the way a groom carries a bride over the threshold. On his lap, Degsy held a pile of photocopies, still warm from the machine.

'I don't know how much it's going to help you though, love,' said Dai to Cameron, passing them over. 'It's mostly letters and numbers.'

Cameron smiled. 'Don't worry,' she said. 'That's just the way I like it.'

'Let's move out,' said Bryn.

The papers which had come out of the safe went back

inside. The safe door swung shut, and locked. So far, the job had been clean and swift.

The raiding party moved quickly downstairs to the loading bay. Exposed to the night air, which was now beginning to freeze hard, Cameron grew chilly, and Bryn rubbed her back and hands in an effort to keep her warm. But he rubbed too hard and she pushed him away. Meantime, Dai had begun to unwrap Degsy's bindings, when movement outside made everyone stop. A torchbeam prodded the lawn, then swung back to the building.

'Shit, Don Jackson,' hissed Degsy. 'Mobile security. How come we weren't warned?'

Too late, Bryn remembered the warning sent him by the phone a few minutes earlier: there had been just one ring, a message that the car had passed Meg or Kati, but not both. Simultaneously, Bryn and Cameron leaped behind a pillar, the same one, about two and a half feet wide. With his back against it, Bryn took up all the available width and there was nowhere secure for Cameron except pressed up against him. He held her with one hand against her belly, one against her chest. He could feel her heartrate increase, but not astronomically. She was alert but not terrified, ready for action but never impulsive. She was also tall, slim, beautiful, wonderful. Bryn wanted her so badly his knees went weak.

Dai meanwhile was desperately trying to tear away the duct tape from Degsy's taut body. In doing so, he must have made enough noise to alert Jackson. The torchbeam jabbed inside the loading bay, searching between the pillars. With his foot, Bryn drew Cameron's booted legs together, drawing her further into the triangle of shadow, bringing her more closely than ever against him. His own heartrate increased, fear of capture melting into joy at Cameron's closeness.

343

'Is that you, Mr Jackson?' yelled Degsy, all of a sudden.

'Jesus, son, there's still a job to finish here,' said Dai, *sotto voce*, or at least *sotto voce* for Dai.

'Who's that?'

'Degsy, Mr Jackson. Degsy Parlour.'

Jackson was invisible to the four people hiding from his gaze, but his torchbeam flashed at ever more obtuse angles now, indicating that its owner was coming closer.

'Bloody hell,' said Dai. Still ripping at the tape with his penknife, he picked up Degsy and held him flat against the pillar, at an angle to the vertical, so the young man's belly was jammed against the concrete, his face poking out into the torchlight. His arms were free at the elbow but still joined at the wrist. His legs were trussed and pinioned like a hospital crash victim.

'Evening, Mr Jackson.'

'Good evening, Parlour. Any incidents?'

'No, nothing. Thought I heard some noises down here, but must have been you I was hearing.'

'Are you alright?'

To Jackson's eyes, Degsy must have appeared at an unnatural angle, arms bizarrely rigid and out of sight. 'Got it,' muttered Dai as the wrists came free. With one massive hand still rammed against Degsy's bottom, he set to work on the lower half, no longer aiming for gentleness, just speed. Degsy moved a hand up to shield his eyes from the torchbeam, the first natural-seeming gesture he'd made. The vibrations still running through his body from the knife-work below and the sudden jolts in his position as Dai's hand slipped must have appeared less natural.

'Absolutely fine, Mr Jackson.' A wodge of duct tape flapped from Degsy's wrist. He pulled it off with a high-pitched laugh. 'There's a lot of mess down here. Might be worth mentioning in the morning. Could be a fire hazard.'

'Got you, you bastard.'

Dai spoke to the last of the duct tape. He moved his hand from Degsy's bum, and the young man dropped with a jerk, painful feeling flooding back into his legs. Dai was on all fours ripping tape from Degsy's trousers, while all Degsy wanted to do was roll over on to his side and weep as his blood rediscovered some much-loved major arteries.

Jackson's torchbeam poked into a pile of packaging material.

'You're right. This lot should have been cleared away. Who's the fire officer?'

Degsy limped to the front of the pillar, still leaning against it, knees and ankles still no match for gravity. His trousers were in fairly good condition except where the tape had passed, where they were massively crumpled and creased. They looked like a pair of trousers which had just spent a couple of hours being tied up . . .

'Fire officer, Mr Jackson?' Degsy was gasping. His legs had been numb in their bandages, but he wanted to scream now that he was released. 'Fire . . . I'll look into it.'

'You OK, son?' Degsy managed a light-hearted wave, with an elbow which still didn't bend. 'Yeah, fine. You want coffee or anything?'

The torchbeam disappeared for an instant while Jackson must have consulted his watch.

'I'll go on with my rounds. You get that packaging seen to.'

'Yes, sir, Mr Jackson,' cried Degsy, weeping in painful relief.

The torchbeam flashed back for a moment in surprise, then moved away, more and more distant until it was gone.

'Bloody hell,' said Dai.

Degsy said something worse. Cameron stepped forward, away from Bryn, leaving him to ache with loneliness. She

345

picked up her papers from the ground, calmly, as though she always spent her Sunday nights in a black catsuit thieving information from beneath the noses of security guards.

'Dammit,' said Bryn. 'Fire hazard. I should have thought of it sooner.'

Without a further word, he dashed off into the building, returning in a few minutes with the bundles of papers from the bottom of the stationery cupboard.

'What've you got there?' asked Cameron.

'Lot of old junk,' said Bryn. 'Causing a fire hazard. Best moved.'

No further explanation came, not then, anyway. From the front of the bay, Degsy checked the path of Jackson's torchbeam.

'Better wait a while,' said Degsy. 'He's checking the Manor before heading out.'

'Thanks again, Degsy,' said Bryn. 'You'll let us know – or let Meg know, anyway – if you get any grief over this?'

'Lose my job, you mean? That'd be a tragedy and a half.'

Bryn smiled. 'You're still welcome to work for me.'

'Now you know how honest and trustworthy I am.'

'If you turn me down, Meg's going to want to know the reason why.'

'Meg, now there's a girl . . .' Degsy tailed off in love-lorn silence.

They waited till the coast was clear, then moved off into the night.

5

The night stretched peacefully across the silver lawns and dense black woods. Somewhere in the silence there were three dogs, two guards and their next target.

Gathering themselves for the run, Bryn, Dai and

Cameron sprinted across the lawn, hastening for the shadows where they were less immediately vulnerable. Panting and breathless beneath the twisting rhododendrons, they checked back the way they had come. Degsy, lost in the depths of the loading bay, was invisible. The remaining guards and dogs betrayed no sign of having seen them, if they had.

They dumped their winnings so far over the wall in black bin liners, and a call to Meg brought her car rolling quietly down the road to collect them. Whatever happened from now on, the principal prize had been secured and, with luck, should pass without detection.

'Now the sheds,' said Bryn, sniffing as a sudden breeze brought a foul smell to their nostrils.

It was hard work beating through the bushes. The rhododendrons formed a dense black screen overhead and little light filtered down to the ground beneath. What made the journey twice as hard were the twisting trunks and branches. Just as you thought you'd identified where one bush rose from the ground and moved to avoid it, another branch would smack you in the face, bruising and freezing at the same time. Silence remained golden, but Dai's version was a stream of swearing, given forth in a loud mutter. Cameron was silent, but occasional grunts told Bryn that she was finding the going as hard as the two brothers.

Eventually, they arrived. At a clearing in the bushes, the moonlight suddenly bright on their night-accustomed eyes, they found what they'd come for. Four sheds of galvanised metal, each one maybe forty yards long by ten wide. A pair of forklift trucks stood like gawky sentries in a dirt-turning circle, which was frozen solid now but which would turn to mud as soon as the cold released its grip. The smell was intense, strong and choking, as though the stink was enough to drive all oxygen from the air. Dai gave his opinion of the standard of animal care in a couple of well-chosen words.

The door of the first shed was closed with a crude hasp and padlock, Bryn noting the signs of Altmeyer's miserliness which had been invisible in the main building. Dai applied bolt-cutters to the lock until the metal pinged and clattered in surrender. Bryn swung the door open. Inside the shed, the building was formidably smelly. It took a few moments of careful breathing to reassure them that life was still possible under these conditions. Cameron found a lightswitch and turned it on.

A string of dim bulbs brought a ghastly picture into view. Animals, kept for research, hunkered in tiny cages, squatting in their own shit. A thousand eyes flashed in the gloom. Despite the crowded life all round, not a sound emerged. Depression, apathy and fear lay as dense as fog over everything.

'Jesus Christ,' said Cameron. Although a scientist and a biologist, her work had never inured her to the suffering of animals and she was instantly horrified by what she saw.

'Bloody hell. Bloody sodding hell,' said Dai, shock robbing him of imagination.

More than the others, Bryn had known what to expect, but even he was appalled and horrified. The cages were ranged along two aisles running the length of the unheated building. There were trays of mice and rats, the commonest species by far. Rats are intelligent creatures, who love confinement about as much as humans do. The crowding was incredible. Some of the trays were just six inches high and almost half full of the beleaguered animals. Many were missing tails, their fur was weak and patchy, and scabs and open sores bore witness to the savagery that this cruel treatment engendered in its victims.

Beyond the rodents, larger cages, stacked one on top of another, held larger prisoners. Cats mewed and hissed in their tiny cells. The poor ruined things, stinking with their own faeces, stared from the bars with lamp-like eyes, shrinking back if anyone approached, and still the awful silence continued.

'There, puss. There, there, pusscat,' said Cameron, poking a finger through the bars.

The cat she spoke to was a tabby, with bare patches on her skin where she had rubbed herself away against the bars of her prison. The cat shrank back, then, in terror, lashed out, slashing Cameron across her fingertips. Blood dripped on to steel bars, an image encapsulating the whole barbarian place. 'Poor puss, poor cat,' said Cameron, licking her fingers. She was white-faced now, with a silent, burning determination to avenge the wrong.

Worse was to come.

In the largest cages at the end, black shapes squatted in fear. Strong arms cradled frightened heads, a hundred dark forms crouched in the foetus position. Monkeys, chosen by science for their similarity to humans, awaited their tortures in cages no jungle had ever prepared them for. Rhesus monkeys, macaques, chimps: the wider human family gathered in bestial reunion.

There was no need for Bryn to give orders. The plan was clear and no one needed further incentive. Bryn took the video camera and began to film. He filmed the rats, their tiny cages, the terrible state of their coats. He filmed the cats, the soiling, the desperation, the crowding. He filmed the monkeys, terrified and defeated, cages piled on top of each other, awaiting the forklift trucks which would one day come for them, to transport them to the next nightmare chapter in their unhappy lives. Bryn wondered if any human hand would ever comfort them, or if the next touch they felt would be the experimenter's hand, jabbing the needle, watching to see if the noxious substance inside killed or spared.

He made his film coldly and carefully, sparing nothing, collecting every detail. Only when he was completely done did he rush to help the others. The cages were closed by simple catches operable only from the outside. Since Altmeyer expected his grounds to be secure, there was no need of further security inside the sheds. Cameron was already taking trays of rodents and spilling them out on to the floor. They tumbled out in shades of grey and white, falling two or three thick over her booted feet. Uncertainty was the strongest emotion visible from the rats' behaviour as they found their footing on the chill concrete. All their lives, a couple of crowded footsteps had taken them to the walls of their world. Now, all of a sudden, those walls had fallen away, and decisions were required. Some of the rats found the walls of the cages stacked along the floor and shouldered up against them, feeling comfort in the security of familiar bars. Others, more active, darted forwards, only to turn and turn again, unable to believe in the possibility of freedom. But others, the smallest proportion, found immediate release, as though they'd been dreaming of just such a possibility for years. They ran for the smell of clean air coming in from the door, disappearing one after the other into the winter night.

'Go on, you lot. Shoo,' said Cameron, stirring the wriggling heap beneath her with her feet.

'This'll get them moving,' said Dai, opening the doors of the cats' cages.

At first the cats shrank back, lashing out at any attempt to remove them. But Dai was unlikely to be put off by any number of cats and, wearing protective gloves, he reached in and dug them out, one by one, dropping them on the floor. Cats, mice and rats, all at large, remembering their primaeval selves.

A skin-and-bone ginger cat was the first to move. Surprising itself, it made a pounce, catching one of the innumerable rodents between its paws. The rat wriggled and the cat let it escape. But the pounce was like the princess's kiss, the gesture that broke the spell. The cats began to behave like cats, the rats and mice like rodents. The surge towards the door was faster now, spurred on by new hunting attempts by the ginger cat. And – more wonderful yet – the horrid silence ended. A mewing, whining, chattering sound filled the room: sounds of distress from a thousand throats, horrible to hear, yet many times more welcome than the dreadful silence which had preceded it.

Bryn, Cameron and Dai were all now slipping catches, shaking out the reluctant animals. Only the cats and rodents had a real chance of escape into a normal life, but the raiders reckoned that the monkeys would be better for a taste of freedom, however brief. Bryn and Dai between them hauled the chimps out into the shed, as Cameron teased the smaller monkeys from their perches.

The releases proceeded in silence until Bryn, checking his watch, told the others that he would go and film in the other sheds. He left them to continue, and by now there was a steady stream of animal life moving out of the door, into the woods, Noah's ark in reverse. Wishing to get outside, Bryn found his way blocked by a chimp that had gambolled quickly to the doorway, then stood stuck on the threshold.

'On your way, lad,' said Bryn.

He tried budging the chimp over the threshold, but the chimp resisted, one burly arm hanging on to the thin wooden frame round the door, easily shrugging off Bryn's efforts to dislodge him. 'Have it your way,' said Bryn, and, leaving the chimp in the doorway, clambered over him instead. The monkey sat thoughtfully, watching a sea of smaller life swirling out over his legs, feeling the unaccustomed night air blowing freely over his face.

Bryn made for the other sheds. Each one held the same

general tale of horror, though the animals varied: pigeons, rabbits, chinchillas. In the third shed there was a small office area containing records on feeding, breeding, delivery dates, and so forth. Bryn wrenched open the filing cabinets, scattering the papers, doing his best to cause as much confusion and muddle as he could. Then on with the camerawork. It was hard to walk steadily down the aisles of woe, video camera in hand, when all his impulses were to release the animals and wreck the cages, but Bryn disciplined himself. He did his filming, released a few catches, spared a few lives.

Weary now, and sickened, Bryn left the fourth shed, the camera tucked back into his belt. Dawn fought silently for control of the skies and was gaining perceptibly over the retreating darkness. Bryn felt annoyed with himself. They should have left sooner than this. He began to hurry.

As he emerged into the dirt circle, he saw something which made his heart leap into his mouth. A guard was running into the shed where Dai and Cameron were still at work. Leading the guard, almost yanking him forwards on a leather leash, an alsatian strained to get at the intruders. Bryn wanted to call out a warning but didn't dare to, in case of attracting further attention. He ran.

Struggling not to step on any in the continuing stream of liberated animals, he burst in after the guard. The bare ceiling bulbs were enough to reveal what happened next. The guard, still running, met Dai. A massive fist flew through the air, big as a cannonball. With the feeblest of groans, the guard collapsed to the ground, unconscious.

But the guard wasn't the problem.

During the short-lived contest, the dog, briefly distracted by the surge of animals all round, had temporarily deserted his master. No longer. Snarling, and with teeth for wolves to envy, the dog hurled itself at Dai.

Dai fell to the ground as he wrestled with the beast, grabbing at its neck in an effort to keep its teeth away from his throat. The dog accepted the invitation, and sunk its teeth into his arm instead. Dai was too much the man to shout in pain, but an agonised gasp escaped him involuntarily, as though forced out through the double set of puncture wounds. Wrestle as he might, Dai only gave further assistance to the deeply embedded teeth. Bryn leaped forward.

'Where's bloody Cameron?' panted Dai.

'Just hold still,' said Bryn, manhandling the dog out of the way to improve his position.

Dai understood his brother's intention. 'Oh Christ,' he muttered, but he held his arm steady, bringing the dog's head outwards and upwards, the back of its skull against the concrete floor. Knotting his hands together to make a club, Bryn drove downwards with all his strength. It was enough. Dai hollered, the dog slumped, its teeth still knotted into the Welshman's arm. 'Bloody sodding shitting buggering hell,' said Dai, giving due weight to every sentiment contained in his brief summary. 'Where in buggery is that doctor of yours?'

First things first. Bryn hooked his thumbs into the dog's mouth and yanked the jaws open. The dog's tongue lolled stupidly from its mouth, but it breathed normally and would wake with nothing worse than a serious hangover. Dai examined his arm, which was badly gashed. 'Bloody hell,' he said, reverting to his normal, more laconic, assessment of the situation.

Dragging the dog, Bryn pushed it into one of the empty monkey cages, checking its position to ensure its tongue wouldn't block its throat and choke it. He closed the door and latched it. Dai meanwhile did the same with the guard, although he was none too gentle as he squelched the man backwards into the monkey shit which had for so long been somebody else's jail.

'Count yourself lucky, you sod. You'll only be there a few hours,' he said, locking the catch.

'Now, Cameron,' said Bryn. 'Where the hell is she?'

The question was soon answered.

'Guys . . . guys . . .' Cameron's voice, sounding small.

Now Bryn thought about it, he realised the sound had been present in the background for the last couple of minutes, unattended to in the hubbub.

'Cameron?'

It was strange looking for her. The ceiling bulbs weren't bright, and the cages cast strong shadows. Meanwhile, the floor was full of life: the cats, rats and mice which hadn't yet found the door; the whining monkeys, clinging to each other for comfort, feeling touch for the first time. Several times, Bryn thought he saw Cameron, only for the shape to resolve itself into a monkey as he drew close.

'Cameron? Cameron?'

Eventually, a small sound by his legs stopped him.

'Bryn? Down here.'

Bryn crouched. Deep inside one of the larger cages, a big chimp hunkered back in the shadow. Folded into his burly arms was Cameron, squashed against him like a comfort blanket.

'Jesus. Are you OK?'

'We're kind of cosy. I think the big guy's taken a shine to me.'

Dai arrived on the spot as well, but there was only room for one of the two men to get inside the cage to help. It was Bryn, of course, who took the plunge, squelching into the shit, head grazing against the slatted bars above.

Monkeys are famous for their ability to use legs like arms, feet like hands: an ability used to full effect right now.

Cameron was fastened by two huge arms across her body, two legs folded tightly over her own. Her face was pale but composed. 'Big daddy here thought he'd audition for King Kong. I'd say he was doing pretty well.'

Bryn took the chimp's outer arm and hauled. Though unfit and maltreated, the chimp remained a large and powerful animal. One-handed, Bryn would have stood no chance. But bracing himself with his feet and using both hands, he gradually tugged the outer arm away, forcing it against the side of the cage. Cameron wiggled, but it was a token gesture. She was still held as firmly as ever, and the moment Bryn shifted his attention to the second arm, the first one came back, like a steel clamp.

'There, there, sweetheart,' murmured Cameron to her captor.

The animal was still frightened, still in need of its comfort blanket. It had suffered years of maltreatment and an open cage and a few soothing words wouldn't do much for its hurts.

'Hell,' said Bryn, thinking of the growing light outside, and the stupidity of being caught and jailed.

'In my belt,' said Cameron. 'The syringe. If you can reach it.'

Bryn fought silently with the chimp to gain access to the precious belt. The contest brought forth grunts from both of them: heavy, laboured ones from Bryn, small noises of surprise or offence from the chimp. Eventually, Bryn forced his hand through to Cameron's waist. He could feel her belt and her body beneath.

'You OK?'

'Round to the left. Further. OK? Yeah, kind of . . . I just hope that damn needle's intact.'

Inch by inch, Bryn fought his way. He found the right tool pocket, drove his hand inside. The chimp was beginning to get annoyed at the interruption to its comfort session. Its grunts had a hostile edge now, its fuse was running short. Cameron's breaths became increasingly laboured as the chimp tightened its grip.

'Got it,' said Bryn. 'The needle's OK because I've just stabbed myself.'

The needle had indeed lost its plastic sheath, and the hardest part of the whole exercise was withdrawing the syringe while protecting the fragile needle. The chimp adjusted position, folding Cameron even more tightly against him, starting to snuzzle her hair with peeled-back lips.

'Get off my hair,' she said, 'and I was planning on holding on to that ear as well.'

'Done it!' cried Bryn, holding out his prize.

'Stick it in anywhere, doesn't matter.'

Bryn drove the needle into the chimp's arm, squeezed home the plunger.

There was no effect.

Whereas the dog had simply keeled over, the chimp still blinked with dark eyes, its arms still holding its precious trophy. 'Sod it. It hasn't worked.' The smell of monkey shit doubled in intensity for some reason, forcing tears to Bryn's eyes.

'Give it a minute. It's got a much greater bodyweight, it probably won't even be knocked out. But it'll be dopey, that's all we need.'

She was right. A minute passed, and the chimp began to loll stupidly. Bryn resumed his battle with the great hairy arms, and this time won with ease. He dragged Cameron from the cage, clasped her into his arms. He hugged her with abandon, relief overpowering all thought of the distance it was proper to keep between them. She let him hug her. She had been more frightened in her hairy prison than she'd let anyone see. Bryn kissed the top of her head, rubbed her back, wanted passionately to kiss her lips but was not allowed.

After a short time – more than she wanted, and far, far less than he wanted – Cameron pushed him back.

'OK, OK. It was only a monkey, for heaven's sake.'

It was time to go. They made their way outside, Bryn and Cameron cleaning themselves as best they could, though they'd have won no prizes in a fragrant body contest. The shed was now almost empty. Only the monkeys still lingered, as though knowing they had no chance of escape except by death.

'Bye, guys. Good luck,' said Cameron, turning back at the door for one last look.

'Let's leave our calling card,' said Bryn.

Drawing aerosol sprays from his belt, he handed one each to Cameron and Dai, keeping one for himself. Taking a shed each, and working together on the fourth, they sprayed.

'ALF', in huge letters – Animal Liberation Front.

'Animal rights not human profit'.

'Chimps wouldn't do this'.

'Stop the animal torturers'.

Dai's can rattled as it gasped its last. 'Bastards,' he said. 'Wish we'd had time for the other sheds.'

But they didn't. The sky was light now, and the twisted rhododendrons were little more than an annoyance as they raced towards safety. Finding the hole in the wire, they threw themselves over the wall and into the getaway cars that they had summoned. They drove away fast, exultant at their triumph, shocked at the horrors they'd left behind.

6

The journey home was mostly silent. Cameron slept in the back of the car, as Kati drove. She tried to avoid leaning up against Bryn, but in the end tiredness overwhelmed her and she snored away, her head on his shoulder. Just twice, she woke up.

The first time, she said, 'Thanks for getting me out of that cage, by the way. It was getting kinda scary.'

'You're very welcome.'

'That chimp was a nice guy and all, but . . .'

But what, Bryn never found out, as she closed her eyes and slept.

A while later, as the car began to jolt through the congested London traffic, she woke again.

'How did you know we'd find all that? Those sheds, those poor animals . . . Meg didn't know, nor Degsy.'

'Oh, that was easy. I'm a banker, remember.'

'Huh?'

'Amazing what you can learn from a balance sheet.'

It wasn't exactly a satisfactory answer, but Cameron was asleep once again.

The truth, however, was simple. When Bryn had searched Companies House for the facts about his property company, he'd also slipped in a request for Altmeyer's accounts and used them to dig down to his major sources of profit.

Altmeyer's business had three legs. First was the research outfit, not contributing so much profit now, but a potential goldmine if they hit on a useful product. Given the way biotech companies were valued these days, the research organisation was likely to be the most valuable part of the business, the key to everything else.

Second was Altmeyer's original business: marketing drugs which other people had researched and developed.

358

With his showiness, self-confidence and willingness to deceive, Altmeyer would always be a good marketer. But the third leg of his business, and the second biggest generator of money, came from a less expected source: Chirpy Chimps Ltd. The name – Altmeyer humour at its most disagreeable – and the description of the company's activities were enough for Bryn. The company described its business as 'the breeding and logistics of laboratory animals', both for Altmeyer's in-house research work and for the British drugs industry at large. The profits were enormous, with margins approaching a stunning fifty per cent.

Gazing with tired eyes at the flickering screen, Bryn had understood the whole dirty economics. The big drugs companies certainly wouldn't slash costs by maltreating animals, but if there was an operator who offered to lower their overhead by managing the whole breeding cycle himself, they certainly wouldn't be over-inquisitive about animal welfare. Bryn saw the outrageous profit margins. He heard Altmeyer's malevolent snicker ringing through the company's jaunty name. He knew enough of Altmeyer's greed and cruelty. He'd heard Meg talk about the pong coming from the grounds when the wind was wrong. He'd known what to expect, and he'd been right.

They'd already made a phone call to the news desk of the local paper, calling themselves the Animal Liberation Front and reporting a victory over the locally-based MA Research Associates. By now, long after dawn, Altmeyer's people would have found the wire, found the unconscious guard and the doped-out dogs. They'd be chasing over the grounds, retrieving the monkeys, swearing as the cats and mice eluded their grasp. It wouldn't be tough to figure out what had happened, and there'd be no reason at all to believe that the central building had been burgled. Anyone reporting lost documents would be told to take better care of them in future, while the contents of the safe itself were all present and correct.

But, as they drew closer to London, Bryn's self-satisfaction dissipated fast. The raid had been successful, but the tough part was yet to come. He was anxious, desperately anxious, and for the time being there was nothing more he could do.

TWENTY-SEVEN

1

Across the country, the radio begins to talk. This is an hour of the day which belongs to farmers, an hour when everyone else is in bed, when the airwaves belong to the Yorkshire dales, the East Anglian agro-factories, the Devon creameries, the Welsh hill farms.

Mervyn Hughes stirs in bed and switches on the radio. Gwyneth wakes up. Muttering his thought of the day ('Bloody hell' – same as it was most days) Mervyn heads off to the bathroom. Gwyneth looks at him going with amazement.

'Are you getting up?' she asks.

''Course I'm getting up, woman. I've a farm to run.'

'That's right, you have.'

Mervyn repeats his thought for the day a couple of times and splashes around in the bathroom, making the old pipes gurgle and slam as he switches the water on and off. He emerges, shaved, and with hair that looks as though it had seen a comb, however briefly. He starts to get dressed.

'Best not to have breakfast ready until eight this morning, love,' he says. 'I've a fair bit to catch up on.'

Gwyneth is astonished, but she keeps her astonishment to herself.

'Right you are, dear. Breakfast at eight.'

2

Still an hour before daybreak, twenty-four hours on from the break-in. A swollen red sun is preparing to haul itself up over the horizon, but for now struggles to free itself from the grey towers and dull air of London's skyline. The first petals of rose-coloured light begin to bloom on the cold winter water round Bryn's barge. A gentle wind, in opposition to the current, rocks the boat: the perfect lullaby for a man with a few hours' sleep still ahead of him.

Perfect in theory; irrelevant in practice. Cameron is up already, has found herself locked out of the boathouse, is hammering at Bryn's door asking for keys.

'Bloody hell.'

Echoing his father, Bryn rolls out of bed. He sleeps as God made him and he can't find his dressing gown. He grabs a towel, wraps it round his waist and goes to the door, which he throws open. Clean chilly air folds itself around him, waking him.

'Cameron. What a delight. Such an imaginative time to call.'

'I need keys to the boathouse. Some fool's quadruple-locked it.'

'Some fool is me,' says Bryn. 'I'm stepping up security for the race to the finish.'

'Uh, good idea.'

'D'you just want keys, or do you want some breakfast too?'

'Uh. It's kind of early. You probably want some more sleep.'

'Want some,' says Bryn, scratching his chest. 'Yes, want some.' He motions her inside. 'Not going to get it, though. Too awake.' He blinks himself another few notches more wakeful, and rubs his chest again, self-consciously. It is a fairly small towel he's wearing and he's a big lad. 'Sorry about the towel.'

She shrugs, looking at him dispassionately. 'I'm a doctor. I've seen worse. Dissected worse, actually.'

'I'm flattered.'

'Don't be. Decent cadavers were tough to come by.'

'Cadaver shortage. Rough. I'll shower, you make coffee.'

'Uh, sure.' Cameron is a brilliant scientist and a woman of a thousand virtues, but her kitchen skills wouldn't pass muster in a kindergarten. Her voice is as uncertain as if Bryn had asked her to play the violin or sing an aria.

'OK,' he says. 'I make coffee, you shower. No? Then I suppose I'll just do everything.'

He takes a six-cup espresso maker from the shelf, and loads its perforated tray with two spoons of mild Colombian, one spoon heaped with a fierce dark Brazilian roast. He tamps down the coffee, checks the aroma, adds a little more of the darker bean, then fills the jug beneath and sets it on the stove to brew.

'Hey, I forgot,' he says. 'You don't drink coffee.'

'I do today.'

'Can you boil an egg?'

'Sure, absolutely, no problem,' says Cameron. 'If you tell me how.'

Bryn sets her in charge of four eggs, a saucepan of water, a half-dozen slices of wholemeal bread and a toaster, and lets her loose. He showers and dresses, and returns to the kitchen, just as toast is bursting joyously from the toaster, the espresso maker is fizzing its head off in satisfaction, and Cameron is (at some risk to her fingers) draining water from the boiled eggs. Bryn sets the table and watches as Cameron begins to wolf her food.

'Do I pay you enough?' asks Bryn.

'I think I might have forgotten to eat yesterday.'

'I think maybe you skipped a biology class somewhere. I believe there's a connection between eating and staying alive.'

Cameron shakes her head vigorously, mumbling through her egg. 'That's a myth. Perpetrated by the farming community. Shame on you.'

They eat some more. Cameron devours both her eggs and is well into the toast. Bryn scrambles a couple more eggs and brings more toast, and they both gobble until full.

'That was real good,' says Cameron. 'Maybe I should learn how to cook.'

Sunlight is entering the barge more or less horizontally now: literally entering through the windows on one side and leaving through the equivalent windows on the other. Light streams across the breakfast table, casting long shadows amidst the litter of toast crusts and eggshells. Steam from the coffee pot is airbrushed in gently waving silhouette on the wall. It's time to talk business and they both know it.

'Well?' asks Bryn.

'Well.' Cameron shrugs. 'The material we collected is pretty helpful. I've been through it all now.'

'Excellent.'

'You know, respiratory disease really isn't my area. No matter what Kati tells you.'

'I know. It's a very, very long shot. We both know that.'

'I'm missing some important data. To be honest, it's absolutely vital that Mungo can get into Altmeyer's system. I'm dead in the water otherwise.'

'Let's hope he can.'

Outside, a river-barge is being hauled upstream by a tugboat. A heavy bow-wave begins to slap at Bryn's barge and the shadows on the table lift and fall amongst the eggshells. Silence prolongs itself. There's a question floating between them, and they both know what it is.

'If you get everything you could hope for . . . ?' prompts Bryn at last.

'If I got everything . . . I'd have to say, I doubt if I can do it in time. I may not be able to do it at all.'

Bryn nods. It's crushing news, but not unexpected. It would be almost too much to hope that they could save the clinic at this late hour.

'We're doing our best,' he says. 'That's all we can do.'

She nods, thinking about her research, her work of a lifetime. In twenty-nine days, most likely, it will all belong to Max Altmeyer and his friends at Corinth. Tears jab at her fiercely beneath her eyelids. She tries to look on the bright side. 'Even if they get everything,' she says. 'Corinth, I mean. The clinic, the research, the peptides, the patents, the Schoolroom. Even if they get all that, at least I can still publish, still tell the world what we've been doing here.'

In sudden horror, Bryn stares at her, mouth open, eyes wide.

'Right? That's true, isn't it? I'm only repeating what you told me months back.'

Bryn tries moving his mouth. His tongue is sandpaper, moving in a bed of ash. He can't speak. He can hardly even gurgle.

Cameron's voice grows more forceful. 'Listen, Bryn. We agreed that I would always be able to publish, and that's what I'm damn well going to do. I'm a *scientist*, for heaven's sake, and if there's one thing we aim to do, it's to get our work published.'

Bryn still can't speak, but he can shake his head.

'What are you saying?' says Cameron. 'Speak to me. If I can't even publish, then we'll have saved nothing from this catastrophe. *Nothing.*'

He drinks some coffee and uses the bitter fluid to get his tongue working again, though his voice clacks like a broken bone.

'Cameron . . .' His mouth produces one word before drying up again. This is hopeless. He swallows more coffee, forces more words to follow. 'That contract you signed, early on . . . you assigned intellectual property rights to the company . . . It's going to be a problem.'

'Problem? Why? You own the company. I asked you about publishing my work. You told me no problem. We agreed that I could publish whatever I wanted, whenever I wanted.'

Bryn tried again. 'We're in default on our loan agreement. Technically, that is – I know it's a bullshit sort of default – but technically is what matters. It's only sort of my company now. Really, it belongs to the creditors – to Altmeyer – until he gets his money or takes his shares.'

'And if he isn't getting his money?'

'He gets his shares. Correct.' Bryn exhales heavily. Not all the coffee in the world could make up for what he had to say now. 'And once he gets his shares, the company is his. Cameron, if we lose now, everything belongs to Corinth. Everything.'

Silence.

Another tugboat hauls a barge full of rubbish up the Thames. The waves rock as before, and, as before, the steam from the coffee wavers in silhouette, but this time, no one notices or cares. Cameron faces the loss of everything, and across the table is the man who's lost it.

'That contract,' she says, after a long while. 'About my intellectual property. You told me it was for insurance purposes. Is that true? It was about insurance?'

Bryn has broken Cameron's heart, so it's only fair that he breaks his own. 'No,' he tells her, 'the insurance company never gave a damn. It was me. I wanted to bind you to the clinic. It was pure selfishness ... I lied to you, Cameron, I lied.'

3

Friendships survive difficult things. That's how you know they're friendships.

Your best friend snogs your boyfriend? What the hell! The guy was a waster, best gone. Your best friend nicks your credit card and flies himself first class to Bangkok? Who cares? Lighten up. He sent a postcard, didn't he?

But some things, friendships will struggle to survive. Cameron cared about her work with a passion. From early in her life, she had realised that she had been born with a gift, entrusted with it – a gift that was of enormous value not just to her, but to the entire human race. For many long years, Cameron had more or less cancelled any trace of a personal life to devote herself to work. This last long year with Bryn, she had thrown herself into fighting Corinth and defending her precious Immune Reprogramming with all her heart and soul and brain.

And Bryn had sold it.

In effect, he'd sold it to her worst enemy for casual gain. By the standards she set herself, his crime was atrocious – perhaps even unforgivable.

4

She rose to go. There was nothing else to do.

Bryn stumbled to his feet. He was desperately in love with her, but now knew for certain he could never have her. His earlier, forgotten selfishness had unwittingly blown up the most precious thing in Cameron and his heart along with it.

'I've got something for you,' he said hoarsely. He blundered into his cabin and came out a moment later, holding some papers. 'It just needs a couple of signatures.'

'Another contract? You think I want –'

'It's a share transfer memorandum. I want to transfer half my shares in the business to you.'

'Transfer, as in sell?'

'No, no. Transfer, as in give. I should have done it a long time ago really, but I hope it's better late than never.'

'Now that we're on the point of being finally destroyed, you mean?'

There was no answer to that. Cameron signed the papers where indicated, and Bryn took one copy, leaving her with the other. She only barely managed to say, 'Thanks'. The word was strangulated. Her voice was harsh and strained. She left the barge.

Away in the boathouses, an unearthly shriek troubled the air. '*Uncha gossa, uncha gossa, uncha gossa.*' It sounded like a pronouncement of doom. From an upstairs window of the boathouse, a podgy parrot launched herself into the air and flapped awkwardly downstream. She didn't come back to the boathouse that day, or the next, or the next, or the next. Mungo finally pronounced her disappeared or dead. They folded away her perch, and wondered how to break the news to Meg.

TWENTY-EIGHT

1

A decent video recorder hits the shops, priced around four hundred pounds. The same item, second hand and stolen, retails in the right sort of dodgy shops for about thirty to forty quid. The price to the thief is maybe ten quid, fifteen tops.

It's one thing to steal. It's another to benefit.

2

The first three fingerstrokes were as clear as could be. In super-slow motion, the short, rather too hairy fingers rose and fell.

'F – 3 – a,' said Kati, deciphering each finger as it rose and fell on the keyboard.

'Mixed case, mixed character set,' said Mungo. 'Nasty.'

The security tape, which Degsy had taken and sent on to them by courier, was sharp as a pin and clear as a bell. Cameron, who was acutely nervous about this, the last critical stage of their burglary, began to relax.

The fourth character was blurred a little by the man's left shoulder, but the three watchers agreed that Altmeyer's head of IT had almost certainly typed an upper-case K. But

369

as he was typing the last three digits, an unseen colleague called to him across the room, and he swivelled in his chair, rotating his shoulder and completely obscuring the keyboard for the last three strokes.

'Damn!' cried Cameron, deeply upset.

Kati gave her a hug of comfort. 'It's not so bad. We've got four characters out of seven.'

'Not so bad?' said Cameron. 'Any key on the board, including numbers and punctuation marks makes about forty possible keys. Forty doubled, because you're talking upper case and lower case for each one. Twice forty is eighty. Eighty keys in any possible order, that's eighty cubed' – she paused very briefly – 'that's over five hundred thousand combinations! Five hundred and twelve thousand, to be exact.'

''S forty-seven, actually,' said Mungo. 'Standard keyboard. 'S forty-seven doubled and cubed.'

Cameron frowned, silently calculating. 'Eight hundred thousand,' she said at last. 'Eight hundred and thirty thousand, five hundred and I don't know – five hundred and some . . . Oh my God, we'll never –'

''S that all?' said Mungo. 'Star.'

'Mungo! That's like a standard three-digit combination padlock, where to try out each different combination you have to crack a whole new three-digit combination lock.' Cameron's voice began to waver as the scale of their failure began to unfold.

'Lovely-jubbly.'

'Come on, Mungo,' said Kati impatiently, thinking of Cameron's feelings. 'Don't mess around. This is heartbreaking.'

'Don't go breaking my heart,' Mungo wailed. He forgot the next line of the song, and repeated what he knew a couple of times more, losing the tune a little more on each iteration. Then he got serious. 'I'll get going now and crack it over the weekend.'

'You're joking.'

'Nope. Password-guessing software. Coupla days sniffing the wires, use SMB Packet Capture to nick the encrypted passwords, then use L0phtcrack to crack it. Eight hundred thousand combos . . . I mean, that shouldn't be more than an hour or so, max.'

'It's that simple?'

'Yep.'

'And we can get in whenever we want?'

Mungo closed his eyes in a silent prayer for patience. 'Listen man, when I get in, I'll be the sys-admin, king of the network. I'll set up a back door – Back Orifice 2000, prob'ly – and stroll in whenever I want. 'S no prob-er-lemo. Might even get some sleep.'

And what Mungo promised, Mungo delivered. By Monday morning, he was as well off as Altmeyer's sys-admin himself, king of the system, opening his kingdom to the hungrily thieving fingers of Cameron and Kati.

3

Cameron could no longer ask for more information. She had everything she wanted. But it was still tough. She pored over the information till her eyes blurred with fatigue. Her Post-it note habit rose to new heights, and she became withdrawn, difficult and moody. Bryn guarded her like a mother bear. He allowed no one to disturb her or her Post-its. One time, Bryn found Rauschenberg clearing notes from the patients' consulting rooms. Bryn bawled him out. 'Leave those bloody notes, leave them!' Rauschenberg must have muttered something in reply. Bryn boomed back again, 'So what? She's a genius. For all I know Einstein doodled on the wallpaper or used marker pens in the toilet. I don't care. Just leave her be.' His big voice smashed around the clinic. It ascended right up into Pod Mungo where Mungo chuckled and cracked open another box of Twiglets in his jubilation. It burst its way into the lab, where Cameron smiled and felt angry, laughed and looked upset.

But those were the highlights. Mostly, it was just hard, grinding, difficult work. One morning, Kati wandered into the boathouse lab to find her partner snoring over a pile of papers, her labcoat rolled into a pillow, sunlight streaming in through the window. She woke her gently.

'You should get some proper sleep,' she admonished. 'It's no good killing yourself.'

'It's only work.'

Kati settled next to her partner, squatting in the papery nest. 'How's it going? Do you want to talk about it?'

Cameron straightened with a couple of audible clicks from her maltreated spine. She stretched.

'How's it going?' she repeated. 'Realistically, it's not going far enough or fast enough. I mean, we'll always be able to put something together, but whether it'll be good enough to persuade Altmeyer, I just don't know.' Cameron pulled on her labcoat, began to button it, then pulled it off in annoyance and threw it away from her. 'I just don't know.'

Kati opened her mouth to say something, then stopped.

Cameron raised her eyebrows.

'Nothing,' said Kati. 'I was just thinking maybe . . .' She stopped. 'Nothing.'

'Allen? You mean, ask Allen?'

Kati nodded.

'Bryn'll go ballistic.'

'Well,' said Kati, dubious about any deception, 'I guess he doesn't have to know.'

372

Cameron shook her head. 'You're right. I agree. It's not like I'm doing so great without him. I'll ask him tonight.'

4

That day Cameron left early, meeting Meg off the train from Cambridge and dragging her across London to Allen's flat. 'Sorry to bother you, Meg, but it's kind of important.'

'Big romantic do, gorgeous? Call in the pros. Just this once I'll let you off, even though *I* had a big date tonight.'

'Degsy?'

Meg nodded.

'What, again?'

Meg nodded.

'Every night so far?'

Meg nodded. 'Or day. Or evening. Or whatever.' Anytime neither of them was at work would be more accurate, and though Bryn had been anxious that Meg shouldn't draw attention to herself by resigning too quickly, he hadn't quite been prepared for the depth of her commitment to staying in the Cambridgeshire fens.

'You guys are pretty serious, huh?'

Meg went coy. 'I don't know. I've only known him eleven days.'

Cameron explored her friend's face. 'Uh-uh, Meg. I give you about a month before you two move in together.'

Meg blushed. 'I *do* like him.'

Cameron laughed, pleased to have roles reversed for a change. 'You can't cook by any chance, can you?'

'I can boil an egg,' said Meg. 'At least, I bet I could, but I've never actually tried it. I'm a demon with the microwave, though.'

'I was kind of hoping for something a bit more stylish.'

'We'll get some stylish food and bung it in the microwave.'

And they did. Cameron took a taxi to the restaurant in Covent Garden which had been the scene of her and Allen's first date and came away with a tray of goodies, comprising, as far as she could remember, all of Allen's favourite foods. Meg meanwhile cleared the flat, removing all Cameron's science papers to her paper-bombed spare room and removing the pink and yellow prayer flags of Cameron's Post-it notes. That done, she selected music, arranged lighting and laid the table. By the time Cameron got back, the flat sparkled, a rose stood in a tiny crystal vase beneath a pair of candlesticks ('which looked better minus the Post-its, babe') and Mozart bubbled gently from Allen's hi-fi.

'Time to dress and impress.'

There was a brief debate, during which Cameron argued in favour of something long and black and backless, while Meg's hotly preferred number was equally black and backless but only half the length. ('Go for the jugular.') But Cameron had her way, and by the time she was dressed and ready, Meg was won over.

'It's sickening, Cammie. I've spent my entire life since I was eight going on diets, slapping on moisturiser, war-paint, ten different types of cleanser, bunging Charles-Worthington-this, John-Frieda-that on my hair, plucking, tweaking, shaving, tanning, bleaching, dyeing, you name it. You've done bugger all, and it's still the princess and the piglet, you and me.'

Cameron, whose height was emphasised by the fall of the long dress, did indeed look as lovely as a princess. Smiling, she steered Meg into one of Allen's swanky suede sofas and sat down next to her.

'You look great. You think Degsy would want you any different?'

'I wasn't really complaining. I get results. I'm just pissed off that you're ten times more gorgeous. You'd think all that bloody plucking would get you somewhere.'

'I owe it all to you, Meg.'

'Oh, bollocks, you were built gorgeous. And brainy. *And* nice. God, when you think about it, it really is sickening.' Meg looked genuinely shocked at the world's injustice.

'I didn't mean that. You know, before you came along, I guess I was always lonely, but I had my science to run to. The more I ran, the lonelier I got, so the more I ran. That's why I needed a Megging.'

'Well, you turned it around, Cammie, not me . . . Hey, if you're so grateful, do I get to ask you a personal question?'

'You need permission?'

'If I ask, you've got to answer honestly. Swear to God, cross your heart, hope to die.'

'All that and some,' said Cameron, crossing herself and gazing piously upwards.

'OK. Question is: are you over Bryn? I know you think you are, but are you? Honestly, honestly, honestly?'

'Ha. Bryn – Bryn, Bryn, Bryn.'

'That's the one.'

'Oh, Meg, you know I'm so unhappy with Bryn at the moment. For a long time, I'd have sworn I was over him. Everything was going so well with Allen.'

'Yes.'

'Then, I don't know, I had a phase when I kept wondering. I kept picking up these messages that he . . . had feelings for me, I guess. So I don't know. I was confused. I thought maybe if things didn't work out with Allen, it was possible that . . . I don't know what I thought, Meg. I just know I was confused.'

'And now?'

'Oh, now I know, I know for sure.'

Meg raised her eyebrows (what remained of them after twenty years of plucking) as high as they would go. *'And?'*

'And the answer's no. Meg, d'you know what he did? He made me sign my research over to the company, right at the start. He lied to me to make me do it. *Lied.* Some garbage about insurance companies. He did it just because he wanted to stop me leaving.'

'He's got his selfish side,' admitted Meg, 'but I think he's got better, actually. It's that bitch-troll wife of his, Cecily, that I blame.'

'He lied to me, Meg. And because he lied, then if Altmeyer gets control of the company, I've lost every right to my research for ever. I won't be able to publish. Jesus, I won't even be allowed to *see* my own data.'

'Bloody hell, Cammie, I didn't know.'

'And you say he's got better. Well, as far as I'm concerned, that's somewhere between a maybe and a certainly not. I don't really care. The way I see it, he's never once done anything which is just about me, or just about my science. When it comes down to it, it's money with him every time.'

Cameron paused, temporarily caught up in her own emotions. Meg was no piglet, but her companion on the sofa did look like a being from another race. Tall and beautiful, Cameron also had another virtue which separated her from ordinary mortals: she had virtually no consciousness of her own good looks, no flirtatious mannerisms now buried in the topsoil of ordinary behaviour. That meant that there was something extraordinarily direct – magnetic – in her displays of feeling: the sort of property that movie stars sometimes have on screen, hardly ever in real life.

'That's not quite true, is it?' said Meg. 'Didn't he just give you shares in the company? Free of charge and everything?'

'Sure, but that's exactly it. Just look at his timing. He

only gave them to me when he was pretty much certain the company was dying and the shares were worthless. Quite literally. He asked me how I was doing with the Altmeyer stuff. I told him I thought it was going badly, and only then . . . Meg, after all these months, it was only then . . .' Cameron's voice broke and she looked away.

'I'm so sorry,' said Meg quietly.

'I don't know if things will work out with Allen. And I don't know if we'll be able to save the company . . . But, well, whatever happens really, I think maybe I'll go back home.'

'Back to the States?'

'Maybe Boston. Maybe Chicago. I'm sure Allen would be OK with the move, assuming that he – you know, assuming that we . . . any event, all I mean is, once things are settled here one way or the other, I'm kind of a free agent. There's a lot of extra work I want to do. I could do it most anyplace. I think it might be good to get away from Bryn.'

'You can't go, I'll miss you.'

Cameron hugged her friend. 'Yeah, me too.'

'Alright, well you can go, but I'm coming too – only can we make it New York?'

''Course we can.' Cameron looked at her watch. 'He'll be here soon.'

Meg nodded, kissed Cameron, and got up to go. 'Good luck.'

5

Allen had come in late, but not too late. 'A celebration, huh?' he asked, sweeping his gaze around the spotless apartment and candlelit table.

'Kind of.'

'Kind of?'

'Celebrating the fact that you're about to be the world's loveliest boyfriend and my own favourite respiratory scientist.'

'I wasn't before?'

'Sweetheart, I'm always crazy about you, but right now I also need your help.'

Something in Allen always brought out the girlish in Cameron. Partly it was the way they'd come together, with Allen as the confident, experienced lover and Cameron as the anxious novice. Partly it could even have been Allen's height. At slightly over six foot six, he was one of the few men who reduced Cameron's five foot nine to something like charming inconsequence. On the other hand, there must have been something else going on as well, because for a long time, their conversation had avoided their one obvious common interest, the world of science, where Cameron's forceful mastery always ended up bringing them into conflict. But right now, standing girlishly with her weight on one leg, looking up at him through her fringe, her hands loose on his hips, she was hard for him to resist.

'Help, sweetheart? Of course. What with?'

Cameron wheezed theatrically. 'Help with the airways. Respiratory disease.'

'You're working on respiratory disease?' His voice rose in surprise.

'Uh-huh.' Cameron swivelled from side to side, rotating on her weight-supporting leg and moving her hands gently from his hips to his buttocks.

'You're growing out of all that terrible immune support nonsense?' joked Allen. 'Good girl. About time too. You want to talk about it now?'

'Uh-uh. Later. First of all, I want my favourite boyfriend to come eat with me.'

The flat was perfectly tidy, the pale parquet floor for once

378

uncluttered with Cameron's papers, the steel worktops in the kitchen wiped clean and ready for action. To Cameron the flat looked too sterile when clean, something like a cross between a battleship and an operating theatre. But still. He preferred it this way. She succeeded in putting food into the microwave without either incinerating it or leaving it cold.

'This is great,' said Allen as the first couple of courses slipped by. 'And you managed to tidy the flat. I mean, you didn't just start to tidy it, you actually succeeded in making it tidier. You must really want my help.'

'I do, yes.'

Allen raised his eyebrows in an invitation to her to tell him more, and so she did. Not the real story, of course. Allen had never been convinced by Cameron's conspiracy theories, nor would he have had any time at all for burglary and theft. So Cameron invented a tale: how her laboratory was beginning to take on outside contract work as a way of raising additional money. They were doing some work for a third party in the area of respiratory disease, and Cameron badly wanted help with some of the technicalities.

'They came to you for respiratory work?' said Allen in surprise.

'Well, we have a pretty good reputation, you know.'

'Of course, immune support, maybe, whatever that really amounts to. But respiratory?' He shrugged. 'Anyhow, what's the problem?'

Cameron began to explain some of the intricacies of the problems she was looking at. Once again, as so often before, Allen was silently struck by Cameron's astonishing command of an area of medicine miles removed from her own field. He said none of that, however, but used his own superior knowledge to begin to guide her through the maze.

'You know, sweetheart,' he said at one point. 'You

shouldn't really be asking me this. A lot of it sounds fairly confidential. I'm sure if you ask your clients they'll be able to help.'

'Maybe, but I want to ask you.'

'That isn't standard practice, though. In fact, it's really quite unorthodox.'

'Please, sweetheart, please, please, please.' She dropped kisses, like little cherry tomatoes, on to his mouth. 'Please, please, please, please, please.'

'OK, OK,' he said, laughing. 'If I help you, will you promise to keep the flat tidy?'

'Yes, yes, yes, yes, yes.' More cherry tomato kisses, one per word – even though Cameron hated cherry tomatoes and didn't normally kiss like that.

'Romantic dinners every night, long dresses, maybe a massage or two?'

'Yes, yes and yes.' Still more kisses. 'Oh, and sweetheart, this has to be our secret. Nobody else is to know. Not ever. Not ever, ever, ever.'

'It's a deal.'

TWENTY-NINE

1

Time passes, hurtling by at high speed.

What lies at the end of the tunnel? A chink of light, or a wall of rock? The company's death or its miraculous salvation?

At present, it's impossible to say. The only thing certain is this: they'll know soon enough. One way or another, they'll know.

2

Everyone's busy. Cameron has her super-top-secret work. Bryn too is always occupied. And on top of it all, there's the General Medical Council investigation, which is a nuisance that needs seeing to.

The investigating officer from the GMC was a nice guy. 'To be perfectly honest with you, we don't anticipate any kind of problem,' he admitted early on. 'The trouble is when we get complaints, it's essential for us to follow them up. In the present climate, we just can't afford to look anything other than highly responsive ... and with novel medical techniques like yours, it's always better to be on the safe side.'

Bryn and Cameron made a bid to see if they could bring things to an early close, aiming to end the enquiry within Altmeyer's thirty-day envelope, but there was nothing doing. 'Being on the safe side' meant, apparently, that the investigation would take 'at least three months, I'm afraid, and realistically these things do have a tendency to drag on'. So Bryn and Cameron supplied the data the GMC required, and sent Rauschenberg to sit, stony-faced, in front of endless committees of enquiry. There was no chance that the enquiry would have a negative outcome, but no chance either that they would escape Altmeyer's hammerblow. Time continued to hurtle.

3

Twenty-five of the thirty days have passed. Elsewhere, people are enjoying their Christmas holidays, opening presents, getting drunk, listening to their kids scream. But not here, not now. There's work to do, and work, as ever, must come first. Bryn intrudes on Cameron's space, high up in the tower. Once again, it's dark. The streetlamps of London glow orange through her windows. Cranes are lit up with strings of fairy-lights, strewing jollity on the frozen air. The silent Thames rides softly, sixty feet below. It's a little like the first time they met: the brilliant scientist, the alien banker.

'Hi.'

'Hi.'

They're still uncomfortable with each other. Bryn's disastrous lie continues to hang between them. But Bryn is here to build bridges.

'Good news,' he said.

'Oh?'

'My dad. He's getting a lot better.'

'Really? I thought –'

'I know. My mum put your pills into a milkshake and whizzed them up, so he didn't know he was taking them. Now that he does know, he takes them even without the milkshake.'

'Bryn, that's great, absolutely great. How are the symptoms? Brain-fog? Lethargy?'

'Better, all better. He's not a hundred per cent, but Mum says he's stronger every week.'

'And the chemicals? You know it's critical that –'

'Dai does all the chemical work. Or me. Dad's promised not to go near them again.'

'That's great. I'm so pleased for you, I really am.'

'You're a star, Cameron. An amazing person and a wonderful doctor.'

'No, it's nothing, really, all I –'

'It's not nothing. You brought a man back to life, when his own doctor was just poisoning him more. That's not nothing.'

'OK, I didn't mean –'

'Cameron, I know ... Look, I know you're still upset with me. I understand why. I don't expect that ...' Bryn halted, inhaled, took control. 'Cameron, in five days' time we're about to meet Altmeyer and fight for the future of our company. I don't think we should do that with you still furious at me. I think we need to patch things up, not just for our sake, but for the good of the company.'

'Uh ...' Cameron could hardly help but agree. Ever since Bryn's awful revelation on the barge, they'd barely spoken to each other. When they had, they had been polite, but strained. It was no way to behave when so much was at stake. 'What did you have in mind?'

'I thought maybe a weekend away. Perhaps, you could come down to the farm, meet my parents. My dad would absolutely love to say thanks directly.'

Cameron scrunched up her face, as though chewing bitter lemons. 'Meet your folks, huh? I don't know, there's still a lot of work to do.' She drummed her fingers on the mountains of paper that lay around her. 'I'd been kind of figuring on working up to the last minute.'

He shook his head gently, and lowered himself cautiously on to a stack of paper. It wasn't a particularly firm foundation for two hundred pounds of Welsh beef, but it was a skill you needed to develop when calling on Cameron at work. 'That's not quite true, is it? The lawyers are going to need their hands on your stuff any day now – before the weekend, anyway. If you don't want to come then just say so. I'd understand.'

'You really want me to meet your parents?'

'Yes. But more than that, I want to mend fences. You don't have to forgive me, but . . . well, we're going to need to look united and strong in front of Altmeyer. At the moment, you either look like you want to strangle me or you want to scream. I thought a weekend away from all this might help us.'

She nodded.

Things *had* been getting very claustrophobic recently. It had been good working closely with Allen, but she could tell that his patience with her work intensity was beginning to wear off. A weekend away would do their relationship good. And Bryn . . . ? Well, Cameron wasn't necessarily prepared to forgive Bryn as such, but in her heart she knew that he was a basically good guy. Maybe a bit selfish. Certainly more concerned with money than her beloved medicine. But everyone had their faults. She didn't have to love him, just work with him. 'Of course. Good idea. Sure.'

'Great, fantastic. I'll tell Mum you're coming.'

'Oh, *damn*.' Cameron halted abruptly. 'They live in Wales, right?'

'You've finally got it, have you, woman?'

'Shoot! I won't be able to come.'

Bryn raised his eyebrows. 'May I ask . . . ?'

'It's stupid. It's just my passport is away for renewal . . .'

Bryn laughed, the merry sound ringing through the darkened room.

'What the hell? We'll just have to slip over the border by cover of night.'

4

Crossing into Wales turned out to be surprisingly easy, border guards most noticeable by their absence. Rain and darkness accompanied their journey, and the last twenty miles passed in a midnight patchwork of steepening slopes, lanes narrowing between wet hedges, the occasional flash of headlights, the sounds of sheep baa-ing and the rush of tyres on slippery roads. They drove mostly in silence, each lost in their own thoughts.

It was Gwyneth Hughes – nervous, dressing-gowned, starting to show her age – who opened the door to them, cautiously because of the unaccustomed lateness of the hour.

'Oh, Bryn,' she said, arms tight round his neck. 'Bryn.'

He hugged her attentively before gently shaking her loose. 'Mum, this is Cameron.'

'Oh, Dr Wilde, please . . . You're very welcome.'

Gwyneth Hughes was thrown by the appearance of authority – medical authority at that, rain-soaked and on her doorstep – and she made a bizarre little gesture, more like a curtsey than anything else, her pink-quilted dressing gown lapping against her ankles as she bobbed. Cameron responded graciously. 'Mrs Hughes – Gwyneth, is it? – hi, real nice to meet you.'

'Mum, do let's come in, Cameron's getting soaked standing there.'

They bustled into the sitting room where a Christmas tree twinkled in the corner and a fire was dying in the hearth. Gwyneth at once started hurling logs into the grate, as though she'd been given one minute to create an inferno.

'My husband, Dr Wilde –'

'Please, it's Cameron, please just call me Cameron.'

'Oh, yes, Dr Cameron, my husband, you see, he's in bed, a farmer you know, has to be up early, otherwise –'

Otherwise nothing. From the top of the broad wooden stairs came heavy footsteps and a crashing roar. In pyjama trousers and a towelling robe which instantly shook itself free of its cord, Mervyn Hughes came pounding in.

'Dr Wilde!' he bellowed. 'Cameron, is it? I can call her Cameron, can I, Bryn? Bloody medical miracle, you are. Bloody miracle, and, by God, a pretty one. Eh, Bryn?'

'Mervyn, dear, your language.'

'Bloody miracle. I went to my GP and told him about you. Don't give out any of those head-pills, I told him. Enzyme P450, I said. Bloody miracle stuff!'

'It's not exactly –' Cameron began, but even she could tell that Mervyn wasn't going to have much interest in the finer points of her treatment programme.

'You've got her a drink, I hope?' Even by his own fireside, Mervyn used the voice he used with Rhys and his other dogs, high on the slopes of the windy Beacons above. The sound roared around inside the room, a multiple echo giving him the voice of Jehovah. Gwyneth's one minute of pyromaniac frenzy had already produced a blaze that pressed the two new arrivals back into their seats, while Mervyn came over with tumblers and a bottle of whisky.

'Just a little,' said Cameron faintly, as Mervyn complied

by leaving a couple of fingers' breadth of air at the top of the glass.

'Water?' he roared.

If he added water like he poured the whisky, Cameron would have ended up with a lapful of Famous Grouse. 'That's fine,' she said bravely.

'Just how she likes it, Dad,' said Bryn, smiling, feeling at home.

'Bloody miracle worker –'

'Language, dear.'

'You know what?' he roared on. 'I've come to a bloody decision and all. Go organic. Forty pound a head, that's what they're selling the organics for. Forty pound a lamb, instead of ten pound if I'm lucky for the ordinaries. By God, that's a profit. And best of all, you just wait till I tell Jones the Poison.' Jones the Poison was the local distributor of agricultural chemicals. 'None of your bloody muck, I'll tell him. Enzyme P450s, that's me, and my bloody sheep, too. Eh? Forty pound a head.'

The blaze blazed, Mervyn roared, Gwyneth remonstrated, her voice like a seagull's protesting against the tide, the whisky disappeared and came again, even in Cameron's glass, and when the time eventually came to go to bed, and Bryn took Cameron to her room, she said, 'Real nice people, your parents.' Then she belched like a donkey and slipped happily into sleep.

5

The next day, Bryn took Cameron off to see the farm, but really to talk, free of Gwyneth's over-solicitous hospitality.

'I'm sorry if the food isn't quite what you're used to,' said Bryn, sitting on a sandstone block fallen from the steep mountain slopes above. His mother, awed by having a

387

doctor in the house, and a female and American one at that, had felt obliged to press a new sort of cake on Cameron at least every hour. Despite Bryn's staunch defensive work, Cameron had already swallowed more refined carbohydrate and animal fat than she usually got through in a fortnight.

'That's OK. She wants to be welcoming.'

'Yeah, she does.'

Silence, as the grey cloud swirled over the summits above, and brown bracken plunged steeply down to the roaring brook.

'Cameron, I wanted to say sorry again for . . . for lying to you about that contract. It was totally selfish of me. I was thinking of the money, not you. I'm truly sorry.'

She bit her lip. The wound had been keenly felt, had not yet healed. 'It's OK.'

'No, it's not OK, really. We just have to hope for a good outcome. That still isn't impossible.'

'No, not impossible.'

The day before, Cameron had finished her work and handed it over to a bunch of well-paid lawyers who knew what to do with it. Whether it would be enough, time alone would tell.

'We're all set?' she asked.

'All set. We're meeting Altmeyer on his yacht. Just you and me, no lawyers. Portsmouth, this time, not Cannes, alas.'

'He was OK about meeting on the boat?'

'I told him we knew his tricks there, didn't want to meet in a whole new place. He didn't care, really. Too vain about his yacht.'

He let go into silence, looking down the valley to the land rolling away to the east. In this landscape, his shape and size made sense. He looked like a boulder tumbled from the same mountain he was sitting on.

Cameron let the silence run for a while before speaking again. 'I don't know what to say about that contract business. I feel so . . . Oh, hell, you know what I feel. But I also know that at the same time you've done a lot of really big things for me. Getting me out of Boston, persuading me about Corinth, getting the whole business set up and funded. It's too obvious to say I couldn't have done it without you, but I couldn't.'

'Yeah, well, likewise.'

Bryn glanced across at his companion. Dressed in jeans and an Aran wool sweater, beads of rain sitting in her windswept hair, she looked like a CD-cover for Celtic music. He wanted her more than ever, and had to force himself to approach gently. 'You and Allen,' he said. 'How are you two getting along these days?'

'Good.' The question made Cameron defensive, and her tone came out sharper than she'd intended. She was defensive because, deep down, she worried about involving Allen in the last, most dangerous, stage of the clinic's fight for survival. She hadn't told Bryn about his involvement, and she'd sworn Kati and Meg to absolute secrecy. But there was a bigger reason for her sharpness. She was defensive because she hated to seem incompetent in matters of the heart in front of the man who'd once described her as the last thing on earth he needed. To Meg or Kati, she might give a more complex story. In front of Bryn, she was only ever going to present the truth at its most rosy. 'My relationship with Allen is absolutely fantastic. The best thing that's ever happened to me.'

'I'm pleased to hear it.' Bryn was almost too crushed to speak. Had he been nuts? Recently, he'd started to wonder if Cameron was as deeply in love with Allen as she made out. He'd started to wonder, to hope whether . . . But here was the blunt truth. She loved Allen, just as she should, just as her hands had typed. He turned his head away, pain replacing blood in his veins. They both sat silent, and the world filled with the bleating of sheep and the cry of birds.

'You and he . . . I guess you must be thinking of . . . You know, making yourself a permanent fixture,' said Bryn after a pause.

'Huh? Getting married, you mean? Uh, I don't know if marriage is my thing . . . But we might move back to the States. We've talked about New York, maybe, or Chicago.'

'Back to the *States*? What about the clinic? What about your work?'

'We're pretty much done, aren't we? In another few months, we'll have got all the peptides we were after – assuming we're still in business, that is.'

'I thought you said your work would never be done? I thought – '

'That's true, but it doesn't have to be done in England.'

'But what about the clinic? My God, we'll be lost without you.'

'I thought you said the clinic would soon be ready to turn into a market-led organisation, instead of a research-led one.'

'But that doesn't mean . . . You're really thinking of going?'

'Yes. Really.'

Bryn nodded. Even the best relationships break up. Until Cameron was actually married to Allen, he wouldn't have to give up hope, but if she was thinking of leaving England, she couldn't possibly care for him, not at all. Bryn looked out over the wind sobbing through the wet grass. If Cameron was going, then there would be nothing left for him in London. Once again, he would be rootless, on the move.

'How about you?' she asked, changing the subject. 'If the business succeeds, you'll be rich.'

'In one way, yes.'

Cameron raised her raindrop-threaded eyebrows. 'What do you mean in one way? Like having a lot of money, that way?'

'Yes, in that way.'

'Which is the only way that matters to you, right?'

'I suppose.'

'What will you do with it?'

For a long time now, Bryn hadn't thought of the money. His aim was to defeat Corinth, preserve Cameron's work, bring it to the broadest possible public. His long-term ambition had been to work alongside Cameron, building the clinic into the best possible platform for her research. If he couldn't be her lover, he could at least be her champion, doing what no one else could do. But if she was gone, would he really stay with the clinic and all its memories? More likely he'd sell up, move on. 'I guess I might move back here,' he said. 'My dad's farm has always been tough to manage, high up on the hill as it is. If we bought some land lower down, in the valley, we could really get a decent operation going.'

'You'd go back to farming sheep?'

'I don't know. Maybe. I don't know.'

'I thought multi-millionaires were meant to have helicopters, and big houses in the sun?'

'Yeah, well, maybe I'll get a big house in the sun and bring in sheep, rain, grass and beer from Wales.'

Now it was Cameron's turn to feel upset. Despite everything, despite Bryn's betrayal, despite her conviction that Bryn cared nothing for her – despite all this, part of her still minded about what he thought of her. And, though she knew he was joking, she realised she'd been hoping he

391

would say something else, something about the clinic, about medicine, about her.

She kicked herself for being a fool. The two of them had nothing in common, she reminded herself. He liked money, she liked medicine, and there was an end to the matter. There and then, she made up her mind that, come what may, she would return to the States, with or without Allen. She'd start her life anew, get Bryn out of her life for good.

They continued to talk, but to all intents and purposes, the weekend ended there, on the rainswept hillside between the tumbled boulders. Bryn's dreams were in ruins, Cameron's feelings settled beyond doubt.

THIRTY

1

The English Channel is not the Mediterranean, and Portsmouth is more than a film festival short of Cannes. It's a grey, choppy morning and a grey mid-winter rain slants down over the sea. Smaller boats nose down the waves till their bows smash into the trough ahead of them, then lift abruptly as the stern wallows. But Altmeyer's yacht is big enough to carve right through the waves, and the rain doesn't pierce the gilt-and-mahogany vulgarity down below.

As a host, Altmeyer is as obnoxious as ever – no, an understatement. This is his hour of victory. He's more obnoxious than ever. He's told Bryn, three times already, that the *Sally Jane* is to be sold off following this deal, and a new, larger yacht purchased in its stead. The new boat is to be christened the *Bryn Hughes*. Bryn bears the goading in silence. There's one difference, though, from previous occasions. There's not been one crack about Cameron – not one – since she came on board. The memory of black Mediterranean waves and a spine bent miles too far over the boat's rail holds Altmeyer back.

It's thirty days since the GMC announced its investigation; thirty days since Altmeyer sent his gloating fax to

Bryn, asking him to repay the ten million pounds. It's thirty days on, Christmas has come and gone, and Bryn hasn't paid a penny. Today, if Altmeyer wants to, he can convert his loan to shares and take control of the clinic. As early as tomorrow morning, the entire operation could be in Corinth's hands.

They head out of the harbour. It's still early – barely eight fifteen – but the harbour entrance is busy enough that it requires the captain's careful attention. Bryn has a preference for empty waters, and Altmeyer is happy to oblige. They head for a spot three miles out beyond Selsey Bill, the southernmost point on this stretch of coast. In the radio room, the captain's gloomy assistant radios a short message stating the co-ordinates of their intended position. Bryn hears the message, certain that Altmeyer is keeping Corinth closely informed.

Meanwhile, a smaller boat pursues a parallel track, holding to the shore. On deck in the needling rain, Bryn doesn't notice it. He has his eyes glued to the furrow unfolding at their stern, a long chain of white bubbles, a temporary necklace for the gloomy sea. Boats come and go, but nothing appears to be following them with purpose. After a short cruise, the distant shore of Selsey Bill comes into view on the port side, occasionally blotted from sight by a sudden hard drumming of rain. They drop anchor. Bryn relaxes, Cameron too.

They're alone in the world, ready to fight for their clinic, win or lose, stand or fall, live or die.

2

As they turned to go below, they stepped down into the seating area they knew so well. Gone were the white canvas awnings, the deep-blue cushions, the hot salt smell of the

Mediterranean. Instead, everything was bare, wet and cold. Bringing up the rear, Bryn lingered briefly. He looked closely at the speakers, and with a thick finger prised back their weather-proof covers. Along with the woofers and tweeters and all that hi-fi malarkey, there was something else, something that shouldn't be there: a microphone. He snapped back the cover and walked on.

The passage to the stateroom passed the tiny communications booth.

'May I look?' asked Bryn.

Altmeyer hesitated, then nodded, shooing the glum-faced radio man out of the way. 'Everything top of the range. Canadian-built. Good enough for the *Bryn Hughes.*'

'This is the radio?'

'Solid mahogany. Not a veneer.'

The casing and dials were sham 1930s, but the steel box inside was up to date and tough, screwed to the worktop to avoid movement in heavy seas. From the back, cabling ran upwards to the mast.

Squeezed into the tiny room along with Bryn and Altmeyer, Cameron looked at the equipment incuriously. There was nothing here to interest her. Dressed in sand-coloured jeans and a chunky woollen sweater, she looked every inch the hardy sailor. For whatever reason, possibly excitement, she felt not the slightest tremor of seasickness, despite the rolling of the boat. She rooted in her bag for something, ignoring the men.

The only other item in the room was a steel cupboard, green-painted, with no markings. Bryn considered it carefully, took a screwdriver from his pocket.

'And this would be your bug collection?'

Jamming the blade of the screwdriver in between the cupboard doors, he prised away. Although the lock held, Bryn was able to bend one of the doors back like a flap. He put his hand inside and pulled hard, causing both doors to burst open in a snarl of metal. Inside was a set of labelled switches: deck, stateroom (port), stateroom (starboard), bedroom, dining room, bar, bathroom. A set of headphones hung from a clip, and there was a rack of blank tapes as well as a row of three built-in recorders.

Altmeyer looked first pained, then delighted.

'You've spoiled my cupboard! You know what, though? I won't send you the bill. Just my little way of thanking you for the company you're about to hand over.'

'Don't count on it, Max.'

Before Altmeyer could answer, there was a sound, a metallic snip. Altmeyer whirled around as fast as he could in the tiny space. Using a pair of pliers, Cameron was cutting all the wires running between the masthead and the radio below.

'Are you mad?'

Altmeyer would have stopped her, but Bryn's hand on his arm was enough to restrain him. Cameron finished her work with care. She hadn't just cut each wire. She'd cut a metre-long segment out of each cable and tucked each one into her bag. The damage would take hours to replace, hours and hours.

'Privacy?' said Bryn. 'Ain't it great?' He took a grip of the cables running into and out of Altmeyer's eavesdropping equipment and ripped. The wires twanged and surrendered. 'So important, don't you find?'

Altmeyer's pudgy face was lost in calculation. Should he head back to shore where his communications would be unimpeded? Or should he stay out here and ride things out? But as he thought about it, his offensive grin began to reappear. If the boat had no communication, then Bryn had lost his ability to conjure money from nowhere. Altmeyer chuckled. 'If you wanted privacy, Bryn, you only had to ask.'

'Don't even try to fix that, Max. Just for today, we thought we'd like it if it was you, me and Cameron, and none of your heavy-footed friends from Corinth.'

'Corinth? Corinth Laboratories? I don't –'

'Don't even bother. I know all about it.'

Altmeyer opened his mouth to deny the connection, but then dropped the pretence. 'It's not a boat anyway, Bryn. It's a yacht. Racehorse's arse, remember.'

'Your tub. Your slab-sided, foul-bottomed, bitch-rigged mud-creeper.'

Chuckling at the insult, Altmeyer led on into the state-room. There, on the heavily carved table between the ugly black leather sofas, was a pair of identical documents, entitled 'Notice of Loan Conversion'. Bryn's signature on those documents would put the new shares into Altmeyer's name, and the clinic into his control. If Bryn refused to sign, then Altmeyer would go to court and force Bryn to hand over the shares. For Max Altmeyer, a signature today would be nice, but ultimately unnecessary. His pudgy face was already gloating in triumph.

Down the corridor, the captain's mate re-entered the radio room, his gloomy face for once alive with a smile as he looked at the blank section of wall where a string of wires ought to be. He twiddled the dials and heard the sound of silence. The thought of fixing the wires hadn't even entered his mind.

Three miles to the north, on the restless waters a hundred yards out from Selsey Bill, a fishing boat bobbed at anchor. The boatman cast glances between the white yacht standing out on the horizon and the bare pebbles of the shore. He didn't seem concerned by anything much. His nets were idle.

3

Modern ship-to-shore communications technology is a complex business, and Bryn couldn't be blamed for not knowing more about it.

When Cameron cut the wires and disabled the radio, a smart chip inside the casing registered that transmission had been cut. Instantly and automatically, the chip ran a self-test program which revealed the extent of the crisis. Again, instantly and automatically, a distress signal was sent, using a different frequency and relying on a transmitter housed inside the radio itself. The only sign that the distress program had been activated was a tiny red lamp, winking on and off, on and off, on and off.

4

Chancery Lane – a pretty name for an ugly street.

At nine o'clock, congestion has loosened its grip, but the melting of the jams has left an ugly, ill-tempered residue. Private cars speed by, late for work, all accelerator, brake and hair-trigger horn. Taxis jerk forwards, brakes squealing like a sackful of cats. And then there are the motorcyclists, screeching around in the short but happy interval between the wave goodbye at rehab and the welcome home at accident and emergency.

Chancery Lane is home to the British Patent Office, and at nine o'clock on the dot Meg was there, Degsy was there, Kati was there, Mungo was there. Kati held a packet of documents. The documents were a monument (one of the many) to Cameron's genius, but this set bore the fingerprints of another set of people too: the patent lawyers, that breed which profits from other people's inventiveness. It was an important packet. That was why Meg and Degsy insisted on coming too. That was why Mungo was blinking in the unaccustomed light of a London morning. That was why Meg, thrilled to be in something a tiny bit like a spy movie, was shooting glances up and down the street, as though an ambush was in any way expected.

The others were teasing her for her suspiciousness, when she shot out a finger.

'There!' she cried, 'Other side of the road, black Mercedes.'

Everyone followed the line of her finger.

Mungo's face emptied of blood. He looked as pale as if he'd been shot. 'Oh shite, shite, shite,' he said, old fears erupting. 'It's freako, it's Janssen, the Darth Vader himself.'

Kati's heart stopped, staring in shock at the frozen-faced man, leather-gloved at the wheel. Arctic blue eyes stared back at her, colder than snow. Something like a smile carved a short-lived channel in the icefield of his face and disappeared. Involuntarily, Kati shuddered.

Janssen. Why was he here? How on earth did he know? Kati's brain raced as she began feverishly to assess the damage. Somehow – God only knows how – Corinth must have got wind of Bryn's plan. Janssen was here, presumably, to check if those suspicions were true, and then – what? There was only one answer.

'Oh, bugger,' cried Meg, 'now they'll up the ante! They'll just bribe the bastard till he can't help but accept.'

'What?' said Mungo. 'What's going on?'

Kati explained. 'Corinth has already offered one bribe to Altmeyer. We don't know how much, but enough to get him to invest in the clinic and make the loan. Now, if they think there's any chance that the bribe isn't enough, they'll increase it. They'll just increase and increase it, till he has to say yes, until he signs the clinic over to Corinth.'

'Oh widdle.'

Mungo's exclamation was heartfelt, but Degsy meanwhile had been using his head. As Kati and Mungo had been speaking, he'd been dialling on a mobile phone, without success. He snapped it shut and said, 'Not necessarily. I'm not getting through to the boat by phone. And by now they should've cut the wires. It looks like all communications have been cut off. Janssen can know all he likes. Doesn't matter if he can't get a message through.'

They all stared back at the car, now noticing its long aerial, the boxes of dark metal communications equipment crowding the passenger seat. They studied Janssen. By rights, he ought to be on the radio now, sending a warning, an offer, a new bribe through to Altmeyer. But Janssen was motionless, his radio equipment untouched and silent.

'Ha!' screamed Meg. 'You're stuffed, matey.' She began a victory dance, with Degsy joining in. A big truck, belching its way down the road, snorted diesel fumes in their faces and momentarily blocked their view.

As the truck drew away, Meg's joy evaporated. Janssen was turning the key in his ignition. The big black car began to nose out into the traffic. 'Oh, piss,' said Meg. 'He's going to go out there.'

A black cab emptied a passenger on to the street, and Meg leapt into the now-vacant cab, followed breathlessly by all the others, except Kati, who still had to take the documents to the Patent Office.

'Follow that car!' screamed Meg, pointing at Janssen's Mercedes, which was already beginning to glide away. If Janssen got to Altmeyer in time, he'd ruin everything.

They had to stop him. *Had* to.

5

'Champagne?' The ice-bucket was silver, clasped at waist height by a gilt statuette of a naked nymph. 'You can remove the bucket, you know.' Altmeyer demonstrated, chortling. He handed Bryn the Notice of Loan Conversion – a death warrant with a fancy name. 'I've kept it simple. You give me the shares. I get the clinic.'

'Simple enough,' said Bryn.

'Shall we?'

Altmeyer produced his rolled-gold fountain pen and adorned the document with his signature. Bryn picked up his own pen, as usual a cheap biro.

'You're sure you want to do this, Max?'

'Pretty sure, yes, I'd say I was pretty sure.'

'How much is Corinth paying you for this?'

'They're paying me plenty, thank you. You've got a lovely little company, Bryn. So sorry I won't be able to keep it.'

'I hope you think it's worth it.'

'Worth it? They're giving me three times my money, Bryn, I'd say that was –'

'Before deductions, Max. Three times, before deductions.'

'What d'you mean? There aren't any.'

'Oh, there'll be deductions alright. Cameron?'

Cameron smiled thinly, drawing a super-thin laptop from her bag. She booted up and, as the computer sorted itself out, she began to speak. 'Damn right there'll be deductions. First up, though, I want to tell you about some work we've been doing.'

'Certainly, my dear.'

'It's on respiratory disease. Should be right up your street, huh?'

Altmeyer's head jerked up. 'What do you know about respiratory disease?'

'Sit back. I'm about to tell you.'

And she did. She spoke about the background of respiratory disease, the chemical assaults on the modern lung, the nicotine, the pollution, the traffic fumes. She spoke about recent research, the major new routes being explored – then began to discuss the very specific treatment being investigated by Altmeyer's people, the treatment he thought was his and his alone. Outside, rain still pattered down on the grey water and the pale yacht, but Altmeyer was in another world, a world of sudden alarm, a world of startled calculation.

'Where did you get this information?'

Cameron smiled angelically. Her grey eyes were as intelligent as usual, but right now they were calm, even relaxed. 'Just brainstorming, really. Tossing ideas around.'

Altmeyer swallowed nervously. He attempted to put on a front of confidence, but he had his fingers in his mouth and was biting at his nails in his anxiety.

Cameron continued. She named the very chemicals that Altmeyer's team had been researching. She summarised the research bulletins that his very own scientists had compiled for him. She even discussed some of the problems that his staff had run into.

Altmeyer tore another nail. 'How did you get this? No one has been researching the area. No one except us.'

'Well now, that's a very curious statement,' said Cameron. 'You see, if no one had researched this area except you, then I couldn't possibly know all about it, could I? And I do.' She smiled.

Altmeyer sucked his finger. 'You've bribed one of my scientists. You've nicked a couple of ideas and pretend to know everything. I'm not fooled.'

'Have it your way.' Cameron shrugged. 'I just wanted to let you know what we've been working on.'

402

'And anyway, who cares how much you know? Without patents, it's all worthless. Why should I care?'

'Very true,' said Cameron. 'You need a patent to make money.'

'Like this one,' said Bryn, tossing down a patent application.

'Or this one,' said Cameron, laying down another. 'Or these.' She laid down a whole sheaf of them. Ten patent applications they'd made altogether, covering every base they could think of. 'Kati Larousse, my research deputy, handed these applications in this morning. They're intended to be fairly broad. We wanted to cover all the bases. I'd be very happy to run you through the specifics if you wanted.'

Altmeyer tweaked nervously at the patent applications, reading the description of contents. Failure was beginning to stare him in the face. His research project hadn't just run into a cul-de-sac, it had ridden into a nightmare of dead ends and failed effort – the jackpot scooped from under his nose. Before he'd even finished looking, his hand flew back to his mouth, which began to gnaw another finger.

'I can't say . . .' he croaked. 'I'd need my scientists to evaluate this . . .'

'Sure, I can see that,' said Cameron equably.

Gathering conviction, Altmeyer said, 'And these products aren't ready to be patented. There are loose ends, issues to be resolved . . . These patents probably don't even hold water.'

Cameron considered the proposition calmly. 'You may be right. We did some work of our own to tidy up the loose ends, naturally. But of course, if you challenge the applications and they collapse, then no one owns them. Not us, not you, not no one.'

'I'll need to review things. I don't have my scientists. I don't –'

403

'Trouble is,' said Bryn, 'you don't have time. We won't give it to you.'

Hand in mouth, Altmeyer's gaze drifted to the phone, and the empty corridor outside.

'No phones,' said Bryn. 'No calling your buddies at Corinth to bail you out. It's your call, Max. You take our company, we trash yours.'

'I'll challenge you in the courts. I'll say you stole our research. In fact, you *did* steal our research. It wasn't those bloody animal huggers, it was you. You could go to jail. You –'

Bryn smiled. 'Max, Max, Max. You say we stole your research. I say we didn't. Can you prove it?'

Altmeyer's mouth opened and closed, but made no answer.

'Plus,' said Cameron sweetly, 'I don't really give a damn about these patents. Unless you give us back our company, we're going to license these patents out free of charge to anyone who wants them. Anyone in the world.'

'So then,' said Bryn, 'you wouldn't just have to sue us, you'd have to sue everyone in the world.' He smiled brightly. 'Everyone in the whole wide world.'

6

Dense traffic, thinning out.

Janssen's Mercedes was darting ahead of them down the fast lane, coming within a metre of the bumper of the car ahead, then flashing and honking to get its way. For a while Meg and the others followed in their cab, matching Janssen, turn for turn, honk for honk, swearword for swearword.

But as the traffic began to thin, their cab driver refused to bump his speed up any further. Eighty miles an hour was his limit, while Janssen hit a hundred and ten where the road allowed.

'A3, M3,' said Degsy. 'Must be Portsmouth. He knows where he's going.'

'Oh, shit,' said Meg, watching the Mercedes disappear, knowing there was nothing more they could do. She tried the phone again. No signal. That was good news in one way. If Bryn had no signal, then nor did Altmeyer. But Bryn's plan had never reckoned on Janssen, tearing towards the yacht, a speed demon on a mission. With Corinth's billions at his command, Janssen could ruin everything, ruin it for ever.

But there was nothing to be done.

Meg dropped her phone in an admission of defeat. The cabbie, meter still burning, turned and headed back into London.

7

Exhibit number two: a bundle of dog-eared papers, yellowing and brittle with age. The bundle was a careful selection from the fire hazard heap that Bryn had rescued from the bottom of Altmeyer's stationery cupboard on the night of the raid.

'Recognise these?' he asked. 'Memory Lane.'

Altmeyer poked through the papers. He shrugged. 'Marketing stuff on Rogulaine, Keraplek, a few other dumbass products. Ancient history. Ten years old, some of it.'

'That's true. Some of it – this one here – is eleven years old.' Bryn shoved one of the documents under Altmeyer's nose, who inspected it half-heartedly.

'Good stuff, eh? Those marketing puffs got me my first million.'

'Good stuff,' said Bryn. 'Tremendous, awesome, incredible, and false.'

Altmeyer chuckled. 'Some of it was true. "Fastest

growing drug in its category". That was true by the time I'd finished.'

Bryn chuckled with him. Then: 'And what about the stuff that was never true? The scientists you bribed with fifty-pound notes and brand-new cars to produce falsehoods for you to peddle? The fake studies, the pretend endorsements, the made-up case histories?' Bryn pulled out a couple of sheets of paper – his homework of the last three weeks – which documented every single lie, every single deception involved. It was a long list, typed small. 'How do you think the authorities would feel about this? Marketing drugs on the basis of out-and-out lies?'

'Everyone does it.'

'Absolutely, everyone does it, but nothing as wild as this. You know damn well the authorities will kick your arse to kingdom come.'

'A rebuke, maybe. A fine.'

'A big fine, Max. A big rebuke. And they'll certainly suspend your licence, even if they don't revoke it altogether. That piece of your business is dead, Max. Time to wave it bye-bye.'

Altmeyer's mouth chewed dryly on the air. The core of his business was his precious respiratory research company. Cameron's patents had blown the heart out of that – but now the second leg of his business, the original drug marketing side, looked like being history too.

'I don't care,' he said. 'The drug marketing side is a sideline now, anyway.'

'That's true,' said Bryn contentedly. 'Your research company was the most important part of the business. I say *was*, because we own the patents now, remember?' As he spoke, he drew an unmarked black video cassette from his briefcase and laid it on the table.

Altmeyer swallowed, his eyes nervously following Bryn's

406

every movement. Then a thought struck him. 'Just a sec,' he gasped, and walked – almost stumbled – from the state-room. He walked down the corridor to the tiny communi-cations room, and with rough hands grabbed the radio. He searched it briefly for what he was looking for, then found it: the tiny red light, winking on and off, a distress signal calling for help on a frequency that only Corinth was moni-toring.

Altmeyer straightened up. A long, juddering sigh of relief swept through him. He was safe after all. The cavalry were on their way.

He composed his face and walked back to the stateroom.

8

Selsey Bill, Portsmouth.

Janssen ran clattering down on to the shore, damp pebbles skipping away under his leather-soled feet. A little way out, well within hailing distance, the boatman was there, still thinkering with his nets.

'Hi, there. You! Come in, please.'

The boatman, a heavy man, slow in movement, turned his head. Over the grey sea, the light rain still pattered down.

'Please! Can you come in, please. I need a lift to the yacht out there. I'll pay you.'

The boatman said nothing, just stared at the smartly dressed new arrival. On the horizon, Altmeyer's yacht still rocked at anchor, white sides greyed out by the falling rain. As though speaking to a foreigner or an idiot, Janssen tried again. He pulled out his wallet, withdrew a whole wad of notes. He waved them aloft, where the crisp notes began to gather the damp.

'I'll give you a lot of money. I want to go out to the yacht.'

The boatman looked at the money and responded with a shrug which could have been a nod. He hauled slowly at his anchor and began to free his boat.

As he waited, Janssen stole a glance inside his coat. Carefully holstered in the lining, there was a knife, black-handled, long-bladed, deadly sharp. Janssen tested its position, checked he could reach it easily, then, satisfied, he closed the flap of his coat and waited, as the boatman brought his boat gliding slowly, slowly to the shore.

9

'What's this, Bryn?' said Altmeyer as he walked back into the stateroom. 'You've brought a video? How thoughtful. Shall I order some popcorn? I'm sure we –'

'Let's just watch it.'

A huge-screen TV filled one corner of the stateroom, with a VCR in a mahogany cupboard to the side. Bryn pushed the eject button, and a video popped out. Bryn raised his eyebrows at the title: '*Matron Spanker and the Ten Naughty Boys*, Max? That would be an art movie, would it?'

'Give me that.'

Altmeyer leaped into life, snatched the video, and watched as Bryn inserted his own video into the machine. He hit play.

Animals. Animals in cages, animals piled on top of themselves, animals with fur patchy and skin torn. Animals cowering in fear, animals huddling in misery. Twenty minutes of tape. The same thing non-stop.

Nobody spoke. Bryn looked grim. Cameron watched the first half-minute, then left the room, and they could hear her pacing about on the rainswept deck. The tape ran to an end, the screen filled with black. Nobody moved. Bryn turned the TV off.

There was a long silence.

Cameron came back into the room. Bryn took a sheet of paper from his case, passed it to Altmeyer. 'A list of names,' he said. 'We've got fifty copies of this video all ready to mail. They go to the police, the RSPCA, the animal rights crowd, your customers, the telly, the papers. You'll have a media outcry, protesters at your gates every day, security costs through the roof. And, of course, your customers will piss off. For ever.'

'We can make it legal,' said Altmeyer faintly. 'Improve conditions.'

Bryn didn't bother to answer. Altmeyer knew as well as anyone that it was far too late in the day for that.

'Think about it, Max. You wreck our business, we'll wreck yours. We'll wreck yours so badly you can't get restarted. Not now, not ever. We'll blow your three legs off, one by one. If you sell us to Corinth, it's the last deal you ever do.'

Altmeyer wandered to the ice-bucketed nymph, and tore the foil from the top of the champagne bottle. The cork boomed briefly in his hands, and he filled three glasses.

'Hurry, hurry, hurry,' he complained. 'You're always in a hurry, Bryn. Calm down. Have some champagne. Maybe we should get some lunch ordered? I think we've got some cold pheasant somewhere in the galley.'

Bryn and Cameron exchanged glances. They'd played their last card. By rights, Altmeyer should have surrendered. By now, he was meant to be begging for peace on any terms.

'Sod lunch,' said Bryn. 'I think you need to decide what you're going to do about all this.'

'Decide?' said Altmeyer. 'I have decided.'

'And?'

'And, I've decided I owe you a big debt of thanks. Both of you. I'm much obliged.'

409

'What the hell are you talking about?'

'Oh, come on, Bryn, you're a banker. You know as well as I do that a decent auction needs at least two bidders. Before today, I had to accept whatever Corinth offered me. I mean, they're a generous bunch, their offers were always reasonable – but this way, I can play them off against you, force them to raise their bid, see how high I can get them to go. It should be fun.' He glanced at his watch. 'I expect them any minute now.'

Cameron and Bryn exchanged glances once again. Their breath was completely synchronised now, short, rapid, shallow. All of a sudden, Cameron leapt up and ran to the communications room. She came back a moment later, grim-faced.

'It's true,' she said simply. 'The boat's been sending out a distress signal all this time. He's right. Corinth is on the way.'

10

'Can't you go faster?'

A hundred and ten miles an hour on the road, now this ridiculous crawl over the sea. The boatman wore no rain-jacket, only a thick-ribbed woollen jumper, thick with lanolin, on which the water beaded like pearls on a party frock. The boatman shrugged.

'Old engine. Better rested.'

Janssen dolloped money down on the wet boards like so many dead flounders.

'I'll buy you a new engine, a new boat. Get me there as fast as you can. Please! As fast as you can!'

The boatman looked at the cash, left it lying there. He increased the engine speed, though still short of full, and their bow-wave curved white as they cut faster through the water.

'What line of business you in, then?'

The boatman speaks, thought Janssen. The idiot has words.

'Healthcare,' he responded curtly. 'Freelance.'

The boatman dropped speed to curb engine noise. The bow sank down as the thrust died off. 'Healthcare? Doctoring? A big responsibility, that.'

'Yes. Please, our speed.'

The boatman throttled up again, water sparkling in his hair and eyelashes.

'My dad was ill once,' he said.

'Yes.'

'Doctors said there was nothing to be done.'

'I'm sorry.'

'Offered him head pills, you know, psychi-what-nots.'

'Psychiatric medication.'

'You're quite right.' The boatman paused awhile in admiration of Janssen's medical skill, then resumed. The boat kept its course straight through the water. They were more than a mile from land now, Janssen's Mercedes just a flash of windscreen in an empty car park. 'Head pills, but it wasn't a head problem.'

'Uh-huh.'

'Then, you know what?'

An answer was expected. Janssen did what he had to do to keep the boat in any kind of motion. 'No, what?'

'Came across a doctor who said he didn't need head pills.'

'Really?'

'Said the problem was to do with poisoning.'

'Oh.'

'Said you could help the body detoxify itself. That means getting rid of the poisons.'

'Yes.'

'Gave my dad loads of pills. My mum had to whizz them all up into a milkshake to get him to take them.'

'Uh-huh.'

'Worked a treat, worked a bloody treat.'

'That's good.'

'You want to know her name? The doctor, I mean, not my mum.'

'Uh-huh.'

'Cameron Wilde she was, a bloody miracle worker.'

'Oh!'

Janssen's exclamation was different this time. His frozen face held no expression, but there was a brief scamper of fear in his eyes, which was almost immediately replaced by something else: an extra hardness, a hint of cruelty. A quick movement inside his coat produced a knife blade six inches long, plenty long enough to reach the heart. He held it expertly, his arm against his side, protected from attack, ready for the lethal jab forward. Dai Hughes, boatman for all of four hours, let the engine die.

'Bit of a bloody surprise,' he confessed. 'I was expecting to head you off, not give you a bloody boat ride.'

Janssen said nothing, letting his body grow accustomed to the swell of the boat on the rocking waves, letting his nerves and muscles do the arithmetic: the moving boat, the shifting weight, the sudden lunge.

'Still,' said Dai, 'it's nice to have a chat, it's more friendly, like.'

Equidistant between far-off yacht and far-off shore, the little boat rocked in silence. Then movement. Janssen darted forward, keeping his hand by his side except for the final lethal plunge. There was a flash of silver, a dull groan, a spatter of blood, the thump of a body crashing backwards.

The knife span briefly in the air before falling to the floor of the boat. Silence returned.

11

There was silence on board the yacht as well. Three glasses of champagne had been poured, but only Bryn and Altmeyer were drinking theirs. Cameron was lost in thought. Altmeyer didn't know about Dai, of course, but Dai was alone and unarmed – what if Janssen had brought a weapon? What if Janssen had managed to evade Dai? What if Janssen was even now preparing to climb up the ship's side?

Suddenly, her head jerked with an entirely different thought and she leaned forwards.

'It's not only about money,' she said.

'Patients?' said Max. 'The darling diddums little patients? D'you know what, Cameron, sweetheart? I don't really give a –'

'Not the patients,' she snapped. 'Your liberty. Your treatment of those animals isn't just illegal, it's an offence, a felony – a criminal, jailable offence. Unless you co-operate with us now – and I mean *now* – I'll see you imprisoned for what you've done.'

Seeing the value of Cameron's new initiative, Bryn leaped in to support her. 'She's right, Max, dammit. And the more the publicity around the incident – the more the newspapers get their teeth into it – then the bigger the jail sentence. You need to work with us, Max. It's your only hope.'

Altmeyer's face looked white and shocked, genuinely uncertain about how to react.

'It's nasty, prison,' said Bryn, rubbing it in. 'And going in there on a charge of animal cruelty . . . I hate to think what the other prisoners would do to you.'

Altmeyer's shock deepened, but then his face changed. He smiled and took another sip of champagne, with hands that weren't even shaking. 'You know, I hadn't thought of that,' he said, 'but it's a good one. You see, the more you threaten me, the more Corinth will have to pay. I mean, don't get me wrong, prison would be horrendous, but if I demanded – oh, I don't know – say five million pounds for every month I serve, then I'd be pushing for the longest sentence I could possibly manage. I'd get my lawyers to supply you with any material you *don't* already have.' He shook his head, mouth smirking, eyes dancing. 'Oh Bryn, Cameron, I love you people. Absolutely love you!'

12

Out on the ocean, Janssen rubbed his head, which was singing like a thousand angels. He hadn't even seen Dai's blow as it crashed like a ton of metal into his skull. The knife stroke had torn Dai's jumper, but had only grazed a rib, sketching a thin line of blood beneath his heart. The two men sat motionless once again, as the bows of the boat were nudged round by the wind.

Warily, keeping his eyes fixed on Dai's beef-barrel fists, Janssen stretched out his toe towards the knife and drew it to him along the floor of the boat. Moving cautiously, he reached down towards it, keeping his body ready for sudden action, found the blade first, then the handle. He retrieved the knife, cradling it once again like the expert that he was. Dai watched expressionlessly all the while.

Back in starting positions: Janssen with the knife, Dai calmly waiting.

Janssen tried to find his rhythm once again, but the boat had twisted in the water and was corkscrewing awkwardly. Its simple one-two pitching motion was overlaid now with the complex beats of roll and yaw. Besides which, Janssen's head was still ringing like the end of a wedding.

But still, the fight needed decision.

Janssen thrust forward again, but the knife never came close to its target. Another huge fist swung through the air, catching Janssen in the same place as before, right on the temple. The knife spun out of his hand, tumbling over the boat's gunwale into the sea. Janssen leaned over the wet thwarts, groaning, blood dripping from his nose where he'd smashed against the wood. When he righted himself, his own wet banknotes had glued themselves to his cheek.

'D'you ever watch rugby?' asked Dai conversationally. Since silence greeted him, he continued, chattily. 'Good game, rugby. Golden rule is never stop thinking about defence just because you're on the attack.'

Janssen unpeeled a ten-pound note from a cut on his knuckles and licked the wound. Dai reached into a locker at his feet and pulled out a yellow life-jacket. 'Where's the bloody air hostess, then? That's what you're thinking, isn't it?' He threw the jacket across the boat to Janssen.

'Oh, God! No.'

'No idea how to put it on, I'm afraid. I'm sure you can work it out. Don't even think it would fit me.'

'Jesus.'

Janssen drew the ugly yellow bib over his head, pulled a cord to inflate it, tied straps to fasten it. He nodded in readiness.

'OK,' said Dai, nodding. 'Nice meeting you and all.'

Face to face with the gunmetal sea, Janssen hesitated, drawing back from the gunwale. Seawater slopped over the side, soaking his shoe, sending bile up to his mouth in a sudden retch.

'I said OK,' said Dai, making the tiniest of gestures with his arm.

'OK, OK.'

Janssen heaved himself to the side of the boat. His head was like a migraine convention and the idea of the cold seawater made him nauseous. He dipped a foot in the water to test the temperature and gasped with the shock of it. 'Jesus,' he said again, teetering unstably on the edge.

'Oh, bloody hell,' said Dai. 'I almost forgot. Wait around.'

Janssen looked up gratefully, hoping for a reprieve.

He didn't get it. Standing up in one deft motion, Dai swept his leg round and caught Janssen in the backside so hard that he was lifted clean into the air and only hit the water several feet from the boat.

'Jesus Christ, Jesus!' Janssen spluttered, as his head broke the surface again. Cold water, English sea, pissed in by herrings, shat on by gulls, slopped into his mouth. His arms beat the waves. 'Jesus.'

'That was from Bryn,' called Dai. 'He said to let you know that if you ever touch a little lad called Mungo or his sisters, then you'll be getting a load more of that.'

Dai restarted the engine, letting it idle. He bent down and picked up the remaining banknotes, one by one, scattering them on the water around Janssen's head. With a nod of farewell, Dai released the motor, ratcheting it quickly up to full speed. The engine boomed, and the boat raced away to join Altmeyer's yacht.

Janssen looked at the distant shore, many times more remote now than it had seemed from the boat. Wearily, hating the sea, hating everything, a funeral march beating in his head, he began a slow front crawl back towards shore and the glint of his deserted Mercedes.

THIRTY-ONE

1

On board the yacht, Altmeyer, Bryn and Cameron waited in hideous suspense, with no way of knowing what was happening outside.

Eventually, there came a bang against the ship's side, then shouting and the tread of boots. Altmeyer greeted the noise with a loud crow of delight.

'Let the auction commence!' he cried.

A gust of damp salt air blew down the corridor into the stateroom, cold and with a smell of bodies. The boat's captain stumbled backwards into the room, brushed aside by a rainswept man of the sea. Altmeyer leaped forwards to greet his rescuer, then, seeing it wasn't Janssen, collapsed backwards, disappointed.

Dai looked about him, the naked gold nymphs, the leather sofas, the painted ceiling. Making straight for the champagne bottle, shaking raindrops from his head and jumper, swigging long draughts from the bottle, belching like a horse and drinking again, he spoke: 'Bloody hell, Bryn. It's a ruddy pimp's palace in here.'

2

Even then, the game wasn't finally won. Still believing that a rescue could be imminent, Altmeyer teetered on the edge of further defiance and it was only Dai's quick thinking which snuffed out the last vestiges of opposition.

'Funny little man came down to the seashore just now,' he said. 'Face all kind of . . . stiff, I don't know, like the poor bugger didn't know how to smile.'

'Janssen? Yes? He's coming?' said Altmeyer eagerly, scenting a possible way out.

'Was coming, laddie, sorry. He asked me how far it was out to the boat. I told him about three miles, and that my brother was out there, all set to bugger up your company. He was bloody pissed off to be honest with you, pardon the phrase. Made a phone call to some chap. Oozing? Hoozen? Something like that.'

'Huizinga,' Altmeyer muttered the magical syllables like a prayer.

'Huizing, that's right. Shouting he was, with all the rain. Couldn't catch it all, but basically, they have a chat about how much it's all going to cost them, and the stiff-faced bugger just closes up his phone and walks away. Didn't even want to come out and tell you. Bloody cheek, I thought. I mean, if you're dropping somebody in it, the least you can do is tell them face to face.'

Confronted with the destruction of his own business and in the absence of a counter-offer from Corinth, Altmeyer had no choice but to give up. 'What do you want me to do?' he said forlornly.

Bryn explained, Altmeyer listening attentively as his fate was mapped out. Bryn said they'd hand over the patents to Altmeyer free of charge, and destroy all the marketing material they stole. As for Chirpy Chimps,

418

they were giving Altmeyer thirty days to clean up his act.

'After that,' Cameron said, 'I'll be on your back. I'll inspect what I want, whenever I want. Not just for a month or two, but for ever. Any abuse, any abuse at all, and I swear I'll break you.'

'And if the animals are OK, you'll do nothing?'

Bryn nodded.

'I'm going to lose money,' complained Altmeyer. 'That place is only profitable because . . . because I'm very cost-conscious.'

'Bullshit,' Cameron came blazing in. 'Bullshit! Those animals are living creatures. You have no right, no right at all . . . By God, I'd like –'

'Max,' said Bryn. 'We don't honestly care if you make money or not. But you treat those animals right or you suffer the consequences. Is that understood?'

Sulkily, Altmeyer bowed to the inevitable. 'And my shares? And the loan?'

'You get to keep them, Max, but with a difference. We reclassify your shares as non-voting stock, and we amend the loan agreement so that you can't call in the loan for any reason at all for the next seven years.'

'No votes? Can't call in the loan? That's not economics, that's hostage-taking.'

'How nicely put. Exactly. You'll get your dividends, you'll get your interest payments. When we float the company on the stockmarket, you can cash in your shares. But no control. Not now. Not ever.'

Altmeyer pondered. Bryn thrust a contract at him which would make the entire agreement legal and binding. Given how things stood, Bryn's offer was generous, and both men knew it. With shaking hand, Altmeyer signed.

3

The boathouse rafters rang with victory. Bryn had ordered celebration champagne by the crate-load, and the staff of the now-large research organisation and the ever-swelling clinic chinked glasses and tucked in, as though they'd never seen booze before. But not everyone was happy. With a strained and anxious face, Cameron pulled Kati away into a side-room, the stationery cupboard, as it happened. There among the ringbinders and paperclips, the smell of manila envelopes and plastic wallets, Cameron found out what she had to know.

'Janssen was there? Waiting? He knew you were coming?'

Kati shrugged. 'We can't be sure, but . . . Oh, Cameron, I'm so sorry – yes, it certainly looked like he was expecting us.'

Cameron nodded. She was crushed, devastated.

4

That evening, Cameron and Allen, alone together in his high-ceilinged flat. The parquet floors, hard white walls, minimal steel furnishings made the sounds clicky and repetitive, like an argument born in hell.

'Allen, please tell me. Did you tell anyone – anyone at all – about the respiratory work I've been doing recently?' Her voice was strained and loud.

'For God's sake,' said Allen, tall, priestly and handsome as ever. 'Calm down. There's no need to shout.'

'I'll shout if I want to. Did you or didn't you?'

As it happened, Allen was dressed in a dark suit, with a dark-blue shirt underneath. Cameron was in a cream shirt and stone-coloured jeans. They looked light and dark, good and evil from a morality play. But Allen wasn't going to play

420

Cameron's interrogation games. He wandered with exaggerated calm into the kitchen and began to take sushi from the fridge and lay it out on a black china plate.

'I've a right to know,' said Cameron, storming after him. 'Did you or didn't you?'

'Rights?' said Allen. 'You're talking to me about rights?' He fished around for the wasabi sauce, and a dish to put it in. 'Perhaps you'd like to explain something to me, something you never told me the whole time I was helping you.'

'Yes?'

'Where did your background data come from? Who was your third-party client? How did they come to pick your laboratory?'

'Why is that important?'

Chopsticks. The next essential was chopsticks. Allen had three sets: one lacquered in black, one lacquered in white, one stainless steel. Cameron's backside was up against the crockery drawer, and she pulled out some chopsticks at random, white ones that didn't match the black china Allen had selected. He raised the chopsticks in complaint, saw Cameron's glare, and stifled his objections.

'Those issues are important,' he said, 'because there's such a thing as property rights. There's such a thing as patent law. There's such a thing as legal ways of doing business and illegal ones.'

Cameron paused. There was so much to say, and yet so little point in saying it. Instead she just said, 'You still haven't answered my question.'

'Which was?'

'Did you tell or did you not tell anyone about my work in respiratory?'

Allen stared at Cameron, not with hatred but with a kind of cold hostility. He'd picked her up, almost as a compliment to himself: the handsome man with the beautiful flat needed a beautiful intelligent girlfriend to go with it. But intelligence was nothing if it was soiled by too much emotion, and Cameron was acting more than a little hysterical.

'I didn't tell anyone, no.'

'You didn't?' Cameron was astonished, taken aback, hopeful.

'I didn't have to. Do you know the name Jed Scarlatti? He's the head of Corinth in Europe, no less –'

'Spare me!' interjected Cameron.

'I had lunch with him the other day, and –'

'Lunch? *Lunch?* What the hell were you doing having lunch with Scarlatti?'

'I was eating,' Allen snapped, then reined himself in. 'When I withdrew my application to Corinth Respiratory, they generously said they wanted to come back to me, see if they could persuade me to change my mind. This lunch was a part of that.'

'I see.' Cameron spoke quietly, her burst of anger having passed.

'Jed Scarlatti was there – fairly impressive, I had to admit. He'd heard about you. He said he understood that you were working on respiratory disease.'

'And?'

'And what?'

'What did you tell him?'

'He seemed to know already. I didn't lie to him. This was Jed Scarlatti, for God's sake, one of the most respected men in the industry. If one can't trust a man like that . . .'

'So you told him. After everything you promised, you just went ahead and told him.' Cameron broke off, too appalled to continue. This wasn't about the clinic any more. The clinic was safe, and her research along with it. But her heart was important, too, and right now she felt betrayed and abandoned.

422

'I did not tell him,' snapped Allen with a mouthful of rice and dead sea creature. 'I only confirmed what he knew.'

'Of course he didn't know,' murmured Cameron, almost to herself. 'If he had known, he wouldn't have needed to ask.'

The whole dirty story became clear to her now. Altmeyer hadn't had the wit to connect the supposed animal rights break-in with Bryn and Cameron, but Janssen had been more subtle. He'd joined the dots, guessed what was going on, and brought Allen and Scarlatti together to confirm his conjecture. In a remote sort of intellectual way, Cameron found herself admiring Janssen. He was a vicious man, for sure, but clever with it, an opponent of rare ingenuity and intelligence.

'Perhaps you can explain this,' said Allen, trying to recover ground. 'Scarlatti had someone with him, strange name, strange guy, actually.'

'Janssen,' said Cameron dreamily. 'Elijah Janssen. Dead nerve cells in the face give him a kind of rubbery appearance, loss of facial expression. Sure, I know him.'

'You know him?' A pink and green rice ball stopped en route to Allen's mouth in surprise.

'Know of him. A friend of mine's been giving him swimming lessons.'

Allen didn't even attempt to make sense of that one. He paused and shook his head before continuing. The pink and green rice ball continued its journey safely to its destination.

'It was Janssen who knew that you'd been working on respiratory disease. He was under the impression your data were stolen – literally stolen, I mean, actual burglary. I went out of my way to defend you. I said I respected your integrity. I said I was sure you wouldn't use data if they had been unethically obtained.'

Cameron nodded, her anger completely gone. She looked

423

at the dish of sushi and saw only blobs of colour on an ebony palette. Things with Allen had lost their meaning.

'I stuck my neck out for you,' continued Allen, angrily. 'Frankly, I don't know where your data came from. Your concept of ethics is much too loose for my liking.'

'Maybe that's the problem,' she said. 'Zapatone, Corinth's big anti-AIDS drug. There was a British study which showed three quarters of patients had their lives shortened by it, but Corinth continues to sell it. Tell me, is that ethical?'

'We've changed the administration protocol –'

'Don't bullshit me. The change in protocol is meaningless. You know that.'

'The drug has been licensed. There's a competitive market. If the authorities have a concern, they can intervene.' Allen was expert with chopsticks. He caught a bit of seaweed-wrapped rice with a thin layer of raw tuna on top, dipped it in the wasabi, and popped it into his mouth. Cameron nodded. She looked around at the steel-and-white flat. It wasn't a place to live. Real apartments were meant to have clutter and personality and smells and photos and knick-knacks. In Allen's flat, there wasn't a single photograph, not even of her.

'You said we,' she said. 'We've changed the protocol. They made you another offer, didn't they? You accepted.'

Allen nodded. 'I –'

Cameron shook her head. 'Doesn't matter. It's not important. I'll be back tomorrow. Clear my things.'

5

London's grey-and-brown winter began to blossom into a brown-and-grey spring.

Cameron's work was almost done. The peptides were found and patented, safe from Corinth for all time. The

424

Schoolroom was being developed by an outside manufacturer to meet all of Cameron's demanding specifications. The last touches were being applied to blood juicing techniques, which would bring the whole thing together. Preliminary human trials were extremely positive, but Cameron postponed the full trials until she could guarantee near-perfect results. She was becoming increasingly well-known, and had been nominated for a couple of prestigious science awards.

Through all of this, she continued to keep her distance from Bryn. She liked him, she admired him, and the whole contract betrayal issue was now firmly behind them. But she understood now that she would always be vulnerable around him, attracted to him against her better judgement, when it was clear to her that he would never make her happy. She had decided to make a clean break of it. She would return to America as soon as possible, and her plans to leave London became clearer and sharper with every passing day.

Meantime, Bryn grew more busy, not less. He had to turn his business into one capable of mounting a worldwide sales drive, fighting and winning a global marketing war. His hours became ever longer. As the company outgrew the boathouses, its original home, he worked in one building, Cameron in another. They seldom saw each other. Plans for the company's stockmarket flotation raced ahead.

At the same time, and to everyone's delight, Corinth began to stumble. As the clinic's breakthroughs became better known, senior doctors began to question publicly whether Corinth's brand of medicine was any longer appropriate. The company's stock price began to nudge down instead of up, and Huizinga's place at the top came under mounting pressure.

On the romantic front, Meg and Degsy were happily

moved in together. Meg, in fact, was two months pregnant, and though she hadn't yet told anyone, except the delighted father, she was over the moon with joy. Meantime, after two long months had passed, a thin, almost scrawny-looking parrot returned to the boathouse. 'That's never Tal-lulah,' said Bryn, but when the blue-green visitor eyed him up and screeched, '*O-shi, matey,*' it was clear enough that the prodigal had returned.

Kati and Thierry Thingummy were also doing well: engaged to be married, trekking all over London looking at houses to buy.

And Mungo was chirpy. One evening, Kati came out of work to see Mungo chatting with an attractive teenaged redhead and her twenty-something boyfriend, lolling against a beat-up car.

'Hey, Kati, Canadian Kate!' yelled Mungo. 'Come an' meet JoJo and her number one guy.'

Kati came over to say hello, recognising in the flame-haired young woman a suddenly matured version of the foster-farmed street-kid of Mungo's photo. Mungo was as proud as an Ivy League parent at a graduation do.

'This is Jeff,' said Mungo, 'and look. Car – ' he said, patting it – 'job' – he said, with a poke to Jeff's ribs – 'and believe it or not,' he twirled Jeff's keys from his hand, and held them up, a housekey to the fore, '*mortgage!*'

Kati laughed and congratulated them all. According to Mungo, JoJo's shoplifting habits were calming down ('lit'rally only make-up stuff now, which is sort of a basic human right, far as she's concerned') and Dar was a handful, but only in the way that adolescent girls are meant to be. He didn't say so, but a huge load was beginning to lift from his young mind and with his precocious parenting duties on the way to being successfully completed, he found time to think more about himself. He continued to work for Bryn, but was growing bored with the routine. 'Cracking's what I love, man, only I'm getting a bit grown-up jus' doing it for fun,' he complained one evening.

'So don't. Do it as a job,' said Bryn.

'Samurai work? Like I used to? Trouble is the suits, man. Too many suits.'

'No. Set up a proper consultancy business. Ask-Mungo.com.'

And so he did. With cash and advice from Bryn, and plenty of moral support from Kati, Meg and Cameron, Mungo set up shop. After a tough start, he scored a sensational and deserved success with a major client, and business began to flood in.

''Magine that,' said Mungo, staring down at his very first legitimately obtained cheque. 'Mungo the capitalist.' He tweaked his grubby T-shirt and looked downwards at his ballooning refugee trousers. He wiped his nose on his hand, and his hand on his bum. 'What d'you think, man? Maybe it's time I got myself a suit.'

6

One night, exhausted and unhappy, Bryn was finding it impossible to sleep. Grabbing a sleeping bag and a bottle of wine, he took himself off to the roof of his barge, lying under the stars and listening to the movement of the river beneath. Cameron was still in his thoughts, every day, every hour, sometimes even every minute. The deluge of work that threatened to drown him was welcome, in part, because it filled his mind and devoured his day. He drank his wine, saw shooting stars destroy themselves in the upper atmosphere, and watched the dark lamps of moored boats splash hide-and-seek reflections over the gently rippling Thames.

Then, at about two in the morning, a light came on in

the boathouse. He sat up, watching. From his own private office, lamplight splashed outside into the darkness. As Bryn continued to watch, he saw a dark shape passing across the illuminated window.

Bryn's pulse automatically accelerated. Now that the war against Corinth was won, he had dropped most of the alarms and keys and security codes, but he still didn't want to give thieves the satisfaction. Pulling on a pair of soft-soled shoes, he ran lightly across the roof, down on to the creaking jetty, and let himself silently into the clinic. At the entrance, he paused a moment to let himself grow accustomed to the layout of the dark, familiar space and the brooding silence of the vaulted roof above. His office light had now been switched off, but the door leading into the research area had been left open, and there was a light on at the stairs.

Breathing through his mouth, Bryn groped under the reception counter for a wooden bar which was used sometimes to prop open some of the higher windows. Bryn hefted the weight in his hand, preparing for a fight.

He crept in silence to the research area and waited, listening. There were quiet noises making their way down from upstairs, and Bryn crept silently up. The first-floor laboratory area was dark and deserted, but lamplight came filtering down from Cameron's tower. The intruder, whoever it was, was in there, in Cameron's office. He grasped his stick and ascended, stopping a few stairs before the very top. He could hear the sound of a human being, papers rustling, light and purposeful movements, but even after a few minutes not a word of conversation. Whoever it was, there was only one person, not several.

Bryn shifted his weight on to his toes, flexed his fingers round his truncheon and slammed open the door. The movement alerted the intruder, who whirled round to face him.

It was Cameron, dressed in a silk taffeta evening dress of infinite-blue indigo.

'Good evening,' said Bryn, laying down his weapon.

'God, you startled me.'

'Whereas I find it perfectly normal to see someone poking round my office at two in the morning.'

Cameron was holding a stack of papers, which she raised in explanation. 'Sorry. I'd left some papers in there which I needed. I just popped in to collect them.'

'This is a regular two in the morning habit? At least you dressed for the occasion, I see.'

Cameron looked awkward, putting her hand to the neckline of her off-the-shoulder dress as though feeling suddenly naked. 'It was the awards ceremony tonight. Research Scientist of the Year. Remember?'

'Oh, yes, of course. Did you . . . ?'

Cameron smiled, half-nodded, and shrugged, almost apologising for her success.

'Well done,' said Bryn. 'That's fantastic. Well done you.'

'Thanks.'

She looked down at her desk, and, following her gaze, Bryn spotted a glass and silver trophy that hadn't been there before. 'Next stop, Stockholm,' he said, referring to the Nobel Prize awards which were always held in Sweden.

'I doubt it.' She was embarrassed. There was a single anglepoise lamp on, but mostly the room was full of starlight and the shimmer of streetlamps. 'Actually, it's good you found me. There was something I needed to tell you. I've been kind of putting it off, I guess.'

'Yes?'

Cameron swallowed. This was hard. 'I wanted to collect up my papers because I may be leaving soon.'

'Leaving? As in . . . ?'

'Leaving the clinic. Leaving London. Going home.'

429

'You're kidding.' Bryn had long known that Cameron would leave, but the very fact of it was more than he wanted to handle. 'When you say soon . . . ?'

'In the next week or two. I've been offered a job. Heading up a research institute in LA. It's a great opportunity.'

'But the clinic? Isn't there more work to do? I mean, we haven't yet begun the full-scale human trials. I thought it would be months at least . . .'

'You don't need me for that,' said Cameron gently. 'Honestly, Kati can manage it all. Rauschenberg knows a lot about running human trials. Probably more than I do. I grew up with rats, remember. If you do ever need me, I'll be on the first plane over.'

'Need you?' Bryn spoke like a broken toy. He needed her a million times over, but no longer had any reasons he could give her. He was almost overcome by her beauty and his own hopeless desire. 'Need you? We'll be fine, I suppose, if we have to be.'

She smiled at him with real kindness and affection. 'Look, I'm sorry about barging into your office earlier. I guess I feel awkward about going. I wanted to make my exit as clean as I could. I was going to come in and tell you, of course. I just didn't want to muddle things up by running around after papers and suchlike.'

Bryn smiled back and nodded. He thought he had been heartbroken before, but at least as things stood now he got to see the woman he loved from time to time. To feel like this about her, but not to be able even to see her, was almost unthinkable.

'Tell you what,' she said. 'Why don't I come by tomorrow? We'll spend the afternoon together. A kind of farewell, I suppose.'

He nodded. 'I'd love that.'

She studied him in the meagre lamplight. Most of his

face was hidden from view, framed in black by the dark river beneath. 'Are you OK?'

He nodded. 'Fine.' He spoke like an automaton.

'Sorry for waking you.'

He shook his head. 'I was awake.' He poked his pole with his foot. 'Sorry for startling you.'

'My fault, I guess.'

She riffled absent-mindedly through the stack of papers she'd brought up from his office. And as she riffled, he noticed that she'd accidentally taken too much: there were some papers at the bottom that weren't science papers but financial documents, which he still needed. He came forwards and gently detached them from the bottom. The dark-blue and gold of the Berger Scholes logo gleamed up at them.

'Berger Scholes?' she said. 'Isn't that your old bank?'

'That's right.'

'What are you doing with them?'

Bryn shrugged. 'We need to float the company on the stockmarket. They're one of the firms pitching for business. This is their presentation.'

'May I see it?'

'It's your company as much as mine. I'd send these things over to you, only you've never shown a lot of interest.'

She laughed at him, her clear laugh making the room ring like a bell. 'No interest at all, right?' She bent over the presentation, skirts rustling as she moved. She flipped the colour pages through to the end. 'They're valuing the company at *four hundred* million pounds?'

'That's right.'

'Six hundred million bucks?'

'Uh-huh.'

'Jeez.' Cameron was visibly astonished. For the first time, despite Bryn's long years of evangelism, she had understood something about the market economics of medicine. 'That's six hundred million bucks supporting *our* technology? Fighting off Corinth and everyone else in the marketplace? Not just in Britain, not just in the States, but everywhere, right? Our patents work everywhere?'

Bryn smiled at her amazement and flipped to a page of the presentation that Cameron hadn't properly studied. 'See there,' he said. 'A few hundred million is only the beginning.'

Cameron looked at the page, absorbing its message. 'They're saying there's a problem because we haven't yet conducted our full human trials on Immune Reprogramming? Hey, that's not right. We've done the preliminaries. The full trials will only confirm what we already know.'

'Not exactly. They're not saying it's a problem, they're just saying the marketability of the company's shares will improve drastically once the results are out. Assuming they're positive, of course.'

'Oh, they'll be positive. These days we can do humans better than I ever managed with rats . . .' Cameron's voice tailed off as she examined the numbers in the banker's presentation more carefully. 'Three *billion* pounds? That's what they estimate the company will be worth if we succeed? Three billion pounds?'

Bryn nodded. 'Thirty per cent of that is yours. A billion pounds, near enough.'

'I'm speechless.'

'No need to join a research institute, Cameron. You can buy one.' She lapsed into shocked, astonished silence. At that moment, the moon emerged from behind a cloud, and the glass-walled room suddenly whitened as the moonlight picked out every object in silver and black.

'So then there'll be three billion pounds supporting our technology,' she whispered. 'And you. I mean, the company has always relied on you. Three billion pounds and Bryn

432

Hughes. Jesus. Nothing will stand in the way of Reprogramming now.'

Bryn shook his head.

She was silent again, seeing a vision – the vision that had been born in Bryn a year and more ago, one snowy night in Boston. The vision was of her technology sweeping brilliantly across the globe, supported not merely by that unreliable ogre, Truth, but by that immense and unstoppable giant, Money.

When she looked up again, tears sparkled like diamonds in her eyes. 'My God,' she said. 'I'm so grateful. I couldn't have picked a better ... You couldn't have been ... I'm sorry I didn't always appreciate you. You always told me and I never understood.'

'Don't be silly. You've been absolutely fantastic yourself. Working with you has been – it's been ...' Bryn was too choked to speak. He didn't just want to work alongside this woman, he wanted to marry her – wanted to marry her a thousand times over. The light revealed that Bryn's eyes were blurry too. He dashed his tears away with the back of his hand, determined that if he had to say goodbye to Cameron, he would at least do so with dignity.

'You must be pleased,' she said.

'Pleased?' For a moment, Bryn could think of nothing at all to be pleased about.

'You'll be a billionaire. Isn't that what you've always wanted?'

'I suppose so.'

They were standing opposite each other now, able to look each other up and down. Cameron studied her bear-like counterpart. He appeared so strong, so invincible – and yet as so often recently there seemed to be so much feeling, sadness even, in his face. She steeled herself. 'You know I said I'd come by tomorrow?'

433

Bryn nodded.

'I hate partings. Maybe . . . Would it be alright if we said goodbye now?'

Bryn nodded. Tears were welling up in his eyes again, and he leaned to knock the lamp away from his face, to prevent Cameron from seeing. But big emotions made him move clumsily, and he knocked the blue-and-gold presentation from her hand. Quicker than him, she bent to retrieve it, and as she did so noticed a sheet of paper which was tucked inside and had only come unstuck in the fall. Bryn hurriedly bent to snatch it from her grasp, but she twirled it away from him.

'What's this?'

'It's nothing. Give it here and I'll put – '

'If it was nothing, you wouldn't mind me seeing it.'

'It's not really – '

'It's my company, right? As much as it is yours?'

Bryn nodded.

'OK then.' Bending over the golden lamplight lying like a pool amongst the moon's silver, Cameron began to read the sheet of paper. It was a letter to Bryn sent by a senior director of Berger Scholes. The date on the paper was two weeks after the date on the presentation. She read it once standing up, then took it to her desk, where she read it again sitting down. Her voice hardened as she said, 'Can you explain this?'

'It's nothing,' said Bryn. 'It's just a strategy I wanted to explore.'

'That's a lie. This letter states that your decision is irrevocable. You've actually given up the right to exploit the company's patents.'

'That's not true,' said Bryn. 'We can exploit them. It's just – ' He took a deep breath. The truth was this. Most of the company's value lay in its patents of all the peptides

434

Cameron had discovered. Owning patents meant you had a monopoly. It's patents which explain how the market value of a drug can be as much as fifty times what it costs the company to produce it. But from the patients' perspective, patents are a mixed blessing. They push up the price of drugs, and they mean that only one company gets to sell them in a competitive market. Knowing all this, Bryn had taken the decision to let anyone in the whole world have free access to the clinic's peptides. The clinic would exploit them, for sure, but anyone else could too. Bryn explained all this, stumbling awkwardly over his words.

Cameron listened to him intently, deep grey eyes drilling for the truth. She turned back to the letter. 'It says here, that, following your decision to give the patents away, the maximum market value of the company is likely to be just a few hundred million. They say that's a generous estimate.'

'It's still a lot of money.'

'You've given away millions of pounds here. No. You've voluntarily given away *hundreds* of millions – billions.'

'I'll have enough. I assumed you wouldn't mind. I'm sorry. Maybe I should have asked you first.'

'You've given away . . .' Cameron calculated. 'You've given away about two and a half billion pounds,' she said. 'Your share of that is around seven hundred and fifty million.'

Bryn nodded.

'Well? Don't you mind? I thought you only cared about money. Obviously not. What *do* you care about?'

'Cameron, I –'

'You do honestly care about the patients, don't you? My God, seven hundred and fifty million. That's a crazy amount! Even *I* feel kind of queasy, when I think . . .'

'Of course I care about the patients. You've done a wonderful thing, Cameron. It's only fair we let as many

435

people share it as possible. As many as possible, as quickly as possible.'

Bryn moved towards Cameron, meaning to hug her, but she flamed away from his grasp, a fiery intensity in her gaze.

'When I asked you what you cared about, you looked really upset. Something's really upsetting you, isn't it?'

'It's nothing, it's late, I'm upset about you going. I –'

'You're lying to me. Don't ever lie to me.' All of a sudden, Cameron froze, her face burning like a pale flame above the deep-blue silk of her dress. 'My God! Bryn, you . . . you . . .'

He nodded. 'I'm crazy, I know, but, yes, I love you. Head over heels. I'm sorry for letting you know like this. It would have been better if . . .' His voice sounded jangled and abrupt.

'How long?'

'God, how long have I . . . ?' Bryn shrugged. 'I only knew about it that night we came back from Altmeyer's boat in Cannes. If I hadn't been a lumphead, I'd probably have figured things out sooner. I only wish . . .' Bryn opened his hands and dropped them again, at the uselessness of his wishes. 'Nothing. I only wish nothing.'

Cameron stood open-mouthed in shock, so still you could have mistaken her for a statue. She had one hand to her mouth, the other hand by her side, holding the fateful letter. A moment passed. The letter dropped uselessly to the floor, joining all the rest of Cameron's clutter, lying like silver treasure in the moonlight.

'You should never lie to me.'

'I'm sorry. I didn't want –'

'I don't care what you wanted. You should never ever lie to me.'

'OK.'

'Jesus.'

Bryn found his tongue again, seeking dignity in defeat.

436

'I didn't want to spring this on you. I wanted to keep quiet about it. I hope you're happy in LA.'

Slowly to start with, then more quickly, she shook her head. Her mouth was open, and her breaths came in short hard pants.

'Screw LA,' she said.

'Screw . . . ?'

He never completed his question. In a single leap she was across the room, in his arms, kissing him with a passion, their two bodies melting together in the embrace. On the roof of the world, shooting stars burned their hearts out and, just outside, the River Thames ran softly to the sea.